DAY

OF

JUDGMENT

Uncommon Bonds – 4

A Novel by

WILLIAM E. NOLAND

FIRST EDITION SOFTCOVER
ISBN: 1622537211
ISBN-13: 978-1-62253-721-1

Editor: Lane Diamond
Cover Artist: Kris Norris
Interior Designer: Lane Diamond

EVOLVED PUBLISHING™

www.EvolvedPub.com
Evolved Publishing LLC
Butler, Wisconsin, USA

Printed in Book Antiqua font.

BOOKS BY WILLIAM E. NOLAND

UNCOMMON BONDS
Book 1: *Playing with Fire*
Book 2: *Hammer to Fall*
Book 3: *From the Beginning*
Book 4: *Day of Judgment*
Book 5: *Cause and Effect* [Spring 2024]
Book 6: *Birds of Fire* [Spring 2025]

DEDICATION

For my cousins, Nancy, Cathy, and Suzanne,
whose voices ring in my head whenever Olive speaks.

CHAPTER 1

Some things, it seems, were simply never meant to be.

Apparently, this included a nice, relaxing vacation in Italy. Lotte and Eric had come here for vacation, but the whole "nice and relaxing" part...?

Yeah, not so much, Eric thought as he dug his shovel into the gravely soil, awakening whispers of pain from the ghosts of old injuries.

Additionally, this wasn't just *any* vacation. This was their honeymoon, planned for months, with an itinerary only an obsessive overachiever like Lotte could concoct. Like so many past plans, this ambitious agenda had been blown to bits at the eleventh hour, as if magical forces had intervened, intent on keeping Eric from ever seeing the historic and artistic treasures of the wondrous Italian peninsula.

He chuckled to himself. *As if!*

He knew full well that magical forces had *very much* intervened. They were the reason he and Siddique now had to dig and sweat as the heat of the late May morning asserted itself.

"What's so funny?" Siddique asked. His shovel hit the dirt as Eric dumped his on the rapidly growing mound next to the incision they'd sliced into the hillside.

"Oh, nothing. Just reliving another experience like this... fate scoffing at our vacation plans."

Siddique wiped his brow and took a sip of water. "Not how you pictured spending your honeymoon, huh? Digging a hole with me? Unless this was all a setup to get us alone together, *hmmm*?"

Eric laughed. "No. You're a hot ticket, but I'm not nearly that crafty."

Siddique grinned as he swallowed his water. "True, that. I don't think you have a deceitful bone in your body, except maybe sometimes toward yourself. Are you laughing to hide what you really feel?"

Eric was somewhat taken aback by that.

Over the past year-and-a-half, he and Siddique, and of course, Lotte, had become fairly good friends. Lotte had needed Siddique's help in processing her kidnapping, in which Siddique had played a significant role. "DIY restorative justice," she had flippantly dubbed it, but Eric knew the seriousness that lay underneath.

Additionally, both he and Lotte had agreed it would be better to have Siddique on the inside of their little "secret," rather than having an unknown and unpredictable commodity on the outside. So, there were ample forces at work, not so subtly, or particularly gently, prodding the trio's orbits to collide. There was tension at first, but somehow, the driving lessons had really broken the ice.

"I can't believe you never learned," Lotte sang from the backseat of Eric's now banged-up and venerable Mazda 3.

"In Freetown, I had a scooter," Siddique somewhat defensively replied, his words accented by his native Temne tongue and the Krio he had spoken on the streets. "It was all we could afford. Besides, you're one to talk. It doesn't look like you ever learned either."

"I did, in high school, but then I didn't drive for years. I suppose it's like falling off a bicycle—you never really forget how. Except now I've totally lost my confidence, especially after that stupid Jeep accident in Tuscany."

"You mean, you lost your motivation," Eric jokingly scoffed. "I think you just like people driving you around, especially me." In the rearview mirror, he watched as she playfully stuck her tongue out at him.

Siddique quizzically eyeballed both of them, unsure whether they were having a real fight or not.

"It's all right," Eric reassured him. "We're just kidding around. Be forewarned, though, you'll be Lotte's chauffeur once you learn. You ready?"

He nodded, and off they went.

Eric had chosen the quiet roads around the old Sturman Building in Southby for their lessons. The rail cars and engines had once been built in this location, supplying the town's livelihood for a time. Now, the monumental brick edifice stood in mute decay, the great opening, where gleaming new carriages and locomotives had once rolled off the assembly line, looking like the broken gap in the mouth of a seven-year-old who had lost her front teeth.

Eric had seen the building a thousand times as a kid, walking the old rail lines through the woods with his buddies. Somehow, the structure's desolation and dereliction now appealed to him more, now that he was older and had come to realize that things had endings as well as beginnings. The town had been debating renovating and repurposing the old girl for decades, but to Eric, that just smelled like another one of those things never meant to be.

In any case, it made a perfect place to teach Siddique to drive, and because this was such a *normal* activity, maybe it made Siddique less threatening in Lotte's eyes. She laughed as he fumbled like a child to put the car in drive, surged forward with too much pressure on the gas, and screeched to a halt with a heavy foot on the brake. Then again, maybe it was simply his open, innocent smile, eyes bright with carefree mirth, that offset, to some degree, his complicity in all that had happened.

Who knows?

It didn't matter. What mattered was that once they'd lurched and screeched and fumbled and laughed for a good portion of the morning, Lotte asked Eric if he could take a walk for a little while so she and Siddique could talk — and that was really the beginning.

Since that time, they got together with him quite regularly. Weekend mornings or afternoons brought driving lessons, with some time alone for Lotte and Siddique to continue their conversation, followed by a visit to Eric's parents' house. Alternatively, they might go to dinner at Peaches with Margot and Jennifer, especially if Margot was playing later in the evening when the music started.

They helped Siddique secure an apartment of his own, co-signing the lease due to his largely nonexistent credit history. It was just a simple studio in downtown Worcester, but he didn't need much space. He was overjoyed to finally have a place of his own, even if it did eat up a huge chunk of his paycheck. When Siddique settled in, he proudly invited them over to share casava leaf stew and rice, a dish ubiquitous in his native Sierra Leone.

After Siddique passed his driver's test in April, Eric convinced his dad to purchase an extra vehicle for the business. Of late, Schneider Industrial Flooring had found themselves in frequent need of an added white cargo van, especially since renting at Vitis Brothers had become a somewhat chilly experience.

Sorry, Dad!

Siddique was given charge of the van, agreeing to drive it anywhere at any time. He always sought extra hours, but the vehicle also served as his personal transportation. It was a responsibility, but Eric vouched for him, and so far, Siddique had exceeded all expectations.

Defying every shred of reason, a relationship that had started with a kidnapping and a knifepoint standoff had turned into a friendship. They came to know Siddique in a totally different way. He came to know them as well, Lotte in particular, though Eric sensed the unexpectedly canny and perceptive Siddique also had a pretty good bead on him.

Lotte was always quiet after her talks with their new friend, pensive in the car after they drove Siddique home, a brief squeeze of hands their only goodbye. It took a while for Lotte to come back to Eric after these encounters, but he knew to give her space, and of course, time—that precious and so misunderstood commodity.

These liaisons with Siddique had seemed to make a subtle but noticeable difference in Lotte's demeanor, though it crossed Eric's mind that his proposing to her on that chilly November night a year-and-a-half ago had contributed as well. Perhaps this had been the final step in forcing his way past the barriers she had placed around her heart, the walls that granted solace and protection from infinite heartache while simultaneously depriving his love of the joys of unfettered intimacy.

Then again, maybe cleaning out her office had been the key, laughing together at the uncaring mess she'd made. The clutter had reminded him of the floors of the closets in her old wardrobe where she'd casually tossed shoes, purses, and belts, all intermingled with wayward, black band t-shirts that had jumped suicidally from their hangers into the bedlam below. For the girl with better things to do, there was always tomorrow for cleaning and organizing... and tomorrow... and tomorrow.

There was also the addition of the couch in her office. Eric now spent a good portion of his evenings there, reading a book or reviewing work for Schneider on his laptop, while Lotte sweated out the complexities of modeling and managing fuzzy measure theory, uncertainty, optimal sampling strategies, and scale and spatio-temporal effects in analyzing the structure, properties, and possibilities of archaeological data—her dizzying dissertation in the making.

In the end, maybe all those things, wrapped inseparably in some impossibly complex formula, like the ones Eric saw endlessly scrolling past on Lotte's computer monitor as he spied over her shoulder, had brought about the great changes.

Whatever had caused it, life had become, for Eric, as close to perfection as he could ever have conceived possible. He imagined the sound of something clicking into place, like the satisfying *snap* he now heard when his shoulder popped into proper alignment—never quite right after their encounter with Charun, or the beating he'd taken from Ninurta.

Of course, a few hitches still surfaced here and there, one particularly curious and vexing, related to the otherworldly being with whom their lives had become irreversibly entangled. Overall, however, it seemed that Lotte had noticeably "settled in," almost as if the volume of her life had been turned down ever so slightly. Not so much you couldn't still feel the pulse of the bass rattling the floor or hear the resounding crash of the cymbals when one of those complex calculations on her screen rang true, but rather, just enough that sometimes, while Eric nestled into the little couch reading or working on a typical evening, Lotte might unexpectedly announce from her desk, "Let's go for ice cream!"

"You do realize it's February and it's freezing outside, right?"

"I don't care."

Her smile said it all. It showcased a deep-seated happiness that Eric had never seen before. Actually, that wasn't true. He had seen it, just not for a long, long time. It was like... like....

"Like back when we were in high school."

"Sorry?" Siddique said. "I don't follow you."

Eric looked up from the large furrow they were digging, almost surprised to find he still held his shovel. "No, I'm sorry. Your question kind of surprised me. I was just pondering the answer."

"And?"

"Well, I hadn't really considered it. You're right: sometimes I do laugh when I feel like crying... or screaming... but the truth is, this time it's different. I was definitely a little resentful when this happened before. Back then, I went along with changing our plans because it was so important to Lotte, then I felt like she left me hanging. This isn't like that. Now, we're in it together. Things haven't been like they are between us for a really long time, and it's not just getting married. It's been like this for a while, since North Carolina. It's been... well, I don't know how to describe it. Awesome. It's been *awesome*. So, to answer your question, I'm honestly laughing because this situation is kind of funny. There's actually nothing more to it, and, believe me, nobody's more surprised about that than I am."

Siddique resumed digging.

For a while, they both worked in silence, getting ever closer to the spot where Lotte had determined the object they sought lay buried, tucked in some small crevice in the porous volcanic rock. The entrance seemed to have been intentionally concealed by other rocks, and then the whole spot buried. At least, that's what the data from the WHG had told her when they'd scanned early this morning—time, and the vegetation, had done the rest, layering centuries of organic material on this plot beneath Monte Sant'Angelo's plentiful trees.

"All right," Siddique finally said. "I believe you. You just do this... this thing where you make a joke, even when it's serious. In fact, you do it *more* when it's serious. So, it's hard to tell."

Eric paused, unsure whether to be amused or annoyed, though he couldn't really deny it. He'd been like that since he was a kid. He'd always thought of it as "finding the humor in anything," but he could see that, to others, it might seem a bit evasive or cynical, even downright obnoxious.

Eric said, "Did Lotte tell you that, or is this from your own observation?"

The slightest smile creased Siddique's lips, but he didn't stop shoveling. "I admit, I asked her about it. You can be hard to read. Her too, but with her... well, we talk, you know? I can ask her what she means. Sometimes, she don't even know, and she has to think about it. With you, it's different, so I asked her. She said it's just your weird sense of humor. *Snaky*, I think she called it."

It took a moment for Eric to get it. "Yeah, I think the word you're looking for is *snarky*."

"Snarky! That's it! Funny word. I hope it's not, like, a bad thing."

Eric laughed. "No, it's not bad. Well, it can be, depending on the circumstance. It sort of depends. Anyway, I don't take it as an insult. I definitely do that, and I can see why you might be confused sometimes, but like I said, this isn't a case of my snarky humor. I'm really not upset about what we're doing. In fact, I think it's pretty damned exciting!"

"So do I," Siddique echoed. "I'm glad you brought me. I'm glad for everything. I can't believe you pay for me to visit home on the way back. I know this was partly just a cover story so people at work wouldn't know I was with you and Lotte on your honeymoon, but my family will be so happy to see me. It's just too much, though. I can never repay what you both have done for me."

"Yeah, I hear you, but don't think about it that way. We need you. We have one shot at this, and there's no way we could do everything that has to be done by ourselves. You're earning every penny of what we spent right now, digging this hole, not to mention helping us out last fall when we *really* needed you, and that van!"

Siddique solemnly nodded.

"Then there's Lotte, of course, and everything you've done with her, which kind of goes without saying. Really, Siddique, it's fine to be grateful, but you don't owe us anything. You and Olive are part of the team."

He chuckled. "We feel like more than that. I mean, you bring us on your honeymoon... and we all stay in that rented house together. That's pretty serious! Why is it that you have to do this now, instead of being on some romantic getaway alone with your new bride?"

"Don't you know this *is* Lotte's idea of a romantic getaway?"

"I think this is what you call *snarky*, right?"

"Yeah, basically, though there is a grain of truth to it. But seriously, why now? Well, the timing is just sort of coincidence. It has to do with Lotte's field of study, and a chain of events that goes back about four years. Although, I guess things really started a couple of months ago."

On one of those typical weeknights, sometime in late February or early March, Eric had fallen asleep on the little couch in Lotte's office. She woke him with a shout, likely staring at her screen and oblivious to his state of unconsciousness.

"Eric, look at this!"

He was surprised to find it was after midnight—unusual even for Lotte to work this late. She must have been completely engrossed in something. He reluctantly extricated himself from the couch and stood next to her chair.

He yawned and said, "What is it?"

The top and right side of the screen showed a narrow band of green, accented by a few dots and streaks of blue. A blank, white space at the bottom left cut an undulating U shape into the lime-like monotony.

"It's the Bay of Naples," she replied, using her mouse to adjust some settings on the bottom of the monitor. The greens got a bit greener, and the blues a bit bluer.

"Wow, glad we're not going there on our honeymoon. Looks dull as hell."

"Ha, ha. I put a lot of bloody work into this."

He wiped the sleep from his eyes to make sure he wasn't missing anything. "Well, that's a lot of work for a big field of green with a few blue splotches."

"And?"

"And what? What am I supposed to be looking for?"

"Don't you see the yellow?"

He blinked a few times and got closer. The contrast was horrible, but now that she mentioned it, in addition to the blue, he spotted some flecks of yellow here and there, embedded in the strip to the top and side of the white space that presumably represented the water of the bay.

"Jeez," he said, "the graphics on this look worse than *Might and Magic III* when I was ten years old. That was a cool game, though. There was a Minotaur at the end. He was tough to beat."

She icily stared up at him from where she sat.

"What?" he nervously asked.

"Well, you've just spoiled the ending for me, haven't you? Now there's no point in playing the game, is there?"

"I... I had no idea you'd ever *want* to play *Might and Magic III*. I'm sorry."

She half-sneered and half-chuckled. "Well, I don't, really. I was being sarcastic. Are you quite done now?"

"Yes, I'm done. Sorry. Show me what you want to show me. I'll keep my mouth shut."

Cranky as she was for being over-tired, she gave a little snort of amusement as she turned back to the computer. "What you're looking at is sort of a heat map of magnetic polarity. It's impossible to make any sense of the raw data."

She clicked a button, and the green band that contained the blue and yellow splotches disappeared, replaced by an inconceivable scattering of overlapping numbers that made Eric's head swim. With another mouse click, the colors returned.

"I've been experimenting with it for a while," she continued, "but I'd never had a dataset like this to play with before. Werner gave me access to their computers last year when I was in England on the Stonehenge project. That worked out so well, they let me keep it. I'm off hours from them anyway, so I don't tax their system. Late last year, Sven Henriksson was appointed as a lead consultant to the dig team at Pompeii."

"He's that Swedish guy from the National Geographic specials, right? I watched some of those. He's great! He did one on Minoan Crete that was amazing — really informative."

"Yes," she said somewhat dismissively. "He's got the gift, all right — the gift of gab, mostly. Reminds me of Mason. I guess he knows his stuff, but what he's really good at is using his charisma and reputation to get funding for big projects, for which he takes all the credit, of course. *Whatever.* In any case, he got funding from the Italian government for a big push at Pompeii. Most of that money went to the Werner Institut, and not just for the hand-held devices, mind you. He got a major fly-by — every bit of Werner's sensory equipment packed into helicopters and drones for a huge survey."

"Wow," Eric said, impressed.

"Wow, indeed. Even better, they scanned the entire area north and east of the bay. In addition to far more details of Pompeii and Herculaneum, they were hoping to find anything else that might have been missed around Vesuvius. The whole area is rife with history, though, and the city of Naples thought they might also benefit from Werner's sophisticated GPR scans. They figured, 'why not,' and kicked in some money as well, so the scans cover the large band all the way to the west coast." Her tone changed. "If anything major turns up, Dr. Henriksson will be like the second coming of Schliemann."

"You say that like it's a bad thing."

"Oh, it just bothers me that it takes all this glitz and glamor to get anything done. The team at Pompeii is highly qualified. If the government had given *them* the money, they could have done what Henriksson is doing. People just seem to be drawn to these personalities. They see a face on TV and think that person is some kind of expert, when usually they're just charismatic mouthpieces. It's frustrating. Besides, you know that *I* want to be the next Schliemann. This bastard is stealing my thunder!"

She laughed, so he laughed as well, even though he wasn't totally sure if she was kidding or not. "Okay, so you have this big dataset. What are you trying to do?"

"Well, a couple of things. First off, I just wanted to see if this idea works. You know that Werner's equipment uses triple-frequency stepped ultra-wideband pulses that combine the advantages of pulse and stepped frequency radar, along with a magnetometer to measure concentrations of magnetic materials that might disrupt the radar readings."

"Umm, I guess I knew that. I knew that you knew that, and that's what's important. Right?"

She rolled her eyes. "*Dummkopf.* Try to pay attention. Werner integrates the magnetometer readings with their GPR and compensates for magnetic conductivity and interference to give you a better picture of what's actually there. That's really the extent of what the magnetometer data is used for, but the system stores all those magnetic readings — quite handy for my purposes. I started by normalizing that underlying data by magnetic strength. Then, I had to strip out and isolate the variables relating to polarity and assign a color range to varying degrees of polar differences, red being a highly positive charge, violet being highly negative."

"I see no red or violet on the screen. Am I missing something?"

"That's because it's zoomed way out. I'm looking for anomalies, places where the polarity is extreme in one way or another. The areas of blue and yellow are of great interest to me, because they point to spots where a pretty large anomaly is present. I can zoom in on those and look at what might be causing the unusual reading. For example... here."

She zoomed in on the city of Naples. With each successive increase in magnification, colors began to separate. The green field became a maze of interconnecting blues and yellows, with occasional oranges and hints of purple.

"It's pretty rough," she said, "especially in an area like this, but here, you can see that the blue area I focused on has now become quite purple. If we flip to the satellite map, we can see a large building. There's a helicopter pad on top with a red cross. It's a hospital. There's something inside causing the magnetism to skew negative—MRI machines, or some-such. I don't know, but for me, that explains the irregularity."

"So, it seems to work, but what good is it? You found a hospital. I could have found that for you on Google."

"Quite so, Mister No Imagination, but tell me if Google could have found this?" She zoomed back out to the original view, then selected an area to the west of Naples where a tiny, yellow dot sat in the field of green.

Eric had to squint to see it. "How did you find that, and why are you looking way over here? Aren't all the really big deal archaeological thingies closer to Vesuvius?"

"Think about your history, Eric," she said as she started zooming in on the yellow speck. "More specifically, Etruscan history."

It had been one of the first areas of study Lotte had encouraged him to pursue once he'd finished his books on Mesopotamian history and myth. He had to think back. "Where are we, Naples? That's Campagna, right? Yeah, I remember now. The Etruscans had a pretty substantial colony down here for a while. They lost it after that battle of... Cumae, right? Big naval battle."

"Exactly!" She sounded genuinely pleased. "Good for you! The ancient acropolis of Cumae is about ten kilometers almost due west of this spot. It was a Greek city. The Etruscan colony was centered a bit farther north in Capua. They'd been squabbling over control of this very fertile region between the two cities for over a century."

"Right, the famous Phlegraean Fields."

Lotte seemed surprised. "My goodness! Something actually *has* stuck in your little brain, hasn't it?"

"I just remember that because it was in *Might and Magic III*. It's where the Minotaur lived. Not really, I'm just making that up. That was a fun game, though. I wonder if I still have it."

She sadly shook her head. "Really, like a six-year-old. Please try to focus."

She returned to the computer and increased the magnification. The yellow area rapidly turned orange, and then, as she zoomed in further, a red speck appeared. "There. Look how that little spot is affecting the polarity of this entire area—enough that it registers at the lowest magnification. Let me zoom in a bit more, then we'll flip over to the map."

When she did, Eric was surprised. "It just looks like trees. Dirt."

"Exactly. There's nothing there to explain this anomaly. There are no buildings around here. It's an undeveloped hillside—Monte Sant'Angelo. It looks like a big park, with hiking trails. Whatever's causing this irregularity must be buried in this spot. It might be an electrical junction of some sort, but it would have to be *huge* to impact such a large area. Why on Earth would they put such a thing up there? It can't be that."

"So, what do you think it is?"

"Well, what do *you* think it is?"

"How the hell would I know? You're the archaeology geek! You're the one who... hey, wait a minute. You're asking me about Etruscan history. You don't think this is... like... I mean, it couldn't be, could it? What are the odds? You can't imagine every magnetic anomaly you come across might be Vanth's portal. Is that seriously what you were looking for?"

"It seriously was," she calmly replied. "Why else would I go to all this trouble looking at stupid magnetic polarity? The only reason the Werner equipment scans for magnetism is so their algorithms can filter out the interference it causes. I mean, this data might have some industrial or geological uses, but as far as archaeology goes, *meh*... except for this one application."

Eric was incredulous. "Are you sure you're not just seeing what you want to see in this data? Think about it. You set out to look for Vanth's portal, and hey... lucky you... you found it! That doesn't seem a little suspicious?"

"It absolutely does. I'm totally with you, but understand, I didn't set out to find Vanth's portal. Yes, I was developing a technological methodology whereby one might go about *looking* for something like that, but I had no expectation to find the bloody thing down here. I was hoping to eventually get scans like this in Tuscany. I felt sure we missed something around Sarteano, and if some of the packing materials in the box had partially decayed like the one Mason and Emilia found, then the pieces of the gateway would mix and begin to produce a magnetic signature."

"Okay," he prodded, still skeptical, "but how do we get from developing technology to thinking we've found a portal?"

"Well, I had to investigate each of the magnetic irregularities I found to see what might be causing them, just to understand the types of things I might need to account for or filter out on later trials. There aren't that many, as you can see. So, I just started looking at them, yellow first, starting at the left part of the scanned area. This is the western shore, coincidentally near the ancient city of Cumae. I eventually got to this weird spot, and I couldn't explain it. There's more, though. Hold on."

Again, she accessed the menu at the bottom of the screen. Several smaller windows popped up, all appearing to display the area she was reviewing in different ways. She selected one that showed pinkish lines, marking what appeared to be elevation levels, punctuated frequently by greenish circles of varying sizes.

"This is a visual representation of stratigraphic data, a 3D model of what's up to about ten meters underground. This is really the crux of what Werner technology produces, using their advanced GPR data run through the algorithms on their mainframe, then further manipulated by someone with the proper programming and interpretive skills. The WHG gives us data like this, just in very small areas. The equipment on helicopters and drones collects it over large areas, though in slightly less detail. The pink lines show how deep you are in meters. In this case, I've filtered the data so that the green circles are open spaces—caves and crevices. Obviously, having found this magnetic anomaly, and thinking in the back of my mind what it might be, I wanted to see if it was located in some sort of underground structure, like the temple Mason and Emilia found."

Eric looked at the spot at the center of the screen. An open space clearly encircled where the red dot emanated its magnetic signature. "That space is too tiny. It's barely a meter in diameter, if I'm reading this right."

"You are," she affirmed. "It's not any kind of underground structure or cave, that's for sure — just a hole in the ground, or a crevice in the rock. I'd need a more detailed scan to tell for sure... but look at this." She zoomed out a bit, and then moved to the left, in a westerly direction. "I wanted to see what else might be around here, something that might be connected to this magnetic spot. I looked back over some of the area I'd already scanned at a higher magnification, and I found this!" She stopped panning left and again magnified the screen.

It took Eric a moment to catch it, but once he did, it was plainly obvious. "That spot there... it's perfectly rectangular! It's like a perfectly rectangular hole in the ground. Actually, it's a hole in a hole. The rectangle is surrounded by another, larger open space. How the hell did you find this? It's so small."

"Well, I knew what I was looking for, so I just snapped the whole area to a grid and started going up and down. That's what's been taking me so long. Even more interesting, but harder to catch, is this wall here. Look. It's perfectly straight. That's not natural. The rectangle is about a meter wide and about three-quarters of a meter deep and high — almost exactly the description Mason gave for the ceramic box containing Charun's portal. This straight wall is almost exactly as wide as the one Mason carved for the portal frame on that plateau above his house in New Hampshire, and the one we made on the hill in the hiking area. This cannot be a coincidence, Eric. It cannot be."

"Okay," he admitted, overwhelmed, "but if that magnetic spot is supposed to be the contents of the box, why is it buried like a half-mile away?"

She flashed him a sly look. "Well, that's what we're going to need to find out, isn't it?"

"Wait a minute," Siddique interjected. "Lotte told me these things had been in the ground for... what... like, two thousand five hundred years, right? Why don't you do your honeymoon like you planned and then come back later? It's not like they're going anywhere!"

Eric chuckled. "Point taken, but there were a few reasons why it had to be now. The most pressing is that, unlike the WHG's magnetic information, which only Lotte would have thought to process and examine, the stratigraphic data is available to anyone who wants to look at it. We're lucky that Pompeii lit up like a Christmas tree, because that's where everyone is focused right now. At some point, though, some bored grad student is gonna start poking around. Small as it is, if anyone sees that rectangle, the game's over. Lotte loses potentially the find of a lifetime, and this hill would come under much more scrutiny. Also, the Werner hand-held devices, like the one Dr. Henriksson so graciously loaned to Lotte yesterday, won't be at Pompeii forever. Lotte felt like this was the moment, and honestly, I agreed."

"Plus, this is her idea of a romantic getaway, right?"

"Exactly! I think you're beginning to grasp the concept of 'snarky' quite nicely."

"Well, I hope you both get what you want out of this."

Almost as if on cue, Eric's shovel made a loud scraping sound. "I think we may have hit the rock. We're about six, seven feet in, which is roughly where she said it would be."

He grabbed one of the pristine trowels they had bought at the local hardware store and scraped away dirt, which Siddique shoveled aside to keep a clear and open channel. After laboriously removing some bulky stones, the nature of the rock changed, no longer large blocks, but smaller stones of various composition. Eric removed one, then another, then another, and then....

"Holy shit!"

The last of the rubble he touched pushed inward and disappeared. Eric put his hand through the opening. "Empty space back here. Lotte was right. It's some kind of little crevice in the rock. The opening had been covered up with these other stones, then buried. I'm gonna call her. She'll want to see this for sure."

Both Eric and Siddique stood covered in dirt and sweating as Lotte marched breathlessly toward them, a bedraggled Olive in tow.

"How'd it go on your end?" Eric asked, offering each a fresh bottle of water.

"Fantastic!" Lotte gushed. "We got all the readings we need. Thankfully, it's not a big area, but it's on a very steep and uneven hill. Olive, you were such a champ! Thank you so much. I couldn't have done that alone—so much climbing around."

"You're welcome." Olive panted between gulps of water. "Now I know what a mountain goat feels like! I guess that was good for me, given I have to get into shape if I want to get a job as a police officer, but if I never see that dang ol' contraption again, it'll be too soon! You never even said if we found anything."

Lotte smiled and put her hand on Olive's shoulder. "I have to analyze the data. That area was much larger than this little hole, and it was deeper. Maybe tonight, after Werner has shut down, I can get on the system and run the data, but I'm certain we found something. We knew it was there. This just gives us more details. Anyway, what's the status here? Any more progress?"

"See for yourself," Siddique replied, handing her a flashlight. "There's something in there, no question."

"We cleared out more of the opening," Eric added, trying to contain his excitement. "We thought you'd like to do the honors."

"You two are so sweet. Thank you!" She took the flashlight and traversed the narrow channel toward the hole. She had to crawl on her belly to access the little crevice and push her upper torso through the slender opening.

Eric noticed that she didn't flinch. This was her element, and nothing would stop her from exploring.

Her muffled voice sounded from inside the hole as they crowded around behind her. "There's quite a bit of mud and dirt in here. I'm clearing it away. Oooh, it looks like there might have been a fabric of some kind, probably a bag or sack of some sort. It's horribly degraded, just the barest fragments, and it's all mixed up in this debris. It's a shame we can't save any. There just isn't time for proper conservation. There's nothing for it. I'll just have to dig in."

She was silent for a time as she squirmed in the trench, trying to get a better position from which to examine whatever was inside. Then she was still... and then....

"*Scheiße!*" she whooped. "Pull me out, pull me out, pull me out!"

Eric grabbed one leg and Siddique grabbed the other. Gently but urgently, they pulled while Lotte extended her arms out straight to reduce friction against the sides of the hole.

Once clear of the opening, she stood, handed the flashlight to Siddique, and brushed herself off.

"What is it?" Eric asked. "Did you find anything?"

She smiled broadly. "Did I? How about this?"

From her other hand, she held out what looked like a highly polished stone—a strip about five inches long and maybe two inches wide. It had slightly beveled edges, with a triangular point on one end, and a triangular recess the same size on the other, and... it was as white as the cream that Eric had poured in his coffee that morning.

CHAPTER 2

He looked like a Nordic god.

To strains of applause, Eric watched as Dr. Sven Henriksson sashayed toward the podium, his every move seemingly larger than life itself. Once situated, his alert and sparkling blue eyes drank in the crowd, drawing them like moths to his flame. A warm and euphoric smile beckoned on his face. His thick blond hair with just the barest trace of gray haloed his broad and ruddy face in the soft lighting of the Encounters with the Americas Gallery in Harvard University's Peabody Museum.

This is just the kind of phony spectacle that usually makes Lotte's skin crawl, Eric fretted. As he looked at her next to him, however, she seemed relatively Zen, certainly not fighting to keep her characteristic eye rolls at bay from the seemingly feigned and overwrought sincerity that Dr. Henriksson projected.

Eric lightly stroked her back in support, and she returned a somewhat feeble smile. She was clearly a little nervous, and really hadn't seemed comfortable at all since she'd returned home yesterday afternoon.

Honestly, she hasn't seemed especially happy for several weeks now, which is weird since she seems to be getting everything she's ever wanted.

A hush settled over the crowd that redirected Eric's attention from those thoughts. It left no time for any final words of encouragement.

"Dear friends," Dr. Henriksson began, his English diction as perfect as the figure he cast. "I welcome you to this exciting event. Those who know me are well aware of my commitment to collaborations. Today, no one person can know everything, do everything, see everything. Today, there is more data available on my phone than there was in the library at my school when I was a boy in Gothenburg. So much has changed."

Grandly, he swept out his arm, drawing attention to the monumental totemic sculptures of the gallery, between which the cocktail tables, crudités, and the bar had been strategically interspersed.

"Still, however, the past calls to us, and as much as we advance, if *advance* is indeed even the right word for our endless groping and questing, the faces of our ancestors continue to call us. They guide us, warn us, remind us that, once, they too thought their societies immortal and unending, but their ruins tell us otherwise. Are there lessons here for us... in what they believed, how they lived, how they died?"

Again, his blue eyes scanned the room, and even Eric felt a distinct tingle when Dr. Henriksson's pleasant but penetrating gaze focused upon him.

"Fortunately for us, there are those who feel such lessons are there for the learning, and today, they bring new knowledge and approaches in how to recover, conserve, and interpret the treasures of our past. When Lotte Schneider-Schwarz first contacted me in the spring of this year, asking me for my assistance, I quickly came to realize who I had encountered. Lotte is at the vanguard of a new breed of archaeologist, steeped as much in the science of computers as the delicate art of the brush and the trowel. Lotte helped us find the proverbial needle in a haystack of numbers and data readings. She looked with new eyes, and what she helped us find was nothing short of a wonder. I know her grandfather, Gordon Reynolds, who so famously discovered the artifacts of the mysterious *Sadat Alnaar*, would be infinitely proud of Lotte, as would her mother, Alice Reynolds-Schwarz, whose spirit still inspires us all. And let us welcome, of course, Lotte's father, Herman Schwarz, who we are so pleased to have with us here today."

The audience again burst into applause as Mr. Schwarz beamed and took a few short bows. Eric felt Lotte grasp his arm as she smiled and waved to her father, who gave a little wave back before retreating to the anonymity of his cocktail table.

"So, without further ado," Dr. Henriksson continued, "I'll let Lotte give you a little taste of what we've found, and maybe answer a question or two. But let me just say, collaborations are what make all this possible. Without the support of Harvard University, The Werner Institut, the funding the Pompeii Project has received from the Italian Government, and of people like you in this room tonight, none of this could have happened. So, thank you all. I'd also like to say that I look forward to many fruitful future collaborations with my new colleague, Lotte Schneider-Schwarz. Please welcome her to the podium."

Eric felt Lotte pull away as she began her short trek across the room.

Again, the audience applauded as Dr. Henriksson greeted her with a tremendous hug. She settled herself and took a deep breath.

Eric knew she had some jitters, but she appeared totally in control. She was also utterly ravishing. He hadn't seen her dressed this nicely and looking so beautiful since the wedding.

Their wedding had been a small affair, but a special one. Saturday, May the 20th, 2017, turned out to be a beautiful day, not a cloud in the sky and near 70 degrees. From the stone patio, the spring vista in the valley below was stunning. Eric considered this cosmic payback for having to postpone the ceremony the year before.

In the spring of 2016, Lotte received an incredible invitation through the Werner Institut to participate in data collection around Stonehenge. The English government had been considering constructing a tunnel literally under the Stonehenge World Heritage Site. The outcry about potential damage to the famous rock formation, and possibly other archaeological treasures, had prompted study of the area, for which the Werner technology was perfect.

It was an incredible experience for her, but with the month spent collecting data, then an intense summer of analysis, the wedding had to take a back seat. Lotte had been concerned in January of this year when the government gave the project an initial go-ahead against her interpretation of the findings, but the matter remained under review.

They stood near the stone steps leading down to the lower yard and the trees beyond as the Justice of the Peace solemnized their union. Eric thought of Lotte, sitting barefoot on the low perimeter wall on a fall day as beautiful as this one twelve years before, when she drank a Coke as she egged him on in their German session. Once, she had napped on this porch, when sleep in her own bed had eluded her, tormented by nightmares.

So many memories here.

How Mr. Schwarz had finagled it, nobody knew. He'd always had an infectious enthusiasm. Had the new owners of 246 Holton Hill Road been charmed by the smiling, friendly man at their door, or had it been the financial incentive of renting out their house for a day to people who had once lived here, and for whom it remained a special memory? As it was, the owners entertained often and were thrilled to serve as hosts, happily attending the ceremony amongst their new friends.

Also happily in attendance was Olive, who acted as de facto maid of honor. She hadn't quite graduated from Savannah State University, having switched her major from history to criminal justice, but with the little she had to complete, they'd let her walk earlier in the month. Sadly, Siddique couldn't come. It would have created the wrong impression, inviting him and not the rest of the Schneider crew, though Margot and Jennifer, along with Keisha from Schneider's business office, were there.

Luckily, Siddique understood the need to keep their friendship on the Q.T., and there had been time enough in Italy for the team to celebrate together, which they most certainly had done.

Lotte began her talk, interrupting Eric's pleasant memories.

"Thank you all so very much for coming. I'll keep my remarks brief, which is easy, because what we don't know about the magnificent discoveries that were made far outweigh what we do."

She picked up a small remote on the podium and pressed a button. The video projection beside her sprang to life. The logos of various partner and sponsor organizations disappeared to reveal a photograph of a wide channel of dirt dug into a hillside. At the end, a hole was flanked by two massive stones, with another boulder forming the top of the opening.

"This is the cave the Werner scans revealed on the northwestern slope of Monte Sant'Angelo, due west of Naples in the city of Pozzouli. By scrutinizing the Werner stratigraphic data, I was able to determine that this cave contained items conforming to the parameters of man-made structures. Dr. Henriksson was kind enough to loan me a *Werner Hand Gehalten,* a hand-held data collection device, which at the time happened to be on site at Pompeii. With that, I was able to take more detailed scans, and get a better sense of what lay under the soil."

Again, Lotte clicked the remote and the picture advanced.

"This shows the cave before the great rocks that had concealed the entrance were removed. Two more are still buried there. You saw the bottom of one of them in the previous photo. We didn't need to remove them all to gain access to the cave. These rocks had been cut specially, placed to conceal the cave entrance, and then the gaps had been filled in with smaller stones. The entire area was then buried. Quite a project. It must have taken several months. We were tremendously fortunate there wasn't anything of archaeological interest in the dirt layers. That allowed us to quickly access the cave."

The next photo drew a gasp of exhilaration from the crowd.

"This is looking in from the entrance. In front of us, we see a statue of a female, perhaps half-a-meter tall. It's been knocked over by dirt and mud that over time has streamed into the cave. Around this statue, we found a large number of coins, Greek in origin. The numismatic analysis isn't complete, but it's thought that these coins date from roughly the middle of the sixth century, BC. To the upper left, you can see the ceramic box, placed on an outcropping they'd somewhat crudely sculpted to receive it. To the right and toward the back, you can just barely see the wall, carved to produce a flat area which is recessed slightly into the rock."

Again, a flip of the remote elicited a chorus of "oohs" and "aahs."

"This is a close-up of the front of the box. It's caked with dirt and mold, so it's a bit hard to see, but on the right, you can just catch a glimpse of that rectangular pattern. On the bottom left, you see a smaller rectangle sitting on what appears to be a stand of some sort. It's connected to the larger rectangle by this line, implying some kind of force or transmission. Currently, it's too dirty to see, but it's thought there are two more smaller rectangles on stands above this one. Here's why we believe this...."

The next photo was taken from the top of the box, part of which had collapsed inward.

"We're not sure what happened to the top, whether a rock fell on the box from above, or it was intentionally broken. Inside, as you can see, there's quite a bit of debris, a mix of stone and broken pottery, so it will take some time to sort that out. If you look to the right, however, you can see what is almost undoubtedly one of those stands depicted on the front. This one's been broken, but there are two more, deeper in the box, that seem to be intact. Here is a photo of one side of the box—the other is completely covered in grime. This one is fascinating, though, because you can clearly see the image of a key. If there is a scroll on the other side, then it's likely this box is associated with Vanth, a chthonic figure in Etruscan funerary art. It's possible her torch is also depicted on the front of the box, but it won't be visible until the object has been removed and properly cleaned and restored."

Again, the screen projected a fresh image.

"This is our final photo, the carved wall. It has a rectangular outline, likely echoing the larger rectangle on the right front of the box. It appears that something was inserted into the corners, as there are little indentations there. It's possible there was an outline, or frame, around the entire recessed surface area, but we can't say for sure. You can also see many small indentations scattered around the recessed surface. Their function is unclear."

Dr. Henriksson interjected. "No objects like this have ever been found in Etruria, or for that matter anywhere in the classical world. They are utterly unique."

"Dr. Henriksson?" The question came from a man near Eric's table who seemed to be connected with the University. "Can you tell us anything about the purpose of these items?"

"Not a tremendous amount, Professor Morgan, but we have guesses. As Lotte mentioned, in Etruscan belief, Vanth is associated with funerary rites. She accompanies the dead to the next world and is often depicted as doing so through a doorway. This interpretation of the items, especially the carved, recessed wall that echoes a passageway, seems most likely, though it's possible that there's a component of divination as well. The front of the box seems to imply *receiving* something coming from that doorway — some *force* which perhaps those items on the ground capture in some way, possibly divine knowledge of some sort. That is, of course, complete conjecture."

A woman with a British accent called out. "Marjorie Stafford, BBC. Why do you think the whole thing was buried? Who buried it?"

Dr. Henriksson nodded, and Lotte fielded the question. "Again, our conclusions are speculative, but it appears the Greeks buried it. Preliminary soil samples tell us some time around 525 BC, near the time of the Battle of Cumae."

"Darling," an older gentlemen interrupted. "Your history is a little off. The Battle of Cumae was fought in 474 BC."

Lotte appeared to take his patronization in stride. "Perhaps I should have been clearer. I meant around the *first* Battle of Cumae, which was fought in 524 BC, almost exactly fifty years prior to the more famous sea battle to which you refer."

That shut him up, Eric noted with pleasure.

"In any case," Lotte continued, "there's other evidence pointing to the Greeks, and the timeframe. The Greek coins, for example, none of which appear to be earlier than about 530 BC. Also, the statue, which we believe is a representation of Soteria, a goddess of safety, deliverance, and preservation from harm, was placed at the entrance to the cave facing inward. The coins are likely votive offerings to the goddess for the gift of her protection, quite possibly protection from the items in this cave. The Greeks could have destroyed the box, but other than the damage at the top, which is of questionable origin, it's not actually clear the Greeks set foot beyond the entrance. It's highly possible they feared this place, and what these items represented."

A woman whom Eric couldn't see spoke from behind one of the Mayan monoliths. "Rehana Bennani, Maghreb Arab Press. Speaking of items, perhaps I can ask the question that is likely on everyone's minds. What else was in that box?"

Lotte smiled. "You saw the picture. Sadly, that's all there was, though we still have some analysis to conduct. If there were ever any other items in that box, it's possible the Greeks took them. They won the first Battle of Cumae, as they did the second. Both had deleterious effects on Etruscan power. It's also possible the Etruscans made off with them, likely in a hurry, as they weren't able to take the box with them. Were I to guess, I'd lean toward the latter explanation. The Greeks seemed to want no piece of these items. They buried this place and forgot about it. It could be that this cave was established as a ritual site in anticipation of the first battle, which was fought on land somewhere nearby. The Greeks may have overrun the Etruscan positions, and everyone had to flee with only what they could carry."

Or bury, Eric mused, fully aware that this is exactly what Lotte had deduced: fearing capture by the Greeks, the priests had tucked the portal material into the rock crevice, disguised it as best as possible, and then tried to sneak back unencumbered to Capua. They were likely caught and killed, because the materials remained hidden and buried for the next 2,500 years.

Most unfortunate was that they appeared to have kept the rings with them. Those had not turned up in the hole despite a thorough search. Two other possibly critical items were missing as well. They had found a solid, cone-shaped object, slightly concave at the wide end that could be interpreted as a torch, but there was nothing corresponding to Vanth's signature key and scroll. Eric knew all of this was moot, of course, as Lotte had no intention of opening the portal, but it was intriguing, and somewhat troubling, that pieces of this material might still be out there somewhere.

"Obviously," Lotte went on, "the hunt will continue, but I'd be surprised if we ever found objects that could be confidently traced back to having been in that box. Then again, surprises are what draw us to archaeology, aren't they? I thank you all for your kind attention. I'm happy to answer more questions one-on-one if you have them."

There was more applause, then a deluge of people swarmed toward the podium to speak with Lotte and Dr. Henriksson.

Eric grabbed a bottle of water from the cocktail table and forced his way through the crowd. "Here you go," he said as he pressed the bottle into Lotte's hand. "You were awesome!"

She turned her attention from the man she was speaking with and smiled gratefully. "Oh, thank you. So sweet! Professor Morgan, this is my husband, Eric...."

And so it went, Eric now trapped behind a throng of people, each wanting to speak with the stars of the moment. Lotte seemed to genuinely appreciate the support, however, and she skillfully passed the hobnobbers and schmoozers off to him when conversations started to wear thin.

She was more gracious with members of the press, though they seemed to know when enough was enough. The woman representing the Moroccan news organization, who turned out to be exquisitely beautiful, gave Eric a kiss on the cheek as she departed. Her citrus perfume distractingly lingered in his nostrils for some time, but he chalked up his fleeting attraction to having missed Lotte so much.

After they'd sent Siddique and Olive on their way last May, each with a portion of the portal materials carefully packed in their luggage, Eric and Lotte had finished what remained of their rather bizarre honeymoon. As planned, Lotte had turned over her WHG data relating to the larger cave, asking that she at least be mentioned in helping with the discovery. Dr. Henriksson had been quite overwhelmed.

Lotte had assumed that would be the end of it, but in late June, he contacted her about returning to Pompeii to discuss a possible collaboration. She flew to Italy for a deeper interview, stopping in Berlin on the way back to coordinate with Werner. By early July, details had been worked out for her to spend the next several weeks in Naples working at the dig site, and off she went again.

Those weeks had turned into months as the painstaking process of excavation encountered inevitable delays and unanticipated obstacles. It wasn't until yesterday, the seventh of September, that Lotte had finally come home, and this would be for barely two days. Tomorrow morning, they were off to New York City for a repeat performance of tonight's presentation, then back to Naples.

Lotte promised this would just be wrap-up, as well as helping Dr. Henriksson run some analytics on Werner data related to Pompeii. In a couple of weeks, she assured him, things would be back to normal.

Eric had been hearing that since August, but he wasn't really mad. He'd long accepted that life would be like this from time to time, but he found it difficult dealing with constantly changing dates and managing unmet expectations.

To her credit, Lotte had maintained frequent contact, but she had been terribly distracted and seemed under quite a bit of stress.

Eric simply bit his lip and tried to be supportive. This wasn't her fault, and she was doing everything she could to be there for him. She didn't need his shit right now. She needed his support, and he resolved to give it to her. This was his moment to prove to her, and to himself, that he was capable of doing that.

The crowd finally started to thin out. "You want some more water?" he asked.

"No, I'm good. Go get yourself some, you poor thing. Thanks so much. I know this isn't your forte, events like this, but you handled it like a pro!" She gave him a little pat on the bottom as he squeezed out toward the bar.

Glass of water finally in hand, Eric naturally gravitated to the periphery of the room. Lotte was right: things like this were definitely not his specialty. Her gratitude, though, made all his effort feel worthwhile.

He spied Mr. Schwarz, happily talking with Professor Sprich, Lotte's doctoral advisor. He seemed as pleased this evening as her father. He knew the professor was eager to have her back on campus, but the positive attention she had garnered with the publicity around the find, not to mention the association with Sven Henriksson, had been impossible to resist. Harvard had organized this event at the Peabody Museum for just that purpose.

Carolyn Booth, Mr. Schwarz's girlfriend, chatted nearby with some people Eric didn't recognize. She would always serve as a reminder to him of what had happened, though with the passage of time, Dr. Esfahani had finally seemed to largely slip from Carolyn's thoughts.

It was all now in the past, frozen, but still quietly shaping his and Lotte's futures. Eric understood, perhaps better than anyone, that this was the way of things, though what practical benefit that knowledge granted him was often difficult to discern.

"You're a quiet one."

The woman had approached him unnoticed from behind. She had olive skin and deep brown eyes that matched her curly hair. For this event, her dress was quite casual, but she wore a Peabody Museum identification tag around her neck, so he assumed she must be staff.

"Sorry, didn't mean to scare you," she said. "I'm Rebecca Geller. I work here at the museum. I know Lotte. Well, I know *of* her. Pretty much everybody does now, huh? I've seen her around campus, though, sometimes with you. You're her boyfriend, right?"

"Husband, actually." He smiled and held up his hand to display his simple, gold wedding band.

"Right! Sorry, I totally forgot. You guys just got married, didn't you? Congratulations! That's so great!"

"I definitely think so. We've known each other for a long time, back to high school, actually. I'm Eric, by the way."

Rebecca shook his hand. "It's nice to meet you. This is a great event. You must be really proud. Does this mean Lotte is back from Naples? I'd heard she'd been over there for a while."

"No," he answered, trying to keep his frustrations from showing. "She has to go back tomorrow, just to finish things up. She'll be home soon. Things just keep getting delayed."

"Hmmm...." she said with a slightly troubled look. "Listen, I was just kind of passing through on my way out. I have to go, but I was hoping to connect with you. I know you're gonna think this is weird, but there's something I'd really like to talk with you about. I can't do it now – not here." She looked past his shoulder toward the podium. "Could I get your number? I know this sounds crazy, but it's not what you think. There's just something I feel like you ought to know."

Eric wasn't sure what to make of this. He felt suspicious, but also quite intrigued.

What in the world could this woman, who I don't know at all, have to tell me? What could this possibly be about?

Rebecca's nervous smile didn't seem to convey anything sinister. She seemed pretty genuine... friendly, even.

Curiosity won the day, and Eric went for his phone. "Sure," he said. "Give me your number, then I'll text you mine. What the hell? My battery is almost drained. I charged my phone right before we left tonight. Lotte couldn't take hers because she's in her nice clothes that don't have any pockets. I think there's just enough juice left."

Rebecca gave Eric her number and he typed it in. In addition to a low battery, it seemed his phone had no reception, either. "Can you get reception here? My phone seems to be freaking out."

"I don't usually have a problem," she answered. "Listen, why don't you just tell me your number? I'll type it in and call you later."

"Not necessary," he said with relief. "It just went through. Whew! Did you get it?"

"Got it," she affirmed, checking her phone. "Listen, I'll give you a call in the next few days. Maybe we can grab a cup of coffee or something. I have to run, but trust me, you'll want to hear what I have to tell you."

With that, she quickly shook Eric's hand and bounded toward the exit.

"Who was that?" Carolyn asked as she joined Eric where he stood, trying to diagnose what might be happening with his phone.

"Oh, nobody," he said dismissively, not wanting to raise unnecessary questions. "Somebody who works here. She just told me to give Lotte her best."

Carolyn sighed deeply. "That's nice. Donya would have been so proud of Lotte. She practically worshiped at her mother's feet. There's simply no justice. Whoever killed her will never face judgment or pay for their crimes. Maybe she's up there, looking down on us right now. Wouldn't you like to think that was true?"

The thought gave him chills. He felt Dr. Esfahani's gaze on him more than Carolyn could ever know. He just smiled and hoped that experience remained precisely where it was now: frozen in the past.

They were supposed to have gone to dinner with Lotte's father and Carolyn, but Lotte had begged off. Now she slumped in the passenger seat of the Mazda, looking exhausted and even paler than normal.

"You okay?" Eric asked. "We'll be home soon."

"I'm fine. I just don't feel too well. The thought of food right now is just... *yech*! I think I'm over-tired, probably jet-lagged. We're also leaving so early tomorrow. I just need to go to bed. Eric, I'm so sorry. We've barely had any time together."

So noted, he ruminated, but he kept the observation to himself and tried to change the subject. "I thought tonight went well. Nice deflection on that 'what else was in the box' question."

"Thanks. I knew someone would ask. It's the proverbial elephant in the room. Do you realize how lucky we were? If the portal material had been in that box, we'd have never gotten it. We couldn't have possibly accessed that cave by ourselves, and someone was bound to have discovered it eventually. They would have found everything with no understanding of what it was and no rings to bind the creature if she had somehow gotten loose. It just terrifies me. I'm glad we have it safe and sound, even if we broke every archaeological protocol to get it."

"Me too. You were even able to make a little hay with that cave discovery. Dr. Henriksson sure spoke highly of you. Future collaborations, huh?"

"Mmmmm...."

"Has your assessment of him changed any since all this happened?"

"Well, yes and no," she said somewhat reluctantly. "Sven is actually quite an excellent leader. He listens. He empowers people to do what they do best. He balances a million priorities, but always makes anyone he's talking to feel like they're the most important person in the world. His hard science days are largely behind him, but what he does is critical to the process. I underestimated that."

"You seem to have hesitations, though. Are you not excited to work with him?"

"Oh, it's complicated. It's certainly a tremendous opportunity, but Sven can be... well... demanding in certain ways. He gives a lot, but he expects a lot too — a whole lot. He's dying to work with someone like me. He didn't have to give me any more than a casual mention in connection to this discovery. I got way more than that, as you can see, but there's quite a quid-pro-quo. A lot of the delays with me getting home have been due to things he's wanted... things that will advance his projects and priorities. That's understandable, but it's just a lot of expectations and... well... entanglements. *Alter!* What a mess!"

Where did that come from? This didn't sound like Lotte. This is what it had been like with her for weeks. The situation just didn't seem to justify her level of consternation and anxiety. They'd gotten what they were after in Italy in the spring, and her expectations of receiving credit for finding the cave had been overwhelmingly exceeded. Yes, it meant a lot of extra work for her, and inevitable separation for them, but that came with the territory.

Eric couldn't understand why things had become so torturous for her. "Are you sure there's nothing else bothering you? It just seems like you've been on edge for a long time."

She closed her eyes and threw her head back into the seat. "Well... umm, I don't know. There's just a lot to think over. I'm not sure if it's going to work out or not. The timing may not be right. It's going to depend. I haven't had a chance to piece it all together. I need to get home, and that just keeps getting delayed. We'll talk it all through when I'm back. I promise."

He didn't completely understand what she was saying, but sensed he shouldn't push too hard. "It's fine. Take your time. I just want you to know I'm here for you, whatever it is. It'll be okay."

She reached out and took his hand. He felt the fire opal engagement ring he'd gotten her pressed against his finger, now joined by a sculpted gold wedding band with small diamonds. It was unusual, but the pieces complimented each other, and she seemed exceedingly proud of them, especially having never been much for jewelry.

"I know, my love," she whispered. "I feel you always. You can't know what a comfort that's been over these past two months. We'll talk when I'm back. We'll figure it out. I just need to decide what I want. I just need to decide. That's all."

CHAPTER 3

A lovely fall Saturday afternoon flourished outside, but Eric couldn't have cared less.

He sat morosely in the living room where he'd been most of the day, idly scrolling through inane YouTube videos. The strains of opera from downstairs told him Mrs. Binson had returned from shopping, or wherever she'd gone earlier, but he still silently moped on the couch, not wanting any company just now.

He figured he was due. He'd held it together through the summer, working his ass off at Schneider and never complaining to Lotte, even when the date of her return kept getting pushed back... even as she became ever more distressed and distracted in their phone and Skype sessions.

Today, though, the disappointment of her visit, her tentativeness in bed on Thursday night after such a long separation, and her abrupt departure this morning, all conspired to overwhelm his emotions. His will to keep pushing through was simply exhausted, and he'd given in to the bitterness and irritation that had been building for some time.

Dr. Henriksson—*or should I say*, Sven?—had arrived in an Uber at 6:00 a.m. Lotte didn't even want Eric to take her to the airport.

"Don't bother," she'd said. "It's such a hassle. Just go back to sleep."

Like he could sleep anymore after that. Like he wouldn't have preferred another hour with her, even just a dreary drive to the airport. It felt like payback for how great things had been.

I guess the honeymoon is now truly over.

Somehow, the thought worried him more than it should have, as if there were more to it, but he couldn't exactly put his finger on what.

"This *sucks*," he exclaimed, as if the empty room had been monitoring his train of thought. He slapped his laptop shut and trudged into the kitchen. Dishes from his meagre lunch still rested unwashed by the sink. Langsam poked her head hopefully out from under the clay shelter in her terrarium. Figuring that taking her for a little walk outside might clear his head, he pulled his jacket off the rack by the door and grabbed his suddenly fluky cell phone from the kitchen table where it sat charging.

He saw a text message and, hoping it was Lotte, swiped his password, pleased to see the damned thing finally registered a full battery.

It wasn't Lotte. It was a reply to the text he'd sent last night to Rebecca Geller. Intrigued, he opened the message:

RU busy tonight? Know Lotte is away. Dinner my treat?

He stared at the message for a long time, as if it were written in Sanskrit and he had to parse and translate the possible meaning of every word. Something didn't feel right about this. He was unclear whether it was the impropriety of meeting a woman alone under unknown pretenses, or if it was something darker, more sinister.

What could she possibly want?

She wanted to tell him something, something she felt he needed to know.

What if this is important? Well, duh, obviously it's important, assuming Rebecca is telling the truth and that's what she really wants. Why would she lie, though?

He wracked his brain, trying to figure out what this might be about, and came up with only one plausible explanation.

Lotte!

It had to be about Lotte.

That only increased his anxiety, but in his gut, he felt he was right.

He checked the time of the message: 2:37 p.m. It was now 3:20. With shaky fingers, he typed his reply:

Sure! What time and where?

The answer came with remarkable speed:

How about Orinoco near Harvard Square. 5:30?

Having never been there, he looked it up. *Venezuelan food. Cool!*

It was about a forty-minute walk from his apartment. He could clean up a bit, change, then walk for a while, try to burn off some of his frustrations and the nervous energy coursing through his veins. He punched out his response:

Great! See you then!

"Sorry, Langsam, I'll take you out when I get back, or maybe tomorrow. Don't look at me like that. Well, okay... I did piss the entire day away. It's reasonable for you to be upset. I know you miss Mommy, too. We both do. It'll be all right... at least I think it will. You really have no idea what I'm saying, do you?"

He shook his head and went to change.

This is fucking ridiculous!

Eric fumed as he stormed back to his apartment. This had been the final straw of a day he hoped would soon be over for good. Of course, then there was tomorrow, and the day after that, and the day after that to contend with, but this had just been too much.

He'd sat in the restaurant for forty-five minutes before texting Rebecca:

I'm here. Running late?

No response.

After an hour and fifteen minutes, he'd ordered some food to accompany his beer. He'd been starving and had started to sense that the wait staff was looking at him as if he'd been stood up for a date. In a sense, that was true. He'd texted again, several times, and each time, no reply. It was as if she'd vanished, and his phone was again virtually drained of juice.

Probably a faulty battery. As if I need this shit on top of everything else!

By 7:30, he was full, and he'd had enough of the looks of pity — *or was it derision?* — from his waitress. He'd brusquely paid the check and bolted.

He'd had a couple of beers. *Or was it three?* He wasn't sure, and didn't know if they had calmed or stoked his rising anger, but they loosened him up and relaxed his normally tight grip. Almost as if he were watching a stranger, he paid the cashier, grabbed the brown paper bag off the counter, and exited the liquor store that had ambushed him on the way home.

I'll probably pay tomorrow, but tonight, I just want to be sedated.

It was suddenly just too much, and he knew he couldn't cope. He doubted he'd be able to sleep, and he just wanted that familiar warmth to take him away.

It's just one night. I can handle it. I'll pour the rest down the drain tomorrow. Tonight, though, I need this. I deserve it.

The brisk walk home did little to diminish his rage. He skirted around the side of the surprisingly dark house.

Mrs. Binson must have gone out again, he deduced.

Still, he went up the back way, not wanting to unexpectedly encounter his good-natured but chatty downstairs neighbor and landlord. He wasn't in the mood for any company tonight, other than Langsam... and Captain Morgan.

He dourly ascended the stairs to the small second floor balcony. Reaching for his keys, he suddenly froze. Their back door stood slightly ajar.

Fucking shit, did I forget to lock the damned door?

That was impossible. The outer handle was permanently locked. You could only open it with the key, and he always pulled the door shut and gave the knob a little twist when he left. *Always!*

It appeared dark and quiet inside. For a moment, he wondered if he should call the police.

Could this day get any more insane?

Not hearing any noise, he threw caution to the wind, stepped inside, and clicked on the light. Every drawer and cabinet in the kitchen stood open. Boxes, cans, dishes, and glasses had been placed on the counter. Nothing had been broken. The garbage can and cleaning supplies had been removed from under the sink and sat in the middle of the room. The ceramic shelter in Langsam's terrarium had been overturned, but she seemed unharmed.

Someone was clearly looking for something.

A wave of panic washed over him. He reached for his phone to call the police. It had about twelve percent juice left, but when he dialed 911, the call wouldn't go through.

Fuck! What the hell is it with this damned phone?

He stuffed it back in his jacket pocket, figuring he'd have to use Mrs. Binson's landline downstairs.

Holy shit! Mrs. Binson!

Disregarding his fear, he bolted into the hallway and clicked on the light. As he rushed by, he observed similar disarray in Lotte's office to that in the kitchen. Items from her desk and the bookshelves sat piled on the floor, not as if they had been haphazardly thrown, but simply removed and placed carefully on the ground.

He'd deal with that later. Right now, he feared for his friend, so he shimmied quickly down the stairs. As was typical, Mrs. Binson's door stood open, but the apartment was dark.

"Mrs. Binson? Gloria? Are you in there?"

He heard a noise emanating from the sofa near the big front window. He threw on the light and beheld Gloria Binson lying face down on the couch. Her hands were bound behind her back with twine, probably from her kitchen. Her feet were likewise tied together. A dish towel gagged her as she struggled to emit a cry for help.

He rushed over and untied the towel. "Gloria, what happened? Are you okay? My phone isn't working. I need yours to call the police!"

She was desperately trying to say something, so he gave her a moment to catch her breath as he untied her hands. "Down... down...

downstairs! The basement. Eric, she's... she's still there... still down there!"

He froze, and then slowly turned to face the door to Mrs. Binson's basement. He'd been down there many times, rooting in boxes for books from her deceased husband's collection, helping sell her daughter Melinda's old furniture, and of course loading in all the custom flight cases containing the Afrit's portal, as well as the large duffel bags where they stored Enki's gateway to the Abzu.

The door stood open. The darkness of the basement stairway yawned, silent and forbidding. There wasn't time now to call the police. If the intruder still lurked below, they might hear, if they hadn't already.

As quietly as possible, he finished untying poor Mrs. Binson, urging silence as he freed her. He then crept toward the dining room and grabbed a large brass candleholder off the table. Removing the candle, he grasped it upside down, so the heavy base was on the business end of his makeshift weapon. So armed, he walked to the basement doorway and flipped the light switch.

Cautiously, he descended. The well-worn wooden steps creaked with every footfall. Surprise was meaningless now. Whoever might be here had surely heard him call out earlier. Soon, they would be revealed — there were few places to hide in the basement's largely open space.

When he'd cleared the cellar ceiling, Eric peered past the stair railing. The naked bulb above the washer and dryer buzzed in the cavernous silence. With intense trepidation, he set foot on the floor, looking to his left to be sure no one crouched in the space invisible from the stairs. Empty.

He walked past the stacks of book boxes he knew so well. To the right, he could see cement steps leading to the bulkhead door. He pulled the dangly little string on another bulb that lit this area and peeked into the cobweb-infested alcove. Vacant.

The bulkhead door was tightly sealed from the inside by its formidable iron bar. No one had left this way as it was impossible to reseal the door, and if Mrs. Binson was to be believed, no one had come back up the stairs. His only companions in the dingy space were the aging washer and dryer, the boxes of books, an old ironing board, and a shelf full of cleaning products against which leaned a tall box labeled:

"Xmas Decorations."

The large space behind the furnace and chimney that had once housed Melanie's furniture, and later the two portals, echoed with complete emptiness. Of course, this came as no particular surprise to Eric. He knew full well why the priceless boxes and cases no longer resided in Mrs. Binson's basement.

It was a chilly late October morning in 2016, about two months after Lotte had returned from her Stonehenge project, and almost eight months to the day before the wedding, when the noxious buzz of the alarm startled Eric from the bliss of sleep. Usually, Lotte would whine until he shut it off. She hated the insufferable noise, but it remained the only way to get either of them out of bed, neither especially being "morning people."

Thus, it surprised him when her side of the mattress remained silent. He vaguely recalled her getting up at some ungodly hour, likely to pee, but he'd fallen back asleep. Reluctantly, he dragged himself to his feet, pulled on some sweats, and staggered to the kitchen. His hopes of her phenomenal coffee were quickly dashed. No aroma wafted from a steaming and steeping French press, which sat forlorn and empty on the kitchen counter.

Okay, I'm projecting. It's me that's forlorn and empty... empty of coffee, that is. She must be in her office. Probably had some wild idea she had to get down before it slipped out of her mind.

This happened from time to time — no big deal. He crossed the hall into the front bedroom that Mrs. Binson had so graciously allowed them to colonize.

It sat dark and empty.

Did she go out? Seems a bit early for that. Am I not remembering an appointment she had?

Just then, he heard a noise from down the stairwell, near the front door. It sounded like a sort of scraping sound, followed by a bump. *Scrape, scrape, scrape, bump...* then a pause... then the pattern repeated. He padded around the corner and looked down.

Lotte stood at Mrs. Binson's door, pawing pathetically, fingertips and knuckles raw and bleeding. Then, with a step forward, she banged her red and swollen forehead into the door. It didn't make much sound, and with her touch of hearing loss, Mrs. Binson was a heavy sleeper. Eric realized this must have been going on for hours.

He took a couple of steps down and she turned.

Her neck was hideously bent, left ear literally touching her left shoulder. Her eyes were white, pupils rolled back in her head. Her tongue listlessly dangled out of her slacked and quivering jaw, and a stream of foaming spittle dripped down her chin. She twitched unnaturally, as if pulled from a thousand unseen strings. Of all the ghastly images he had seen in his life, what he'd come to think of as his personal carousel of horror, he sensed this one might qualify as the most terrifying.

"Lotte?" he whispered to her, unable to find breath for more.

Slowly, a sound rose from her throat... at first a deep moan, it rapidly became a groan of despair and agony, before morphing into a nightmarish screech of seething anger, coupled with the deepest yearning and frustration.

Eric stood for a moment, unbelieving and paralyzed, until he dashed down the stairs.

The second he reached Lotte, Mrs. Binson threw open the door. "What in the world is going on?"

Immediately, the terrifying noise ceased. Lotte turned to Mrs. Binson, a look of horror and confusion on her face, then collapsed in a heap onto the floor of the foyer.

Eric hurriedly carried her into Mrs. Binson's apartment and lay her gently on the couch while Gloria ran for some water and a washcloth.

"I'm so sorry," Mrs. Binson effused while Eric dabbed Lotte's forehead with the damp cloth. "I shouldn't have said anything or disturbed her. I didn't realize Lotte was a sleepwalker."

"Neither did I," he dazedly replied. "This is a first for me, too. I think she's coming around."

Lotte's eyelids flickered and her body spasmed as she regained consciousness. "Where am I?" she puzzled, a look of confusion and fear on her face. Soon, tears streamed down her cheeks.

"Oh, honey," Mrs. Binson said, trying to sound encouraging. "You're in my apartment. We think you were sleepwalking. I didn't mean to wake you up. I'm so sorry. Do you need an ambulance?"

"Here, drink some water," Eric offered.

Lotte spoke through shaky gulps. "It's all right, Mrs. Binson. I was... well, I must have been really tired, in a very deep sleep. I'm sorry if I frightened you. I think I'm okay now. Eric, can you help me get back upstairs?"

Despite Gloria's concern and objections, Lotte insisted on returning to their apartment. Though still highly agitated, she was stable on her feet while Eric escorted her up the stairs.

Once inside, she directed them to the living room. "Make sure you close the door behind you."

Eric complied, then joined her on the couch, wrapped a blanket around her shivering shoulders, and sat beside her. "What is it? What's going on?"

"*Shhhh!*" she said, finger to her lips. "We can't let Mrs. Binson hear. Eric, you're not going to believe this. It's the Afrit!"

"What? You mean the dreams have started again? Are you telling me Chuckles somehow got stuck in another mirror?"

"No, it wasn't like that. It was a dream, but... oh, Eric, the *power* I felt... *calling* me! I couldn't resist it. I was utterly compelled. It's like nothing I've ever felt before."

"Calling you? Calling you to do what?"

"To come forth. It wants... it wants to *speak* with me. It yearns for... you're not going to believe this. It wants *companionship*."

Eric stared in wide-eyed shock. "What do you mean? Are you telling me the fucking thing is *lonely?*"

"I... I can't explain it. I've never felt anything like this from the creature before. It must be Ninurta! Absorbing his power has made the Afrit exponentially stronger. There may be other changes as well. I can't say for certain."

"Maybe it wasn't such a good idea feeding Ninurta to the Afrit after all, huh? I guess that ship has sailed."

She nodded. "Quite so, but we didn't have much of a choice. I wasn't about to argue with Enki about it. The creature doesn't seem angry, though. There was just this... well... this insistent *longing*. It wants me to come. It wants to speak with me, and it won't give up. This won't stop until I give the Afrit what it wants."

"How the hell are we supposed to do that? It's not like we can conduct one of our little Afrit seances in Mrs. Binson's basement."

"There has to be another place. We have to find a way, and we have to do it quickly. Today, if possible. Look at my hands! The creature's power is too great. This is going to destroy me. Help me think of something... please!" The look of desperation on her face said it all.

It didn't take him long. In truth, he'd anticipated the need arising to call forth the beast at some point, though he'd never imagined the reason for summoning the infernal entity would be that it wanted to hang out with its "homegirl."

"Hold on," he said as he got up to retrieve his phone. By the time he returned to the living room, they could both hear the ring in the speaker and the sound of someone answering.

"Hello? Eric?"

"Siddique! Yeah, it's me. Lotte's here too. Listen, where are you?"

"Going to work, man. I'm just about there. What's up?"

"What time are you off?"

"About four, depending on how it goes. Why, what's going on?"

"We need your help. Can you ask Ernie if you can cut out on time, or a little early if possible? We need you to drive to our place. You've got the van, right?"

"Of course."

"Perfect. Whatever plans you might have had for tonight, better cancel them. It's gonna get a little crazy, but this is important. Really important. Understand?"

"I understand. I'll be there. Whatever you need."

When Siddique arrived late that afternoon, they rapidly removed the flight cases with the un-mirror and other materials out of Mrs. Binson's basement and into the van.

Their landlord took in the activity with curiosity. "Where are you taking it?"

"I just need my equipment at school," Lotte explained. "We'll bring it back in a few days."

In the absence of anywhere else to go, they went to Siddique's apartment. It would be horribly disruptive in the relatively small living space, but he didn't balk. Fortunately, he lived in a converted warehouse, so the stairs and hallways were navigable with the bulky cases.

Siddique made pepper chicken that gave the apartment an exquisite smell while Lotte and Eric finished setting up the frame and the black marble board. At her direction, they placed only one candle in each of the bowls, but kept more aside if needed. After silently eating their dinner, Lotte settled herself in front of the great un-mirror, which they had assembled along the weathered and irregular brick wall that gave the room a cozy charm.

"I'm just going to talk with it," she explained. "Give me some time. I'll let you know if I need anything."

Siddique and Eric sat at the kitchen table as Lotte lit the candles and sat cross-legged at the apex of the black marble slab in which the bowls rested. Soon, her head bobbed as she incanted, summoning the supernatural creature within its realm of fire. It didn't seem to take long.

In quiet tones, Lotte conversed with the beast. Mostly, she listened, occasionally interjecting a question. Her hushed voice prevented Eric from hearing the details, and the Afrit's projected thoughts from the portal seemed to extend only to Lotte. Two words, however, finally rang clear in the tense silence.

"That's impossible!" Lotte's tone was desperate.

Eric started up from the kitchen table, but she immediately shot out her arm, palm facing him with an order to stop. She leaned intently over the bowls on the board in front of her, straining toward the glass of the gateway and forcefully whispering. Whatever was happening, the conversation grew intense.

Finally, Lotte sat back and deeply sighed. "Eric, come over here."

He sat next to her on the floor. "Are you okay? What is it?"

She was sweating and slightly pale. "I'm fine. You need to listen to me, and you need to trust me and do as I say. Place two more candles in each of the bowls and please light them."

"What are we doing?"

She met his worried gaze. "We're summoning the Afrit. It wants to come out."

"We can't do that! You know this, Lotte! You know what it means to summon this thing. Someone has to die. Why? Because this fucking monster wants to sit on the couch with you to have a little in-person chat? There's no reason for this. I can't be a part of it."

"No," she tried to explain. "It's not like that, not this time. This is different. The Afrit has... *changed*. No one will die. You have to believe what I'm saying. It won't give up until it gets what it wants, but I think it's telling the truth. Its word has always been good. The creature just needs a small taste of our world, then it will go back. Tomorrow... I swear to you. It won't give up, Eric. It won't. We have no choice. You have to trust me."

Trust.

So much power behind that one little syllable. Eric knew all too well what a long and hard road it had been for Lotte to trust him: first, to not judge her; then to keep her secret; later to help her; and eventually to find his way back to her. Finally, the hardest part of all: to never leave her — never, ever — because he held her heart in his hands, and despite external appearances to the contrary, her heart was fragile, having once been so unbearably broken.

In contrast, all he had to do to trust her was to believe she was right. In comparison, that was easy, because Lotte was always right.

The summoning was the same, but the result was shocking. Only a sliver of the normally thick tendril of sparkling black ash twisted from the cloudy glass of the portal. Siddique was transfixed, having never witnessed the near miracle firsthand. Eric, however, almost laughed aloud when, after the whirling particles had coalesced, an Afrit barely a foot tall stood assembled before them — a perfect miniature of the hulking obsidian monstrosity with whom he and Lotte had become so hopelessly entwined. Strangely, the little creature now bore some dapples of orange, as if magma coursed in places under its ashen, pumice-like skin.

Its wings flexed as the little beastie quested achingly toward the window of Siddique's apartment. Lotte rose, pulled the curtain aside, and opened the room to the chill of the night. The little monster launched into the dark sky as if shot from a bazooka.

Lotte closed the window and turned to face them. "It'll be back tomorrow, and we'll return it to the Eternal Flame. This portion of it will carry its experiences back to the whole, and this will satisfy the creature... for a time."

"For a time?" Eric incredulously asked. "You mean we'll have to do this again? How often?"

"I don't know, but I'm guessing with some frequency. It must be some part of Ninurta's energy that's caused this, perhaps his human desires combined with his godlike power. I'm not certain, but whatever it is, the creature wants to talk with me, and it wants to fly free in our world. No deaths, and no bargain is needed, not for this small incursion into our realm, but it's going to want this, and it's going to want it with regularity."

"Oh, man," Siddique chimed in. "That's gonna be a lot of moving and driving!"

"Obviously, that isn't practical," she replied. "We'll have to find another solution to Mrs. Binson's basement."

The next morning, Eric called all of Schneider Industrial Flooring's Boston-based suppliers in the hopes someone might have some spare warehouse space. They needed something indoors, and reasonably climate-controlled, but not monitored too closely like a rental storage building. It also needed to be in a remote enough area that their activities wouldn't be noticed.

As luck would have it, one of his old contacts in the business office at Peterman's said they lived near Andrew Square in South Boston, right across the street from an old factory building that had been converted into artist spaces. Tucked into a small triangular plot at the intersection of Ellery and Boston Street, the structure was too close to the railroad tracks to have been converted into loft apartments, as so many others of its kind in the area had been. As it turned out, they had a fairly undesirable space in the basement with no windows, but it sported a secure steel-reinforced door with sturdy locks. Best of all, it sat right next to what had formerly been the loading dock, so they would have easy and essentially unmonitored access.

At $162 per month for the unit, it was pricey, but space in this area was half the cost of that in Somerville. Additionally, the building was only a short walk from the Andrew Square T stop, a straight shot south for Lotte from Davis Square on the Red Line when Eric couldn't drive her. It was perfect.

They secured the lease and moved the materials in the following week.

They kept the fire portal set up for her roughly monthly visits. Lotte would carry the impish Afrit out in her backpack, releasing it to the night sky and returning it the next evening. Enki's gateway, and later the materials of Vanth's portal, were also stored there, though not entirely.

The silver rings that had once commanded Charun, now void of their black ornaments, which had shattered in the magnetic maelstrom, along with one piece of the gateway to the Abzu, and later, after their honeymoon, one milky white piece of Vanth's portal, were securely hidden in Lotte and Eric's apartment.

Or are they? Shit!

Eric bounded back up the basement steps two at a time and burst into the living room where Mrs. Binson sat on the couch, still seemingly immobilized by fear.

"Did you find her?" she urgently asked.

"There's no one down there," he replied, knowing full well how that would be received.

"That's not possible! I saw her go down there—just barely, but I saw her, and I haven't taken my eyes off that door. Nobody came back up. Nobody! Did she leave by the bulkhead?"

"No, it's sealed tight from the inside. Listen... we have to call the police. Can you do that? There's something I have to check on upstairs. I'll just be a second."

"Eric, I'm scared to death!"

"I know, me too, but I really think the house is clear. I'll go up, and then be right back. Can you call the police?"

Warily, she rose and lurched toward the kitchen.

He didn't hesitate. He shot up the stairs, past Lotte's office and through the door into the kitchen, where he hung a hard left down the hall. He halted in front of the bathroom. The light was off, so he reached inside and flicked the switch.

The metal grating for the heating vent lay on the floor next to the toilet. He saw the screws scattered haphazardly on the floor as he bent to inspect the hole in the wall. The little bag containing the rings and the white stone were gone, as was the curved, hollow piece of Enki's gateway. It was almost inconceivable someone could find the items here, but find them they had.

Lotte, Eric, and in some sense the entire material plane of existence, had just been robbed.

CHAPTER 4

"Eric! Where are you?"

"Coming!" he called in response to Mrs. Binson's ever more agitated queries as he frantically twisted the final screw holding the metal vent cover in place. He couldn't let the police see that in the condition he'd found it. When finished, he ran to the kitchen, ditched the screwdriver in the utility drawer, and bolted back down the stairs.

Gloria stood in the foyer, gazing anxiously upward. "What in the world were you doing? I'm just so afraid!"

"I'm sorry, I'm sorry... there were just a couple of things I had to check. It's all OK. Why don't you come inside? Let's sit down and maybe you can tell me what happened while we wait for the police."

She weakly nodded, and he directed her gently to the couch. The loosened string and limp dish towel lay in testimony of her ordeal. "I still can't believe it. I must have fallen asleep. I was tired after I went shopping after lunch, and when the opera finished, I must have nodded off. All of a sudden, I woke up and felt somebody pushing me down onto the sofa. I tried to fight back, but... it was like I was paralyzed. I couldn't move a muscle!"

"Could you see the person's face?"

"No, I think she intentionally turned my head toward the back of the couch so I couldn't see her."

"So, how do you know it was a woman?"

"I'll get to that. Once she had me face down, I heard her rustling around in the kitchen. She came back with that ball of string and started tying me up. I still couldn't fight back. I couldn't even talk or scream for help. I've never felt anything like it! Once she'd secured me, she went off and started opening drawers, searching the house—kitchen, bedroom, dining room, bookshelves... everywhere. Slowly, the feeling started to return to my hands and feet, then my arms and legs... just enough so I could move a little. It was hard, but I got my face turned back into the room. Just as I did, I saw her open the basement door and go down. Eric, she was naked!"

"Naked? Like, no clothes naked? Nothing?"

"Not a stitch on her."

"What did she look like otherwise? Could you see her face?"

She shook her head. "No, I only caught her from behind. Pretty little behind, too, if I may say. She had kind of darkish skin, and thick, curly hair... brown or black. The sun was going down, so I couldn't tell exactly."

"And you say she never came back up?"

"Eric, I could barely move my head. I had nowhere to look but at that door. She never came back up those stairs."

Lights flashing in the street indicated the arrival of the police. Eric let them in the front door and led them into the apartment, one female officer and one male. They introduced themselves, but he didn't even register their names. After a quick recap of what happened, they did a sweep of the house. It was empty, basement included.

An ambulance arrived, and the female officer stayed with Mrs. Binson while the paramedics examined her.

The male officer escorted Eric upstairs. "You say you don't think anything was taken?"

Eric lied but tried to make it look convincing. "Well, I can't be certain. Everything's such a mess, but it doesn't look like it. Honestly, we don't have much. I saw my wife's desktop is still in her office. I haven't checked, but if my laptop is in the living room, there really isn't much more to steal."

"And where is your wife?" he asked, all business.

"At this moment? Either at JFK in New York, or on a plane back to Italy. She left this morning to give a talk at the Metropolitan Museum, which is probably over by now."

"And where were you this evening?"

Eric suddenly had a chill.

Dark skin... thick, curly hair... brown or black. It sounds like Rebecca, but why would she do this? How could she do this?

It didn't make sense, but it definitely helped explain why she'd stood him up for dinner.

She wanted me out of the apartment. She knew Lotte was already gone, but she probably didn't anticipate Mrs. Binson being here. She works at a fucking archaeology museum. Maybe she knows something about these things?

The pieces were starting to add up, but if Rebecca had taken the hidden portal materials, she too would need to remain unknown to the police.

"Did you hear me?" the officer asked.

"Sorry," Eric fumbled. "Crazy day. I had dinner in Harvard Square. Then I walked home."

"Alone?"

"Yeah, alone. I felt like treating myself because I was missing my wife. She's been gone a lot recently. We just got married in May."

"Congratulations," he said with little enthusiasm. "Listen, I'm not sure what happened here. Sounds like some kind of prank to me. I mean, a naked girl running around the house opening drawers? Nothing broken, nothing taken? Don't get me wrong. What she did to your landlord is assault and battery. I could get some detectives here, and we could take some prints, but if it's some weird sorority hazing thing, it's doubtful the girl will have a record. If not, there really isn't a lot we can do. You sure you closed and locked that door?"

They were in Eric's kitchen now, Langsam looking up curiously from her disordered terrarium. "I want to say I'm one hundred percent positive, because we've never had an issue like this. I mean, what are the chances? The *one* time I leave an upstairs back door unlocked, somebody comes in and does all this? It just seems more deliberate than that. So, I'm pretty damned sure I didn't leave the door open. That's the best I can say."

The officer seemed satisfied. After casing the outside of the house, they left their cards, said they'd file a report, and promised a little extra security on the street. The paramedics had already gone, Mrs. Binson having adamantly determined that transport to a hospital was unnecessary.

"They said I might have had sleep paralysis," she explained when the cruiser departed. "That happens sometimes. I guess it's caused by stress, or whatever. Maybe that woman grabbing me and waking me up that way did it. Who knows? All I know is what I saw... or didn't see... meaning a naked woman *not* coming out of that damned basement. I'm sure as hell not staying here tonight. I've called my friend, Doris. She has plenty of room, so she's coming to get me. Honey, do you have somewhere safe you can go?"

"I'm fine, Mrs. Binson. I think the officers were right, that it was probably a prank. I know that doesn't answer what happened with this weird disappearance, and I totally understand how you feel. I just think there's a logical explanation. I'll stay here and guard the house. I have a phone, and I know how to use it."

Actually, I don't. My phone is fucked, but it gave him an idea. "Speaking of phones, mine's been a little fluky recently and is just about out of juice. There's somebody I'd like to call. Mind if I use your landline real quick?"

"Of course. I'll go get some things together. Doris should be here soon."

Mrs. Binson went to her disheveled bedroom. For some reason, the intruder hadn't been as careful in her apartment as his and Lotte's. Her things had been strewn about quite haphazardly, though nothing had been broken. Eric headed to the kitchen, praying his phone hadn't quite died. Luckily, it seemed to still have about ten percent charge left, so he swiped it open and went to his text messages to grab Rebecca's number.

His jaw hit the floor. All his text threads were gone.

Desperately, he looked in his call logs, but no record of her number was there either. He also realized that he'd never entered her as a contact. All traces of her had disappeared from his phone.

Crap! Guess I have the answer about whether this day could get any more insane.

It was about 7:30 a.m. when Eric's laptop started its familiar chime, waking him from fitful sleep. He'd stayed up late rearranging the apartment, and tidying up what he could in Mrs. Binson's place. He'd have preferred to have slept in, but talking to Lotte took priority. He could nap later if necessary.

"Hi!" she said, looking relatively cheerful on the Skype screen after her long flight. "I got your email. I held off calling as long as I could. I know it's early for you, but I have to get some sleep. Tomorrow is going to be insane. What's going on? You said it was important... and what happened to your phone?"

That was a lot of questions to field without coffee. He'd ease into it. "I think it's the battery, but it loses its mobile data and wi-fi signal a lot too. I don't know. I'll probably take it in tomorrow so they can have a look at it. How'd it go yesterday in New York?"

"Oh, the same as the Harvard presentation, more people, but the same dog and pony show. It gets everyone excited, though. I guess that's how the game is played. Sven is really giving me a lesson in the art of publicity."

Eric shuddered. *When the hell did he become* Sven *as opposed to Dr. Henriksson?*

"In any case, what's so important? I'm dying to know."

Oh, you'll be dying all right, he thought with dread. *This is gonna suck.* "Look, I need you to stay calm about this. Promise? We have to keep our heads and think clearly."

Lotte's pixelated and erratic image showed concern. "What is this about, Eric?"

"Last night, we got robbed. Someone broke in, tied up Mrs. Binson, and took something important in our apartment."

"I... I can't believe it! Is Mrs. Binson all right? The poor thing!"

"Yeah, she's fine, shaken up but not really hurt. She went to stay at a friend's house. She saw the thief, or at least one of them. It was a woman. She was totally naked."

"What?"

"That was my reaction, but that's what Mrs. Binson swears she saw. She also said the woman went into the basement, and that she never came back upstairs. The bulkhead door was secure from the inside. I have no idea what happened. Maybe Mrs. Binson blacked out briefly. The paramedics said she might have had some kind of sleep paralysis, so maybe that was a factor. Anyway, nothing got taken from her place."

"Well, what was taken from ours? Don't tell me they took my desktop! You know I suck at backing that thing up to the network. I have no idea what files were on there."

"Nope, not the desktop, or my laptop. Worse."

"*Alter!* They didn't hurt Langsam, did they? Who could do such a thing?"

It almost made him laugh, and he felt cheered by her care for their turtle, but it also made clear the ludicrous impossibility of the portal materials being uncovered. "No, Langsam's fine, not a scratch on her. It's worse than all of that. Unthinkably worse."

Lotte stared in horrified silence. "But Eric, that's impossible! Why on earth would a thief look in a place like that? It would take ages to get that grill off, and gratings like that are all over the damned house! Were all the others removed as well?"

This was an excellent point. "No, they weren't. I didn't even think of that. Whoever did this must have *known* those things were exactly there, or had some way to, I don't know... detect them. Is that even possible?"

She had no answer. He could see her eyes frantically batting back and forth as she tried to conceive the inconceivable. "We have to get them back! We must! Do you have any idea who might have done this?"

This was where it got really tricky. If he revealed his suspicions about Rebecca, Lotte would blow a gasket... probably hop on the next plane out, take an Uber to the Peabody Museum, and beat the living crap out of this woman. Eric doubted he could talk her out of it, not to mention he'd have to explain the rather odd way in which they had met, and that he had planned to meet her for dinner.

He fully intended to try to find Rebecca tomorrow. Staking her out at work first thing on Monday morning was the only way he knew to get hold of her now that his phone had mysteriously erased her number. If Lotte were with him, he'd probably tell her the truth and take her with him. As it was, it just seemed unnecessary. He'd fess up if Rebecca turned out to be the culprit, but for now, rightly or wrongly, he decided to keep that to himself.

"No, I have no idea who did this," he lied, "but I'm guessing whoever did it isn't finished with us. Now that they know we have this stuff, and probably more, I think they'll be calling again."

"Should I come back? Are you in danger?"

"Well, I'm not sure. They didn't really *hurt* Mrs. Binson. I'm guessing they didn't anticipate she'd even be there. They could have easily killed her, and if they'd wanted me dead, they could have broken in and stabbed me, or something. It feels to me like they were trying to avoid some kind of confrontation. The theft happened when I'd gone out. They probably also knew you weren't home."

"How?"

"Lotte, your face is all over the archaeology press. Pictures of what you found are in the news. You're easily traceable to New York City yesterday, and maybe we're not the only ones who know what was once in that box."

"You're right," she reluctantly admitted. "I'm sorry, I haven't had time to think all this through."

"It's fine. I'm not upset, but this is why I wanted you to be patient and not do anything rash. Stay put for now, and let's see what her, or their, next move will be."

"All right, but you have to keep me posted. I have to know what's going on."

"Deal. Gives me a good excuse to Skype you many times a day."

"Little shit! You'd like that, wouldn't you? Actually, I'd like it too. I miss you terribly."

His heart skipped a beat. The sincerity of her words cut through the latency and choppiness of the video. It was exactly what he'd needed to hear, and it was all he could do to keep from crying.

They stared at each other on their respective screens.

"Eric," she finally said, also appearing quite emotional "I... I have to, umm...."

"What?"

"I have to... oh, never mind. I have to go. Send me emails if you can't get your phone straightened out. I'm right here, my love, and I'll come if you need me."

With that, she was suddenly gone.

As promised, Eric took Langsam for a nice walk in the backyard. She enjoyed it, but he had to cut it short when his head started pounding.

Probably stress and lack of sleep. It wasn't the booze. He'd never cracked the bottle of Captain Morgan's, and he had no plans of doing so now.

He did wind up falling back asleep, this time in the living room after surfing through more stupid YouTube videos.

"Who watches this shit?" *I guess that would be me,* he realized with dismay.

He woke a little after 2:00 p.m., feeling refreshed. He tried Mrs. Binson at Doris's house. She'd written the number down for him and, amazingly, his phone made the connection. "How are you? Do you feel like you're ready to come home?"

"Well, yes and no," she replied, sounding far more sanguine than last night. "I'm probably going to sleep here at Doris's for a few nights, but the thought of my place being such a mess is making me crazy. If you were planning to be in tonight, I was thinking about stopping by, maybe cleaning up a little. If you're game, I could cook a nice dinner. I bought all that food yesterday and it will just go to waste otherwise."

"I'd like nothing better," he happily agreed. "I can come get you... five-thirty sound good?"

That settled, Eric focused on his need for some exercise. A nice bike ride would do the trick. He changed, then grabbed his phone on the way out.

"What the hell!"

The phone that was almost fully charged ten minutes ago had drained down to twenty-five percent.

"Fuck it!" He plugged the useless thing back in and left.

He walked down the stairs, unchained his bike, and started walking it toward the street, but then turned around. He resolutely walked back up the stairs, crossed the porch, and checked their door.

Closed, and locked.

Satisfied, he walked back to his bike and took off.

He banged a right out of the walkway onto Rogers, crossed Broadway, and took a left on Boston Avenue toward Tufts University, where there were plenty of nice places to ride. He'd gone a block up Broadway when he felt dizziness and his head started hurting again. By the time he hit College Avenue, it was pounding, and his stomach was churning.

Maybe I should have eaten something? Figuring Tufts was just a bit ahead on his left, he pushed on. There would be places to rest if necessary.

It was necessary. *Acutely* necessary. He was convinced he was about to throw up, or maybe expel an alien creature through his solar plexus. The horrible mixture of dizziness, pain, and sickness finally forced him to abandon his bike and lie down in the nearest grassy patch he could find.

What next? A plague of locusts? The thought made him gag. He reached for the water bottle on his bike, but it seemed miles away. The aching discomfort and nausea were getting worse. Eric began to wonder how much more of this he could take.

"You all right, dude?"

Groggily, he looked up. A dark-skinned young man stood above him. He wore a gray hoody, loose fitting black jeans, and had a backpack around his shoulder.

"I'm not," Eric admitted. "Listen, I have to get home. I don't have my phone, but I have something north of fifty dollars in my wallet. If you call an Uber, it's all yours. I'm only a few blocks away. It has to be a big car, though. For my bike. Please, can you do this?"

"You sure you don't need a hospital?" he skeptically asked.

"I might. I don't know. I have no idea what the problem is. I go to Cambridge Hospital. My house is on the way. If I don't feel any better when I get home, we'll go there. It isn't much farther."

"It is for me, but whatever, dude. You're hurtin'! Hold on." To his amazement and relief, the young man whipped out his phone. "Five minutes. Can you hold on that long?"

"I can if you get me my water bottle."

The Uber arrived and the young man explained the situation.

"I don't want anybody puking in my car," the driver sourly said. "You gonna puke, buddy?"

"I haven't yet," Eric groaned. "I haven't eaten anything, so I doubt it."

"Maybe that's your damned problem. All right. I'll put the bike in the car. You help him get in."

Eric felt the young man tug at his arm. With every ounce of strength, Eric pulled himself to his feet, reeling from the waves of agony that wracked his body. From the back seat, he heard the driver get in.

"How much is it to Cambridge hospital?" his companion asked.

"You asked for 67 Rogers Avenue in your request," the driver curtly replied.

"Yeah, but if he's not feeling better by the time he gets home, I want you to take him there. How much?"

"Hold on. $12.69. It isn't far."

"Listen," the young man said to Eric. "Give me your wallet. I'm gonna take twenty bucks to cover the charge on my card, that's all. This guy will take you where you need to go. I got things I need to do. You're gonna be okay. Is that fair?"

"More than fair. Take more if you want it. I can't thank you enough."

"Forget it. Good deed for the day, right? You take care of yourself."

The Uber pulled away. Amazingly, the motion of the car seemed to do Eric some good. By the time they reached Powder House Square, the nausea had lessened. The driver stayed on College Avenue, then took a left onto Kidder. By the time they approached Rogers on the left, he was feeling much better.

"What'll it be buddy? You need the hospital?"

"No, I think it's passing. Just drop me at home. Thanks."

"Want to thank me? Give me a nice cash tip like you gave to that kid."

Eric happily complied.

Whatever it had been, it had come and gone.

Eric ate some Alpen when he got in, just to put something into his stomach, but no trace remained of the symptoms he'd felt earlier. It was utterly bizarre.

Around 5:00 p.m., he left to get Mrs. Binson. Having never been there, he had little choice but to take his phone for directions to Doris's house. For now, the infernal thing seemed to be cooperating and holding its charge.

When they arrived home, Mrs. Binson cooked while Eric straightened out more of her apartment, benefitting from direction as to exactly where things went. At one point, she even worked up the courage to let him take her into the basement. Everything appeared as it had been, and after a thorough search, Mrs. Binson seemed to finally accept that a naked woman no longer roamed the house.

Too bad. I might have actually liked to see that.

When they were about to sit down to eat, Mrs. Binson put on some music. After a few moments, Eric felt a slight dizziness and his head again began to ache. He excused himself and lay down on the couch.

"Are you all right?" she asked, rushing over to him. "Oh, sweetie, this must have been so hard on you, too. Hold on, let me get you some water." She turned the stereo down on the way to the kitchen, and he almost instantly started feeling better.

"Here you go" she said, handing him the glass. "You're sitting up. That's a good sign."

"Yeah, I think it might have been the music, though I've never known Dave Brubeck to give me a headache before. Honestly, I had a little episode like this in the afternoon... well, maybe not so little. I think you're right. I think I'm stressed out. It's not just about the break-in, though. Lotte's been gone for so long. It's totally wearing me out. It's affecting her, too. I can sense it. Something's just not right."

"Have you talked to her?"

"No, I don't want to make a fuss about something like this when she's so busy, and I don't think either of us want to have a big discussion over Skype. It's so flaky, especially internationally. I heard about this other platform called Zoom. It might be better, but nobody I know has used it. Even if it's more stable, though, I think we'd both prefer to talk face-to-face."

She was silent for a moment, then reached over and gave him a warm hug. "Oh, sweetie, I've known you two for a few years now. I attended your wedding. I've never in my life seen two people more in love than you and Lotte."

He blushed, and felt tears tickle his eyes.

"But let me tell you something... you've picked the hard road. Separation is usually difficult for couples. George didn't go to many conferences, but when he did, both our lives got thrown for quite a loop. It was always so good to have him back. I can't imagine what it would have been like if he were gone for months at a time. So, whatever stress you're feeling about missing her, I'm guessing she's feeling it too, even if her reaction to it may be different."

He nodded. "Yeah, I can't argue with any of that."

"So, you have to talk to her, find out what's on her mind. In my day, we had a crazy little contraption called the telephone. Yeah, you tried not to use it for really sensitive stuff, but sometimes it was the only tool for the job. In the end, though, there's just no substitute for communication. So, skip, or zip, or zam, or zing away, or whatever it was you told me you two do on your computers. Or call her... or get on a plane and fly to Italy! But, sweetie, you have to talk to her. You can't let suspicions and speculations fester. It'll cloud your judgment. Maybe it already has, and that's not good for anybody, is it?"

CHAPTER 5

Eric enjoyed the rest of the evening, though Gloria Binson's words continued to ring in his ears. He pondered them as he walked her to his car to return her to Doris's house for the night.

Maybe "fester" had been too strong a word, but he couldn't deny that he increasingly harbored certain... *notions*. Maybe "petty jealousies" and "irritations" better described how he felt about the way Lotte's project, and how she had been behaving, had interrupted their idyllic lives. He was confused by how she suddenly seemed to embrace a world she'd previously deemed superfluous, and he felt annoyed by the way she now called Dr. Henriksson "Sven."

But do I really think something is going on between them?

He couldn't bring himself to believe she would, or *could*, do something like that. Yet, for some reason, he had drifted down that rabbit hole.

If I don't truly think she's having some kind of affair, why would I do that?

The only answer he could find troubled him: it had to be his own insecurities.

Not that Eric lacked self-confidence. He felt he was a stand-up guy, and knew that people liked and even, in some ways, respected him. He had a good job, playing an increasingly integral part in a successful and growing company. Even when it came to Lotte, he had acknowledged the wisdom of his grandmother's words: "Lotte has made her decision, and she is not one to choose lightly."

He accepted this. Lotte obviously had her reasons for picking him and questioning that was counterproductive. She'd also responded quite positively to his efforts to be more proactive... forging independence through his work at Schneider, forcing himself gently into her world to share the joy of being with her, and of course the most proactive step he'd ever taken, proposing to her. It had all worked spectacularly, yet despite this, he felt at a deficit when he compared himself with her — basically always had.

It didn't trouble him one bit that she pursued her dreams and got all the accolades and attention. Deep down, however, he worried that she might just wake up one day and realize she'd made the wrong decision, that as good as he might be, at some level he might not be able to hold her attention indefinitely, even if he did his very, very best.

So, he noticed little things, and they gently brushed the back of his mind with vague suppositions—fears, really, which only mounted when waters became choppy.

Mrs. Binson is right. We need to talk.

No doubt his reluctance to expose these small but deeply rooted anxieties was inhibiting him from initiating the conversation, as if speaking the words aloud might make it so, that confessing he judged himself in some sense *inferior* might make her cognizant of their inequality and wake her from the slumber that kept her with him.

Eric put the car in reverse and backed out of the driveway.

"You don't have to take me," Mrs. Binson argued. "Doris can pick me up. I'd drive myself, but it's all resident parking around their house."

"It's fine." He smiled to hide his inner disquiet. "It's twenty minutes there and back. I'm happy to do it. Let it be my thanks for cooking and for your great company tonight. It was just what I needed, and believe me, I really heard what you said. It's on my mind."

"I know, sweetie. I can tell. You two will be fine. Trust me."

Nice words, he mused as he banged a left onto Kidder. *Hope she's right.*

They hadn't gone two blocks when the dizziness again assailed his senses.

"Oh shit!" He rapidly steered the car to the curb.

"What's the matter? Are you feeling sick again?"

"Yeah, it's definitely starting. I'm so sorry. I thought it had cleared up. I was fine in the car earlier. In fact, I'd been thinking that the motion might have helped. It's probably some kind of inner ear infection. Maybe that's why the music was affecting me. I don't know."

"Do you need to go to the doctor?"

"I don't think it's an emergency. If it doesn't clear up, though, I may go tomorrow. Problem is, I'm not sure it's a good idea for me to be driving right now. I can feel it getting worse. Can you get us back to the house and call Doris or an Uber? I'm so, so sorry."

"Oh, sweetie, don't worry about it. It's fine. I just hate to see you like this."

He got out so they could switch seats, but he was so shaky he couldn't even make it around the car. He collapsed into the back seat instead.

Mrs. Binson got behind the wheel, banged a U-turn, and headed back toward Rogers.

As before, he immediately started feeling better, and by the time they were inside, his symptoms had disappeared.

It didn't take long for Doris to arrive.

"I need more time before I'm ready to try sleeping here," Mrs. Binson explained. "I'm still just so jumpy! Call us if you need anything. You have the number."

"I will," Eric promised. "Thanks so much. I really had a great evening, despite all this weirdness."

When they pulled away, he sat heavily on the front steps of the porch. It was a nice evening, the chill of fall an as yet unfulfilled promise in the light breeze.

What the hell is happening to me?

There just didn't seem to be any logic to it. Sometimes he went out and he got sick, sometimes he didn't. He'd made the trip to pick up Mrs. Binson just three hours ago — no problems.

And what was with the music during dinner? It just doesn't make any sense.

He went back inside. Mrs. Binson's door was closed, but not locked, so he went inside and clicked on the lights.

He approached the stereo and turned it on. It looked like the CD was still in the player. He turned the volume down low and hit play. The frenetic piano of *Blue Rondo à la Turk* lightly emanated from the speakers. Slowly, he turned up the volume, and by the time the band kicked in, the music was far louder than it had been when Mrs. Binson had played it earlier.

He felt fine.

Ridiculous!

He shut off the stereo, turned off the lights, closed the door, and went upstairs. Upon entering their apartment, he flicked the light switch in the kitchen, and Langsam stirred in her terrarium. Eric grabbed her water bowl and went to re-fill it at the sink. His phone caught his eye where it sat on the kitchen table re-charging.

He considered the strange situation. When he'd returned with Mrs. Binson, he'd come upstairs to hang up his jacket. Using the phone's GPS for directions had drained virtually all of its juice, so he'd plugged it in and left it there. When he'd taken Gloria home later, he'd retrieved his coat, but had left the phone where it was since he already knew the way.

He shook his head.

It can't be, but....

It all started to come to him.

He didn't have his phone with him in the afternoon when he rode his bike, or in the back yard when he'd walked Langsam that morning after talking with Lotte. He hadn't been paying attention, and the ever-adventurous turtle had waddled under the fence into the neighbor's yard behind them. He'd been forced to circle around to fetch her, and that's when the dizziness and headache started, when he got farther from the house — farther from his phone.

It's absolutely batshit crazy, but it's easy enough to test out.

He still wore his jacket, so he slipped the phone into his pocket and went back downstairs and out the front door, making sure it was locked. He turned left, the same way he'd just taken Mrs. Binson in the car, quickly reached Kidder, went left again, and walked to where he'd been forced to pull over.

No symptoms manifested.

He walked home, unlocked the front door, dropped the phone on the stairs, and then went back out to retrace his route. By the time he hit Kidder, the dizziness and nausea again hit him. Before the sickness could overtake him, he reversed direction, and he felt better with every step back toward home.

It made sense now, as much as something like this *could* make sense, but one mystery remained to be solved.

Why did I suddenly start feeling sick when Mrs. Binson played that music... and why didn't it happen when I spun the CD just now?

He went back inside, grabbed his suddenly highly suspect phone, took it back upstairs to the kitchen, and returned to Gloria's apartment. He repeated his music experiment, and strains of The Dave Brubeck Quartet soon loudly filled the room.

He sat and waited, but nothing happened.

What else were we doing? We'd just sat down to dinner. I was dishing out some vegetables while she was pouring wine... we were talking —

He froze.

Talking. What if the damn thing is listening to me? How is that even possible? Then again, how is it possible that monsters and gods walk into my world from different realms through those weird-ass portals?

Given his recent experiences, "possible" took on a significantly different tenor.

It wants to hear what I'm saying. I seem to be in its range, but if the music is too loud....

"I wonder if Mrs. Binson has any chamomile tea?" he asked aloud, his words mostly drowned out by the volume on the stereo.

Nothing happened.

Well, so much for that theory. Unless....

He got up and walked into the kitchen. After turning on the light, he picked up the receiver of Mrs. Binson's phone, which hung on the wall, and dialed Margot's number, one of the few beside his own that he had memorized.

Please pick up, please pick up, please pick up....

"Hello?" Margot's voice rang out in the receiver.

Immediately, he was overcome by nausea and a searing pain in his head. He fell to the floor, reeling, but tried to push through. "Margot... hi... it's... Eric."

"Eric! Why are you calling me on this weird number, and what the hell is that noise in the background? Are you at a jazz club? If so, why didn't you invite me?"

He couldn't bear the pain that felt like a dagger in his skull, and this time he knew he would puke if he couldn't get the dizziness to stop.

"Hold... on," he croaked.

He heard her say something on the other end of the line, but he'd already dropped the phone. Torturously, he dragged himself to the stereo and groped miserably for the volume knob. On the third try, he grasped it and shakily twisted it to zero.

Slowly, the pain and nausea subsided. He got sluggishly to his feet and stumbled back to the receiver, which dangled by its cord about a foot off the linoleum floor of the kitchen.

He heard Margot's voice in the tinny speaker. "Eric? You there? Eric? What's going on?"

He grabbed the handset. "I'm here. Sorry, I just had to turn down that music. Mrs. Binson must be going deafer than I'd thought."

"Where are you?"

"I'm in Mrs. Binson's apartment," he explained, shaking off the last vestiges of this most recent ordeal. "She's cleaning up and I'm helping her. Long story... I'll tell you tomorrow. Listen, my cell phone is fucked up, that's why I'm calling from here. I have to take it in tomorrow for them to look at. I'll be out of commission in the morning. I didn't have anything big on my schedule, but if anyone calls the office, I just wanted you to know where I'd be."

"Cool, thanks for letting me know. You sound funny. You okay?"

"Yeah, fine. It's just been a long day. I'll get in touch tomorrow when my phone is fixed."

"Okay, take it easy."

He closed up Mrs. Binson's apartment and returned upstairs. His phone sat menacingly on the kitchen table. Cautiously, he picked it up. As usual, at least of late, the battery was almost drained. He plugged it in.

He'd need it tomorrow when he went to see Rebecca, and find out what the hell was going on.

Eric's mind raced as he stood in the shade of a building.

He surveyed the main entrance to Harvard's Peabody Museum from across Divinity Avenue. He knew Rebecca worked here. He'd found her name and biography on his computer, listed under the Conservation Department of the museum, but he had no idea what time she came to work, or what entrance she might use to access the building, so he watched, and waited, and worried.

He'd barely slept all night. The thought of his phone in the kitchen eavesdropping on him had invaded his thoughts, made him paranoid and jumpy. He'd considered dropping the accursed thing in the toilet but doubted that would really solve anything.

What if it can see me, too... watch what I'm doing?

That idea had really freaked him out, especially when he was showering. It was just too much to bear. At this point, though, he'd have to take what came. Rebecca was his only lead, and the sole thread in all of this that he could follow.

It was approaching 9:00 a.m. and the Peabody would open soon. If he didn't see her, he'd try to contact her through the front desk. Several people, presumably other employees, had gone in the museum's main entrance. The door had opened and then been locked behind them.

As he battled growing impatience and anxiety, she appeared, using the same walkway beside the Museum of Comparative Zoology that he'd traversed about an hour-and-a-half ago. She looked completely relaxed, obliviously walking toward the Peabody, earbuds attached to a phone tucked in her jacket pocket.

He crossed Divinity and stood on the brick sidewalk that was separated from the street by a row of grass and trees. As she approached, Rebecca seemed to register his presence, but it wasn't until she was about ten paces away that recognition appeared to dawn in her eyes.

She smiled warmly and removed her earbuds. "Eric! What are you doing here? How are you?"

It wasn't the reaction, or the demeanor, he'd expected. That threw him.

"I, umm... I just needed to find out what happened on Saturday."

"What about Saturday?" she asked, now slightly suspicious.

"Uh... you texted me. Remember? Dinner? Five-thirty? Orinoco? Where were you?"

"Eric," she replied, any hint of friendliness now gone from her face. "What are you talking about? I didn't text you Saturday. I was busy."

"But I got three texts, all from your number. You even mentioned you knew Lotte was away."

"Look, I told you, I was busy Saturday, and I didn't send you any text messages. I don't know who texted you, but it wasn't me."

He looked into her eyes and saw genuine confusion. Fear and anger were obviously rising, too, and it dawned on him that she truly had no idea what he was talking about.

He quickly backed down. "Rebecca, I'm so sorry. Somebody's played a really mean trick on me. I *did* get those texts and they *were* from your number, but I can see that it obviously wasn't you. Remember how my phone was messed up? Maybe it got, I don't know... scrambled, or something. Or maybe I got hacked. Every text thread in the damn thing got deleted on Saturday night. Do you still have my number?"

She cautiously pulled her phone from her pocket and signed in. After a moment of scrolling, she held the phone so he could see. His text to her was right there, but no other messages appeared in the thread.

"Satisfied?" she asked with annoyance.

He was and he wasn't. Rebecca clearly hadn't sent the message, but that left him not knowing who was behind all this.

"I'm sorry, really. Those texts, they just... I don't know. I went to the restaurant, and while I was out... my house got... well... oh, forget it. It doesn't matter. I'm really sorry if I upset you. This has just been kind of crazy."

She seemed to sense his sincerity. "It's okay. No harm, no foul, right? I hope you get it figured out. It looks like it's really been bothering you. Listen, I have to get to work. We good?"

"We are, but can I ask you just one more thing? I know you have to go, but while I'm here, could you please just tell me what you wanted to tell me? I'm trying to figure out if it's somehow linked to what's going on."

"I highly doubt it, but okay. It's gotta be quick, though."

He nodded.

"All right. It's probably not my place to say anything, and I'm not trying to stir up trouble, but when I heard Lotte was working with Sven Henriksson, I just couldn't let it go."

Eric felt himself going numb.

"I was an archaeology grad student. Four years ago, I went on a dig in Spain to the Roman city of Italica, where they've also found remains of the people who lived there before the Romans... the Turdetani. That was really my interest. Dr. Henriksson was overseeing the digs that summer, which was a super big deal. I was lucky to get a spot. He was incredible. It felt like he took me under his wing. He's so, I don't know, he's like a... like a—"

"Like a Nordic god."

"Exactly. I see you've met him. He just made me feel so... *special*. He put me on important assignments, arranged for me to stay on an extra month. We started working late together, then going out to dinner, and then... you know the story. I thought I was in love. Shit, I *was* in love! We made plans for me to work with him, to be his collaborator. It would make my career. Okay, he's almost thirty years older than me, but it just didn't seem to matter."

Not that Eric couldn't see where this was going, but he asked anyway. "So, what happened?"

"What *always* happens with Sven. He's a fucking magpie. Whatever the newest bright, shiny object is in front of him, he grabs at it. We were together for about a year, and I spent most of that time marking my territory against a veritable parade of women, most of them younger than me. It wore me out. Finally, I gave up, but he was already gone. He didn't give a shit."

"And you think this may be happening with Lotte?"

"What do you think? How long has she been over there?"

His chest tightened. "Months."

"Months. I don't know, Eric. Lotte isn't me. Maybe she sees through his bullshit game. Looking back, though, I sure wish somebody had warned me. He's just so confident, and makes you feel so indispensable and important—so *loved*. Plus, everybody knows he holds the keys to the fucking kingdom. It's a hard package to resist."

Lotte's words coursed through his mind. Dr. Henriksson—Sven, *that is*—gave a lot, but expected a lot in return. There was a quid pro quo, so many expectations and entanglements. "*Alter!* What a mess," she'd said, and she'd told him that she needed to decide what she wanted to do. Add to this the weeks of delays that had postponed her return, the way "Sven" had rocketed her into the archaeological spotlight, plus the distress, distraction, and anxiety she'd clearly exhibited since at least August, if not before, and it all added up. It confirmed his worst suspicions, even though in his heart, he still felt it just couldn't be true.

"I'm sorry to lay this on you," Rebecca gently offered, "but this ruined my life for years. I'm just getting back on my feet. I was in a relationship with a great guy, and that got blown all to hell. It was awful. I don't want to see this happen again, especially to someone like Lotte, who has so much promise—or you. You seem like a really nice guy."

What's the old saying... something about nice guys finishing last? He'd never really believed that, but now he worried that his dismissal of the aphorism might have been premature.

"Thanks," he unenthusiastically replied. "I appreciate you letting me know. It looks like it's something she and I will have to deal with, one way or another. I'll let you get to work."

"Oh, Eric, I hate leaving you like this. Can I call you in a couple of days to make sure you're okay?"

"Sure," he agreed. "Just give it a few days. I'm having this problem with my phone, and I need to deal with that too... one way or another."

The museum was only thirty minutes from his house, but he took the long way. The phone in his pocket felt like a boat anchor, but walking had always helped him think. Right now, he needed to think, even though exhaustion, and what Rebecca had told him, made concentration elusive.

He tried to take stock of the situation. *What do I know?*

Obviously, whoever monitored him had been after those portal materials, and their surveillance would likely continue until they had the remaining portions in their possession. He sensed they were waiting for him to either show his hand or crack under the pressure, or were hoping someone around him might unwittingly reveal their location.

I'm certain they can hear me. I'm gonna assume they can see me.

He concluded this because the phone seemed to be able to tell when he was speaking to himself in Mrs. Binson's apartment versus when he was talking with Margot. How would it have been able to know that without a visual cue? Plus, it was safer to err on the side of caution and assume his actions could be seen.

The question is, what can it see? Does it see through my eyes, or is it looking down on me somehow? Can it see my hand inside my pocket?

He had no idea, but it was important. He was hatching a plan that depended on at least certain things not being visible. The other big question in his mind was how much they knew he'd figured out about being monitored.

At this point, they must know that I know, and they know that I probably know that they know I know. But how much do they think I know? I Just don't know!

His head started to hurt, and the cause this time had nothing to do with being separated from his telepathic phone. On the plus side, whoever was behind this hadn't taken action just yet, and that gave him some hope. It also gave him a window in which to operate.

When he got home, he plugged in his phone as usual, given that the battery had run down yet again. He then put his laptop into his shoulder bag and verified that his pen was in the outer pouch. It contained a notebook as well, which he rarely used. He slung the bag around his arm and headed out the door.

This is gonna suck.

He backed the car out and headed toward Broadway. At Kelly's Diner, he hooked briefly onto Boston Avenue, then banged a sharp left onto Broadway, desiring to stay on a major road.

The tingling began, but he pushed a bit farther. He wanted to be sure he was out of range. Between Josephine and Willow, the pain and dizziness mounted. Naturally, there were no open parking spaces. Frustrated, he veered off onto Bristol Road and stopped the car, probably illegally, in front of one of the houses. He'd risk the ticket.

Shakily, he reached for his bag, grabbed his pen and the largely unused notebook, and frantically began scrawling a note.

Take the car on Ferris. Park by the entrance to Montague. Hop the fence. Sneak in the back. Get as close to the van as you can. But DON't let me see or hear you! And don't come out until I yell. Trust me. – E.

He rolled down the window of the car and vomited into the street. His head throbbed unbearably, and dizziness wracked him. His hand shook so fiercely he could barely control it, but he managed to fold the paper in half and tuck it into the driver's side sun visor where it couldn't be seen. He grabbed his keys and stumbled out, barely avoiding the ugly mess in the road. After locking the car, he staggered erratically back toward Broadway.

It felt like a thousand miles, his legs rubber, and despite clearing his stomach, nausea still washed over him. He wouldn't have been surprised if his head split wide open, and actually hoped it would if that might serve to relieve the agonizing pressure against his eyes, and the siren's wail blasting through his ears. He reached the street, but that was as far as he could go. He collapsed on the sidewalk, right between the House of Kebab and Taco Factory. The thought of either made his stomach churn.

"Please," he begged to the first passer-by. "Can you hail me a cab? I'm having an allergy attack. I need to get home. I'll give you twenty bucks!"

The woman walked all the way to the curb to avoid him.

Shit! Where is my kind young man now? Come on, people, a little help here, huh?

Three more pedestrians walked by, avoiding him like he had the plague, probably assuming he was a drunk panhandler. They clearly didn't get the idea that he wanted to give *them* money.

Or maybe I actually have the fucking plague!

It became increasingly difficult to focus and keep his eyes open. He felt himself fading, possibly dying, and fighting against the inevitable started to seem like a worthless battle.

A couple approached, walking arm in arm. He thought of Lotte.

Lotte!

He needed her now, but she was a million miles away.

She said she felt him, always... that he was her heart.

Did he feel her? Was she *his* heart?

With a trembling hand, he touched the simple gold band on his finger. The rings bound their pact: he was hers, and she was his. Of this, there could be no question, no doubt. Her blood coursed in his veins, and well did he know, her blood was powerful.

"You look so happy," he rallied to groggily declare. "I don't want to do anything to spoil your day, but I'm having an allergic reaction. Can you please hail me a cab? I'll pay you. Please. I have a wife who I love, and she loves me. It will break her heart if I die here. Please. Help me get back to her."

He wasn't exactly clear what happened next, but after a period of muddled confusion, someone was asking, "Which way?"

"Bang a U-turn," he mumbled, assuming they were still on the far side of the street. He thought his eyes were open, but he couldn't see a thing. "Rogers Avenue. It's just a couple of blocks down, and a block in. Number 67."

"He's right," a woman's voice affirmed. "It's really close. Just go. He's losing it!"

He perceived movement, presumably that of a car, though perhaps it was his ascension to Heaven—or descent to Hell. He had no illusions. He wasn't free of sin. Of course, if Freud were right, both Heaven and Hell were illusions. Right now, he didn't give a fuck. He just wanted to get home, which he knew he was approaching because his physical decline had begun to reverse.

By the time they reached the house, he could see once more, and the jackhammer in his ears had subsided. He still found it difficult to walk, so the kindly couple helped him inside. He made a show of fumbling in the bathroom for ibuprofen, so they'd think he'd taken his allergy medication.

After sitting quietly in the kitchen for some time, his rescuers seemed assured he was okay and got up to leave. He offered them some money, but they refused.

They hugged him, and he hugged them back, telling them they had likely saved his life.

When they left, however, he grasped the ring on his finger, knowing that Lotte had been his true savior, from a million miles away.

CHAPTER 6

After the couple who'd taken pity on him left, Eric grabbed his phone and dashed back to the car.

Miracle of miracles... no ticket!

He drove back home, fixed himself something to eat, and then took Langsam for a nice walk. Back inside, he stocked her terrarium with plenty of food and water, then sat at the kitchen table and tried to work up the courage for the next step in his plan.

It was past noon, and Siddique was likely on break. With all the pieces of his plan in place, it just remained for him to act, so act he did.

He shouted into the empty silence of their apartment. "Let's stop fuckin' around! I know you're watching me, listening to me. I know what you want. It's time to talk about it. You seem to be on pretty good terms with my cell phone. Why don't you give me a call?"

Five minutes passed. He stared at the device on the table as if expecting it to spring to life. If this didn't work, there would be an escalation, but he calculated that was probably coming anyway. The subtle approach hadn't worked. The next logical step would be to beat the information they wanted out of him, and he wasn't certain he'd be able to resist.

The phone's ring startled him. It displayed a number he didn't know along with, "Unknown Caller." No surprise.

He swiped to answer. "Hello?"

"So, Mr. Schneider," said a woman with an accent.

Middle Eastern, maybe?

She sounded vaguely familiar, but he couldn't place where he might have seen or heard her. "Schneider-Schwarz," he calmly replied, in spite of his racing heart. "I got married in the spring."

"Congratulations, I'm sure," she flatly replied. "Let's get down to business, shall we? I believe you have something I want."

"I have a lot of things. You're gonna need to be more specific."

"Ah, yes, you and your new bride seem to have quite the little collection, don't you? I confess, I was surprised when I saw the damaged rings, and more so the piece of clay. If that's what I presume it to be, then it's an extraordinarily ancient and powerful artifact indeed. I'm impressed. The two of you have been busy, and I see now that your discovery of Vanth's doorway was, in all probability, not an accident."

"How did you find those things? They were hidden pretty well. Did you know they were there?"

"I am not here to answer your questions, Mr. Schneider."

"Schneider-Schwarz."

"Quite. I'll tell you what... as a way of demonstrating what you're dealing with, I'll tell you this. I knew the two of you possessed more than you had publicly revealed. Through your phone, I heard you both speaking of Vanth's doorway in the car after the event at Harvard."

Yep... exactly what I'd feared. She was fishing, hoping to hear something relating to the portals, and she heard something. I wonder if this means she was at that event.

"Possessing this knowledge, I arranged a convenient time to investigate your home when you weren't there. I wasn't expecting the woman downstairs. She was easily dealt with, but my presence was no longer a secret. Had it not been for that, you would never have known I was there at all. I would have put everything back as it had been. I detected the items you'd hidden when I came close to them. They radiated a small signature in the air that caught my attention. I think you can see, Mr. Schneider, I have powers, and in the end, you will be no match for them."

"Not to brag, but I've heard promises like that before, and I'm still standing. Why didn't you just sneak in and kill me, or Mrs. Binson, when you found her?"

"Because it didn't suit my purposes. I want information, and in my experience, it's quite difficult to get a dead person to speak. I had no idea what that woman knew, and hoped your conversations with her after what happened might be illuminating. Turns out they weren't, but it had been my hope to get what I wanted and be off without resorting to violence. Now, sadly, my only recourse is a threat to your safety, as well as that of your bride's, and your respective families. Mr. Schneider, this isn't my way, but you've left me little choice."

It was like Blake Harris all over again, except this woman was clearly not of this world, or had learned how to harness the powers of other realms.

Dangerous, he assessed, but he'd known that going in. "So, I assume it's Vanth's doorway you're after?"

"Indeed. We've been seeking it for a long, long time. We were all so excited when the box had finally been discovered, then so horribly disappointed when it appeared to be empty, save for broken ceramics. I couldn't believe it. I decided to see for myself what secrets lay behind this incredible find. Little did I know what I would uncover."

"Just out of curiosity, can I ask why you want this thing so badly?"

"That is none of your concern, Mr. Schneider."

"Schneider-Schwarz."

"Yes. Mr. Schneider-Schwarz, whom I would caution that there is a fine line between bravery and foolhardiness. In any case, what I will tell you is that not all is as it appears. My need for the doorway is fleeting. Again, I bear you no malice. I intend no harm to anyone."

"In my experience, harm comes from these objects regardless of anyone's intent."

"Be that as it may, I will not be denied."

He knew he'd pushed as far as he could. It was time to put his plan into action. "All right. You obviously have me at a pretty major disadvantage. I don't want to die, and I don't want any of the people I love to suffer. I guess I'll just have to trust you, but we're gonna do this *my* way, okay?"

"What do you propose?"

"I don't actually have the rest of the portal, and I don't know where it is. We gave it to a friend who has it hidden, even from us, just in case something like this happened. I can call him and convince him to bring it to a safe location. I'll let him take my car and leave, then you can come in and get it from me."

"Why don't you just leave it, and I'll get it when both of you are gone?"

"Because I want to hand it to you, make sure you get it. I want to hear you promise you won't use this thing to hurt people. I want you to lift the curse you put on my phone. I want you to swear you won't hurt my family... and I want to hear all those words from your flesh and blood lips, while I'm staring into your flesh and blood eyes. This isn't negotiable."

She again laughed. "Oh, Mr. Schneider, you have something up your sleeve. I'd call your bluff, but I grow weary of this game. I have nothing to fear from you, and I'm almost curious to see what little surprise you might have in store for me. All right, we'll do it your way. Where shall I meet you, and when?"

"Do you have a car?"

"I can access one if necessary."

"Can I text you an address to this number?"

"Why not? Feel free."

"Okay, I'll text the address, and then I'm gonna call my friend. I'll use this phone so you can see there's no funny stuff. Please don't block the call. He and I will arrange the time to meet. It will take both of us a while to get there, so it'll be sometime in the mid-afternoon. Wait until you see my car pull out, then come inside. I don't need my friend to get mixed up in this anymore than he already is. Understand?"

"I understand. You impress me. Most in your shoes would be terrified. They would beg, grovel... I've seen it all. You seem different. Perhaps experience has made you so. It would be a shame to have to kill you, but I will if I must, be assured. I will see you this afternoon, Mr. Schneider."

"Schneider-Schwarz," he reiterated as he ended the call.

He took a deep breath, but knowing this mysterious woman still monitored him, he tried to keep his emotions in check. On Google Maps, he found the location he desired and texted the address to the number in his call log, assuming it would vanish mysteriously from his phone at some point in the near future. Then he pulled up Siddique's contact and hit the dial icon.

"Hello? Eric?" Siddique's voice was cheerful as always.

"Hi, Siddique, how's the day going?"

"Oh, fine. We started really early. Busy. What's going on?"

"Where are you?"

"This job is in Milford. Why, what's up? You need something?"

"I do," he replied, intentionally inserting seriousness into his voice. "There's trouble. Lotte's in trouble. I need you to get the materials for the portal we found in Italy this spring, the ones you have hidden. I need you bring them to me."

"But Eric, you know that I—"

He forcefully interrupted. "You have to do this, Siddique! I know this isn't what you expected, or what we planned, but I need you to go home, get your suitcase, go to where the portal materials are, and load it up... all of it."

"But Eric—"

"Then I need you to drive it down to the Sturman building in Southby. Remember? Where we did your driving lessons. Just drive into the big opening in front. I'll meet you inside. Understand?"

Siddique was quiet for a moment. "So, let me get this straight. You want me to get my suitcase. You want me to pack it up, right? Bring it to the Sturman building?"

"Exactly. Pack it up good. I know it'll be *really* heavy, but it should all fit."

"Eric, you know that I—"

"I do! I know that you can do this. We're both counting on you. When can you get there?"

"Job's almost done. Figure... I got to go home... traffic... maybe like three-thirty?"

"Perfect. I'll see you then. Can't thank you enough!"

The wheels were now in motion.

The dilapidated and rusting fence around the Sturman building had been ancient when Eric was young. Barbed wire had once bristled along the top, but now only empty struts angling from the crest of the poles gave any hint of its former presence. The gate had long since been demolished, replaced by a sagging chain from which a corroded "No Trespassing" sign morosely dangled.

He thought about the legions of punk-ass kids who had daringly unhooked the unimposing barrier, asserting their sense of rebellion, their individuality, their utter boredom.

His was an act of need. He released the chain, marched across the crumbling asphalt, and entered the darkened structure.

The interior of the building provided the perfect setting to execute his plan. He'd only been inside once but had never forgotten it. In the open area near the great maw, one railroad track split into two, or two became one. Each line disappeared into a channel where the bones of ancient machinery rose on either side. Walkways loomed above to the left and right, leading to what had once been offices and machine shops along the outer walls. The loading bay where raw materials had once streamed into the facility was located in the back. Like the front, the great sliding doors of the individual bays disappeared long ago, providing easy transit.

Siddique would enter here and slink quietly and secretly along one of the assembly lines, and at precisely the right moment....

Eric heard a noise and peered around the corner of the great opening. Schneider's white van pulled through the gate, running over the now limp chain. He stepped out and waved.

Behind the wheel, Siddique returned his gesture. He drove through the great entrance and parked the van next to Eric's Mazda along an interior wall, out of view from the street. The Southby police didn't come by often, and rarely did more than a cursory perimeter inspection, but better safe than sorry.

Siddique popped out and began to speak, a questioning look on his face, but Eric held up his hand to silence him. "There's no time. Did you bring it?"

Siddique shook his head with confusion, but finally answered. "Yeah, man, it's in the back of the van, just like you told me. It's heavy."

"Perfect. Okay, I want you to take my car. Give me the van keys. I'll call you later and we'll figure out where to meet. Just go get some coffee somewhere. I won't be long." He paused, and then looked directly into his companion's eyes. "My keys are in the car. In the driver's side sun visor. *Got it?*"

This was the part that had him worried.

When he'd arrived at the Sturman building earlier, he'd parked his car, shut off the engine, taken the keys from the ignition, and held them in his left hand. With his right hand, he'd grabbed his phone from his pocket and placed it on the console between the driver's and passenger's seats.

Looking down and right, he'd swiped his password and texted Siddique:

I'm here. Just drive through the gate and come inside.

Meanwhile, with his left hand, he had cautiously and quietly slipped the keys into the folded note he'd written that morning and tucked in the sun visor above his head. He hoped that the person monitoring him could only see through his eyes, or that even if he were being watched, his observer's focus would be on what he was typing.

It was a shot in the dark, but it was the best he could think of. He wasn't ready to go down without a fight.

"Got it," Siddique affirmed. "That it?"

Eric hoped his demeanor and tone had conveyed that something was amiss. "That's it," he replied, extending his hand. Siddique grasped it, and Eric held on for just a second too long, trying to drive the point home.

Siddique slowly turned and strode off toward the Mazda, while Eric went outside to see if anyone was watching. The deteriorating road seemed empty. He heard the engine start inside, and soon the car drove out, his friend giving a little wave as he passed by.

Was that understanding in his eyes? Did his motion signal agreement with my instructions?

Eric would just have to wait and see.

He went back inside, removed his jacket, and sat on the decaying cement stairs leading up to one of the walkways. It was cool in here, but he didn't want any encumbrance for what was to come.

He thought about Lotte, what she might be doing now at 9:30 in the evening where she was. Normally, they'd be together in her office that time of night, often the best part of the day for him.

Rebecca hadn't told him anything he hadn't already feared, at least at some primal level. She'd just made it more real, more plausible. That didn't mean he believed it, but he needed to take some sort of action with Lotte.

But what action... and when?

All of his focus had been on the situation at hand, leaving no time to contemplate how to approach Lotte. He didn't want to seem accusatory, or petty, and he'd come to understand his tremendous reluctance to discuss his feelings of... *inferiority.* He hated that word, which for him hardly captured the nuance of the dynamic, or what a fine and subtle line it really was.

He found it quite hard to broach the discussion, and if something truly were going on, that would make it infinitely harder. They'd managed through difficult things in the past, but this was different. Something in the pit of his stomach told him so, and he wasn't sure what to do.

A shadow appeared in the parallelogram of sunlight that dappled the ground in front of him. He heard no footsteps but wasn't surprised when a figure stepped inside. She looked immediately to where he sat, obviously knowing his exact location because he was holding his phone. Their gazes locked, and the epiphany of recognition came to him.

"You're the reporter," he stammered, reluctantly reminded once again of her exotic beauty. "From Morocco... Maghreb Arab Press. *Shit!*"

She smiled thinly. "Yes, one of my many guises. Never has it served me so well." He got another surprise when she aimed a small but frighteningly lethal looking wooden crossbow at him. "I assure you, it's quite dangerous, despite its diminutive size, and I am quite proficient with it. Shall I demonstrate?"

She fired.

The bolt flew at him with incredible force and speed. He had no time to react as it smashed directly into his sternum. He sprawled backward onto the stairs, a searing pain in his chest. Spasmodically, he flailed and groped, trying frantically to pull the missile from his body, but nothing was there. The projectile sat on the step between his legs. No blood stained his fingers, but the throbbing of his ribs told him there would be a terrible bruise.

"That one was blunt," she casually explained as she efficiently notched another bolt. "The next one won't be. I don't want to kill you, but will if I must. Cooperate and give me what I seek, and you'll have all the things you asked of me. Now, get up."

He painfully pulled himself to his feet, veins pumping with adrenaline. The sharp strike had acted like smelling salts, a jolt of focus and energy that made everything appear hyper-real.

"Where is it?" she demanded.

"In... in the... in the van." He coughed as he pointed, still catching his breath from the unexpected blow.

"Get it out, and don't try anything! I don't need you any longer. I won't hesitate."

He walked slowly toward the van. "Cute trick you pulled there with my phone."

She laughed softly. "Yes, your lovely bride didn't have one on her, so I chose the next best thing. One little congratulatory kiss on the cheek to get close to you, and it was mine. The technological devices of today are such a wonder—already creatures of air, so easy to penetrate and manipulate. Not like the old days, when it was far harder, and infinitely more time-consuming, to imbue an item with the ability to watch and listen to someone from afar."

"Well, I hope you enjoyed the show."

"In truth, Mr. Schneider, I think you lead a rather dreary life. Then again, most mortals do, but here we are, yes?"

"What are you? Are you saying you're immortal?"

"Oh, Mr. Schneider, immortal I am not. I am exceedingly old, but a woman never reveals her age now, does she? I'm certainly old enough, however, to know when someone is trying to manipulate me. Can you please focus on the task at hand and cease your meaningless questions?"

With his delaying tactics exhausted, Eric turned to the back of the van, praying Siddique was close by. He opened one door, then the other, and spotted the suitcase tucked behind the driver's seat. "It's there. Want me to get it for you?"

"Oh, please, Mr. Schneider, that would be so courteous."

"Schneider-Schwarz," he reminded her, to which his antagonist testily raised her crossbow.

With grim resolve, he pulled himself into the white van. His chest pounded, partly from his heart, and partly from the blood coursing through the contusion on his breastbone. He staggered to the suitcase and hefted it.

Jeez, what the hell did Siddique put in here? It feels like lead. It's perfect.

"It's heavy," he warned her, painfully picking it up and cradling it in his arms.

"Then you'll kindly walk it to my car, won't you?" she replied with withering politeness.

Eric estimated the distance. She was only about six feet from the back of the van. He had the advantage of height, and could reach her, but he hadn't anticipated her having a weapon, let alone a freaking crossbow. He needed a wee distraction, just something to draw her attention from him for one brief moment.

The second he reached the back of the van, he jerked his head to the right, eyes wide, as if something had suddenly appeared.

She couldn't resist. Just barely, she flinched and directed her gaze ever so slightly left.

Eric struck.

With all his might, he launched the leaden suitcase. It slammed into her and knocked the weapon from her hand, and sent the woman heavily into the dirty ground.

"*Now!*" he screamed, as he leapt on top of her.

She had managed to toss the suitcase aside, but still thrashed to regain her bearings. For a moment, he thought he had his opponent pinned, but her fragile beauty belied an uncommon strength. Before he could secure her to the ground, she bucked wildly and he flew uncontrollably over her head, landing face first in the dirt.

Under his legs, he felt the woman twisting to her right, toward the crossbow. He reached behind him and batted the weapon farther away, for which she had a rather nasty response. Eric felt a solid contact from her fist directly into his groin. Pain he'd never known possible shot through his guts, and he floundered, immobilized.

His adversary threw his legs aside and righted herself.

He writhed in the dirt, unable to move until he felt a hand on his shoulder. With tremendous force, the woman whipped him onto his back, and he came face-to-face with the point of a crossbow bolt a mere three inches from his nose.

"That was a tremendously foolish thing to do, Mr. Schneider. You're no match for me. I expected some trick like this, and I expected to be compelled to kill you for it. I hope you lived a good life, because this will be its— *Ugh!*"

The crossbow vanished from his face, and his opponent violently struggled while being yanked backward. The stunning shock of pain in Eric's private parts had abated somewhat, so with trepidation, he looked up.

Siddique tightly held his erstwhile captor around the neck and waist. He'd knocked the sinister little weapon from her hand. She fought to free herself, but he had her secured, and when he pulled his arm even tighter around her throat, her resistance ceased.

Eric hauled himself from the dirt. "Perfect timing, my friend. Let me just take this little variable out of the equation." He reached down and picked up the crossbow. Its wooden construction appeared immaculate, at once ancient and primeval, while simultaneously seeming futuristic, as if it had been conceived by a computer and manufactured on a 3D printer instead of carved, likely by hand, from organic material. Its bolt remained cleverly locked into place despite the jostling.

Returning his attention to their captive, he was surprised to see a perverted smile on her face as she wickedly laughed.

"Oh, Mr. Schneider, bravo! Well done! I've been in this realm for thousands of years. It takes much to surprise me. Truly, you and your friend here have outdone yourselves. But you know what, Mr. Schneider? I can be surprising as well. *Surprise!*"

With that, she vanished into thin air.

Siddique stumbled as his arms tightened to his chest, clutching a now empty jacket and shirt. The rest of the woman's clothes collapsed in a heap to the ground.

"Oh, man," Siddique cried. "I don't think this lady's human! What the hell is going on?"

"No time to explain," Eric frantically gasped. "Keep your eyes open. I don't think she's gone."

They both rotated in cautious circles, surveying the room.

"Let's move over to the wall," Eric suggested. "That way our backs are covered. It'll be harder for her to surprise us."

Siddique nodded and started in that direction.

Eric suddenly detected movement behind his friend. "Watch out!"

Completely naked, the woman sprang from behind the cement stairway. She held a large piece of debris in her hand. Siddique began to turn, but she struck like lightning. With a dull thud, the brick bashed into the back of his skull, and his companion crumbled, silent and unconscious.

She whipped around to face him, a vicious snarl on her lips.

The crossbow! The bolt was nocked and the string drawn, so he rapidly aimed and pulled the trigger. With a *thwap*, the projectile shot toward his foe.

Again, she instantly disappeared, and the missile ricocheted harmlessly off the brick wall behind.

Reflexively, he started toward Siddique, but a mighty kick from behind knocked the breath from his lungs and sent him tumbling to his knees. Another blow to his upper back forced his body and face into the detritus near the wall. Some hard, sharp object pushed painfully into his already aching chest. He coughed and spat out dirt before he felt a foot lodge firmly into his back, pressing him downward.

"Oh, Mr. Schneider, tell me please, before I kill you... what will I find in that suitcase?"

He still couldn't catch his breath, and the object pressing against his ribs was becoming unbearable. "Can't... breathe...." He gagged.

The force from her foot lessened slightly, and he just managed to reach in and pull the offending article from underneath him and bring it near his chin. It turned out to be an old, rusted rail spike.

"Come along, Mr. Schneider," she cajoled, nudging him with her toes. "I had to hire a driver to get me to this forsaken place, and the meter is running, as they say. I haven't all day."

"I don't know what's in that case," he breathlessly confessed. "Books? Bricks? Little bags of unmixed cement? Who knows? It isn't Vanth's portal, though, that's for damned sure. Siddique has no idea where it is, and if you kill me now, you'll never get your hands on it either."

She loudly *tsked* as she bent low and grabbed him by the shoulder. "Such a poor decision. It should be clear to you now that you can't defeat me. Be assured the agony you'll soon experience will be far beyond any you have ever imagined possible. Why don't you avoid this unnecessary pain and reveal the portal's location to me? What do you say, Mr. Schneider?"

She started to powerfully turn him over.

"Schneider-*Schwarz!*" he screamed, as he wildly swung the rail spike, still clutched in his hand, at the spiteful woman.

She must not have seen or expected it, because to his surprise and relief, he made contact. The woman collapsed on top of him, her face just inches from his. Again, her citrus perfume pleasantly invaded his senses, contradicting the horror that rapidly unfolded before him.

The spike was old and dull and, for lack of options, he'd clutched it icepick style, never anticipating penetration but hoping to perhaps knock his tormentor out. As it happened, he completely missed her head and drove the thick nail directly into her neck. To his wonder, her flesh had parted as if it were paper. Blood oozed from the wound, and the area around it had begun to turn a grayish black. Tendrils of dark liquid under her skin snaked down her shoulder and up toward her ear.

Even more incredible, the woman's entire body stiffened, and she shook as if having a seizure. Her eyes rolled back in her head, and her teeth clenched as she violently shuddered. After a time, the ferocious trembling lessened, but black tendrils now covered the side of her face and left shoulder, and thick, dark blood rhythmically pulsed from the horrible wound in her neck.

In repugnance at the foul liquid that drenched his fingers, Eric released his grip on the rail spike, which slowly disgorged from where it protruded in Rehana's neck and fell to ground with a dull *clunk*.

The woman's convulsions eased and her eyes gradually refocused. She looked directly at him and suddenly appeared confused and frightened. She voiced some quiet words, perhaps a prayer, in a language Eric didn't know and couldn't understand. Her voice sounded different to him, softer, and lacking the haughty and mocking tone she'd used to intimidate him.

He felt suddenly sad, and contrary to his previous anger, he wanted to provide some solace for the suffering woman who lay on top of him, her slowly moving lips close enough to kiss. Soon, however, her eyes went blank, her head drooped lazily onto his shoulder, and her labored breathing ceased.

He let her lie there for a time... silent... still... and quite dead.

CHAPTER 7

The surprises were not quite over for this unusual day.

Eric eventually pushed the woman's body to the side and got up. The wound in her throat had become a desiccated crater. The flesh around the gash had turned to a dark gray powder that spread in the wake of the black tendrils, which now engulfed Rehana Bennani, or whoever she was, practically from the waist up.

Entranced, Eric watched the morbid process unfold for a few moments before he rushed over to Siddique, who still lay face down on the dirty ground. An ugly lump had formed on the back of his skull, and blood trickled past his ears onto his cheeks. Eric fetched his jacket from the cement stairs and used it as a pillow to cradle Siddique's head as he gently rolled him over. For several moments, small, sharp spasms racked his friend's body until he finally lay still.

This is not looking good. He needs a hospital.

He ran to the van, started the engine, and backed it closer to where Siddique lay. After opening the side door, he went to heft his comrade's limp body into the vehicle, but his chest screamed in agony. After the fight, he could barely find the strength to lift Siddique's dead weight, but necessity drove him, and soon his comrade lay in the cargo space, an old tarp replacing Eric's jacket to support his injured head.

Eric gasped when he painfully hopped out to the ground.

His former adversary's upper body had now dissolved into dust, and the dark tendrils had shot forth into what remained of her buttocks and legs. It appeared that soon there would be no trace of her, not after the wind from the great maw spread the now powdered corpse across the moldering remains of the Sturman building.

Not wishing to leave any evidence of their presence, Eric deposited Siddique's suitcase, the petite but deadly crossbow, along with the two bolts that had been fired, and the woman's clothes— which included a pouch with several more of the fierce little wooden projectiles—into the back of the van. Then he peered outside and looked for the car where presumably the woman's driver was still awaiting his attractive passenger's return.

Indeed, he saw a black limousine with tinted windows parked on the opposite side of the street, about a block past the gate. What really caught his attention, however, was much closer.

Near some old barrels and boxes stacked by the front of the building sat a hard-shelled Rollaboard suitcase. It was open, likely the source of the crossbow that the woman had removed. Not wishing to be seen, Eric crouched down and sneaked toward it.

Packed amongst the clothes was a black case with a form-fit foam interior, sized perfectly for her weapon. His heart truly jumped, however, when he saw one end of the curved piece from the Abzu gateway poking out from a shirt in which it had been wrapped. He breathlessly rifled through the woman's belongings until he also found the little bag that had been stolen from their apartment.

He found Charun's spiral rings and the tile from Vanth's portal, but he was surprised to discover another item tucked into the pouch along with them, something wrapped in a small silk cloth and secured by a couple of elastic hair ties. Unable to contain his curiosity, he loosened the bands and unfolded the material.

His eyes went wide with wonder at what looked like a thick coin about three inches in diameter. A hole near the edge implied it might be an amulet, meant to be worn on a string. One side was perfectly smooth, but on the other, two unfamiliar shapes stood in relief against the flat background.

$$\not{\times} \mathcal{L}$$

For him, however, the most incredible thing was that the entire object was constructed of the same, milky white substance as Vanth's portal. When he gently touched the two pieces together, they clung to one another magnetically.

He suddenly remembered Siddique, and quickly packed the incredible find away, closed the Rollaboard, and lifted it. He slipped back inside the building and jumped into the van. From the window, he could see that the woman's entire body had now turned into a pile of dust. Shaking his head, he steered the van to the great opening, then he gunned it.

Once past the gate, he banged a hard right. He could see the limo in his rear-view mirror, and estimated it was probably too far away for the driver to make out his license plate or read the Schneider Industrial Flooring lettering on the van's door.

He whooped as he pushed the white van to its limit, trying to rapidly put distance between himself and the black car. "Hope you already got paid, dude!" Knowing these roads, he diverted off the main thoroughfare to a side street, then another.

Eventually, satisfied he wasn't being followed, he steered the van toward Route 16. He hadn't made this drive for a long time—twelve years to be exact, when he'd accompanied Lotte to visit her father at the hospital. The poor man had been recovering from an encounter he would never know had been with a creature from an entirely different plane of existence.

Now, Eric traveled to the same hospital, to help another man who had suffered a similar fate, and as he had in the past, he worried that this wasn't the end of his troubles.

More like just the beginning.

"Eric, is that you?" Lotte's voice sounded at once wearied and animated. "Have you fixed your phone?"

"Well, sort of." He wondered if killing the being who had enchanted it legitimately constituted some sort of repair. *It probably wouldn't void the warranty.* "I know it's after eleven your time. I hope I didn't wake you."

"Don't I wish. No, I'm working. I have so much to do. I've been really worried. Please tell me you have some news."

"I'll go you one better. I got our little souvenirs back. I even added one to the collection. Check your texts. I sent you a picture."

"Eric, you've got to be kidding me. How? Who took them?"

"You won't believe it. It was that Moroccan reporter, Rehana Bennani, who was at the Harvard reception... except... I don't think she was really a reporter. In fact, I'm not even sure she was human. She'd somehow invaded my phone and had been watching me, trying to figure out where we'd hidden Vanth's portal."

"Vanth's portal? How could she have possibly known about that?"

"Well, as I say, somehow, she'd enchanted my phone, and she could hear and see what was happening around me. She heard us talking in the car after the reception about having the portal, but I think we'd already been targeted because she suspected we had it in the first place. She implied that others knew about it too. When she doesn't come back, these other people, or whatever they are, might start getting suspicious as well."

"Why won't she come back?"

"Umm... I guess I sort of, like... killed her."

"You what?"

"It was kind of an accident. We were fighting. She pretty much had me on the ropes. I was trying to hurt her so maybe I could get away, but what I did wound up freaking killing her. Then her body just *evaporated* right in front of my eyes."

She paused, obviously taking all that in. "All right. Probably not human. *Verdammt!* Eric, are you okay?"

"I'm fine. A little bruised up, but nothing major. Unfortunately, Siddique is in the hospital. That's where I am now."

"Siddique was with you? Why?"

"Long story. I needed help from somebody Rehana Bennani wasn't watching. Siddique was the only possibility, and he totally saved my ass. Before I killed her, though, she turned invisible, or vanished into the air somehow. Then she ran out from behind some stairs completely naked and hit him on the head with a brick. It's hard to explain. You kind of had to be there."

"I don't know what to say. Is Siddique going to be all right?"

"He's still unconscious. He's got a pretty brutal injury. I'm staying here to wait for an update. Now that my phone isn't *cursed* anymore, I can let you know when I hear something. That's why I didn't call or try to contact you before, by the way—just too dangerous."

"I understand," she said reassuringly. "Actually, I don't *entirely* understand. This is all quite inconceivable, but I get why you didn't contact me. In any case, what is this picture you sent?"

"Have a look. This thing was in her luggage. She'd put it in the bag she took from us with the rings and the white portal fragment. When you see it, I think you'll know why."

"*Alter!* It's just like Vanth's portal, but what is this? I've never seen anything like it among the materials we've found."

"I think it's an amulet. Doesn't that hole look like it would have been for a strap or a chain?"

"Well done! That's exactly what it looks like to me as well. These two shapes look like letters. I'm not certain what alphabet, but someone around here will be bound to know. Maybe Sven."

Eric grimaced.

"Everyone's gone to bed. I'll look into that tomorrow. Oh, Eric, this is incredible. I can't believe it! But you say there may be more beings like Rehana Bennani out there? We may still have trouble. Should I come home?"

Please come home. Come home and never leave again. "Mmmm, let's talk about it tomorrow, once you figure out what those letters mean, assuming you can. I'm not sure how imminent the danger might be, and I don't want you to mess up your opportunity over there. But Lotte... I'm really starting to miss you."

"Oh, Eric, I miss you too. Let me talk to Sven tomorrow, see about getting this project wrapped up. I need to get home, for me and for you. There's so much we need to discuss."

He pondered what to make of that last bit but was unwilling to pursue a deep conversation now if indeed her return was imminent. "I'll be here. I'm always here for you, no matter what. You know that, right?"

"I know you are," she whispered. "I know."

Eric was startled from sleep by his phone as it vibrated and rang on the floor of the van. It was 6:00 a.m., and the call was from Lotte. He swiped to answer and groggily greeted her. *"Guten Morgen."*

"Moin! Did I wake you?"

"It's okay. I have to get back inside anyway. Siddique was still in the emergency room at midnight, so I decided to come out here and catch some sleep."

"Where are you?"

"I'm in the van in the parking lot of the hospital. I figured at least in here I could stretch out. I didn't want to go home, or to my parent's house. I want to be around when Siddique wakes up. He may be confused, and we'll need to get our stories straight about how he got here."

She snickered. "What do you mean? Isn't getting hit on the head by a naked woman who could vanish into thin air a good enough explanation?"

He laughed despite the terrible soreness that rocked his chest, compounded now by a stiff back and neck from sleeping on the hard floor of the van. "Yeah, maybe we'll just stick with the truth, nice and simple! Anyway, it's like noon your time, right? Were you able to get any information?"

"Was I ever! You're not going to believe this. So, as I figured, there are some linguistic experts here. They pretty quickly identified those two symbols as Phoenician characters. The first is the letter *K*, the second is the letter *N*. Actually, since Phoenician is read right to left, it's really an *N* and a *K*, assuming the hole for the string is at the top."

"And that spells what, exactly?"

"Well, it's difficult to say. Phoenician is hard to translate because there aren't any vowels. They're *implied* in some way based on the context. Without that context, you can't really say for sure."

"Well, great work there, Sherlock. That really is unbelievable. Thanks for waking me up at six a.m. to give me that important bulletin."

"Little shit! There's more. I was as stumped as you were, but I wondered if this particular letter combination might be mentioned somewhere else. So, I Googled 'Phoenician Letters N K,' and there was one site that had a perfect hit. Check your text messages. I sent you a link."

He opened his texts and clicked on the hyperlink. It took him to a webpage for a Greek travel agency, "Nikolopoulos Kalabaka Tours." Their logo duplicated exactly the two characters on the white amulet. "Wow, that's weird. They really look the same, but it doesn't say anything about these being Phoenician."

"Scroll down. It's part of their deluxe tour, last stop. Read the description and look at the picture."

He flicked past some incredible scenery. Apparently, Nikolopoulos Kalabaka Tours specialized in trips through Metéora, a huge rock formation in the center of the country where incredible monasteries had been constructed almost impossibly on the mountaintops. One perched on a gigantic finger of stone, a flimsy looking rope precariously connecting the complex to a nearby ridge.

Hey! That one was in a James Bond film! Cool!

He finally got to the last image. This appeared to be a smaller compound, situated at the top of another disconnected stalagmite of rock. An outer wall enclosed a courtyard, in the middle of which rose an octagonal tower. The structure itself was rather unremarkable, quite unlike the dazzling monasteries from the earlier stops on the tour, but the view behind was absolutely breathtaking, which is what drew tourists to this remote spot.

His eyes, however, were transfixed by another feature. A huge round plaque hung near the top of the tower, on the side facing what appeared to be the entrance. Emblazoned in gold lettering on the black background were the same characters from the amulet. Eric rapidly read the brief description.

"See the incredible views from the prominence overlooking the remote and ancient Tower of Heaven and Earth. The Phoenician Letters N K on the tower's crest have come to symbolize the Nikolopoulos family's tour company based in historic Kalabaka. A Nikolopoulos Kalabaka Tours exclusive!"

"Holy shit, that's unbelievable! Heaven and earth, like An and Ki. Could that be what the letters mean, if you added the vowels?"

"Brilliant! That's exactly what I think it means. The tower's name gives the context."

"Okay, so, what the hell is going on here?"

"That was exactly my question, so I decided to call them."

"They have a phone in that tower?"

"Good Lord, Eric. You just giveth and then you taketh away, don't you? No, you idiot. I called the tour company. I wanted to see what they knew about this symbol, and why they were using it as their logo."

"Did you get through?" he squeaked with embarrassment.

"I did. They're an hour ahead in Greece, so they were open. I pretended I was interested in their tour, and when the man I was speaking with started talking about that stop, I asked if anyone lived there. He said yes. In fact, it turns out that the Nikolopoulos family, along with some other locals from Kastraki, another little village nearby, have worked in the tower since the early 1800s. It's not a monastery, it's a private home. That's why it's not really on any other tours."

"So, who lives there?"

"Well, I asked that, but the man at the tour agency didn't really answer me. He said the owner is extremely private and reclusive, and that he didn't want to jeopardize his family's connection by revealing any information. I decided to try a different approach. I told him I'd come across something with those symbols on it, and I wondered if the owner might want to see it."

"Are you nuts? Did you hear the part where I told you about there being more people, or *creatures,* or what-the-hell-ever they are, out there like Rehana Bennani? What if the owner of this place is one of them? What if he, or she, and the entire Nikolopoulos family are hanging upside down from the rafters of that freaking tower waiting to fly out and, well... I don't know... shoot you with a damned crossbow or something?"

"A crossbow? Eric, what in the world are you talking about?"

"Crap! I forgot to tell you about the crossbow. Yeah, our friend Ms. Bennani had a little portable crossbow. She shot me with the damned thing, too. *Bitch!* Never mind that. I'll explain later. Tell me what in the world you were thinking."

"I was *thinking* that if the people in this tower were associated with the woman who attacked you, then they'd know exactly what I was talking about, and they would naturally want me to come. Eric, the cat is out of the bag, or it will be very soon. They already know who we are. They can find us any time, unless we throw everything away and go hide somewhere, but then they'll just go after our families. It's bloody hopeless. We have to seize the initiative, and on the off chance this tower was *not* connected with Rehana Bennani, we needed to know that as well."

"Okay, that makes sense. I surrender. So, what did he say?"

"It was quite interesting, really. He told me to stay away. He told me not to bring any trouble to their door, and to leave the matter be. He also said that whatever I'd found, I should hide it away, and make sure no one ever discovered it, or we'd be in great danger."

"Well, that warning is a day late and a drachma short, but does this make you think these people aren't connected with Rehana Bennani?"

"I think the person who lives in that tower is connected with the amulet you found in her things, and by extension, I think he, or she, is somehow connected with Vanth's portal. I also think they're linked in some way to Enlil and the Rope of An and Ki, but that one, I'm having trouble working out, because the gods of the Abzu were gone by the time the creatures of The Zone and the Afrit were discovered. To answer your question, though, I don't think the owner of that tower is in league with Rehana Bennani. In fact, I believe it's quite the opposite. I think she's exactly the 'trouble' these people are afraid of us bringing to their door."

"So, what are we gonna do?"

"We don't have much of a choice. We have to go there. We have to talk with them and try to figure out what's going on."

"Umm, you do realize that might be extremely dangerous, right?"

"Of course, it's dangerous, my love. That's why I need you to come with me!"

The wheels of the aircraft touched down with two gentle bumps, distracting Eric from his whirlwind of thoughts. He realized with some surprise that he was in Athens.

Well, the airport anyway.

The dull and dusty vista outside the plane's window displayed none of the city's iconic majesty, but it didn't matter. This wasn't a sight-seeing visit, not that he and Lotte ever had sight-seeing visits anyway.

Lotte!

He'd see her soon. In theory, she would be waiting at the gate. He was excited, but also completely exhausted. It had been utter chaos booking an immediate flight to Greece, then organizing everything that needed to be done. His first step after securing a reservation, which depressingly turned out to be in the middle seat of the last row of the plane, had been to call Olive.

"You want me to *what?*" she groggily slurred into the phone, which she surely regretted picking up before 7:00 a.m. "How the hell am I supposed to get to Boston today, let alone get to wherever you said you are."

"Milford," he calmly explained. "It's not that far. Take an Uber, you can have the van to get around while you're here. Somebody has to be here for Siddique, somebody who can explain what happened and make sure he knows the cover story."

"What *did* happen?"

"I'll fill you in when you get here. I know it's a lot to ask, but this is super important. Will it be a problem for work?"

She yawned deeply. "Nah, they can cover for a few days. They don't give me much to do anyway. I'm just a part-time Community Service Officer, and I don't think they like me 'cause I'm a girl, so I get all the shit jobs... pardon my French. So stupid! I'm just doing this so I can get into the academy, but it looks like that won't happen until January, which sucks. Whatever. The only person that will miss me is Mutig, and he ain't even a person."

"What will you do with him?"

"I'm still living at home. My mom will take care of him, just like during your honeymoon. Won't she be thrilled? He ain't no trouble, but man he gets mopey when I'm not around."

Eric wished she could bring the magically enhanced dog along in case of trouble, but on such short notice, it might be difficult to book the flight. "It'll be fine. We shouldn't be gone long, and then you can get right back. I'm sorry to ask, but you know how things like this can go."

"I do. Really, I don't mind. It'll beat the heck out of filing and taking fingerprints for a few days. I'll call you when I have my flight booked."

After talking with Olive, Eric checked in on Siddique, who was still unconscious, but otherwise seemed completely stable. Around 8:30, he initiated his next important call.

"Hey!" Margot answered, all business on her likely busy Tuesday morning. "What's up? You get your phone fixed?"

"Yeah, all fixed, though the solution was a little unorthodox. Listen, something's come up. I have to go out of town for a few days. Lotte needs me."

She hesitated for a moment. "I'll start canceling all your appointments for the next two weeks, or should I make it three?"

He laughed, knowing he deserved that. "I beat you to it. Already done. It's just for the rest of this week, though. If I'm not back by then, I'll never be back."

"What?"

"Just kidding... sort of. I do need to let you know something else, though. Siddique had a little accident. He asked me to help him replace a light fixture on the ceiling of his apartment, so I dropped by late yesterday afternoon. He was standing on a chair, and lost his balance, hit his head pretty good on the countertop. We're at the hospital in Milford. They just moved him to a room, but he's still unconscious."

"Oh shit! Is he gonna be okay?"

"The doctors think so. They say his vitals are fine, and there's no evidence of significant damage, but sometimes people just stay unconscious until their bodies are ready to come out of it, so they're not rushing things. I've already called Ernie, so he knows the situation, but can you sort of keep tabs on what's happening and update everyone?"

"Sure. Should somebody visit him in the hospital?"

"No, that's all set. I called Olive."

"Olive! Doesn't she live in Savannah, Georgia?"

"Marietta, actually. She's back living with her mom now that she's done with school. She's on her way and should be here in the afternoon. I fly out tonight."

"Why would you drag her all the way up here from Georgia? Keisha or I could have stopped by. It's not thirty minutes from the office."

He hoped his lame explanation would get past Margot's bullshit detector. "Yeah, it's cool. Siddique knows Olive from that trip where we all got to be friends a couple of years ago. I don't think she's got anything lined up yet, workwise. This will give her something to do. I'll give her your number, and she can keep you posted too. That okay?"

"It's fine—weird, but fine. You're about right on-cycle to have another batshit crazy episode, but hey, at least this time I'm not having to clear your calendar at the last minute. I'd really like to open up next week, though, just to be on the safe side."

He laughed. "I'll let you know by Friday. Promise."

The final call promised to be the hardest, being a pretty big ask, but it was necessary, especially if he and Lotte actually didn't make it back from their little "excursion."

"Hi, honey! I wasn't expecting to hear from you today."

Eric just shook his head at how his mother could be so predictably cheerful. "Yeah, some stuff has come up. I need to ask you a favor. Are you busy?"

"I'm headed to the middle school," she explained, and he sensed through the phone that she was driving. "I've just started doing some volunteer work there, and occasional substitute teaching."

"Really? Wow, I didn't know you were doing that. Very cool! What subject are you teaching?"

She laughed. "Math, of all things. They gave me work experience credit for the bookkeeping I did years ago. Truth is, they're pretty desperate and will probably put me wherever, since I have unlimited availability, and substitute teaching is really just paid baby-sitting. It's the volunteer work that really interests me, working with kids who need a little extra help, like you did in German."

He winced. "*Yeesh.* You'll have your hands full, then, won't you? Why would you want to work with more unmotivated losers like me?"

"Honey, don't call yourself that! You just needed a little extra push, and you got it. By the way, look how that turned out for you."

"Well, it's sort of a mixed bag. I still can't really speak German that well, but I seemed to have hit it off pretty well with my tutor."

"Exactly! It all works out, even if you don't know precisely how it will all work out. That's what I really enjoy, working with people and seeing how they manage things, how they grow and develop, and eventually how they turn out. It's fun for me helping them navigate the little hurdles in their lives, try to make it go a little more smoothly, or help them do something they thought might never be possible."

Something about that gave Eric a warm feeling, and he thought of the countless ways his mom had done just those things in his life. "Well, I think that's awesome. You're a great teacher. I sure learned a lot from you."

"Oh, that's sweet. Look, I'm almost there, what was it you needed?"

"Right." He grimaced, fearing this would test the limits of his mom's willingness to help things go more smoothly for others. "So, here's the thing... I need to go out of town... out of the country, actually. It's to help Lotte, of course, and I have to leave tonight. Could I ask you to watch Langsam for a few days?"

"Of course, honey, I'd be happy to. Just bring her down. I love having her visit, as long as no worms are involved."

"No, no worms, promise. The problem is, I can't bring her down. I'm in Milford at the hospital with Siddique."

"What happened? Is he okay?"

"They think he'll be fine. He had a fall last night when I was helping him with something in his apartment. Dad will explain the details, but I can't leave here until Olive arrives to watch him. By then, I won't have time to drive all the way to Somerville to get Langsam, then back to Southby to drop her off with you, then back to our apartment to drop off the car, and then catch the train to get to the airport. I was hoping maybe you could go to our place and get her."

"Honey, you know I hate driving into the city by myself. What about Mrs. Binson? Can't she watch Langsam for a few days?"

"No, she's still freaked out about what happened the other night and is staying at her friend's house. I'm not even sure I can get her to go home if I'm not there, and I'm not exactly sure how long this trip might take." *Maybe forever.*

There was a long pause before he again heard his mother's voice, now drained of some of its usual merriment. "Okay, I'll do it. I'm booked up today, so I'll try to go around lunchtime tomorrow when traffic is light. Well, light for Boston, anyway. It always seems like a gigantic mess around there to me. You better appreciate this, mister!"

"Mister. Mister! Hey, mister, you gonna move?"

Eric was startled out of his memories by the understandably impatient woman behind him. He was holding up the immigration line, having almost fallen asleep on his feet after a particularly long delay.

"Sorry," he said as he picked up his bag and shuffled forward. Eric did appreciate what his mom had done, and he'd told her so. She'd never failed him, and he briefly wondered if she could say the same about him.

Almost without realizing it, Eric passed through his passport check. With no bags to claim, he quickly exited into the terminal. To his infinite joy, Lotte stood right at the gate outside the doors.

She looked simultaneously fantastic and awful. Like Eric, she clearly hadn't been getting much sleep recently. The signature black circles to which she was so susceptible had returned under her eyes with a vengeance. She wore the Boston Bruins cap Eric had bought her to cover up the limp mess of her hair.

Her look upon seeing him, however, made all the rest fade. She furiously waved and beamed, seeming on the point of ecstatic tears. He raced directly to her, not even bothering to wind his way around the fence that separated them. He simply reached over, and she melted into his arms. When they finally and reluctantly separated, tears and black mascara streamed down her face.

"What's the matter?" he asked. "Aren't you happy to see me?"

She choked out a little laugh. "Quite the opposite, you *Dummkopf!* I'm just a little... well... overwhelmed. I missed you so much, plus everything that's going on. Are you actually going to walk around so we can go, or will we just spend the next hour here, talking over this fence?"

"You've gotta admit, it's a pretty good fence. Plus, we seem to be putting on a fairly entertaining show. I'm happy here. Why leave?"

"Little shit." The two strode off toward the rental car area. "I've already hired the car, but they'll need to see your license, as you'll be driving. Any word on Siddique, and did Olive arrive okay?"

"Olive got to Milford late yesterday afternoon. We went in the van to pick up my car behind the Sturman building, where Siddique had left it. I explained everything to her on the way. She's cool. She knows what to do. I even have her talking with Margot, which will help control what gets out about what happened. I called Olive when I got to Heathrow on my stopover. She said Siddique is still unconscious, but they're letting her in to see him. She'll try to be around as much as possible so she's there when he regains consciousness."

"What a trooper. We're lucky to have both of them as friends. I had no idea what a can of worms I'd be opening with that cave discovery. I'm starting to regret it. Maybe it was poor judgment to have my name associated with that find."

"Lotte, that cave had been buried for twenty-five hundred years. How could you possibly know somebody, or something, was still out there looking for it?"

"That's the problem. I *should* have known... or guessed, at least. I have to think ahead, have to be better prepared. I should have been more careful. We know what kind of forces we're up against."

"What the hell are we dealing with here, more gods like Enki and Ninurta, or creatures like the Afrit?"

"That's what we're here to find out. If I'm right, the owner of that tower may be able to answer a lot of questions. I just hope it's not too late for us to make use of what we learn."

CHAPTER 8

Eric had the odd sensation of not quite knowing where he was when Lotte gently woke him.

They hadn't gotten far the night before. His flight had arrived late in the afternoon, Greece-time, and he'd been completely exhausted. The pair found a cheap hotel on the outskirts of Athens, ate a quick dinner, and then when back to their room and collapsed immediately into sleep.

"What time is it?" he asked, sensing light creeping past the corners of the room-darkening shades.

"It's after nine, sleepy head" she playfully scolded. "You probably would have slept longer. I hated to wake you, but we have to get out of here or they'll charge us another day."

"Why don't you just book a week and then hop back into bed?"

For a moment, it seemed as if she'd take him up on it, but they were here on business, so he reluctantly shuffled into the bathroom for a quick shower before hitting the road.

By coincidence, the trip north took them directly through Thermopylae, which they came upon right around noon. The memorials to King Leonidas and the seven hundred Thespians, who died alongside the famous three hundred Spartans, lay just off a dusty and unimpressive strip of roadway. He tried to imagine how the iconic battle might have unfolded, but the terrain had been altered virtually beyond recognition by the passage of time and the interventions of man. The truth, as so often happened, hovered just out of view, as if the past were guarding secrets the modern mind was unfit, or unworthy, to grasp.

They didn't have time for the visitor's center, another destination Eric mentally added to those he'd listed for exploration in some more-than-likely fictional future where he and Lotte enjoyed the latitude to do as they pleased. They had time for lunch, however, and he was pleased to see her devour a generous portion of moussaka and stuffed grape leaves. She looked way better than yesterday, obviously benefiting as he had from over twelve hours of solid sleep.

Now, she slumbered in the car, no doubt lulled into a stupor by an excess of carbohydrates at their midday meal, as the imposing and almost unimaginable vista of Metéora unfolded before Eric's eyes.

"Hey," he said, giving her a soft nudge. "You might want to see this. It's pretty impressive."

She stirred and stretched her neck, stiffened by its odd position while sleeping in the passenger's seat. "Cool," she remarked upon seeing the mighty rock slopes on the horizon.

Kuuuul. That just never gets old. "It's close to three thirty. You want me to try to find a hotel?"

She wiped her eyes. "No, I want to check if this tour place is still open and see if we can get anything out of them. It's right on the main street in Kalabaka. Let's try to find it."

Set in the foothills of Metéora, with the mountains looming directly above, Kalabaka was not a large settlement. Unlike Boston or Somerville, Eric easily found a parking space, and he and Lotte walked along Trikalon, their main street, past various souvenir shops and restaurants in search of Nikolopoulos. It wasn't hard to locate. They both immediately recognized the unique Phoenician lettering of their signage, and since the tour agency was connected with a shop that sold the omnipresent t-shirts and painted ceramics of which tourists never seemed to tire, they were still open for business. The two went inside.

A man rather quickly rose from a chair by the counter. "Kalimera," he welcomed them. "Good day. You speak English?"

"Yes," Lotte replied, "or German, whichever you prefer."

He laughed. "My German is *nicht so gut*. Let's stick with English. How can I help you today? We specialize in tours of the area. Would you like to make arrangements for tomorrow? We have several packages. Here... I'll get you a brochure."

"Actually," Lotte interrupted. "We're interested in one particular stop on your deluxe tour. You seem to be the only ones who have it: the Tower of Heaven and Earth."

"Yes, we are the only ones who offer this location. It's on private property, and the tour is the only way you can see this beautiful spot. There's space for tomorrow. Can I book you so you can go see it?"

"Truthfully, we were hoping to go visit the site ourselves. We'd like to talk with the person who lives there."

The salesman's smile faded, replaced by a stony and suspicious visage. "You're the girl who called, aren't you?"

"Was it you I spoke with?"

"No, it was my brother-in-law, but he told us what you said. I see you did not heed his warning to stay away. Were you followed here? Does anyone know of your destination or reason for coming to this place?"

"One person knows we were coming to Greece," Eric interjected, "but I didn't say anything about coming to Metéora, or why." That wasn't strictly true. Olive knew he and Lotte were here to investigate the strange object they presumed to be an amulet, made seemingly of the same material as Vanth's portal, but he hadn't told her exactly where they were going in Greece, so he didn't count his statement as completely false.

The man shook his head. "You don't know what you've stumbled into. Great trouble could come from this. What do you think is so important that you must disobey our wish for you to simply stay away?"

Lotte calmly reached into her jacket, pulled out the amulet that Eric had passed to her the night before, and removed its protective covering. When finished, she held the item up for the shopkeeper to see.

He gasped, and a look of wonder filled his eyes. "I never thought I would see it myself, gone for so many centuries. I began to doubt if it ever truly existed. Where did you find it?"

"It's kind of a long story," she recounted, "but in short, we took it from someone while we were retrieving some things that person had taken from us."

"That was a dangerous thing to do. What happened to this certain *someone*? Did they follow you here?"

Eric cut in. "Let's just say this person is really no longer in any condition to follow anyone, anywhere. I saw to that personally."

"I see," he replied, seemingly satisfied. "Then you traced the object here because of the lettering on our website, which mirrors that on the tower itself, correct?"

Both he and Lotte nodded.

"I confess, I'm impressed, and assuming what you told me about dispatching the person who held this item is true, then perhaps we're safe... for a time. One moment." The man went to the counter, produced a notebook and pen, and began scribbling something. When finished, he tore the page from the book, grabbed a folded brochure from the display by the register, and returned to where they waited.

He pointed at the map inside the leaflet. "Follow the main highway to this road, here. Sometimes the roadway to the tower has security. As I say, it's private property. If you are stopped, show them this letter. When you get to roughly this point, you'll see a dirt road off to the left. Take this and park when it comes to an end. There's usually a Rover parked there as well.

Walk back to the paved road and follow it the rest of the way to the top. Leave all your belongings in the car, especially any electronic devices. They won't work in the tower anyway. Leave your jewelry as well, especially that unusual ring."

Lotte bristled as the man pointed at her wedding band. "Why? This ring isn't dangerous."

"How do you know?" he shot back. "When was the last time you took it off, or the last time you were not near it? You must do as I say! They will not tolerate such things in the tower, and you may never see your precious ring again. Do you understand?"

Thinking of the recent experience with his cell phone, Eric touched Lotte's arm and gave her a reassuring smile. "It's fine, we understand. We'll do exactly what you told us."

"Good. Now, when you get to the top, you'll see a cabling apparatus and a bell. Ring the bell and give them the letter I wrote. They'll either let you in or not. I can't control what happens."

"Can you at least radio ahead?" Lotte asked. "Let them know we're coming?"

"Did you not hear me? There is no radio... no telephone... no television... no cell phones. None of that will work in the tower. This is the way of things. If they let you in, all will be made clear. Go now, and you can possibly return before dark."

They thanked the man and stumbled back onto Trikalon Street toward their car.

"I'm gonna call Olive," Eric decided as they walked. "It's about ten-thirty her time. I want to catch her before we get in a place with no signal."

Their friend was quick to answer. "Hey," she greeted him, a bit flatly as if from lack of sleep. "Glad you called. Great news... Siddique woke up this morning. I was right there when he came out of it, so I told him to just be cool about what happened until I could fill him in on our cover story. He got it, no problem. He said he don't remember much anyway, so he should be pretty convincing. They're giving him all kinds of tests right now, so I'm down in the cafeteria, otherwise I'd let you talk with him. It looks like he'll be fine, though, and hopefully he can go home in another day or two."

"That *is* great news!" Eric beamed, giving Lotte a thumbs-up.

"Are you with Lotte in Greece?" she asked, a bit more perky now.

"Yeah, we're here. We're taking care of what we came to do and should hopefully be back soon. Listen, you're the only person who knows where we are. This is kind of a sensitive thing. Just make sure you don't tell anyone we're in Greece, okay?"

"Who would I tell? I ain't even told Siddique, didn't have time. I'll just keep it on the Q.T. until you're back."

"Perfect. You're the best! If they release Siddique before we're back, you can get a hotel room or go stay with my folks. They'd love to see you again. Either way, it's on us, just like the plane ticket."

"Okay. I might stay with poor Siddique, though, just in case he needs somebody. He's got a pretty nasty lump on his head."

"That would be really nice, Olive. You do whatever you think is best. Sounds like you've got it under control."

"That's a bloody relief," Lotte said after Eric had hung up. "I wouldn't have been able to live with myself if something serious had happened to him — either of them, really. This is all turning out to be more dangerous than I'd ever imagined. I never dreamed anyone else knew of the existence of these portals. I thought I could just collect them up and store them safely away, and no one would be the wiser. I miscalculated that, and it makes me worry what else I might have misjudged."

It seemed a reasonable concern to Eric, but at the moment, neither of them could do much about it. "Let's just finish what we came here for. We can worry about all that later... at least I hope we can. Maybe they'll just toss us over the walls when they get their little amulet back."

She stared at him, aghast, as he started the engine.

"Uh, never mind that last bit. I was just kidding." *Sort of.*

The tower crouched precariously on the top of a gigantic boulder which jutted skyward from the tree-filled depression beneath them. How they'd transported materials for the sturdy structure and its meandering walls was beyond Eric's comprehension. Maybe he and Lotte would come back to Metéora someday and take the Nikolopoulos tour... learn about the history of this wondrous place... snap some scenic photos.

That would be a nice change of pace.

A harsh clanging woke him from his pleasant fantasies, from an iron bell set in a frame on the ground near one end of a rusty bull wheel. That mechanism uncertainly suspended a cable over the chasm between the ledge they stood on and the prominence with the tower beyond.

"Maybe they'll come out to see us," Lotte said with little hope in her voice as she rang the bell once more. "I'm not looking forward to crossing on that pathetic-looking contraption."

Neither am I, but it is what it is at this point.

After a few moments, two iron-bound wooden doors opened in the tower's wall, beneath where the cables disappeared. The bull wheel began to creakily turn, and they could see a small tub-like bucket dangling from a chain clamped to the line as it moved toward them. The bucket stopped when it reached them, and looking inside, Eric saw a couple of rocks.

"I think these are so the note won't fly out," Lotte speculated. "Let's give it a try." She tucked the message the man at Nikolopoulos had given them under one of the stones and again rang the bell.

Once more, the cables surged into motion, and soon the basket disappeared into the opening in the wall of the tower. The wait felt like forever, but finally a slight flexing in the suspended wires indicated activity of some sort.

"*Scheiße!*" Lotte groused in dismay. What looked like a ski-lift chair from the 1890s emerged from the darkness of the orifice beyond and swayed dizzily toward them. "This can't possibly be up to code."

Eric wasn't any happier about it than she was, but all too quickly, he gingerly hefted himself into place next to where she already sat, white-faced and tightly grasping the armrest in the unstable seat. With an unreassuring *clank*, he threw the shaky safety bar into place, then reached over to ring the bell. The apparatus lurched into motion, and swiftly the ground gave way to a stomach-churning view of the plummet into the forest below.

Lotte cursed through clenched teeth. "I might actually prefer to spend the rest of my life in that tower than make this trip again. To hell with archaeology... I'll take up bloody painting!"

Too terrified to laugh, Eric just clasped his hand over hers on the bar to which they both desperately clung. Miraculously, the unsteady mechanism did its job, and he was overjoyed to feel a stone floor under his feet once they'd cleared the opening in the wall. Sadly, the feeling was fleeting, as they met the icy stares of two men and a woman, the latter of whom threateningly waved a pistol in their faces.

Uh oh. We might have stepped into a trap after all.

With some words, presumably in Greek, from one of the men, the woman begrudgingly lowered her weapon.

Nervously, Eric unlatched the safety bar, and the two of them staggered to their feet.

"You will be searched," the man who had spoken announced, this time in English. "Remove the item you brought and hold it in your hand. Also, remove your shoes. We have to make sure you have nothing on you."

Lotte complied, and the woman with the drawn pistol frisked her, even feeling each toe under her socks. Eric received the same treatment from the other man, who had an Uzi slung over his shoulder. When each shrugged and seemed to indicate they'd found nothing, the man who appeared to be in charge stepped forward.

"Let me see it," he demanded, firmly but without anger.

Again, Lotte unwrapped the white medallion and held it forth.

He seemed awestruck. "Incredible. It appears you didn't lie on the phone when you told me you'd discovered something. He will be most pleased to feel its presence once more, and that you brought it to him, assuming you also spoke truly about not having been followed."

"I can't see how anyone could know we're here," she explained. "The person, or rather the being, we took this from is quite dead. My husband killed her himself." Eric saw her flash a quick smile in his direction before she went on. "Who is it you speak of that will be happy to see this again?"

"Naturally, the man who resides in this tower. We are merely his caretakers, though in truth, he requires little care. Companions might be more accurate, and when necessary, guards. He awaits you. I will take you to him. Come."

His gesture was inviting, but after closing the doors in the outer wall, the other man and the woman flanked the pair as they marched down a tunnel that cut through the thick wall. Another sturdy door stood open leading into a courtyard. Structures on the inside of the wall appeared to be residences and storage buildings. The somewhat faceless octagonal tower loomed above them at the center of the plaza, the great black disc with gold Phoenician lettering glittering near the top. The sigil seemed out of place against the austerity of the rest of the compound, almost as if the object radiated a menacing power that entirely enfolded the top of the enormous boulder. The sky above shimmered strangely, though Eric wasn't certain if he was merely experiencing jet lag, or perhaps lingering vertigo from the perilous crossing.

The man in the lead pressed open yet another heavy door, this one made of solid iron and weathered with age, and the entire party entered the tower proper. Only lanterns and candles illuminated the windowless foyer. Each of the three who accompanied them took a lantern, and they directed the two nervous visitors to a wide stairwell that ascended along the left outer wall. The tower stood perhaps four stories tall, though it was hard to tell how many floors it contained, as the landings with doorways to the interior came at seemingly random intervals. Soon, however, the stairs gave way to a short hallway before ending in another large iron door.

"Two warnings," the man in the lead said quietly. "First, if you try anything foolish, you will be killed—no questions, no hesitations.

Second, try with all your strength to contain your reactions to what you will see. He is a proud man, deserving of your respect. Above all else, do not forget this."

With that, their guide opened the door, revealing a large room with a single window on the wall opposite where they entered. Sunlight streamed in between thick iron shutters, which at the moment stood open. A large wooden table, shaped like a half-circle, dominated the center of the room. One chair sat on the straight side, while seven others sat opposite along the curvature, all empty and covered in the dust of disuse.

A man sitting on a stool by the door snapped to his feet. He also wielded an Uzi, as well as two pistols and a variety of lethal-looking knives at his belt. Another woman, similarly armed, rose from her seat near the window. A large and ancient looking wheelchair sat parked next to her, piled high with cushions and blankets that draped over the back and sides. If someone occupied the chair, they faced the window and Eric couldn't see them.

The man who had so far served as their guide spoke again. "Remember what I told you." With that, he exited the room along with the man and woman who had accompanied him, and closed the door.

"What do we do?" Eric whispered to Lotte, feeling the intense scrutiny from the two well-armed guards with whom they had now been entrusted.

She feebly pointed toward the window through which the day's fading light still meekly shone. "I think we have to go over there. Let's just start moving in that direction. I think we'll know rather quickly if this isn't what they want from us."

He gulped and stepped carefully alongside her. Neither guard flinched, so they inched cautiously across the room.

"Recognize the shape of that table?" she asked as they passed.

"How could I not? I see arches in my dreams, and they're not the golden kind leading to hamburgers."

The woman near the wheelchair inclined her head slightly as they approached, indicating they should circle around to greet the occupant. The guard from the doorway assumed a strategic position to the opposite side, machine gun at the ready.

Hesitantly, Lotte and Eric stepped forth, and the person in the wheelchair came into view.

The man before them lay in an unimaginable state of mutilation, and the warning they had received became instantly clear. All that remained of him was his head and torso. The blankets that covered his body hung limp where arms and legs should have filled them. His eyes were gory gouges, ripped flesh sewn crudely shut and left to heal into scars that betrayed the violence of the original injuries. These eyes were not pried from his head, they were impaled by the stab of a sharp weapon. How he had survived the impact was impossible to discern.

"I welcome you." His voice, deep and beautiful with an accent of indeterminate origin, emerged from a jaw permanently offset by a brutal pummeling, and from a mouth that held only the broken shards of what had once been front teeth. "I understand you brought something for me to see. Sadly, that is beyond my ability, but I should be ever so grateful if you would press it to my cheek, that I may once again feel its touch against my flesh."

Lotte didn't flinch. Holding the item up so the guards could see it, she strode confidently toward the disfigured man and placed it gently on his face. With her other hand, she grasped his shoulder, just where the arm had likely been severed from its socket.

He sighed with seemingly infinite pleasure, and despite his grotesqueness, displayed an almost beatific smile. "It returns me to the distant past... to a place that was my adopted home for many years. There, we tried to start anew, attempted to forge peace after centuries of bloodshed that eventually caused the collapse of civilization as we then knew it. How is it that you come to possess this object which was taken from me so long ago?"

Lotte's eyes went wide, and Eric began to realize that the incapacitated man before them might be more than he appeared.

"A woman came to us," she attempted to explain. "She tried to take something from us by stealth, but resorted to force when that failed. My husband, who is here beside me, resisted. In the process, this woman was killed. We found the medallion in her things and traced it here because of the matching symbols on the tower's emblem."

"This woman... you are certain she is dead? How did you accomplish such a feat?"

"Honestly, it was sort of an accident," Eric confessed. "We were fighting, and I stabbed her with the only thing I could get my hands on, an old rusty rail spike. I can't believe it had the effect that it did. It didn't just kill her, she literally evaporated right in front of my eyes."

"It was the iron," he quietly replied. "They cannot tolerate it. It freezes them, and if the wound is severe enough, they are forced from their host."

"Who are *they*?" Lotte cautiously ventured. "Clearly, she wasn't human, but what was she?"

"In truth, she was human, at least in part. Her mortal flesh, however, had been infiltrated by a creature from another realm, what you might refer to as a Jinn. It is the only way they can remain on this plane for any length of time. Long have they inhabited your world, living side-by-side among humans, sometimes in harmony, and at other times making mischief. The one you killed was old, indeed. She must have gotten terribly careless, and severely underestimated the opposition you presented."

"Yeah," Eric affirmed. "That's basically what she said. I don't think she realized how much Lotte and I have seen. We must be sort of uncommon in that regard. It seems like you knew her pretty well."

"All too well, I fear. Her name was Aicha Kandicha. At least, that's how she was most commonly known. Once, she was a priestess of Astarte in Tyre, but not long after I arrived with the Seven, she fled to the North African colonies, eventually settling in what is now Morocco. She was never party to the agreement, but largely stayed out of the way. That changed, of course, when she stole the amulet from my possession, and left me in the condition you now observe. I beg your pardon for not shedding a tear in learning of her fate, not that crying is something I'm especially capable of any longer."

Lotte gasped. "Wait, what you're saying... it's impossible. If she was a priestess of Astarte in Tyre when you arrived, it would mean you're almost three thousand years old!"

The man laughed. "Were only I so young. I go back even further, to the place of my homeland that was once at the heart of civilization, in service to gods whose names are now but a distant memory. In their wisdom, they made me immortal for the merit of my counsel, but as with so many things, the consequences of actions are often unforeseen."

"We... we know who you are," she said, breathless with wonder. "You're Utnapishtim, and the gods you served were Enki and Enlil."

The man jaggedly smiled. "You surprise me. I see now how Aicha might have underestimated you. Long has it been since I have heard my name spoken, or the names of my lords, who are lost to me. I have been in the condition you observe for nearly two hundred years, as a result of the object you now hold in your hand. However, even retrieval of the amulet will not change a thing. This I tried to impress upon Aicha all those years ago, but she wouldn't believe me... not until she had enacted the torment that finally convinced her I spoke the truth. The gateway to which this artifact is linked is long gone, and without it, the amulet is void of significance."

"I sense there may be another surprise in store for you," Lotte enthusiastically interjected. "We have much to tell you, and I think you have a lot more to tell us as well."

CHAPTER 9

"What would you say," Lotte excitedly put forth, "if I told you that the gateway you speak of is no longer lost? My husband and I found it, in Italy. *This* was the very item Aicha Kandicha was trying to steal from us."

"I would say that you are in great danger," Utnapishtim solemnly replied. "Aicha is not the only Jinn eager to find the gateway. There are others, and they will not relent easily."

"We know. That's precisely why we're here. We need to understand why they want it so badly, and what kind of danger it poses to our realm if they take it from us. There are too many things I can't piece together. We know with near certainty that the gateway, or *portal* as we call it, summons a being named Vanth. What's the link between an Etruscan artifact and this Phoenician medallion? What could the Jinn possibly want from Vanth, and how are either of these artifacts linked to the Rope of An and Ki, from which this tower no doubt gets its moniker? Enki and Enlil were gone long before the beings of The Zone were discovered, or so I thought. What's the connection? These are the questions we came here to answer."

Utnapishtim remained silent for a time, seemingly deep in troubled thought. When he spoke, however, he sounded calm. "What is your name, young one?"

"I'm so sorry. How rude of us. My name is Lotte Schneider-Schwarz, and this is my husband, Eric."

"Pleased to meet you, sir," Eric added, also happy to hear Lotte proudly use their joint last name.

"I am pleased to meet both of you as well. The things you tell me are astonishing. It is a wonder what information you have collected, and how much you appear to have figured out. You will have to explain to me how this came to be, but first, I will attempt to address what you have yourselves identified as the most pressing concern. To understand, we must venture long into the past."

Eric was surprised when the female guard offered Lotte her stool, and the other guard retrieved his from near the door. Clearly, the dusty chairs weren't for everyday use.

"As you know, I served Enki and his brother, Enlil. I lived in Eridu and was a notable priest in the E-Abzu, Enki's temple, near the end of the third millennium, BC. It was Enlil, however, who had taken charge nearly a thousand years before that. When he became enraged at humankind's continued inability to live in peace, he threatened terrible destruction. I counseled patience to my lord, Enki, and he carried these words to his brother. You can see, Enlil did not destroy this world, and in gratitude, they jointly made me immortal. This has been a curse to me as much as a blessing, but that is of little consequence. Ironic, as in the end I sense my recommendations were not the impetus for Enlil's change of heart. Both beings feared their tempers were as tempestuous as their father's, and wished not to fall into the same dangerous patterns."

"Yes, Anu," Lotte interjected. "We know how Enki and Enlil pushed away the realm of air and trapped their father there."

"How can you know of this? It is knowledge few have ever possessed, and most of them are long dead. Only the Jinn remain, and they would never share what they know with mortals they do not trust."

"Because we heard it from the horse's mouth... or more accurately, the goat's. You may not believe this, but we're also in possession of Enki's portal to the Abzu, and we've gone to battle with him against Ninurta, who accidentally escaped and was threatening our realm."

"That is impossible! I was told Enki's gateway was destroyed when the Amorites sacked Eridu at the end of the second millennium. How can this be?"

She pondered before responding. "I believe those who did this lied in order to protect the portal's location, and to honor Enki's wish to withdraw from this realm. I'm surprised you weren't there with your lord when it happened."

"Indeed, I was not. I had gone to serve Enlil. Your *Epic of Gilgamesh* promulgates the notion that my wife, too, was made immortal. Would be that it was so, this wishful thinking on the part of scribes who could not countenance the concept of an eternal life lived bereft of an enduring partner. Eridu came to have too many painful memories for me, watching my wife and children, and their children, grow old and die. Much pain you will see if long enough you live... and my life is *endless*. I needed to start anew, and Enlil was more than happy to employ me. Angry as he had once been, and later devastated by the betrayal and imprisonment of his son, Ninurta, the great god redoubled his efforts to make right the promise of a better tomorrow."

Sublimation, Eric mused. *I wonder if we got it from Enlil, or whether he picked it up from humans?*

"Sadly, it was all for naught. The root of the problem lies in the fact that sequestering Anu in the An, the realm of winds, had to be done quickly and in secret. The conspiring brothers could not announce to the beings of air who were then present in our realm that they must leave, or never again see their home. When they found out, it came as a terrible shock, but reopening the doorway in the Rope of An and Ki was simply out of the question. That would surely unleash Anu back into this world. If you feared the threat of Ninurta, I assure you that Anu would make even the stoutest tremble. All was quiet for a time, but then a great war began which lasted nearly six hundred years. Jinn fought on both sides. Some recognized that their fates were now locked to this world and sided with Enlil, while others who demanded to go home fought against us. The conflict culminated in what you would know of as the collapse of the Bronze Age, near the end of the twelfth century, BC, with neither side having much to show for their efforts."

"So," Lotte deduced, "that's the danger. This is why we can't give the Jinn the portal. What I don't understand, though, is how Vanth got caught up in all of this. Why is her gateway of interest to them?"

"Your mind is sharp... I will explain. In 1230 BC, Enlil's city of Nippur fell to the Elamites, who were in league with the rebellious Jinn. We escaped to the island city of Tyre, and the struggle seethed on for another fifty years until everything lay in virtual ruin. Both sides came to realize they couldn't win. All were losers, and all were finally weary of the endless conflict, even Enlil, who was by this time a spent force. He readily agreed to step out of the affairs of this world and sleep for the rest of eternity in the Rope of An and Ki."

"That's when he vanished," Lottes interjected. "This is why Enki couldn't sense Enlil when we later called him from the Abzu."

"Correct. However, before he left, Enlil did two things. First, he set up a Council: Seven Kings of the Jinn, representing as wide a coalition as could be cobbled together, but ultimately answering to human authority. By consensus, this body could call upon the great god's power should the Jinn not honor their word and live in harmony with the beings of this world. All agreed, in principle, though some, like Aicha, simply went far away to pursue their own path, or else chose to spend their existences largely in their immaterial form, only manifesting their physical bodies when they needed to feed."

"Wait a second," Eric cautiously put forth. "There are seven chairs on the arced end of that table, facing one on the straight side. Is this where the Seven Kings of the Jinn met?"

Utnapishtim laughed. "For a time, it was, but that was after the young conqueror finally brought Tyre to its knees. Fortunately, he took a liking to us, sending the Council back to his homeland just to the north of here."

"Umm..." Eric stammered. "That would be Macedonia. You're talking about Alexander the Great, aren't you?"

Utnapishtim's silence was all the answer he needed.

"But why would *you* have this table?" Lotte asked with confusion. "Are you saying it was *you* to whom the Seven Kings answered?"

"Well, I am human—immortal, but quite human. The 'immortal mortal' as some have joked. Yes, they chose me to lead the Council, but many times I tried to extricate myself from responsibility. I was most hopeful for King Solomon in the tenth century. He traded closely with Tyre, bankrolling our ships that brought raw materials back to him from across the Mediterranean and beyond. Sadly, when he died, his kingdom was split in two, and I was again put in charge. So it went, across many centuries."

Eric stared at Lotte, who stared back, appearing to be equally overwhelmed. Finally, she broke the silence. "You said Enlil did one other thing before retreating to his eternal sleep."

"Yes, it is what I have been leading up to. The Rope of An and Ki has an entrance that Enlil can manifest anywhere in this world he so chooses. Before he went into his eternal slumber, he selected a spot where it would be anchored. This location is hidden, even from me, but Enlil entrusted the Council with two items made of clay from the Abzu. The first is a scroll that will reveal the whereabouts of the doorway, which will become visible when the scroll is in proximity. The second is the key that will open the passageway."

"*Alter!* The key and the scroll, two of Vanth's attributed items. That's the connection!"

"Quite so. These would be the method by which the Council could call Enlil forth should the agreement ever be broken. Knowing how angry he might be if we did so, only once was such drastic action ever considered, when Tyre was under siege for over a decade in the sixth century BC. We knew, however, when we received these items that they would attract attention. Despite their acquiescence to the pact, all Jinn were quite aware that if the Rope of An and Ki were somehow penetrated, it would be possible to access, and potentially open, the barrier inside that leads to the plane of air. We had to find a hiding place for the artifacts, and luck gifted us the answer. A refugee named Antenor from recently sacked Troy arrived with a strange grayish volcanic rock his ancestors had found in the ruins of the eruption on Thera, modern day Santorini. This we forged into two most powerful items."

"You made Vanth's portal?" she asked, astonished. "Charun's as well?"

"Yes," he answered. "The material Antenor brought to us was quite raw and inefficient. He used it crudely, though it did provide him with power and influence. We refined the substance into its polar sub-components, unlocking the matter's true potential and summoning beings of far greater power. The Kings had to work through me, as these are materials of the earth endowed with highly magnetic properties, anathema to them and impossible to forge. Good thing I was immortal. The power they brought to bear would kill a normal human. When complete, we gave possession of the precious items to the more tractable of the two mysterious beings that could now be called forth by the newly fashioned gateways."

"Wait a minute," Lotte interrupted. "How could Vanth take these things with her into The Zone? For reasons it's too hard to explain right now, I happen to know you can't put pieces of the portal material back through the gateway. It causes a rather extreme reaction."

Utnapishtim nodded. "Yes, but the material found at Thera is of *this* world. Perhaps it was touched in some way by the energy of The Zone during your universe's creation, but it is endemic to this realm. Vanth could transport Enlil's artifacts with her because clay from the Abzu is formed at the intersection of the domains of earth and water. The items are equally at home in either plane."

"Unbelievable. All right, I understand. What happened next?"

"Antenor agreed to take the gateways with him, far into the west where they would have no connection with Enlil or the Rope of An and Ki. Through Tyre's trading network, we were able to secretly keep track of the artifacts, and by extension, the key and the scroll should they ever be required. This worked well until disaster struck, and Vanth's portal was lost during a battle with the Greeks."

Eric tried to put the pieces together. "So, the key and the scroll are locked away with Vanth in The Zone, only accessible through her portal. What does this amulet have to do with anything?"

"Excellent question, young man. In a sense, the amulet is the key to the key. Care was taken to ensure that these valuable items wouldn't fall into the wrong hands. The medallion, made of the same substance as her gateway, must be presented to Vanth, or she will not hand over the key or the scroll. This is why you are in such great danger, especially if you indeed hold charge over Vanth's lost gateway. You must possess both, and you must know the ritual for how they are used."

"Ugh, the bloody ritual," Lotte said with dismay. "We have Vanth's portal, but we don't have her rings. If the Jinn did get their hands on these things, how would they bargain with her? She'd fly off and start killing people just like Charun did."

Utnapishtim sighed deeply. "The rings would no longer stop her. The power behind them is long past. The Council is no more, and the Seven Kings who once presided over the pacts no longer exist. Any bargain would only be as good as the words of the participants, bolstered perhaps by their belief in a power that is now illusory. There is no longer any authority to which one may appeal, no day of judgment for those who transgress."

Eric was stupefied, and saw that Lotte was as well, though she recovered more quickly. "This is terrifying news for us. We've always wondered what role the rings played in the summoning ceremonies. Charun felt unconstrained when he was called and not bound by the proper ceremony, committing many murders. I can't image what the Afrit might have done."

Utnapishtim turned his sightless eyes toward Lotte. "What do you know of the Afrit? I thought the last of its ilk buried and forgotten."

"It's a terribly long story. It turns out my grandfather found the device used to summon the being in Morocco. It *had* been buried, for nearly fifteen hundred years. Without knowing what they were, I inherited the artifacts, and about twelve years ago when Eric and I were in high school, we had to call the creature forth in order to stop it from torturing me when I slept. Since then, it helped us battle Charun and later Ninurta, and has now grown quite strong. In a sense, the Afrit started everything for us. Are you also responsible for that gateway?"

"In a sense," he answered, turning his empty gaze back toward the ever-darkening sky. "A part of the piteous being was brought to us one night in Tyre by rebellious acolytes of that most nefarious Jinn. Iblis was his name, born in fire when the host he took resisted, igniting a blaze that left him disfigured, both inside and out. Why Enlil suffered this mad creature's restoration after the war is testimony to his desperation for harmony. None were surprised when the intransigent and duplicitous scoundrel again precipitated the manufacture of mayhem, the creature of fire being one plot among many to take possession of the key and scroll. It was Iblis who first summoned the beast. We merely did our best to restore and safeguard what endured of the wretched thing. Much of it remains in some woebegone pit, lost forever when the acolytes were killed and couldn't reveal the location."

"*Scheiße!*" Lotte said, bewildered. "There's more of it out there, trapped even longer than the Afrit we know? Maybe it's for the best those parts stay buried. They might be really quite insane at this point. What happened to Iblis? Were you able to stop him?"

"Sadly, no. Iblis went into hiding far to the east, but later he returned with the Turkmen who finally toppled Byzantium and eventually conquered Greece. This made matters quite challenging, indeed. We battled him across the ages, but through the acquisition of some exceptional power, the source of which we never ascertained, step by step, he was able to isolate and eliminate one King after another, until only three remained."

"Why didn't you just leave?" Eric asked. "Go somewhere the Turks didn't control?"

"That would likely have backfired. The authority of the Council and its ability to keep loyal Jinn in the coalition would have been greatly diminished had we simply run away. So, on we fought. As it was, our proximity and secrecy gave us certain advantages at times in subverting attempts by Iblis to extend his power. In the end, however, nowhere on Earth was truly safe, or safer than where we were, assuming we stayed cautious and loyal. The council had already avoided detection in this tower for hundreds of years."

Eric laughed. "Kind of surprising with that big plaque on the top of the building announcing, 'heaven and earth' for anyone to see... anyone who reads Phoenician, that is."

"Aicha put that there," Utnapishtim shot back, a bit testily. "That crest marks the end of the Seven Kings, and it is what both holds me here, and to some degree protects me from further harm."

"Why would Aicha do that?" Lotte asked with surprise. "I thought you said she went far away and had nothing to do with the Council."

"For a great time that was true, but circumstances change. In the early part of the nineteenth century, our efforts against Iblis began to pay off as the fortunes of the Ottoman Empire declined. A Greek resistance formed, to which we lent our support, but it wasn't enough with just three Kings remaining, so we reached out to Aicha. She had proven herself a formidable opponent of the Portuguese in their attempts to conquer Morocco for well over three hundred years. Feeling we had the situation in hand, we extended a generous offer, and she agreed to assist us."

"But it was a trap."

"Perhaps. It is hard to know what was on her mind when she crossed the waters to join us. It is possible she was sincere, at least at first. Surely, she furthered our cause, providing invaluable intelligence and rallying allies around the world to intervene on the Greeks' behalf. In truth, the fault may lie more with me than her. Humans, unfortunately, lead human lives, however long they may be, and frequently make human mistakes from which they cannot escape. It was comforting to have one around me so conversant in the ancient cities of my birth, and Jinn or no, I admired Aicha greatly — her intelligence, her spirit, her beauty. We fell in love, or at least I fell in love with her."

Where have I heard a story like this before? I hope they don't all end with the guy lying mutilated in a giant wheelchair.

"In my zeal, I fear I trusted her more than I should have, granting her information as to the activities and whereabouts of the remaining Kings to better coordinate all our efforts. Perhaps by design, or maybe just simply sensing an opportunity, she secretly made a pact with Iblis. She passed her knowledge on to him, and he was able to finish off the remaining Kings, leaving me helpless. I fled here, to the tower, but Aicha was able to track me through something she planted in my belongings. I should have known better, but my feelings blinded me, far more so than the eventual loss of my eyes. With the Seven Kings now conveniently out of the way, Aicha, and the Ottoman troops Iblis supplied to her in exchange for the information she provided, took the tower, and I was hers."

Lotte was incredulous. "What could Aicha have possibly wanted with you? The amulet? What's the point? Everyone knew the key and the scroll were lost when Vanth's portal disappeared."

"That is not so. Only I and the Seven Kings knew the gateways had both been lost by the ancient Etruscans. Utter chaos would have resulted had the rest of the Jinn been privy to such information. I tried to explain to her that it was impossible to give her what she wanted. I held out as long as I could, but Aicha's determination and cruelty knew no bounds. I was sadly reminded that my love was not human, and that there was something she wanted which held far greater importance to her than me. Facing an eternity with no ears to hear, or tongue to speak, I turned over the amulet and confessed the truth to her."

"Why didn't she just kill you then? What's the point in keeping you here?"

"Aicha cannot kill me. Even if she immolated my body, my disembodied consciousness would float about for eternity in forsaken misery unless rescued by one of the lords of the Abzu. I sense, in the end, that she believed me about the gateway having been lost. Lost things, however, can be found, and I remained a source of information to her should the artifacts be recovered or clues to their whereabouts emerge. Aicha created the disc you see on the tower to hold me here, thinking it infinitely amusing that I would ever be a slave to the symbols of An and Ki."

"Wait a minute," Eric jumped in. "When I killed Aicha, her enchantment on my phone stopped. If she's dead, maybe the disc on the tower isn't working anymore?"

"Were it only so simple. You are correct about the termination of her conjurations upon dying, but her hold over your device was accomplished quickly and depended upon a stream of energy from her to maintain and utilize. With sufficient time, Jinn can craft powerful and more permanent items out of non-magnetic materials, gold in particular. The enchantments on such objects can persist almost indefinitely, and independently of the life or status of the Jinn responsible for its creation."

"*Verdammt!*" Lotte cursed. "Maybe we could find another Jinn to come up here and counteract the original magic?"

"Sadly, the sigil both holds me here and keeps other Jinn out. I wonder if she meant to protect me from her dubious ally, Iblis, who would surely have roasted me over one of his molten alchemical flames, given the opportunity. Perhaps Aicha harbored some remnant of feeling toward me after all, as an owner might for a particularly loyal dog. In any case, one would have to be in contact with the object for a great period of time to negate the enchantment, and only Aicha, who crafted the sigil, would be able to bypass the barrier to get close enough, and again, only if she were in fairly close proximity. Humans, however, may enter, and can pose a threat, particularly armed with some type of Jinn magic."

"Thus, the guards, I suppose," Eric observed, "and why they searched us so closely. I'm surprised *they* don't still work for Aicha." The man with the Uzi shot him a rather disagreeable look, and Eric withered slightly at his gaffe.

"It was my kindly companions' ancestors who took back this tower from Aicha's Ottoman henchmen in 1829. They represent the final defense should the unthinkable occur. It is why you were searched so carefully, and why they are armed as best as possible against threats both mortal and ethereal. I have tried for two hundred years to convince them this is too dangerous, and that they put themselves and their families at great peril protecting one so undeserving. Regrettably, it is like talking to a ziggurat."

"Quiet, old man," the female guard replied, mild humor in her voice, "or I'll make sure you only get cheap Retsina with your dinner tonight."

"You see?" He heartily laughed. "They are impossible, but I love them so. No, they do not answer to Aicha, who abandoned this place long ago and has not once returned. Likewise, Iblis has never bothered, presumably concluding that Aicha got everything of value from me, and that an assault is not worth the risk or the resources. I imagine their networks inform them of the tower's silence in all affairs, which in the end has proven to provide the best protection of all. I sincerely hope your presence here doesn't jeopardize our hard-won safety."

Lotte impotently shook her head. "We hope so too. What an incredible mess. What should we do now? If Iblis and Aicha were still in league with each other, will he now be coming after the portal?"

"I know not. Surely, Aicha had accomplices of her own, and they will soon know of her demise. If Iblis is involved, then he and his minions would be added to the register of threats. However, the answer to your basic question of what now must be done is obvious. The key and the scroll, which Vanth possess, are made of clay from the Abzu, and you are in possession of Enki's gateway. Had I enjoyed such an advantage, I would have given them to my old master for safekeeping. This is what you must do, and then you, and all who you love, must vanish forever, unless you wish to entrust your safety to a capricious and sometimes selfish god."

Lotte sighed and nodded. "It may be our only choice. Our lives aren't so easy to displace in the manner you're suggesting, and the truth is, most of our friends and family have no idea what we've gotten mixed up with. They'd think we were quite insane, probably lock us up in the loony bin, which actually doesn't sound so bad in comparison to other possible fates."

Eric agreed with that assessment, though the idea of running away with Lotte and hiding out together held far greater appeal. In his gut, however, he knew that neither of these paths would provide an easy way out of their dilemma.

"Do as you will," Utnapishtim conceded. "As always, humans must lead human lives. Hopefully, you will avoid making a human mistake from which you cannot escape. The safest place for the key and scroll, however, are clearly with Enki in the Abzu. Even if my lord's gateway falls into Iblis's or some other Jinn's hands, they will not be able to reach the artifacts. Enki's powers in the deep waters are too great. Do this, and you will have secured the preservation of your world, though your lives will likely remain in great peril."

Lotte dismally nodded, taking in his words. "We'll do as you say. It's the only logical choice. We thank you for seeing us and explaining all this. It's far too complicated for me to have ever figured out."

"I thank you both for your bravery and perseverance. A heavy burden, it is, which you bear, but perhaps we can provide at least some support. Let me speak with my companions. It would be terribly risky, but given what is at stake, they may agree to assist in your protection."

Eric glanced with curiosity at the two guards who stood watching them, but their faces betrayed no hint of what they felt about this proposal.

"Remain with us this night. We will dine on fine foods, one of the few pleasures left to me, and we will talk further of your interesting exploits. I will speak with Eamon, the man who met you at the gate, and we will see what he thinks. Perhaps things are not as impossible as they currently seem."

"We thank you," Lotte replied, much more enthusiastically. "We'll happily stay, and it will be an honor for us to share your company."

Honor was putting it mildly.

Eric had read somewhere that of all the superpowers humans might desire, time travel ranked as number one.

Be careful what you wish for, he thought, recalling his harrowing experience using the Tablet of Destinies to save Lotte. As he listened to Utnapishtim, however, he felt like they were experiencing ancient history firsthand. The minute details, so often lost, blossomed to life before them, spoken by a man who had breathed them in from day to day, and who now casually exhaled recollections of an existence lost to modernity. What Eric would have loved to have asked him, given enough time.

Sadly, the evening passed far too quickly, and Utnapishtim took great pleasure in hearing the details of Lotte and Eric's tale. It seemed the ancient man yearned as much for information about the present as the pair did about the past, and they weren't about to disappoint him. When all were finally exhausted, they bid the ancient man goodnight.

Eamon and the stern woman who had browbeaten them with the pistol earlier escorted them to one of the outbuildings near the wall. The tiny but cozy second floor apartment smelled of antique furniture and the oil of countless lamps.

"I wish we'd brought our toothbrushes from the car," Lotte muttered when their escorts had closed the door behind them. "I'll be damned if I'm going back on that ridiculous cable chair in the dark to get them, though. I'm not looking forward to that ride tomorrow."

"Neither am I," Eric agreed, yawning as he stretched to remove his shirt.

"*Verdammt!* Eric, what happened?"

For a moment, he didn't know what had upset her so, but then he saw her eyes fixed on his chest. "Oh, yeah... guess you didn't see that yesterday. I put on a t-shirt in the bathroom before we went to bed. I told you Rehana — er, I guess that would be Aicha, actually — shot me with her crossbow. It was just a warning shot with a blunt bolt, but you can see it left a pretty nice bruise."

"Oh, my love, I had no idea! Does it hurt?"

He laughed. "Only when I breathe... or move... or get on rickety ski-lift chairs. It should be some comfort that this isn't actually the worst injury I've ever had." To his surprise, she flew into his arms and held him tightly, though mercifully not in one of her spine-cracking hugs.

"You had no idea what you were up against," she said tearfully, cheek pressed to his shoulder. "I could have lost you right then, and there wasn't anything I could have done. This has all gotten too complicated, too dangerous. My obsession with these objects is going to get us both killed, and maybe everyone we know and love. This is all my fault. Why can't I just be normal and let things bloody well be? I make a mess of everything."

There it was again, that strain of doubt and anxiousness, which of late had seemed to regularly pierce Lotte's normal air of cocksure confidence. Eric had almost put his worries aside when she'd been so happy to see him, but now the questions and suspicions again penetrated his consciousness.

Is this the time to talk to her, time to risk voicing my concerns and possibly exposing my own stupid insecurity?

"What have you made a mess of?" he said. "Yeah, maybe you drive the bus a little more than I do when it comes to this portal stuff, but you know what? I'm right there with you. There may have been a time when I questioned all of this, but that's *way* in the past. I made a commitment to you, Lotte, wherever that leads me."

She hiccuped a little laugh. "Right over the cliff, I'm afraid. Some bus driver I've turned out to be."

"What are you talking about? You can't seriously believe you should have known what kind of danger unearthing Vanth's portal might bring. I don't believe it. Anyway, it's seemed like something's been wrong with you for a while, before all this trouble started. What's going on? Is there something I should know?"

She stiffened in his arms. Gently, but firmly, she pushed him away and turned to stare out the window into a night sky dazzlingly illuminated by a near-full moon. Her voice was flat when she finally spoke.

"Oh, Eric, I don't know where to begin. Maybe now isn't the best time to get into all of this. We're so tired, and there's so much happening."

He reeled at what he heard, confirmation in his mind that there was, indeed, something behind his concerns. Truthfully, he dreaded hearing more, but nonetheless, he mechanically recited words he didn't really want to express. "It's okay, go ahead. I'm listening... I want to know."

She sighed with resignation. "All right, I... I suppose there's really nothing for it now. It all began— *What the hell was that?*"

Eric had also jumped at the thunderous noise that shook the room and echoed in the valley below them. "That was an explosion... and gunshots! Get away from the window!"

They both hit the floor and crawled madly toward the door. It swung open just as they reached it. Eamon stood there with a lantern, an accusatory look on his face.

"You see what has happened? They must be here for you, what you possess! We told you not to bring trouble to our door, but that is exactly what you have done!"

"It's impossible!" Lotte shot back, her resilient spirit reasserting itself. "No one knew we came here! They're fishing, hoping they might catch us. Hide us away somewhere and tell them we're not here."

"It's obviously too late for that," Eamon barked. "They've already launched an assault. If any of the attackers employ Jinn magic that can detect the amulet, no place we can hide you will be safe."

Eric knew this to be true, remembering how Aicha had been able to detect the items hidden in their bathroom heating vent.

"We must get you out of here. Come!"

Eamon bolted down the stairs with them scrambling after him. When they exited the building, he led them toward the far end of the tower's walls. Behind them, near the entrance through which they'd come on the chair lift, sporadic gunfire continued.

"They must have crossed by hand on the cables and planted an explosive by one of the lift doorways," the man breathlessly explained. "I hope to God the cables didn't snap. We can hold them, for a time, but eventually they might scale the walls, and our only refuge will be the tower."

"But the tower's entrance is back there," Lotte worriedly said. "Why are we going this way?"

"You shall see."

Eamon led them through an archway into the wall itself. When they reached the end, dark hallways radiated out to the right and left. He chose the left passage, and after a short distance started to carefully feel along the rough stone outer wall with his hand.

"Here it is," he finally announced as he placed his lantern on the ground. "Help me push!"

Eric skeptically did as instructed, wondering what good could come from pushing on a rock barrier built to withstand a siege. To his surprise, however, the section of wall against which they pressed reluctantly gave way, seeming to be on some sort of metal track.

Eamon shuttled the pair through the opening, and they emerged in a small chamber, cleverly nestled in a spot where the true outer wall of the compound jutted slightly outward. The tiny room contained only a set of spiral stairs leading downward.

Eric helped Eamon struggle to return the false wall into position before taking Lotte's hand and following the man, who carried the lantern, down the musty stairs. Distressingly, there was no railing, so all three groped cautiously forward on the uneven wedges that wound ever deeper into the bedrock. The humid and still air smelled of dirt and mold. Clearly, this passage saw little use, and he wondered why they were being taken this way.

The answer became clear when they reached the bottom.

"You've got be kidding," Lotte sniped. "If you think we're getting in that damned thing—"

"There is no choice," Eamon angrily interrupted. "You must get away from here and do as Mr. U. commanded!"

In the center of the room, a large vertical winch connected an ancient and decaying wooden basket to a rope that would, in theory, hoist the vessel up and down. It made the cables and the old-timey ski-lift chair look like a leisurely ride on one of Boston's Swan Boats, and Eric wondered if maybe he and Lotte weren't better off trying to shoot it out with whoever was breaking into the tower above them.

CHAPTER 10

Eamon interrupted their horrified examination of the questionable apparatus before them. "You have the amulet, yes?"

Lotte nodded, somewhat chastened by the man's agitation.

"Good! *You*, help me move this. It's extremely heavy."

By "you," Eamon meant Eric, and by "it's extremely heavy," he meant a really incredibly, unbelievably, almost impossible to move giant iron slab on the floor near the outer wall, rusted with age, but still sturdy due to its tremendous bulk. As instructed, he helped Eamon pull, grasping one of several thick handles. A hole slowly emerged beneath the massive barrier, revealing a straight shot into the moonlit trees, which he guessed were nearly six hundred feet below them. The opening turned out to be about eight feet in diameter, easily big enough for the derelict-looking vessel that rested nearby to fit through.

"Are you sure there's no other way?" Eric feebly asked.

"You can jump!" Eamon brusquely replied, turning his attention to the saucer-like receptacle that he apparently felt would transport them to the ground below. "Help me drag this to the opening."

Lotte moaned as they all pushed. "Is this thing even operational? It looks like it hasn't been used for years."

"It will work," the man said with confidence. "We still use it on occasion to bring up heavier items, though not for some time. It may be a bit, well... rusty. That's my problem. I have to turn the winch. All you have to do is hold on."

The only thing Eric could see to hold onto were heavy chains secured to four thick circlets of iron welded onto plates and bolted to the rim of the wooden basket. When they got the container in place, Eamon crisscrossed the chains over a heavy iron hook, which in turn connected to the thick rope that a series of pulleys conveyed back to the winch. The basket itself seemed more like a deep dish, meant for hauling boxes and bags, not people. Roped netting for additional capacity, or perhaps to transport larger or oddly sized items, draped across large nails at several points along the sides. Most of this, however, appeared to be in tatters.

Eric couldn't believe it. "Why would you put your supply lift way down here behind a hidden door? How do you even get stuff to the base of the cliff? It just looks like trees down there to me."

"There is a path that connects to the road which loops around not far from here," Eamon explained as they carefully lowered the basket through the opening. "This is just an ancillary lift. The larger one is along the wall in the opposite direction, but it is higher and heavier, requiring several people to operate. When our families took charge of Mr. U. in the nineteenth century, changes were made in the ramparts above us to hide this mechanism, for a situation exactly like this. Be glad they did so. It will likely save your lives."

"Assuming we don't die of heart failure on the trip down," Lotte groused. "Really, you couldn't have made it a bit more people-friendly?"

Eamon stared at her. "It's a supply elevator, not a tourist attraction. Just stay low and distribute your weight evenly. It will be fine. In any case, there is no choice, and we must hurry! When you reach the bottom, find the path that leads to the road and try to get back to your car. It's doubtful they know where it is. Maybe you can get away. If they've found it, just hide in the woods. Help will come eventually. It's the best I can do. You're dead for sure if you stay here."

As if to add emphasize to his words, another explosion rocked the top of the boulder, raining debris on their heads. "They may have penetrated the courtyard now or are getting very close. You have to move. Get in, now!"

"After you," Eric said with terrified politeness.

Lotte stiffened. "No, you first... I insist."

He took a deep breath, steadied himself on one of the connecting chains, and lowered his body into the swaying dish below. Being somewhat heavy, it was surprisingly stable once he crouched fairly low near the center.

"Come on," he said encouragingly. "It's not so bad. Grab one of the chains, step in, and then give me your hand."

She gulped but did as he asked while Eamon held the rope to help steady the basket. Soon, the two were settled on their backs, side by side, each tightly gripping a chain for additional security.

"All right," Eamon said, gently releasing the rope. "Just hold on and relax. It'll be bumpy at first until the gears get loosened up, but don't worry... all these mechanisms are far sturdier than they appear."

"Damned well better be," Lotte grumbled under her breath.

Eric took her hand in his, which seemed to calm her slightly. Without warning, the basket stuttered and then dropped a couple of feet. She squeezed her eyes shut and tightly clasped her fingers against his palm. With another unexpected jounce, they again descended, swinging slightly in sympathy to the rough motion.

"It'll take an hour to get down at this rate," she fretted, "and I'll probably be sick if he keeps jerking us around like this."

"Give it a minute. He said it would be bumpy at first. I think once it loosens up, he'll be able to do a smooth circuit on the winch and it'll go much faster. Just hang on."

She didn't bother responding as there was little choice for either of them but to hold on for dear life. Sadly, progress became no less jarring in the near term as they watched the light from the hole above them retreat in fitful increments. More gunshots and shouts came from the top of the rocky outcropping, but they still seemed quite distant, near the opposite end of the compound.

Eric estimated they had dropped about thirty feet when something flashed past them to his left, barely visible in the moonlight and what remained of the illumination from Eamon's lantern.

"What the hell was that?"

Lotte reluctantly opened her eyes. "What was what?"

"I don't know. I thought I saw something fly past... *there!* There it was again! Did you see it?"

"I didn't, but I heard something. It sounded like a bird, or maybe a bat... probably attracted to the light or scared by the noise going on near the tower. I don't think it's anything to worry about."

Before he could respond, a loud *thump* against the side of the basket sent them swinging wildly to one side. Eric felt Lotte's weight press heavily against him as they lurched. He clung to the chain, and planted his feet as best he could against the side to keep from being pushed out. Knowing that she would face the same pressure when they listed the other way, he hooked his ankle around the chain near his feet and threw his right arm around her shoulders.

Fortunately, she also had a tight grip on her chain and was able to maintain balance, but he winced as the iron links dug painfully into his shin. Gradually, the basket's side-to-side motion decreased, and the threat became less immediate.

"Okay," she panted. "Maybe it's something to worry about after all. What the hell kind of bird would do that?"

Eric had his suspicions, but just then their erratic trip downward began anew with yet another staggered drop. He had just recovered from the jostling when, to his horror and amazement, he saw a great owl swooping directly toward them. The bird appeared to be light in color, yellow perhaps, with streaks of gray or black through the feathers of its body and wings, which nearly spanned the diameter of their basket. Bright orange eyes, intent with menace, glared directly at him.

"Oh, shit!" He clung firmly to Lotte, fearing another brutal impact. "Hold on!"

Instead of ramming the side, however, this time the creature grasped the chain near Lotte's feet in its muscular claws. Impossibly, the beast pumped its mighty wings and began to tilt the basket. Again, she was forced into his body, and his chest seared with pain as he fought to hold on and keep both of them from tumbling out.

"Kick it!" he screamed. "We have to force it to let go. I can't hold out here much longer!"

She drove her leg backwards but couldn't reach high enough. "I have to turn around. Let go. Eric, you have to let me go!"

With great reluctance, he withdrew his arm from her shoulders, and felt a rush of panic as she released her grasp on the chain to which she clung. This allowed her the flexibility to nimbly rotate onto her back, putting all her weight on his upper body. The ferocious owl had nearly overturned the basket when she finally caught the beast with the sole of her Euro-styled Adidas sneaker.

The strike caught the creature straight in the abdomen... or, it would have, had the incredible bird not vanished right before their eyes. Lotte's blow encountered only the moonlit darkness of the night sky. The basket plunged back into position with a shuddering jolt, rattling the chains, and loosening the bolts on the plate near her feet that tenuously held their vessel aloft.

"All right," she said in a trembling voice once they'd both recovered their balance and gotten past the worst of the shock. "Definitely worried now. What the bloody hell are we going to do?"

He really had no idea, but fortunately he didn't have to answer.

Eamon hissed at them, silhouetted in the light as he crouched in the opening. "What's going on? The mechanism can't stand that kind of banging around. You'll break the rope or knock it off of the pulleys. What in the world are you doing?"

"It's not us," Eric shot back. "We're under attack here! It's some kind of freaking Genie owl... super strong, and super mean! It's trying to tip over the basket and kill us!"

"Damn," he replied, reaching to his side. "Hold on!"

"What do you think we're doing?" Eric asked with dismay, which only increased when he saw the man now held a pistol pointed downward. "What the hell is that for?"

"There's only one choice! We have to kill the creature, or at least subdue it. I wish I had a machine gun, but this will have to suffice. When it reappears, I'll do what I can."

"Are you quite insane?" Lotte shrieked. "If you miss, you're likely to hit one of us!"

"It can't be helped," Eamon said with no trace of remorse. "If you have a better option, I suggest you employ it. I'm a good shot, trust me."

Trust.

So much power behind that one little syllable. Eric hoped Eamon told the truth because, in reality, no better option existed. This was it.

The gunfire from the top of the great rock had ceased. Eric wasn't sure if that was a good sign or not, but silence had once again overtaken the valley above which he and Lotte wordlessly swayed. They waited, and listened, anxious to determine from which direction a renewed strike might come.

"I have to pee," she whispered.

He gave a slight laugh. "Me too. They should really install a bathroom in this thing. I'll leave that in my Google review."

As if from nowhere, the great bird appeared right above them, its orange eyes glowering with anger. Once more, it clasped one of the chains in its talons, this time closer to the hook and out of reach from another kick. One of them would have to stand to reach the beast, a complex and delicate maneuver in their unstable contraption. The Jinn-owl rapidly beat its wings, dragging the entire basket with it as it flew to the side.

Having grasped the chain so high, the vessel didn't actually tilt that much. Should the creature go far enough and let go, however, the momentum and chaos of the motion would almost surely throw them loose. It appeared to be taking all of the monster's strength, but little-by-little, they gained height, and the danger increased.

A shot broke the valley's silence, and the terrible bird let out a chilling shriek as feathers flew from the beast's wing. It again vanished from sight, and the pendulum of the basket swung instantly back, causing the wood around the iron circlets to creak forebodingly. Lotte and Eric floundered miserably in the increasingly flimsy dish. Fortunately, the height hadn't been great enough to cause the maximum turmoil. After a time, they again settled into a slow swaying beneath the opening above.

"*Skatá!*" Eamon shouted. "I was aiming for the body. The bullet went right through the cursed thing's wing. That won't stop it, but it may slow it down a bit. We'll have to wait for it to come back, and I'll take another shot."

Even in the moonlight, Eric could see that Lotte was turning green from the lurching motions. He knew they couldn't take much more of this but harbored newfound hope now that Eamon had actually hit the thing.

"Just breathe," he encouraged her. "We have to hang on. I think Eamon can do it. We're gonna be okay."

She didn't open her eyes, but her chest began to slowly rise and fall, and the grimace on her face softened ever so slightly. Knowing his own need to conserve strength, he laid his head back and gazed up into the infinity above him. But for the moon, and the lantern's illumination, they'd be able to see the stars perfectly. Even with these impediments, the Greek sky brimmed with a life he rarely saw in light-polluted Boston.

It's gorgeous.

He thought about how the ancient Greeks had looked to these same stars for guidance, or for solace in troubled times.

Eamon cautiously scanned with his pistol, hovering above like some guardian angel.

Eric took a deep, soothing breath, and watched in mute horror as the angel suddenly took flight.

Pitching headfirst through the opening as if stoutly pushed, Eamon screamed and grasped desperately for the rope. It was hopeless. Both he and the gun that fell softly from his hand plummeted toward where Eric and Lotte helplessly lay. Only the swaying of the basket prevented a direct collision. Instead, the doomed man plunged past. His shoulder cracked with a dull thud against the side of their wooden prison before he disappeared in a wail of terror into the depths below.

Lotte shot bolt upright. "What in hell just happened?"

"Lie back down," he commanded, pushing at her shoulder. "That owl thing must have gotten through the opening while it was invisible and then materialized behind Eamon. It pushed him out. He didn't see it coming at all."

"Eric, what are we going to do? This is awful!"

He was dumbfounded. "I... I don't know. I have no fucking idea what to do. I think we might die here."

"Oh, no," she said with anger and determination. "We're not dying here, not without at least putting up a fight."

"What do you propose we do? That thing can pull the basket like it did before and send us flying. There's no gun to stop it this time."

"Then we'll have to stop it ourselves. We need a weapon of some kind. We know the Jinn can't tolerate iron or magnetic metals. We need something like that."

"There are big nails on the side of this thing. They're holding up all that old netting. Could we get one of those out?"

"We'll have to try. It may be our only chance. You look on your side, and I'll look on mine, see if there are any that look like they'd come out easily."

"All right, but stay low. We don't want that thing pushing us over the edge like it did with Eamon."

Warily, he peered over the lip of the basket. Even with the moonlight it was difficult to see the dark nails, so he felt his hand along the outside until he found one. Deeply embedded in the wood, the rusted but still sturdy spike showed no sign of moving. He felt for another. This one stuck out a bit more. He could get the tips of his fingers around the base but couldn't get enough pressure on the head while reaching over the side of the basket.

"I think I found one," he said, "but I have to get a better angle on it to have any chance of pulling it out."

"There's one on my side too that I might be able to wedge out. What do you want to do?"

"I'm stronger than you are. Hold onto that chain with one hand and hold my leg with the other. That'll give me the best angle, and the best chance of getting the thing out."

She wriggled into position, and he felt her tight grasp around his ankle. Her grip pressed painfully against the forming bruises from the chains, but he forced that inconvenience from his mind.

"What is the damned thing doing?" Lotte wondered aloud. "We're like sitting ducks. Why doesn't it just finish us off?"

A valid question, but Eric now fully focused his attention on extending over the basket's side. The rough wood scraped against his bare skin, having been unable to retrieve his shirt before they fled the cozy little apartment where he wished they were both happily sleeping right now.

He still couldn't achieve enough of an angle. He needed to lock his elbows on the outer face to have any chance of generating enough force to dislodge the thick nail. "Hold tight. I need to stretch out farther."

The basket rocked unsteadily as he extended his torso over the edge. Disregarding the perilous drop that unfolded beneath his eyes, the increasing pain in his leg, and the now more urgent need to pee, he intently lodged his fingers under the head of the nail and pressed with all his might. The spike didn't budge. He tried again with even more intensity, his fingers hammering with pain as he crushed them against the rusty iron.

Still nothing. I need something to act as a lever. "Lotte, we need something to — *Ugh!*"

The blow came from above and slammed Eric between his shoulder blades. Sharp talons pierced his bare flesh and forced him downward. For a brief instant, he had the sensation of falling, the moon-dappled treetops his only vista.

Lotte's grasp saved him from plummeting directly downward. Her hand on his ankle forced his upper body back toward the underside of the basket, directly into the tangle of ratty netting that draped raggedly from the side. Desperately, he clenched a handful of the decrepit roping before gravity and momentum ripped her hand away. His legs swung down, and abruptly the full weight of his body hung suspended by his tenuous grasp on the ancient netting. He could hear multiple strands snap and tear above him, and he dropped by another two feet before painfully jerking to a halt.

Steaks of blood tickled his back as he frantically tried to catch his breath. He couldn't hang here by his arms forever. The only chance was to pull himself up and try to get his feet lodged in the netting. Then, perhaps, he could attempt to get back in the basket. Of course, this assumed the Jinn-owl wouldn't just simply swoop in and finish him off.

Above him, Lotte cried out hysterically. "Eric, hang on! Just hang on! Can you try to pull yourself up? If you can get close, I'll give you my hand."

"No," he coughed. "Don't lean over. It'll knock you out too and I won't be there to help. Just give me a second."

"Eric, you may not have a second. That thing is bound to be back, and you're in no position to put up any resistance."

Good point. It's now or never.

He summoned all his strength and tugged hard on the roped netting. The gym he went to in Somerville had pull-up bars, and this was essentially the same. He sucked at pull-ups, usually using the assisted machine to get in any meaningful reps. Unassisted, though, he could rip off a few... maybe four or five when he was fresh.

He didn't exactly feel fresh at the moment, but he didn't lack motivation. He fully realized his life depended on what he was about to do. As he hoisted himself upward, the netting continued to tear, as luck would have it, mostly on his left side, where his shoulder had been weakened by multiple injuries in battles long past. He briefly let go with that hand, hanging completely from his right arm, and reached as far upward and away from where the ropes were giving way as he possibly could.

It worked. With more solid purchase, he inched incrementally upward until he could hook his foot through a dangling loop below him — not perfect, but a damned sight better than his previous position. Only a couple of feet above him, the basket listed where his weight created an imbalance.

Lotte screamed, "Look out!"

Not really being able to look at anything, he wrapped his arm through the torn netting and hung on tightly. The Jinn-owl swooped in from his right, wings tight to its body, and slammed into his bleeding back. The downy and beautiful feathers did little to soften the blow, which felt like being pummeled by a bag of gravel. His head whipped sideways, and his body pitched violently in the tangled jumble of ropes. The loop that supported his leg gave way, and he again dangled by his arms alone.

How such a seemingly delicate creature could deliver a strike like that was beyond him. He credited it to the powers of the Jinn, remembering the superhuman strength Aicha exhibited when they had battled. A couple more blows like that, however, and either the netting, or his ability to hold on, would give way. He again desperately heaved, gained another foot or so, and finally found a fresh toehold.

Lotte called from above, peering cautiously over the edge. "It's injured! It's not flying right. I could tell when it went past. That bullet must have hurt the thing, and now it probably doesn't have the capacity to pull the basket. It's going to try to knock you off, and then come after me."

"I'm so happy it had a Plan B. I really look forward to watching how *that* works out."

"Can you get a bit higher? Maybe we get you back inside before it circles around again."

He doubted that would be possible with the monster out there watching for a vulnerable moment. There wasn't much farther to go, though, and the netting actually seemed a bit more secure the closer he got to where the ropes hung from the nails in the side of the basket.

"Hold on, I'll try."

Just as he hoisted himself upward, the Jinn-owl assailed him once more, timing its strike to grab his right wrist as he reached for a fresh span of rope. Sharp claws bit into his flesh as the creature furiously tried to wrest him away. Lotte's observation had been accurate, the owl's left wing wasn't moving properly, and it appeared to have far less ability to pull. Nonetheless, it was still supernaturally strong, and he couldn't free his arm.

He had only one option. With all his might, he rammed his head into the beast's torso. He made contact but lacked enough momentum to dislodge the monster that now seemed fully intent on dislodging him. He started to lash out again when something from above struck the Jinn-owl squarely in the head. The creature screeched in pain and surprise, looked up, and then immediately vanished as another Euro-Styled Adidas sneaker streaked past into the darkness below.

"Got him!" Lotte cheered while Eric fought for balance after being so abruptly freed. "Come on, quickly, while the thing is still stunned. This may be our only chance!"

Eric summoned the last of his strength and, fighting off the pain of his injuries, again attempted to climb upward. His spirit soared when he felt her hand on his bleeding right wrist. The vessel wobbled unsteadily as he began the delicate process of getting back in, looping his elbows cautiously over the basket's edge.

He had almost scrambled to safety when the Jinn-owl reappeared and forcefully grabbed the fabric of his right pants leg. He tried to shake it away, but it refused to let go. His arms were now too tired to support his body, and he couldn't kick out with his other leg, lest he lose his toehold and risk being pulled away. He suddenly felt the tattered ropes beneath him give way from the pressure, and he fell downward, at the last moment catching his hands on the basket's lip.

"Lotte, this rope is giving out! You have to try to pull me in, *now!*"

She gazed down at him in horror, and past him to where the terrible bird seemed poised to finally assert its will.

"No! Hold on!" With that, she disappeared from his view.

"Hold on?" he screamed. "What do you mean, *hold on?* This thing is gonna kill me, Lotte! What are you doing?" To his great alarm, she didn't answer. "Lotte, are you there? *Lotte!*"

A vigorous yank from the beast caused the rope under his foot to give way. He now hung only by his hands. Briefly, he reconsidered kicking out at the monster, but his feeble grasp would never withstand the motion. Frantically, he fought to pull himself closer to the basket as he groped around with his left foot for another loop of rope. Incredibly, he located one, but it was a Pyrrhic victory. He could hear the netting tear around him. It was only a matter of time now, and precious little time at that.

"*Lotte*! What the hell are you doing!"

"This," she breathlessly gushed as she grabbed his left forearm. "Give me your right hand!"

"I can't let go! It'll pull me away!"

"There's no choice! This is our only hope!"

He reluctantly complied and felt her press something to his hand as he reached toward her. It was a thick, rusty, iron nail, and he knew what he had to do. Almost without thinking, he took it from her, buoyed now by the extra support she provided on his left side.

Knowing he'd only have one shot at it, he looked down and tried to calculate where best to strike. The wings would be easiest to hit, but they were mostly feathers. It was a near miracle the bullet had found an area of flesh and bone near the top edge. He saw where blood from the wound had stained and damaged the fine yellow feathers, but the small spot would be almost impossible to hit, especially as the wing was in constant motion. It would have to be the body, which he figured would do the most damage anyway.

He'd employ a one-two motion, first tucking his leg in as much as possible, then jabbing downward. Then he'd try not to fall.

I guess that's a one-two-three motion. Whatever.

Not wanting Lotte to be surprised, he whispered what he hoped wouldn't be the last word he ever said.

"*Now.*"

He pulled his knee up as far as possible, pulling the terrible bird toward him. The Jinn-owl shrieked and fought against the movement, but this took all the creature's attention. With force, he drove the spike into the beast's back, and then wildly scrambled to regain his balance as he pitched to the right.

No spout of blood appeared, no noise, no flailing about—nothing but a loosening, the abrupt absence of the violent tugging that had threatened to pull Eric to his death. Whether the creature had been immobilized by the iron like Aicha, or had simply vanished again, remained unclear. Nonetheless, this presented his best, and likely last, chance to get back to the relative safety of the basket. He felt Lotte grasp his wrist as he reached up and secured his hand to the lip. Then he hitched his right foot to the now perilously shaky netting. To his wonder and relief, he soon lay on the wooden planks of the swaying dish.

Lotte breathlessly heaved by his side. "I can't believe we did it. I can't believe you held on. I thought that was going to be the end."

"It may still be. We're now hanging here with nobody up there to turn that winch. We'll figure that out in a minute when I catch my breath. What I want to know is, how the hell did you get that nail out?"

"I wedged it out."

"With what?"

"With the only thing I had on me." She held up the medallion.

"Wow, pretty clever. Why didn't we think of that earlier?"

"I guess necessity really is the mother of invention," she said with an unusual hint of sadness.

"Well, I hope necessity gives birth again soon, otherwise we're gonna dangle up here until we starve."

CHAPTER 11

The shaking in his muscles had just begun to subside, and Eric's abraded hands and hyperextended arms had just barely started to regain flexibility and feeling. Time was short, but his body had been pushed to its limit, and his courage well past that. With all his heart, he wished he could just nod off to sleep.

"I think I'll take my socks off," Lotte rather offhandedly remarked. "It'll probably make it easier."

It took a few moments for the sluggish wheels in his brain to register what she'd said. "It'll make *what* easier?"

"Climbing the rope, obviously. I think the socks will be too slippery without my shoes that I tossed at the owl. What do you think?"

Tired as he was, he lifted onto his elbows and faced her. "What do you mean, 'what do I think?' I think there's no way in hell you're climbing that rope. Even if by some miracle you got up there, I don't think you're strong enough to turn that winch."

"I am freakishly strong. At least that's what you always say."

"That's true. You're really strong for a girl your size, though honestly, I think you just *will* yourself to win physical challenges because you hate to lose... but this isn't like that, Lotte. Willpower will only get you so far. In the end, you need the muscles for the job. No way you're going up that rope."

"Well, you're obviously in no shape to do it. What choice do we really have? They're not going to be able to hold out up there forever. The people trying to get in the compound may have heard the shot Eamon fired. They might be headed this way *right now*. I'm trying it. I don't care what you say."

He was shocked when she intently began to remove her socks. "Woah, woah, woah... hang on there. Who says I'm not in shape to do it? Yeah, I'm a little beat up, but hanging off those ropes gave me a pretty good sense of what it's gonna take to get up there, and how to get back down. We're what, like thirty feet or so from the opening? That's basically a vertical first down."

"Excuse me?"

"Never mind, football reference. I'm gonna try it. I think I can get ten yards."

"You can't just *think* you can do it, Eric. You have to be certain. I *know* I can do it, but I'm not as sure about operating that damned winch. Do you *know* you can do it? Because if you don't, I'm trying it anyway."

"No, you're not. You're *not* climbing up that rope. I am. I *know* I can do it."

She smiled. "All right, I know you can do it too. Just hold on a minute."

To his surprise and pleasure, she began to remove her shirt.

"Umm, not that I'm not thrilled by what you're doing, but what the hell are you doing?"

"I'm making a bandage. Your wrist is bleeding pretty badly, and the blood might impact your grip."

He watched as she tore the fabric of her little button-down top, though his eyes were more strongly attracted to her sleek, black bra. He also surreptitiously observed that she might have put on a few pounds, probably feasting on the awesome pasta in Italy while she was working so hard with Dr. Henriksson.

Sven, that is. Whatever.

It reminded him of their unfinished conversation from earlier, but not wishing to create any added tension just now, he kept the thought to himself, as well as any mention of her having gained weight. That would be an express ticket to the trees below.

"There," she announced, having finished her makeshift tourniquet. "That should do for now. Your back is bleeding too. We'll deal with that when we get to the car."

"That's optimistic," he said, and flexed his wrist. Though still painful, at least blood had stopped dripping everywhere.

She leaned over and gave him a quick kiss. "As I said, you can do this. I know you can. If you don't do it now, though, it may be for nothing."

He nodded, stood cautiously, grasped the chains nearest to him for extra stability, and planted one foot on the basket's lip. He reached above the hook and grabbed the thick rope, tight from the weight of the saucer below and, simultaneously pushing with his leg and pulling with his arms, launched onto the rope and struggled to plant his feet on the knobby top of the hook. It took some fussing to find his balance, but once in position, he saw a straight shot to the top.

OK, first and goal to go. Let's just try to pick up five yards with a quick out pass to the sidelines.

He pinched his feet to the rope and pulled himself upward, repeating the process ten times. He felt it working. At the end of his final tug, he stopped to catch his breath, figuring he'd traversed a little less than half the distance.

All right, second and six. Let's hit the defense with a quick snap run up the middle.

His legs had benefitted from the slight rest, but his arms, tired from their earlier exertion, had begun to feel sluggish, and his badly scratched wrist had started to throb. He barely completed a second set of ten pulls and calculated that only about a third of the distance to the top remained.

Damn, this is harder than I thought it would be. I've got two downs left and three yards to go. Do I go for it, or try to get closer? The defense has to be getting tired too, right? I'll take it to the goal line and then bash it in from there.

In agony, he dragged his rapidly flagging body toward the illuminated opening above him. Every muscle in his hands, arms, and shoulders screamed with the distress of overexertion. His legs trembled as he tried to maintain pressure on the rope with his feet, but they were giving out.

The rough stone of the recess leading to the hole hovered a mere foot-and-a-half above him when he had to stop. Just a bit higher and he could swing out his feet and use the rock face for added support, but he had to find the resources to cross that small distance.

Wow, this really is a game of inches, isn't it? Fourth and goal to go. Too bad a field goal isn't an option.

He'd told Lotte he knew he could do it, but now he wasn't so sure — wasn't even convinced he'd ever meant that in the first place. He'd been more afraid that *she* would try it and wind up falling to her death. She hadn't flinched, though. She was about to do it herself, brave to a fault.

He looked at the bandage she'd made for him, already wet with fresh blood. She had known with the kind of certainty only she could possess that he could do it, and she hadn't hesitated when he'd told her that he would. He couldn't let her down now, couldn't let her think that he wasn't the person she thought he was. Sliding back down the rope at this point simply wasn't an option. For a variety of reasons, this wasn't the moment to fall short of her expectations and risk making her realize she had made the wrong decision by believing in him.

Quarterbacks know they're gonna get the crap beat out of them when they run a sneak. Monstrous linemen set a wall, muscular linebackers dive on them, everybody swats at the ball — all the while saying nasty things about your mother. You just have to go low, keep your legs pumping, and embrace the inevitable pain.

Eric had developed a protracted and intimate relationship with pain, and he renewed the acquaintance now with an ecstasy bordering on the maniacal. These were the reps in the gym where you risked hurting yourself, where technique went out the window, and where "anything goes" to reach your goal. They hurt like hell, but as the saying goes, "no pain, no gain," and to his unbounded relief, he began to rise.

When he pulled himself high enough, he caught the rock face with the soles of his Nikes and walked himself torturously upward. Utterly exhausted, he collapsed in a heap on the dirty floor, sweat drenching his body and blood streaming from his wrist and the wounds on his back. Lotte's slightly stifled cries below him reminded him his work wasn't yet complete.

First, however, he had to pee, the only relief he could bring to his battered body.

The winch, a sorry and ancient apparatus, hadn't failed them so far. After a shouted warning, he pushed heavily on the wooden bar, which reluctantly gave a quarter turn and knocked the basket lower by a couple of feet.

Shit! Lotte would never have been able to move this. I'm not even sure I can.

The difficulty continued for some time, taxing what remained of his strength until the rope on the vertical pole began to thin out, and the windings got lower and closer to the lever he was shoving against. As poor Eamon had promised, the ride soon became quite smooth, and he was able to repeatedly circle the central pole without interruption. He was surprised and gratified when the rope suddenly went limp, indicating the basket had reached the bottom.

Now, it only remained for him to shimmy down the rope, surely an easier task than going up, but made challenging by the distance, the dizzying height, and his own diminished condition.

Let's see, six-hundred feet... that's... like... twenty first downs. Hmmmm.

He inspected his shaking hands and the open, blistered wounds on the palms and most fingers. His left shoulder, permanently weakened during his battle with Charun, ached now as it hadn't in years. His legs felt like Jell-O beneath him, and his biceps were tight with fatigue. None of that mattered. He had to do this one final thing.

Just go slow and steady, and then we'll be in the clear.

On the way down, it struck him as odd how one's initial assessments of how to do something were so often wrong. Slow and steady had definitely proved *not* the way, using as much or more of the energy he'd expended going up. After nearly exhausting himself in a careful and controlled descent, he eventually settled into a rhythm of leaning back, loosening his feet, and letting his arms lower him. The lesions on his hands made it painful, especially when he slipped and further burned his palms on the rope. In due time, however, he could hear Lotte cheering him on from below, which brightened his spirits tremendously.

She met him in the basket where the hook now lay, idly disconnected from the iron chains, and beamed as she threw her arms around him. "You did it! It's quite amazing, and really most illuminating. I can't believe it actually works."

He staggered in exhausted confusion. "You can't believe what works?"

"Reverse psychology."

"What are you talking about?"

She shook her head. "You silly. Do you actually think I could have gone up that rope? I wouldn't have gotten two meters. I knew you'd go, though, if I threatened to try it myself. It was probably the only way to get you motivated enough to start moving quickly."

He wavered, both stunned and impressed, but knew she was probably right. Lotte was almost always right. Had she not been about to start climbing herself, he'd have dithered far longer, waiting to recover his strength, plotting strategies for the climb. Her apparent commitment to performing the task had definitely provided a significant boost, as did the confidence she'd later expressed in his abilities.

Still, he felt a little used. "Do you do this to me a lot?"

She laughed "Constantly. It's really the only way to get you to do anything at all."

"I hate you," he said, mostly joking.

"No you don't. You absolutely love me, probably far more than is good for you. That's why I knew you'd never let me try to climb that rope. Plus, I was just kidding anyway. I've never done anything like that before. I saw you lying there and knew what you'd just been through. We needed to act fast, and there weren't a lot of options. Speaking of which, we better get the hell out of here."

He just shook his head, realizing there was almost no limit to what Lotte would do to get what she wanted.

She helped him out of the basket, and it seemed to dawn on her how exhausted and hurt he was. "Oh, my love, I'm so sorry. You can't imagine how proud I am of you right now. I *did* know you could do it. I had total confidence. I'd have never tried something like that if I didn't, but I can see how hard it was. I promise we'll get you fixed up as soon as we can. You're incredible!"

His hesitations diminished with her words, as did, to some small extent, his nagging sense of inferiority. "Thanks. You're pretty incredible there yourself, Dr. Schneider-Schwarz, distinguished professor of Reverse Psychology. Did you find your sneakers?"

"One of them," she replied, morosely holding up her muddy shoe.

"What about... well...."

"Poor Eamon is over there. You don't want to see, trust me. I have no idea where the owl went. I couldn't see past you when you stabbed it because I had to keep my leverage inside the basket. If it turned to dust like Aicha did, then we'd never find it in the dark. If the damned thing lived and flew away, then it's just more reason to get out of here quickly."

No argument from me.

The pair prowled cautiously down what appeared to be the trail leading back to the road. They hadn't gotten far when another explosion furiously sounded from the tower above.

"There were three doors they had to get through," Lotte calculated, "one on the outer wall, one on the inner wall, and the iron door into the tower. This is not good."

"They knew this was a possibility. That iron door looked pretty tough. Maybe the explosive didn't work. Even if it did, just because they're in the tower doesn't mean it's over. That building is pretty defensible, and I can't believe help won't be here soon. Somebody had to have heard those explosions in Kalabaka."

She didn't respond, focusing on moving as quickly as possible while avoiding rough footing, having only one shoe.

Still, it was all he could do to keep up. Exhaustion and thirst made every step a new study in misery. He limply followed as she cut the trail, relieved when she came to a stop and motioned for him to crouch next to her.

"This is the road back to the tower," she whispered. "It's not that far from the dirt path where we parked, but walking will probably take us at least a half-hour to get there."

It might as well have been seventeen years, as far as he was concerned. "What if they found that path and are watching the cars?"

"It seems unlikely. If we hadn't been looking for it, we'd have never seen it, and that was in broad daylight. They'd either had to have known that off-road was there or been informed by the Jinn-owl. The tree cover was pretty thick where we parked, so I doubt either is the case, but whether they're near the cars or not, we still have to be careful. They may be guarding the road, or they may come back down once they discover we're not in the tower anymore. We need to move cautiously, and we'll have to hide quickly if we see something. Are you ready?"

"Yeah, ready to drop dead. I badly need some water."

"I know. I left my water bottle in the car. It's all yours when we get there. That'll be your well-deserved reward."

Her sincere smile in the moonlight gave him ample encouragement to try, even though his legs and back furiously protested when he began to move. Thankfully, progress on the road proved vastly easier than the ancient dirt path they'd been on before. They wearily hiked up the hill, stopping only when they heard the muffled sounds of gunfire from the tower. It seemed the battle raged on, and Eric thought with remorse about the stern but altruistic people in the compound who had been endangered by their actions.

How could someone have found us? Nobody knows we're here. Lotte must be right. The attackers were just fishing in one of the few possible places it made sense to look. Even if we weren't here, maybe neutralizing Utnapishtim as a source of information made sense at this point.

He shuddered thinking what further tortures the piteous man may yet have to endure if the tower fell. Without warning, Lotte grabbed his arm and dragged him forcefully into the bushes by the side of the road. Headlights from a car heading down the hill surprised him, and he realized he'd been blindly following in her footsteps, oblivious to his surroundings. A dark SUV sped past them and wound out of sight in the direction they'd come.

"I think they've figured out where we went," she said with alarm. "This isn't good, but I believe we can still make it. Come on, it's just a bit farther."

She dragged him to his feet, and they set off again, this time moving more quickly. The dirt track leading to where their car and the guard's Range Rover were parked eventually appeared. They monitored the entrance from the side of the road and, once satisfied that all seemed clear, scurried down the path.

Their little hatchback and the Rover sat nestled in the quiet of the dense trees. Lotte knelt, reached behind the front right tire, and retrieved the key they knew wouldn't be allowed in the tower, exactly where they'd left it. All seemed to be in order.

Inside the car, Eric smirked as he passed Lotte's water bottle back to her with a bit remaining. "I guess you're not gonna offer to drive? You gotta admit, that would get me motivated given what a lousy driver you are."

She laughed and gave him a slight shove, which actually sort of hurt given his sorry condition. "Little shit! It wouldn't work because you *know* I can't drive. I think you really believed I could climb that rope, or at least that I'd try."

It was true. He had believed it, and it had genuinely terrified him.

Is that love? Sacrificing yourself in some way so the one you care about is safe, or has what they want or need?

If it were, then despite all his inner misgivings, he'd at least proven that his love for her was genuine.

Lotte did what she could to quickly patch up his back so he wouldn't bleed all over the driver's seat.

He then threw on a t-shirt and started the engine. "So, what's the plan?"

"If I'm right, that car will be parked down the road near where we came out of the woods. They'll be looking for us back where the basket landed. With luck, we can just speed by, and they won't be able to react until we're well past. There's only one problem."

"Only one? I can think of plenty of things that might go wrong with this idea, but please, carry on."

She scowled and stuck her tongue out sideways at him. "Okay, one *big* problem! If somebody is in that car, they'll see us coming. You'll have to drive with the lights out."

That *was* a big problem, one which, in truth, hadn't exactly been on his radar. "All right... umm... I guess I can do that. At least there's some light from the moon, but it'll get dicey if we have to go fast. Let me see what I can do."

Without turning on the lights, he backed out of their parking spot and drove slowly down the dirt path. It was tough going here, the branches thick with leaves blocking most of the light. After nearly steering the car into a tree, he turned on the hazard lights to find the actual road. There, visibility improved, but remained far from optimal.

"Okay, better shut off those lights now," she instructed. "Just go slowly until we see the SUV, then we'll figure out what to do."

That assumes we'll see the SUV. At this point, however, they couldn't really do much else. It felt too dangerous to wait and risk being discovered.

He clicked off the hazard lights and cautiously pulled onto the road, the crunch of the tires on the worn gravel the only sound. Even the noise from the tower seemed to have ceased. As carefully as possible, he navigated the dark roadway.

Boston's light pollution suddenly seems like not such a bad thing.

At points where the trees grew denser, visibility dropped to near zero, and he wondered how he'd possibly be able to steer going any faster than they were now. Tensely and wordlessly, they coasted down the hill.

"There," she called out, spotting the SUV. "Right where I thought they'd be."

They'd emerged onto a slight straightaway on a brief plateau before the hill made its final descent to the intersection with the main road. The SUV sat parked on the right side of the road, not far from where he estimated they had exited the trees. The tower on its boulder loomed above, a grim reminder of their recent ordeal. The vehicle's lights were on, and the engine was presumably running.

"Damn. If there's somebody in that car, they're gonna chase us."

"We can do it," she confidently replied. "Just go as fast as you can and turn on the lights when we get to that next drop off. We don't want them to see our license plate."

He took a deep breath. She was probably right, but he had no idea what the road looked like beyond the little he could see. Still, lacking any better options, and fearing another car might come up behind them, he said, "Okay, hang on!" and hit the gas.

They weren't really going that fast, but in the darkness, it felt like a dizzying speed. The digital speedometer read 69.2 kilometers per hour. He figured that was slightly north of forty MPH, so he pushed it a bit harder when he swung the car wide around the menacing SUV, then sped toward the blackness ahead.

Lotte looked over her shoulder and shouted. "They're coming! Can you go any faster?"

"Not safely, but I guess *safe* is a relative term." He gave the car a little more gas, then risked a quick glance at the speedometer, which now flashed 82.1.

"Eric, look out!"

Another vehicle crested the rise. Having not been concerned with traffic in front of him, he had drifted to the left side of the road, so the lights that suddenly became visible bore directly toward them. With their own headlights off, the approaching car probably couldn't see them and wasn't slowing down.

Sensing he couldn't get back into his lane in time, Eric made a split-second calculation. He jerked the steering wheel to the left and their little hatchback plunged into the underbrush by the roadside. Lotte screamed when the mirror on her side was sheared off by the passing vehicle, while a horrible scraping rang out from the back left bumper as it grazed a tree trunk. Once past the oncoming car, Eric twisted the steering wheel hard right, slammed on the brakes, and screeched to a spiraling standstill.

"*Lights!*" Lotte screamed. "Turn on the lights, now!"

He fumbled for the control, finding it just in time as a pickup truck swerved to avoid slamming into them broadside. This new vehicle abruptly halted in the road and several people jumped out of the back, obviously intent on investigating their car.

"Eric, go! Drive... now! We can't let them stop us!"

He didn't really understand. These were likely the people Eamon had alluded to, who might be coming to help. He wasn't clear why they needed to flee from potential allies, but she was adamant, shaking her arms and shrieking at him to move.

Despite shouts of protest from those approaching, he once again hit the gas, and the tortured little car grudgingly squealed into motion. They rounded a corner just as the sound of gunfire filled the air behind them.

"Are they shooting at us?" he worriedly queried.

"I'm not sure," she distractedly replied, attention focused out the back window. "It could be they're engaged with the people in the car we passed. They were probably here to try and rescue Utnapishtim and the others. If they're shooting at us, it's because they don't know who we are."

"So why didn't we stay and tell them who we were and what happened?"

"Because they might not have believed us! Even if we could have eventually convinced them, that would have taken time... time we simply don't have right now. We can't risk another assault happening while we're still here. We might not be so lucky next time. We have to disappear, and then complete the job we've been charged with. Hold on!"

They'd reached the intersection with the main road, and he'd been about to turn right, back toward town. "What? What's the matter?"

"Go left. We're not going back to Kalabaka. It's too dangerous. Going the opposite direction basically leads north. Eventually, we'll get to something that leads us back to the E90, and from there we can get to Thessaloniki."

"Why are we going there?"

"So we can take advantage of their international airport. Athens is too dangerous for us. They're looking for us, and if they find us, they'll kill us... or worse. Just ask Utnapishtim. He was right. We have to vanish until we've done what we need to do."

"And what then?" he uneasily asked, turning the now banged-up little hatchback in the direction Lotte had indicated.

"I have no idea, Eric. I truly have no idea."

CHAPTER 12

Necessity finally forced Eric to pull their damaged little hatchback into a quiet roadside parking lot before they reached the airport. He collapsed into the back seat, and almost instantly fell into deep and much needed sleep.

Lotte woke him near dawn so they could complete the trip to the city. She'd been busy, re-booking flights and changing the return location for the rental.

Won't they be thrilled when they see the damage? We're, like, the scourge of rental cars. At least it's not Ricky this time. I assume Lotte took the extra insurance.

The flights had been her primary challenge—not a lot of options. Generally speaking, you could get from Thessaloniki to Athens, then to just about anywhere, but it became trickier if you wanted to bypass Greece's capitol. In the end, she'd chosen the most expedient path, and the one she came to feel would also be the safest: two individual flights, which might confuse anyone looking for both of them together. She would fly Aegean Airlines to Frankfurt, then on to Kennedy in New York, before catching a bus from Penn Station to Worcester, Massachusetts, where she'd get in at about 10:00 p.m. on Friday night.

Not a lot of fun, but Eric's journey promised to be worse.

They grabbed a quick coffee and drove the remaining distance to the airport, where the two reluctantly parted ways.

His trip began on Ryanair to Milan. Unable to keep his eyes open and wanting only to be left alone, he found himself in some hellish Home Shopping Club nightmare, constantly being woken up by incredibly loud and obnoxious announcements for products he couldn't imagine any sane person ever purchasing, least of all on an airplane. He'd never considered unleashing the Afrit on anyone before, but he took mental note of the masterminds behind Ryanair should the beast ever need a bargain-completing victim.

After being slapped with the final indignity of a trumpet announcing another "on time arrival," he caught a flight from Milan to Heathrow,

- 137 -

then another to Chicago, before finally touching down in New York's La Guardia airport near midnight.

Unable and unwilling to make the drive to Worcester, he found a cheap hotel to spend the night before he schlepped back to La Guardia in the morning to rent a car.

Eric pulled in just shy of 11:00 a.m. on Saturday morning. Lotte already stood in the turnaround of the Homewood Suites, where she'd spent the night. She waved when she saw him, which brightened his mood considerably. It had been an absolutely exhausting and often frustrating thirty-six hours.

She cheerfully hopped in and gave him a kiss. "How was the drive? Did you get any sleep last night?"

"Some," he replied as he hit the gas and steered back into the street. "Some on the plane too... well, some of the planes. You ever fly Ryanair?"

"No, was it awful?"

"That's one word for it. Whatever. Glad you got in okay. Why did you spend the night here, though? Why not call Olive? She'd have picked you up. Where is she staying, anyway?"

"I did call Olive. She's staying somewhere down in Milford near the hospital. They're not letting Siddique go until later this afternoon or tomorrow, so she's been there this whole time."

"She must be going nuts. I wish there'd been some other way."

"She was certainly worried about us. I got a million questions about where we'd been and what had happened, but I couldn't get into all that on the bus. I told her we'd meet her at the hospital and explain everything in person. I didn't have her come get me because she was so hyped-up. I'd have never gotten any sleep last night. She would have wanted to hear everything. Plus, I still have reservations about getting them more involved at this point given how compromised we are. If I'd somehow been followed, then being with Olive would have put her at risk. I thought meeting today in a more public place would be safer."

"Yeah, makes sense. I just can't believe anyone could track us here, though, and those two will need to know whatever plan we come up with. Like it or not, if we fail, it's gonna be up to them to try and salvage the situation. Speaking of which, any schemes percolating in that oversize brain of yours about how to do all this?"

"I have an idea, but I figured we'd work out the details together. I spent more time doing research, though, and you won't believe what I've discovered poking around on the internet."

"Do tell."

"Well, obviously, there are loads of myths relating to the Jinn, but if you go way back, back to the very earliest stories, it's quite possible they were once revered as demi-divine tutelary entities. In all likelihood, they were forerunners of the Mesopotamian gods, which makes sense as Enki said they were already here when he and his father and brother started visiting our world. Reverence to the Jinn was carried down through history in various ways, among them the possible belief in angels and demons."

"Angels, huh? I haven't met a Jinn yet I'd describe that way."

"Well, maybe *spirits* is a better term, some malevolent, others perhaps not. Jinn were especially feared because they were thought to be able to shift into different shapes, and also turn invisible so they could attack without being noticed."

"That's pretty close to reality. From what I've seen, I don't think they can actually fight after they vanish, but it's a way of avoiding being struck, and also gaining surprise. That's how Aicha was able to hurt Siddique. We didn't know where she might come from, but she still had to rematerialize before she could actually attack."

"Exactly. Speaking of forms of attack, Jinn have also been associated with various illnesses, in particular... get this... sleep paralysis!"

"Holy shit! That's exactly what Aicha did to Mrs. Binson. You probably have to be asleep for it to work, otherwise she'd have just paralyzed me and Siddique when we fought her. That owl would have done the same thing. I assume the owl was actually a Jinn? You say they can shape shift, right?"

"That's what the myth says, but I'm not certain that's accurate. I think they take various forms depending on the type of creature they initially... well... *possess*, for lack of a better term. This form can become invisible, or insubstantial, as it were, but I don't think a Jinn who has taken over a human can become an owl, or vice versa. Jinn were thought to take the forms of many creatures... humans, owls, serpents, scorpions, cats, black dogs, and even onagers."

"What the hell is an onager?"

"It's a wild ass."

He shook his head. "So, you're basically saying eighty percent of the human population are Jinn?"

"Ha, ha... very funny. It's a donkey, you silly. Can you imagine meeting a Jinn donkey? What would it do, try to kill you with stubbornness?"

"To be perfectly honest, after almost being knocked senseless by a freaking owl, I'm really not sure I want to test the waters with a donkey. I'll pass on the Jinn scorpions and snakes too."

She grimaced. "Quite, but you might prefer one of those to bloody Iblis!"

"You found mythical references to Iblis?"

"Oh, yes. Plenty, in fact. Iblis appears in both early Christian and Islamic traditions, where he's identified as either an archangel or as a Jinn. He's commonly placed as living on Earth during the battle of the angels, where he was apparently taken prisoner but allowed to live, and later given a choice when the angels and Iblis were commanded by God to prostrate themselves before Adam."

"Interesting. That sounds a lot like Enlil's decree that the Jinn Council answer to a human authority."

"Precisely. I think this is the Christian account of that incident, transcribed centuries after it occurred and reinterpreted within that new religious framework. This 'war of the angels' is most likely the great war that Utnapishtim talked about, which ended the Bronze Age. It was actually a war of the Jinn. Iblis was spared to secure the peace, but he quickly reverted to his old ways. Certain Christian doctrine actually links Iblis to Satan, an angel who refused to bow down to God because he was born of fire, as opposed to other mortals who were created from clay. It's more ambiguous in Islamic theology, but at root, Iblis emerges as a powerful and ancient entity who in some ways opposes God."

"Great, can't wait to meet him."

"Unfortunately, I think it's inevitable. Hopefully, we can get the key and the scroll to Enki before that happens, and maybe he'll have some idea how we can protect ourselves."

Utnapishtim's words about leaving their fate in the hands of a capricious and selfish god rang in Eric's ears. They were silent the rest of the way to Milford, though Lotte often absentmindedly brushed his shoulder as she gazed out the window, almost as if that touch were unconsciously keeping her tethered to the earth.

With some difficulty, they located the white Schneider Industrial Flooring van in a remote spot of the Milford Regional Medical Center's parking lot, under some shady trees. They navigated the dubious formalities of the front desk, then rushed to the room where Siddique still recovered. With a small rap on the door, Olive sprung from her seat near the window and into first Eric's, then Lotte's arms, giving each a great hug.

"Damn, you two! We was so worried when we didn't hear anything, and then suddenly... you're back! What the heck happened?"

"We'll explain everything," Eric said with a smile. "How's Siddique?"

"Siddique is fine," their friend announced from his bed, which sat obscured by a curtain that separated it from an empty bed near the door. "Nobody here believes this, but it's true. I wish they'd just let me get out of here." Eric shut the door and they all gathered around where Siddique smiled despite his frustration. "I think they just want to make more money off of my head. For a good price, I'd sell it to them!"

Everyone laughed.

"You're lucky you don't have a roommate," Eric observed. "How'd you manage that?"

"I think that's Olive's doing. She was here so much, they either took pity on her, or else the poor person in the other bed who had to listen to her talk all the time complained, so they moved him out."

"Hey, now," Olive playfully interjected. "I don't talk *that* much. That guy was leaving anyway. Besides, I was under orders to watch over you, and I take my assignments seriously."

Siddique nodded, the cumbersome bandage on his head hindering the motion. "This is true. The first thing I saw when I woke up was Olive sleeping in that chair. She's been with me the whole time. I can't get a moment's peace!" He directed a smile to her. "I'm just kidding. She's been wonderful, and we've had fun talking about you two behind your backs. Now, tell us what the world happened!"

"Yes, please do," Olive echoed. "We're dying to know."

Neither of their friends said a word as Lotte and Eric took turns relating the string of events that unfolded in Greece. What started out as exciting soon took on an ominous tone, and Olive and Siddique seemed to realize the danger of the situation, and the perils they may soon have to share. Olive's mood darkened noticeably as they detailed the escape from Metéora and the battle with the terrible Jinn-owl. As always, the story ended with the same question.

"So, what now?" Siddique asked with apprehension.

Lotte proffered her answer. "We have to get the key and the scroll from Vanth and pass it to Enki as quickly, and in as much secrecy, as possible. There's no time to find a location to carve a new doorway in the rock. We don't have the tools anyway. That leaves us only one choice."

"New Hampshire," Eric said with realization. "There are two doorways up there that are already carved. The question is, what condition are they in? We haven't seen those things for four years. Who knows what may have happened to them."

"That's true," Lotte said, "but at least there are two of them, and at a minimum, the sculpting was completed at one point. If they need some repairs now, that will be easier than beginning from scratch, not to mention the amount of time it would take to find an appropriate spot to construct the thing. The other great part about New Hampshire, though, is that there's water right there. Remember the stream that ran through the hills? There must be a place nearby where the water is deep enough to set up Enki's portal. We can do that first, and he can help us if we can't successfully negotiate with Vanth."

"What do you mean, *negotiate*?" Olive skeptically asked. "You have the amulet. You have the portal. That's everything you need to get the key and the scroll from her, right?"

"Well, maybe, but I'm not certain. Remember, these creatures are used to bargaining and sealing their pacts with the rings. We don't have Vanth's rings, only Charun's, and his were broken when we destroyed his portal... and him. Vanth may expect her rings to be present since they're part of the ritual. I know Utnapishtim said they no longer exert any true power, but she may still expect them, and if she doesn't get them, she might become violent. That's why I'd like Enki to be there."

"What about the Afrit?" Eric asked.

Lotte scowled. "Too dangerous. Remember that Charun almost finished off the Afrit with his magnetic properties. The Afrit is more powerful now, but I'm still reluctant to risk it. Plus, it isn't practical. We'd never fit those huge flight cases in the rental car, and then there's the issue of lugging them around, setting them up—"

"Take the van," Olive offered. "I can go and help you. We can do it!"

"That's an extremely nice offer, Olive, but it's also far too dangerous. There's one thing we still have to do that puts all these plans in great jeopardy: we have to retrieve the portal pieces that Eric returned to their hiding place in our apartment. There's an extremely good chance our house is being watched, and if it is, we may be as good as dead. You and Siddique will then be the last line of defense. So, you can't come with us. It would be a disaster if we were discovered all together. Even meeting like this presents a tremendous risk."

"If you're dead, though," Siddique said, "how will we know what to do? You've never told either of us where the portals are hidden."

"We made arrangements for that," Eric clarified. "If something happens to us, you'll get a letter from a lawyer. It will have the keys and the location of the portals. Presumably, the pieces in our apartment will be gone, but without the rest of the portal, they're useless. Best of all, you and Olive are completely unknown commodities. You can do whatever you think is best. It'll be totally up to you. Olive, you've even helped summon the Afrit. If it comes to that, you'll be ready. That's why both of you are more valuable staying on the sidelines for now."

Olive stood up and went to gaze out the window. "You've really thought of everything, haven't you?"

"Hardly," Lotte dourly replied. "If I'd thought of everything, we wouldn't be in this mess now. Vanth's portal would still be buried. Nobody would have any idea where it was."

"It doesn't work that way," Siddique cut in. "You know this, Lotte. If you hadn't unearthed it, somebody else eventually would have. That's why we were out there, digging a giant hole on your honeymoon. Okay, maybe you made some mistakes. So what? We all make mistakes, take it from me. Right? In the end, though, there isn't anybody who knows better than you and Eric what these things mean and how to deal with them. Don't judge yourself so badly. We could all be in far worse trouble. Go and do what you need to do. Olive and me, we'll be here. I'll tell her more stories about how we fooled that nasty devil woman with the crossbow. You like that story, don't you, Olive?"

Olive turned from the window and flashed Siddique an eerie smile.

"All right," Lotte somewhat begrudgingly agreed. "You're right, of course. I just... well... whatever. What's done is done. You can only move forward, make the best decision possible given the realities. I suppose there's no reason to put it off. We should probably get going."

"Y'all sure I can't tag along?" Olive longingly asked. "Not that I'm not having a super great time with Mr. Sunshine here, but I'd sure like to be a little more... well... *active*, if you know what I mean."

"No," Eric said, putting his arm around her shoulder. "Like I explained, we need you right where you are. After all, who's gonna take Mr. Sunshine home when they finally release him? Hopefully, we can get all this done safely and quickly. Trust me, though, even if we do, this won't end it. The day will come when you two *will* be needed. No reason to rush it along."

The four friends delivered hopeful but somber farewells before Lotte and Eric reluctantly exited.

Olive accompanied them to the car, possibly hoping they would change their minds and take her along after all. "Where'd y'all park?" she asked as they left the lobby.

"Right next to the van," Eric replied. "When we finally found it."

"Oh, good. I need to get some stuff out of there anyway."

"Why the hell did you park so far from the building?"

"I get tired of being in that dang hospital. It smells like crappy dish detergent. I wanted to park near some trees, where I could be alone and just breathe some fresh air."

It made sense to him. He'd never been a fan of hospitals. *Of course, who really is?*

When they reached the vehicles, Lotte asked for the car keys. "Let's reorganize our things, make sure we have enough room for the portals. Whatever we don't need, we can drop at home, which I assume will be our first stop?"

If they were discovered, it surely would be better to not have the remainder of the portals on them. "Yeah, that's the plan," he affirmed, helping her with their bags while Olive got her things from the van. Eric was sorting through his duffel bag in the trunk when Lotte rather stiffly called to him from the back seat. "Eric? Can you come here, please?"

He laughed. "What's the matter, you having trouble going through all the crap you brought that you probably never wore?" *Actually, that's not fair. She's been gone a long time and probably needed everything she took with her.* "I'm sorry, I was just kidding. What do you need?"

He rounded the car's bumper and stopped dead. Olive had exited the van's side door and was pointing Aicha Kandicha's fully loaded portable crossbow directly at Lotte's chest.

"Olive, what the hell are you doing?"

"Oh, H-E Double L, Mr. Schneider, I'm fixin' to shoot your pretty little wife right where I shot you before... unless you do exactly as I say and get in this here van. You too missy! I must say, this accent really is a treat. I haven't had so much fun in millennia!"

Eric was dumbfounded. "Aicha! How... how? How can you be alive?"

"A lucky stroke!" Olive's voice and face spoke the words, but Aicha's manner projected clearly. "The iron spike you stabbed me with fell out of my neck just in time. My host's blood was poisoned with rust, and I couldn't remain in that body, but it gave me a moment to escape. Sad... I'd been with her for thousands of years, a comely little acolyte of Astarte. Fortunately, your dark-skinned friend was unconscious nearby, otherwise I surely would have perished. I went into his body and kept him comatose until I found the perfect host, or hostess, as the case may be, conveniently sleeping in the chair by my bed. Frustratingly, you'd kept both of your little friends ignorant of the gateway's location. I called my associates, who tried to capture you in Greece, but somehow you eluded them and killed one of my oldest companions. You really are something, Mr. Schneider, and the brilliant and talented Ms. Schwarz, of course. Now do as I say and get in the van... both of you."

"You don't need Lotte," Eric barked. "Take me. I'll do what you want."

"Oh, but I do need her, Mr. Schneider. Ms. Schwarz is my insurance policy. You see, I know almost everything Olive does... certainly the big, important stuff, like how much your *dear Lotte* means to you, and how brokenhearted you'd be to see a crossbow bolt pierce that bosom that attracts you so. You'd willingly surrender your own life, but not hers. I know it all, Mr. Schneider — *everything* — and I'm sure you know what *that* entails."

He gulped. Olive was the only person on earth — well, human person, anyway — who knew that he had offered up his grandmother's life so that Lotte could live. True, Grandma had accepted willingly, but it would devastate Lotte to know the truth. Also, in the back of his mind lurked his fleeting attraction to Olive and their rather awkward kiss two years ago. They'd both gotten past all that, but it would come as a shock to Lotte, as much for having kept it from her as the reality of it happening at all. He realized with dismay that Aicha didn't need to shoot his wife in the chest to break her heart.

"The only thing I don't know," Aicha coolly went on, "is where that gateway is located, and we're about to rectify that. In fact, I think we'll take that little trip you were planning to New Hampshire as well. It just sounds downright peachy to me, and it will save so much time and trouble. Utnapishtim had to make things so difficult, damn him, but you seem to have it all figured out. Now, as I say, shall we all get in the van, or shall I just kill you now and wait to conveniently inherit the keys to the kingdom?"

"You'll just kill us in the end anyway," Lotte drily observed. "Why should we help you?"

Aicha sadly shook her head. "Just like your husband, always jumping to conclusions. Despite appearances to the contrary, I am not human and I'm not subservient to the vindictive and petty emotions that govern your pitiful existences. I have no need or desire to kill you. I merely want what I want. Give that to me, and I'll happily be on my way."

"Small comfort," Lotte retorted. "If you reopen that passage to the plane of air, Anu will return to our world. I've seen what kind of destruction a far less powerful being can cause. It will be disastrous for us. Why would we aid you in bringing about such an outcome?"

Aicha scoffed. "Utnapishtim! He fills your heads with partial truths. Yes, Anu will likely return here, but do not overestimate his power, at least at first. He has been separated from the Abzu for eons. He'll need time to recuperate and restore his strength. His first target will likely be the Abzu itself. Perhaps your friend Enki can stop him?"

"Enki is also weak," Eric interjected. "The Abzu is depleted, and it regenerates slowly. I'm not sure he'll have the power to stop his father."

"Perhaps, but if the deep waters hold so little energy, then that's less for Anu to call upon as well, yes? You see? All may not be as hopeless as it appears. I sense that you're skeptical, however, so let me sweeten the pot a bit. Assuming I get what I want, which it appears I will, one way or the other, and Anu does get loose... who on earth is better equipped to devise a strategy for stopping him? It's just as your friend Siddique said: there isn't anybody who knows more about entities like me and the gateways through which we enter your realm than the two of you, the illustrious Ms. Schwarz in particular. I promise that if you help me without resistance, I'll let Lotte live. That's your best shot, and clearly represents humanity's foremost hope. So, you can die now, or you can gamble that I'm telling the truth, like I have been all along."

Eric stared at Lotte, who returned his gaze as if waiting for his reaction. What Aicha said made some sense. Even Ninurta and Sharur had to eat to replenish their strength before acting. It wasn't clear how long they might have, but without Lotte, and to some extent himself, there would be no chance of stopping Anu before he did terrible damage. In the end, though, it really came down to a question of dying now or dying later... and Eric preferred the latter.

"All right," he gravely consented. "We'll take you. I swear, though, if you hurt her in any way—"

"I gave my word. That's the best guarantee you're going to get, Mr. Schneider."

"Schneider-Schwarz," he whispered.

"Don't push it. Just get in the van so we can be on our way."

At Aicha's command, Eric drove to the repurposed old factory in Dorchester where the portals were stored, and where Lotte could freely summon the Afrit. The wily and calculating Jinn maintained a safe distance as Lotte unlocked first the large iron door leading from the loading dock into the dank basement of the building, then the metal door to their windowless unit. A coat draped cleverly across her arm shielded the small crossbow she intently wielded from easy observation.

When Lotte turned on the lights, Olive's eyes went wide with Aicha's astonishment. The multicolored stone of the Afrit's portal danced in the light from the naked bulbs. The massive frame and the thick, ancient glass it enclosed dominated the far wall of the long, narrow room. The semicircular black marble board sat on the floor at its base, empty of the bowls lined with precious *Alkuartiz Alnaar*, which were safely packed in their boxes nearby.

As many times as Eric had seen it, the monolithic structure, and the power it represented, never failed to send a shiver of awe down his spine.

"All these centuries, I thought it lost forever," Aicha said with wonder. "I never imagined I'd see it with my own eyes. Well, with the eyes of another who serves me, at any rate. You realize it was my magic that you undid when you removed the silvering from that glass?"

"*Your* magic?" Lotte gasped. "How is that possible if you've never seen the item?"

The Jinn's glare softened slightly as she seemed to momentarily revel in ancient memories. "It was a complex time. Islam had swept across North Africa and was poised to soon move into Iberia. The land in which I lived, modern-day Morocco, had been largely subjugated. It mattered little to me. I have given allegiance to many rulers—Babylonian, Canaanite, Carthaginian, Roman, Greek—all are the same for me. As always, it remains only to ingratiate oneself with the new management, and for whatever reason, the servants of the Caliph wanted the Afrit and his handlers out of the way."

"But why?" Lotte asked, incredulous. "This is what I've never understood. What could the Afrit possibly have done to fall so out of favor?"

"I know not, but were I to hazard a guess, I'd put it down to a perceived lack of obedience and control. The beast, or the infamous *Sadat Alnaar*, or possibly both, had at times defied the wishes of those in charge of the armies of Islam. Only so much of that would be tolerated. The creature appears to have its own... well... *principles*. I once witnessed its loyalty firsthand, as well as the monster's rather prodigious talents in the art of combat."

Lotte spoke the words Eric was thinking. "You *saw* the Afrit? When?"

"The night before it was imprisoned. I was in Ceuta, then called Septem, with my benefactor of the moment, Count Julian. The city lay under siege, and he realized the end was near. Having no love for Roderic, the Visigoth King of Hispania who had impregnated his daughter, Julian was in discussions to capitulate and flip sides. However, there was one final chance to salvage our independence. When I passed on the materials I had concocted, along with instructions for their use, to the Arab spies who would turn the Afrit's gateway into its prison, they warned me that the creature was being sent to intimidate Julian into surrendering. They meant it as a warning so I would stay safely away, but knowing their plan, I thought it might be worth trying to strike a bargain with the creature, which would make a powerful and deadly ally."

"But it turned you down," Lotte said, "because that would have meant betraying the *Sadat Alnaar,* which the Afrit would never do."

The Jinn nodded. "As I say, the beast is faithful. Perhaps knowing as I do now from Olive's memories the monster's preference for women, I'd have delivered the offer myself rather than observe through the keyhole of a safely closed door. My words would likely have met with equal failure in unraveling the rather *uncommon* bonds this entity forms with its trusted associates. Had I won its trust, I wonder at the things we might have accomplished."

"You had another chance," Lotte retorted, her tone condescending. "The artifacts were found buried in Morocco, right under your nose. Why didn't you investigate that discovery the way you stalked us after we found Vanth's portal?"

"For such a supposedly astute historian, you appear to know little of the past. The digs that uncovered those items were conducted in secret, partly to discourage looting, and partly to avoid the outcry over yet more ancient treasures being sold to former colonial powers to help subsidize the recovery from the very colonialism they inflicted. Corrupt and inept local governments didn't help the situation, but it wasn't like it is today, where someone farts and it's immediately broadcast worldwide on every social media platform. Despite my rather extensive network of contacts, I never became aware of the artifact's recovery until the sale was completed, well over a decade later. By then, the trail was cold. Your grandmother had passed away, all her possessions auctioned off, and of course there had never been any official mention of the mirror, because it was, in fact, *looted*! I should have followed the child, your mother, but it seemed a dead end. To my knowledge, not even Iblis pursued it, but then, the Afrit conferred far less advantage with the Seven Kings gone and Vanth's portal lost. It was that to which his attention turned, as did mine. So, take the items that you will need to summon forth the bearer of the scroll and the key, and let's be off. We've dallied here long enough."

They next stopped at their apartment on Rogers Avenue. As it turned out, no danger lay in wait for them. The true threat had unknowingly penetrated Lotte and Eric's closest circle, and the pair were already in as much trouble as they could be. They retrieved the bag with the piece of Vanth's portal and Charun's broken rings from behind the heating vent in the bathroom, and at Aicha's insistence also took the section of the Abzu's gateway.

"I'll be taking possession of this," she coolly explained. "I wouldn't want Enki making another grand entrance to save the day at the last moment. We'll just leave him to his beauty rest, agreed?"

Neither of them felt inclined to argue.

Mrs. Binson had left a note for them saying she was staying at Doris's house, still fearing sleeping alone after her ordeal, and to call her when they were back in town.

I'm not certain we'll ever be back in town.

Eric was cheered, however, to see that his mother had picked up Langsam. At least their turtle would be safe.

Thanks, Mom.

They got on Interstate 93 and headed north just past lunchtime. Aicha nestled in the back of the van on a bevy of blankets she'd obviously pilfered from the hospital in Milford. This had likely been her home for the past several days, which appeared to suit her minimal needs, and better explained the remote parking spot.

Traffic got lighter as they approached New Hampshire. It wasn't peak leaf season just yet, so there weren't throngs of tourists from New York and elsewhere clogging the roads, only the normal flow of weekend escapees from Boston. Eric could hear Aicha murmuring on her cell phone, even though the language she spoke was incomprehensible.

"I think that's Canaanite," Lotte whispered from the passenger seat, "or maybe even Akkadian. Incredible, to hear a dead language spoken fluently. What we could learn from these beings if they were more open about their existence. Given our tendency toward intolerance and cruelty, though, I don't blame the Jinn for being reclusive."

"Maybe," Eric said. "Enki told us the Jinn were on a path toward dominating our world. They may have basically gone their own way because they just aren't that concerned about humanity. I mean, look at what Aicha is doing. As long as she gets her way, it doesn't seem to matter one way or the other what happens to us. Some Jinn may be more resigned to living in this world than she is, but that doesn't imply they have any great love for us. They live their existences, we live ours. In the end, that might be better for everyone."

"You have a point. Maybe it *would* be better if they found a way to get back to their own realm. It's possible this coming together of such disparate creatures was all a gigantic mistake. Enki and Enlil certainly seemed to come to that conclusion. We just want and need such different things."

"Silence!" their captor announced, apparently done with her call. "What are you whispering about? If you wish to talk, speak clearly so I can hear you."

"We apologize," Lotte said with deference. "I was intrigued to hear the ancient language you were speaking, that's all. What was it?"

She laughed. "Ever curious, you are. You would perhaps call it *Punic*, related closely to the language of the Canaanites. It was the tongue I spoke for many centuries before the Romans sacked Carthage and salted the earth around it. Odd that I would use it now to arrange air travel. Apparently, Olive didn't bring her passport, and I have no intention of wasting time retrieving it. I have a good friend who has a private plane. We've made plans to meet once I have the key and scroll in my possession. He'll be most interested to see all the wonders I've uncovered."

"Iblis," Eric murmured with dread.

"Indeed, Mr. Schneider. His skills will be most necessary to penetrate the barrier once we're inside Enlil's hidden fortress. Typically, he prefers to work alone, but by taking the risk of securing the artifacts, I guarantee a place by his side when we venture back to our realm — a partnership of mutual benefit, much like ours. Speaking of which, you can stop and get something to eat if you wish. I have no need for food or sleep, though I do both for pleasure from time to time. I just don't want my little ol' colleagues starving to death."

"Aren't you concerned with us escaping?" Lotte dubiously ventured.

"With those happy hugs in the hospital, I took control over both your phones. Your husband can explain what that means... if he hasn't already. You largely can't do or say anything I'll be unable to monitor. I strongly suggest you not test the limits of this enchantment again, Mr. Schneider. I won't be so easily fooled a second time. I'm extending this offer as a courtesy. Don't make me regret my solicitude... y'all."

"If you care so much about us, why don't you and Iblis help us contain Anu while he's still weak? It could save untold deaths and destruction if Eric and I can't figure out a way to stop him."

"An interesting proposal, but Iblis was a disciple of Anu. They shared the vision of using this world for its energy and exploring the material universe... much as Ninurta plotted. Oh, yes, I know all about that little adventure from Olive's memories. In any case, if you fail to stop him, then Iblis will perhaps rejoin his former master in such a venture. It matters little to me. I know it sounds awful, but in the end, my kind view humanity as energy... sustenance. We feed when you sleep and are vulnerable, mostly taking just what we need and leaving you temporarily paralyzed as a result. We can take more, however, if we wish—enough to kill, and enough to power greater feats."

"That's horrible!"

"Is it? Is this not exactly what you humans do with the animals you harvest for food? Your revulsion is the product of insecurity, existing as you have for such a relatively brief time at the top of the food chain. Now, you chafe when something bigger and meaner comes along, who would do unto you exactly as you have done unto countless species. I fully understand and share your will to survive, but it's no different with any living being, sentient or not. Some must give their lives so that others may thrive. It's nothing personal, Ms. Schwarz, certainly no more personal than you and your husband eating a dead cow for lunch."

Eric flashed Lotte a "told you so" look, though he took no pleasure in being right about the Jinn's cold lack of regard for humanity. He realized what a dark and lonely place the universe could be, or the multiverse, which seemed even darker and lonelier. You grasp for love and happiness as you can, pushing out of your mind the grim reality that everything could all come tumbling down at any moment. The curse of sentience, however, are the moments when the truth penetrates that thin barricade, like the barrier keeping Anu from returning to Earth, the flimsy shield of denial and fantasy which preserves one's hope, and sanity.

Aicha broke the tense silence. "So, as I said, would you like to stop and get something to eat?"

Neither of them felt hungry anymore, so they drove sullenly on toward their bleak and suddenly ever-more-uncertain destiny.

CHAPTER 13

Little to nothing appeared to have changed in Bailey, New Hampshire since their last "visit," if that's what you could call it. Eric steered the van through the two scanty blocks that constituted downtown, noting the single municipal building where poor Vern had once been headquartered.

There must be a new deputy now. I'm not sure if having the police involved this time would be good or bad. Bad, he finally decided, doubting a lone and ill-prepared law enforcement officer would do much to thwart their captor's plans.

"Can we take you up on your offer?" Lotte meekly asked. "There's a little grocery here. We could just pop in and get something to go."

"Hungry now, are we?" Aicha coolly replied. "Very well, but be quick about it... and don't dare try anything."

It was still disorienting to hear harsh commands such as this spoken through Olive's voice. Eric wondered if their friend was still in there somewhere, conscious of what was happening, but like them, unable to stop the seemingly irreversible momentum toward Aicha's goal. He also pondered the troubling question of what might happen to Olive's body and mind if the Jinn successfully made the transition back to her realm, or if somehow, they were able to find a way to kill her. What then? Would Olive also be dead like the woman she'd possessed for thousands of years?

He pushed these concerns aside and pulled the van into the small parking lot. He and Lotte both hopped out, making sure to bring their phones. It was just past 5:00 p.m. They still had about two-and-a-half hours of good daylight left to investigate, and possibly set up, the white magnetic portal, assuming either of the carved rock faces were still in a condition to accommodate the artifacts.

The market hadn't changed at all, though Trudie wasn't at the register. Eric picked out some energy bars while Lotte got some fruit. He also selected three potted plants from an assortment of locally grown perennials the store had on proud display. Any suspicions he had that

Lotte might be considering an escape attempt vanished when he saw her standing by the register with apples and oranges in hand.

It frustrated him not being able to talk with her or plan any coordinated action. Aicha's little trick with their phones made this impossible. Anything they saw or heard, she could monitor, and any attempt to separate themselves from the enchantment would surely be met with a stiff reprisal. Eric assumed Aicha was also blocking calls or texts from Siddique, who was probably frantic about what might have happened to them. As Olive, perhaps the Jinn had developed some sort of cover story to calm him down, but it just cemented in his mind the knowledge they were truly trapped. The best course forward was to cooperate, and trust their captor would be true to her word.

"Look as *this!*" Lotte said with amusement when he joined her in the checkout line. She grabbed a somewhat homemade-looking pamphlet with a poorly reproduced photo on the cover.

"You've gotta be kidding me," Eric said with hilarity. The staple-bound booklet, entitled *The Baily Smasher*, included a photo depicting the derelict building of the gravel mine from which Lotte, Eric, and Mason had barely escaped with their lives.

"It's all about the murders," she said, flipping through the pages. "It looks like they're making it out to be some kind of occult thing, maybe tied up with drug distribution. *Alter!* There's a picture of Mason here. They think he might have been involved because of the similar rock carving behind his house. His poor family, thinking their son was connected with something like that."

"Well, in fairness, he was involved in some pretty nefarious shit. If you think about it, the occult isn't even that far off. I get your drift, though. Theft is one thing, but thinking their son was an accessory to grisly murders has gotta be hard. I wish we could tell them the truth."

"I doubt they'd believe us. That will probably be our fate in the end: dead in some strange place under even stranger circumstances, our families and friends left to cobble together some explanation that will never really make any sense at all. Maybe that's a fitting epitaph for the girl who thought she knew everything and could do it all herself—a senseless death capping off a senseless life. How apropos."

"Lotte—"

"Forget it," she cut in, slamming the pamphlet shut. "I'm just in a crappy mood because I'm starving. Let's get this booklet, though. I want to see what they say and who they talked to. I wonder if they interviewed Ethan McCarthy. If so, I'll feel a bit better, especially if he told them the truth. Nobody will ever believe it. Although, these days, who knows? Everybody seems to be abandoning reason and believing all manner of garbage. It makes you wonder if there's anything worth preserving in this stupid world at all."

Her words and mood disturbed him, and he felt certain it tied into what she'd almost told him in Metéora. Now, however, wasn't the time to get into it, especially given that if Aicha killed them, it wouldn't make any difference anyway. They jumped back in the van and ate their hastily assembled meal, then he drove past town, toward the left turn onto New Speck Lane, which led up the mountain that rose above them.

"What are the plants for?" the Jinn asked suspiciously.

"We need the pots as stands for parts of Vanth's portal," Lotte explained. "The general store was closed, or we'd have bought empty ones. We'll have to do a little work on them to cut a groove. Hopefully Siddique's toolbox will have a file that will work."

"We'll stop at Mason's house first," Eric offered, sensing Aicha was satisfied. "That carving is on private property, so it's less likely to have been damaged. The problem is, if anybody's home, we won't be able to get to it without being seen, and I'm not sure that's what you want."

"The less attention we attract, the better," Aicha agreed. "Your plan seems sound. We'll investigate and move on if necessary."

The familiar road brought back memories for Eric, remembrances of a time when he and Lotte were as far apart emotionally as they'd ever become. That trip to New Hampshire had been make or break for them. "Just friends" wouldn't have been possible for him. He'd known he loved the dark and determined young woman who sat next to him then, as she did now, more than anything in the multiverse.

Similarly, the task at hand again seemed of less importance to him than finding his way back to a happy stasis with her. So it had ever been, for the most part, the adventure serving merely as a means to the end of being with the person who brought purpose to his life. Like his mother driving to Boston to pick up Langsam, he'd do almost anything to make Lotte happy, distasteful as it may sometimes be.

The drive on the dirt road to the house remained as bumpy as he recalled, and forgetting the exact route, they had to backtrack once until the familiar curved driveway came into view. To his dismay, a Jeep sat parked near the stone steps that led up to the cottage, and smoke rose from the chimney to the fireplace that had once been his companion in sleep. A large dog chained near the dilapidated bench to the side of the house began to bark as the van crept nearer.

He stated the obvious. "I think we have a problem. You have to cut right through that yard to get to the path up the hill. That dog, and whoever is in the house, won't be too happy about that."

"Very well," Aicha begrudgingly acquiesced. "If the other rock face is unusable, however, we shall return here. Dogs and houseowners can be dealt with, if I'm making myself clear."

With a shudder, he turned the van around, noticing a woman at the door to the cottage as he did so. She appeared far too young to be Mason's mother. The family probably sold the house in the wake of what happened, unlikely to ever return to a town where their name had become synonymous with murderous scandal.

He took a right off the dirt track and back onto New Speck Lane.

Lotte called to him. "Pull over for a second. Have a look at this." She held out the pamphlet they'd bought in the grocery store, which she'd been perusing.

He stopped the van and took the booklet, open to a page of photographs.

"That's a picture of the crevice we carved out on the hill near the trails. There's some graffiti, and it looks like maybe some part of the middle has been damaged, either gouged out or shot at. It's hard to tell with this grainy little reproduction."

He flipped to the front. "What's the date on this book? Here it is. It came out about two years ago. There's no way to tell what condition the doorway might be in now. All the damage seems to be in the middle, where the little holes are. The outline is still clear, and obviously the recession is still there. We'll have to bring the tools with us. Maybe we can fix it up enough to be usable."

Having no option other than letting Aicha kill the people in the cottage, they drove on. As he made the right onto the dirt road leading to the trails, Eric recalled facing off against Charun and losing Mason through the roof of their beat up, white rental van. It had been a long time since that particular memory had forced its unwelcome way into his consciousness, and he felt momentarily beset by the shock and sadness of holding his unlikely friend's severed arm and trying vainly to will it back to life.

"Are you all right?" Lotte gave him a concerned glance. "You look pale. Do you need some water?"

"Sure, that would be good. I'm fine. Just a lot of... well... *memories* around here, if you know what I mean."

"Do I ever. It's like a flood. Not all those memories are bad, though. I mean, what we did here brought us back together, right? Although come to think of it, maybe that's not such a good thing... for you anyway."

"Don't be ridiculous. You're still the best thing that's ever happened to me. Even if everything ends here now, it will have all been worth it. I don't regret anything, other than not getting on a plane to go find you right after college. You found me, though, and I'm glad you did, even if I don't always...." He choked on the words.

"What? What is it?"

Measure up, he thought, but couldn't bring himself to say it aloud. *Be as bright and shiny as you and get the admiration and accolades for my brilliant accomplishments... not because I give a rat's ass about any of that shit... but to continue to hold your attention.* His inner fears had become all too clear to him, but if these were truly to be their last moments together, that wasn't the direction he wanted the conversation to take.

"Oh, nothing," he finally coughed out. "I don't always show my appreciation, that's all."

"Now *you're* being ridiculous. I don't think anyone feels more appreciated than I do, and most of the time undeservingly. We'll get out of this, Eric. It's not all going to end here, I promise."

"Sadly, Ms. Schwarz," Aicha intervened, "you're not in a position to be making promises of any sort. It's up to *me* what happens. So far, you've cooperated nicely. Well done... but I suggest you both continue in this manner if you're sincere about wanting any sort of future."

They had no time to discuss it further. The van emerged from the overhanging trees and into the rounded clearing that marked the entrance to the trails. Two other cars were parked there, one in the exact spot where Vern had left his police cruiser on that final day.

Once more, Lotte and Eric hopped out of the van and began unloading gear, while Aicha stood a safe distance away, her crossbow again at the ready.

Lotte dumped the luckless perennials into the bushes and brought the pots back to the van where she added them to the bags containing the portal materials. Siddique's toolbox was too heavy for her, so Eric took that and slung one bag over his shoulder, which was still painful from the battle with the Jinn-owl. Lotte picked up the other bag, and the three began their trek up the mountainside. Apparently, it had been dry, recently, the trail not slick with mud as it had been four years before. Still, it was rough going, especially once they'd passed the green trail on the left and the hill became steeper.

It all felt familiar, but different. Foliage had grown, and the vagaries of time and memory made exact distances difficult to recall. Only when they reached the rocky slope of the hill to the left of the trail, the one they'd first taken to the top, did Eric recognize where they were.

"We've gone too far," he said, exhausted. He put down his bag and the toolbox to drink some water. "There's no way I can get all this stuff up that slope. We have to circle back and go up the other way."

Aicha stepped aside, reached into her pocket, and donned a pair of thin but sturdy black gloves that she must have retrieved from her suitcase. "That's a waste of precious time, Mr. Schneider. Leave the toolbox where it is and lead the way. I can take it easily."

Why the hell didn't you say so before? he groused, but he didn't dare to voice the thought and risk losing the Jinn's assistance.

After catching his breath, he again hoisted up his bag, and they began the ascent. It was quicker this way, though more exhausting and treacherous. He looked over his shoulder at their captor, who walked casually behind them as they struggled, not even breaking a sweat as she hefted the heavy toolbox in one gloved hand while wielding her nasty little crossbow with the other.

"How do you do that?" he asked between cautious and laborious steps. "Olive's body can't do what you're doing right now, and real owls can't do what that Jinn-owl did to us. How is that possible? Or is this one of those, 'I can tell you but then I'll have to kill you' type of things?"

Aicha laughed heartily. "It isn't a secret, Mr. Schneider, any more than the Jinn themselves living within your world isn't a secret... to some. Once you know that, a few additional details are of little consequence. We are creatures of air, and even separated from our realm, we can still control this element in certain ways. It can make us strong, or fast, or hard, or permeable. This power is not without limits, and the energy used requires eventual replenishment, but it conveys many advantages over mortals."

"Counterbalanced, it appears, by certain disadvantages," Lotte observed.

"Sadly, this is true. We have our susceptibilities as well, and in a world increasingly made of iron and steel, our fortunes have waned considerably. Before the lords of the Abzu trapped us here, it mattered little. If the body we inhabited was dispatched, we simply floated back to our realm. Immortal, in a sense, though it takes great effort and no small amount of fortune to establish a presence here. Duplication of that process is never guaranteed, nor is a transfer from body to body, which is why we tend to stay with the hosts we've chosen. Not knowing the full extent of the injuries I dealt Siddique, or how long he'd be stuck in the hospital, I took great risks moving from him to Olive, but I expect great rewards will be mine as a result."

They approached the top of the rock slope where Lotte and Eric had once toiled to establish the configuration in the stone cliff required to set up Charun's portal. The rise of the nearby hill, where the beast had consumed his prey, slowly came into view, as did the largish stream that ran through the little valley, and the dreaded double-hillock where Charun had established his lair. It was like walking in a vivid dream. The events that unfolded in this place seemed so uncanny that the entire experience felt fictitious and imagined, rather than truly lived.

Over the short rise where once the Afrit's portal blazed into the western sky, the ghostly outline of the recessed stone doorway gradually revealed itself from beneath a miasma of graffiti. "Hail Satan" competed for attention with a host of other proclamations like, "God Will Prevail," "Die in Hell You Sick Fuckers," and "For a Good Time Call Selena Diaz." The number on the latter inscription had been crossed out and then spray painted over so many times it was now completely illegible.

Beer cans and cigarette butts littered the scraggly grass that clung in clumps to the rocky soil, but the debris and the graffiti appeared pretty old. The spot seemed to have once been a hotbed of attention and interest, but its remoteness and relative inaccessibility had protected it from becoming a true pilgrimage point for the disaffected youth of Bailey, or for the lurid thrill seekers who came to gawk at a spot where unimaginable and titillating atrocities had actually occurred.

The impatient Jinn intruded on the almost cathedral-like silence. "Will it work?"

"Give us a moment," Lotte solemnly replied. She stood almost exactly where her battered body had landed after the implosive collapse of the magnetic portal. She moved toward the stone face and Eric fell in step behind her.

The damage was piecemeal, mostly near the center of the doorway, with occasional hunks missing from above and below. Clearly, the carving had been used for target practice, but with the ledge so close by, the range was minimal, so most of the damage clustered near the center. Others appeared to have hacked away wedges of stone, which contained the small holes that anchored the marble-sized spiked magnetic balls responsible for creating the gateway itself. The rim around the perimeter where the larger pieces formed the frame remained basically intact.

"A lot of the little holes have been shot or gouged away," Lotte explained. "Also, the surface isn't as smooth as it was before. I'm not sure if that matters or not, in terms of creating or sustaining the magnetic field.

There's enough stone left that we can drill more holes, but they won't be distributed evenly unless we put some in the scooped-out areas. Plus, we'd need a drill, which we don't have."

Aicha put down the toolbox and stepped back, then motioned with her crossbow. "Come here and open this up. Look inside and we'll see if there's anything that can be used to make those holes."

Eric complied, opening the box and rooting through various compartments. "There's a mallet here, and some bigger nails that would probably be wide enough. The holes don't have to be deep. There's enough iron ore in the rocks around here that the marbles will basically stick, as long as the spike has something to cling to. This is granite, though. It's hard to cut into, which is probably why there's anything left of the surface at all. It took hours to make these holes with an electric drill. Doing it with a mallet and a nail will take forever. I'm not even sure I'm strong enough to drive a nail into this stuff."

"Why don't you give it a shot, Mr. Schneider? We'll see what happens."

He shrugged, picked up the mallet and a large nail and returned to Lotte's side by the stone face. He selected a spot on the smoother surface where he could get a good angle and maximum force, then raised his hammer to strike, but Aicha stopped him.

"Mr. Schneider. Aim carefully. Trust me, you don't want to miss the head of that nail."

Having banged a finger or two with a hammer in his life, he wholeheartedly agreed, though he didn't understand why Aicha would really give a crap. He again positioned the mallet above the head of the nail and gave a sharp strike. With a loud *crack*, the granite split and splintered as if a bullet had hit it. He couldn't believe the force he'd brought to bear. It was like hammering into wood. The little gouge in the rock was just a bit too small for the spike, but one more tap like that would finish the job. He suddenly felt relieved that he'd taken Aicha's advice. A miss would have likely broken his finger.

"I assume this is your doing?" he asked without looking back.

"Yes, Mr. Schneider. A little aid to help the proceedings move a bit more quickly. Now, do you think you can do it, and will it work?"

He nodded. "I can do it. I need to be careful, but these nails are big, and pretty hard to miss. I have no idea if it'll work or not, though. I'll space them as evenly as I can and try to keep them all on the same plane... but in some spots that won't really be possible. We'll just have to try it and find out."

"Then I suggest we get busy, Mr. Schneider. The day is not getting any younger."

Aicha's assistance made the process of creating the holes vastly easier and more expedient. Eric's only delay came from his frequent need to refresh nails, which were quickly dulled or bent. Lotte filed grooves in the bottoms of the clay flowerpots to support the three larger, slightly curved pieces of the portal. These would be placed at the perimeter to complete the magnetic arc.

The two worked in silence under the Jinn's watchful eye. Not much they could say anyway, but occasionally their gazes would meet, and he would return her encouraging smile. Despite the circumstances, she looked beautiful, cheeks full and slightly flushed, which for Lotte was a veritable panoply of color. The dark circles under her eyes had diminished since Athens, meaning she had gotten more sleep recently than she'd been getting in Italy, which he found a bit scary given how crazy things had been.

With the holes complete and the marble-like balls hooked into place, assembly of the remaining portion of the portal proved a simple matter. The roughly five-inch beveled pieces snapped easily together, anchored by corner segments to complete the frame around the stone recession.

Lotte placed her modified flowerpots, one each to the left and right of the doorway, and the final one dead ahead.

Eric wedged the larger pieces into the notches she had carved, and soon only the final, central piece remained to be placed.

"We're ready," Lotte quietly announced. "When we lay down this final stone, the field will activate, assuming the holes are placed properly. Then we take this triangular, funnel-like piece and let it go into the magnetic area. If everything works, it should travel to the center and begin to spin, and that'll complete the process of opening the doorway. At least, that's how it worked with Charun's portal. If this one's different, we'll have to improvise."

Aicha looked around her and took another couple of steps back. "All right, carry on. One more warning, however. No tricks! You've done well so far. Don't spoil things now. If I get what I want, you'll both live to see tomorrow, which is the best promise I can make."

Lotte gave a slight bow, then turned to Eric and took the final large, curved piece from his hands. She secured this segment into its groove, and turned the flowerpot so the curvature faced the doorway. Immediately the familiar low thrum emanated from the ground, and the signature bluish-white glow steadily expanded to encompass the area between the rock face and the three white stones at the perimeter.

"Well, so far so good," she remarked with a slight chuckle. "We'll see if the uneven holes will actually support opening the gateway."

With that, she dropped the funnel-like piece into the magnetic field. It immediately shot to the center of the area without touching the ground and began to slowly rotate. The low noise and the intensity of the aura increased as the triangular object spun ever faster, and soon the glow from the collection of marble-like balls within the frame became a field of near blinding white light.

All save the spinning funnel remained still for what seemed like an eternity, but finally a shadowy figure appeared in the glowing doorway, silhouetted against the piercing luminescence. Cautiously, the outline of a head peered outward, framed by the points of wings to each side. The creature appeared to take its time observing what it saw, and Eric began to worry that maybe the being would decline this offer to again walk in their world. He breathed a sigh of relief when first one claw-footed leg, then another, emerged from the doorway and warily inched toward the blur of the spinning triangle.

Lotte groaned with distress and pity. "*Alter!* This is awful."

Vanth appeared diminutive in size compared to Charun. Where he had been muscular and stout, she appeared sleek and elegant. Instead of the azure-gray feathers of Charun's head, wings and upper legs, hers were instead a light tan with brownish tips. Vanth's smaller beak lacked the menacing boar's tusks, and she was void of her counterpart's thick beard, heavy brow-ridge, and fibrous strands evocative of snakes. Save for the pink nipples of her bare breasts, her skin possessed a luminous white tone compared with the somewhat sickly pale blue of Charun's flesh.

At least it should have.

Instead, horrible splotches of desiccated, mottled gray spotted her body like some creeping rash. Vanth walked with a debilitating limp, dragging one clawed leg behind her as if paralyzed. Skin sagged from her bone-thin arms and abdomen, and many of the beautiful hazel and coffee feathers were missing from her sparrow-like wings and delicate dove-like head.

Of great interest, however, were the two items that clung tightly to the sad creature's waist as if glued there. One was clearly a key, though of primitive design: a large circlet of wood-like clay from the Abzu, connected to a roughly six-inch shaft with three protruding bumps on the end. The other object simply appeared to be a circular rod made of the same substance, roughly one foot log and perhaps three inches in diameter.

To Eric, it looked more like a scroll case than an actual scroll, but he had to assume these were the artifacts Aicha coveted.

With arduous and punishing effort, the no longer mighty Vanth hobbled to where the funnel spun in the magnetic maelstrom. The black dots of the bird creature's pupils narrowed in her still gleaming orange-yellow eyes, and with a lighting fast movement that belied the disheveled appearance of her body, she plucked the small triangular piece out of the air and held it aloft. Like Charun's hammer, the object began to grow once in her grasp, becoming a torch about two feet in length. At the top, a haze of purplish light battled for visibility within the wash of the blue-white field that sizzled all around. Despite her decrepitude, Vanth seemed to flush with pride, and to Eric's amazement let out a triumphant cry that was so devastatingly beautiful, both he and Lotte collapsed to their knees.

'Long has it been!' she screeched, her words understandable in their minds despite the alien nature of her vocalizations. 'So long! Why was I abandoned? Why was I left to fight for the scraps of our ravaged realm and then waste away in misery when one pole inevitably overshadowed the other? And why now do you call me forth? What is it you could possibly want from me after you've taken everything!'

"Scheiße!" Lotte cursed under her breath. "This is really awful." Somehow, she pushed aside the effects of the mental assault, which Eric felt keenly, and rose to face the anguished and enigmatic bird. "Great one, hear me, please! The gateway which allows you passage to our realm was lost. It happened centuries ago by the way we mark time, long before my husband or I were born. We don't know how that came to be, but recently we uncovered the artifact. We want nothing from you, but the creature who stands behind us does. She appears human, like us, but she's not. She's a Jinn, and she wants only two things from you: the key and the scroll with which you've been entrusted."

Vanth cast her gaze past Lotte and examined Aicha where she skulked near the ledge.

"I have the amulet," the Jinn offered. "I show you this and you have to give me the items, correct?"

'Negative!' the bird cried. 'The symbol must be placed in my hand within the arc, this is the protocol. If you do not know this, perhaps you are unfit to receive my gifts.'

"As the girl explained," Aicha replied, obviously attempting to keep her temper in check. "Centuries have passed. The specifics of rituals have been lost in the mists of time. It was impossible that any of us could have known. Is there no other way to complete this exchange? I find being too close to magnetism... *uncomfortable.* Can we not simply bypass the formalities?"

Vanth's predator eyes narrowed and the feathers around her neck expanded threateningly. *'You mock me. You call me here and trivialize everything for which I have existed since this doomed association with your world began. My word is my bond... sacred. I fought to retain my life when all seemed lost because the ones who found and nurtured me to strength told me it was important. Critical! I did not let them down as they did me, and I will not do so now. If you cannot complete the process, leave me in peace!'*

"It's just getting better by the second, huh?" Eric quipped. "It'll be interesting to see how Aicha gets out of this one."

Before Lotte could respond, their captor spoke. "Very well, we'll do it your way. I can't complete your hallowed ritual, but one of these two can. Let's see, who shall it be? Ms. Schwarz, I think this duty falls to you, yes? You're the smooth talker who has Afrits and Abzu gods wrapped around her little finger, aren't you? Let's see if you can be a good little girl and go fetch my artifacts from the belly of the beast. Pretty please with sugar on top?"

CHAPTER 14

To Eric's surprise, Lotte didn't flinch. She marched directly toward the haughty Jinn, a determined and perturbed look on her face. When she got within a few feet, Aicha raised her little crossbow.

"That's close enough," the Jinn warned. Without taking her eyes from Lotte, she pulled the little pouch containing the amulet from the case of extra bolts around her shoulder and gave it a quick toss to the ground between them. "Pardon my ill manners, but we can't be too careful, can we?"

Eric saw Lotte's shoulders slump as she sighed with disdain. Nevertheless, she grabbed the little bag, removed the medallion, and strode purposefully back to his side.

"Is this dangerous?" he asked. "I mean, would Vanth actually harm you if you can't give her what she expects?"

"I imagine so. She wants what she wants and doesn't appear to be in an especially good mood. It also looks like she's starving, and my energy would make a nice little meal."

"I'm going in with you."

"No. You have to stay here. If I make a mistake, you might have a second chance at it, learn from what I did wrong. We have to do this. If we don't, Aicha will simply kill us both. Completing the task is our only hope of surviving and limiting a massive amount of damage in this world. Annoying as she is, Aicha is right. I've dealt with these creatures before, and I'm good on my feet. It's that oversize brain of mine, right? It'll be fine. I think I can do it."

When Lotte died on that beach in South Carolina, Eric's world had collapsed. Risking his own death or mental incapacitation to get her back had never been in question. Now, he had to watch idly as she walked into danger once again.

When you play high stakes games, you know the consequences of losing, but the reality of it, like death itself, always seems remote. That is, until you come face-to-face with the moment of truth.

Having cheated death before, Eric had shrouded himself in the illusion that they were, to some extent, in the clear, and that the threats to their happiness were now largely in the past. With sudden and complete clarity, however, he realized this wouldn't be the last time he and Lotte would face a moment of truth. He saw, cascading before him, an endless string of them—one, after another, after another, after another—until finally... their luck ran out. It was the logical outcome of the path he'd chosen, the one he'd selected because, in the end, he'd never have been able to live with himself if he weren't by Lotte's side, even in death.

This is it. This *is my life.*

"I guess that means I have to pay attention, huh?" he joked, holding back the tears stinging his eyes. "This material might be on the test."

Incredibly, the humor found its mark. She gave a little snort of melancholy laughter, holding back tears of her own. The two clasped hands and gently touched their foreheads together before she stretched her neck and shoulders and proceeded in a businesslike manner into the magnetic arc.

"I'm not armed," she announced to the ominous bird being. "I carry nothing but this amulet. I wish merely to complete the transaction in the manner prescribed. May I approach?"

Vanth hesitated momentarily, then beckoned her forward. Lotte stepped directly up to the creature, who, despite being smaller than Charun, still towered almost a foot taller than the young woman before her.

Lotte's voice sang out as she held the object forward. "In exchange for this amulet, I ask that you return the items entrusted to you, the key and the scroll, which you have guarded so vigilantly."

The beast's head darted from side to side, but the fierce orange-yellow eyes never strayed from Lotte's hand. As if plucking a fruit, Vanth reached out and carefully grasped the medallion in her bony fingers. Immediately, the cadence of the low hum began to quicken, and the bluish-white light intensified, as if the artifact were suddenly contributing to the magnetic field.

Vanth trilled with satisfaction. '*It is authentic! Eager I am, to relieve myself of this burden and end all connection with this realm forever. Your kind intervenes recklessly, causing unanticipated damage to systems that cannot be easily repaired. True, we were fools to answer your call, but The Zone is not like your world of growing, dynamic things. Rock changes at a miniscule rate, and the energy of fragile polar fields is easily destabilized and rapidly depleted. You said you would feed us, replenish what had been lost. In the end, you either lied, or again could not foresee the potential for mayhem. Let me return to the ruins of my home forevermore. May the rings bind this final pact!'*

Oh, shit! Eric thought with dismay. *Just when it looked like we might get out of this in one piece.*

Lotte was also clearly taken by surprise. "I... I... well, you see... umm... we don't actually have... well, we do... kind of... but kind of not. It's a bit complicated...."

'Why do you blather?' Vanth loudly squawked. *'Produce the rings so we can be done with this! I grow weary of your ignorance. Either complete the ritual, or I'll feast on your energy and take my leave.'*

Lotte stiffened, obviously chastened by the great creature's irritation. Shaking her head, she reached circumspectly into her pocket and pulled out the little bag. Charun's broken rings were the sole remaining contents. Reluctantly, she dropped them into her palm, and offered up the larger of the two for the bird being's examination.

Vanth's predatory eyes again focused their attention. Still holding the medallion, she extended one thin finger and gently brushed against the spiraled silver ring that Lotte held forth.

The beast's feathered head tilted with a look of curiosity and surprise. *'This is not* my *ring. It is too large, and it is broken. Like mine, something was once set on each of the ends, but those pieces are missing. What is this, and how has it come into your possession?'*

Lotte took a deep breath. "You're correct, this is not your ring. In truth, it was made for your mate, Charun. It's his ring, or rather, it was. Charun's gateway and his rings were destroyed."

Vanth recoiled. *'So, he exists forever in this realm? Odd, I sense him not. He must be far away, indeed, unless I am vastly weaker than I imagined.'*

"No," Lotte said with trepidation. "Knowing The Zone could no longer support both of you, it was Charun's intention to remain in our world so you could survive, but this meant feeding regularly on our kind. You can understand, perhaps, how this would be intolerable to us. We had to... well... put an end to him... right in this very spot. I'm dreadfully sorry. There seemed no other way."

The once majestic bird raised her head to the sky and let out a tremendous shriek. This time, no words were behind the beguiling and beautiful noise that again sent them reeling to the ground—only a fathomless scream of pain, sorrow, and loss. When finished, Vanth furiously scoured the ground with her eyes, then abruptly dragged herself toward where Eric knelt near the large, curved segment at the apex of the arc.

Fearing she was about to kill him, he scrambled to his feet and retreated backward. He could hear Lotte crying out behind the advancing beast, but there was little she could do. Fortunately, the bird creature stopped at the portal piece and gave it a feeble kick, knocking it from its ersatz stand. The magnetic field and the low thrum immediately ceased, while the light around the gateway instantly returned to that of a normal New Hampshire sunset.

Vanth then raised her arms wide, amulet in one hand, torch with its luminescent purple flame in the other, and began to twirl in place. All around, the ground began to roil and swirl as small black particles of rock emerged from the dirt and shot into the air like a great swarm of gnats.

They stung Eric's skin as they whirled upward, collecting in a great cloud of matter just out of reach above their heads. It took him a moment, but he realized these were the tiny shards and fragments of Charun's shattered portal, lost from view after four years of intermixing with new layers of soil and grass.

Vanth cried out with anger and despair as she surveyed the floating wreckage. *'What have you done? The one who completed our circle gave his all for me, made the only choice possible given the damage wrought within our realm... damage you caused! You deny him survival in the same world where he was once sent forth to harvest the lives of those deemed unfit? You creatures are mad! We should have turned our backs on all the meaningless bargains and reveled in a banquet of your blood!'*

"Oh, piteous creature," Aicha sardonically spat as she approached. "You yourself admitted to the mistake of trucking with these pathetic beings, equally unable to foresee the consequences. You blame them for wanting to salvage their insignificant lives? Trust me, were the tables turned, you would have acted no differently. Your mate's death changes nothing. Hand over the objects you possess and return to your precious Zone. All will be as it was, and his sacrifice to you will not have been in vain."

Vanth lowered her head and turned with unhurried grace to face the Jinn. *'Return, I shall, but these items will come with me. The ritual is not complete, and I begin to harbor mistrust for a being that cannot enter the arc to bargain properly. Is this not the precise reason the gateway was so constructed, to prevent the likes of you from getting their hands on the artifacts? No, it shall not be. You can all suffer in eternity without them!'*

Aicha countered with a sinister snarl. "That is not an option! If necessary, I'll take them by force. You've lost the protection of your little magnetic shield, and it doesn't appear—ah, ah, ah, Mr. Schneider. Do please step away from that flowerpot. We'll just leave the gateway shut down for a spell. Ain't that a grand ol' idea?"

Eric dejectedly backed away from the portal segment and the upturned flowerpot, where he'd hoped to surreptitiously restore the magnetic field.

"That's better. Now, where was I? Ah, yes, you poor creature. Why don't you just hand over the key and the scroll now so we can both be on our way. It doesn't appear you're in any condition to resist me."

Vanth howled. *'Appearances can be deceiving!'* With that, she thrust forth her glowing torch, which shot out a beam of purplish magnetism directly at Aicha. The Jinn seemed surprised, but when the energy made impact, Olive's empty clothes crumpled to ground along with the abandoned crossbow and case of bolts.

Sensing an opportunity, Eric again dove for the curved white block that still lay nearby. He had just grabbed it when Lotte screamed from behind.

"Eric, look out!"

The blow felt as if being hit with a sledgehammer and caught him unaware. The portal fragment flew from his hands while the rest of his body slammed agonizingly into the rough soil.

Lotte rushed to his side and helped him sit up.

As he did so, he saw Vanth prostrate on the ground between them and the ledge.

After Aicha had casually dispatched him, she had clearly pummeled the great but weakened bird from behind, knocking the torch from her hand and causing it to revert to its miniature size. Now the Jinn's, or rather Olive's, naked body walked back toward the dazed avian, preparing another punishing strike.

"Wow," Eric observed. "I didn't know Olive had a tattoo there."

"Neither did I," Lotte breathlessly replied. "Eric, what are we going to do?"

There wasn't really much either of them *could* do. Aicha stiffly kicked the helpless Vanth, whose head slashed sideways before flopping back into the dirt. The Jinn then brought her foot down forcefully on the prone creature's back, horrifically splitting one wing with a hideous crack.

"Don't want you flying away now, do we?" Aicha cackled. "Are you done, or do you need a bit more convincing?"

Vanth's hand twitched, and the small funnel shot out in response to its owner's desperate plea. Aicha, however, was too quick. Her bare foot deftly pinned the object to the ground. Then, with obvious distaste, she kicked the milky white funnel over the ledge.

"Really, no more of that," she said, shaking her foot to free it of any residual dust and magnetic energy. "You'll never hit me anyway. I'm too fast. Now, can we please just conclude this unfortunate business?"

Aicha flashed a stern look back at Lotte and Eric, who sat, stunned and immobilized. Nodding with satisfaction, she grabbed the helpless bird creature by the shoulders and flipped her over.

Eric remembered the move. It was the one Aicha had been attempting on him when he'd nailed her with that rail spike.

Sadly, Vanth's hands were empty of weapons, and her pathetic attempts to keep the Jinn at bay were met with a brutal smack that ended all resistance.

With acrobatic ease, Aicha hopped to her feet and stood over Vanth's unmoving head, turning her body to address Eric. "Like what you see, darlin'? I know you do. Why don't y'all just come on over here and help little ol' me out? You get that key and scroll off her, and I'll overlook your tiny *indiscretion* trying to restore that magnetic field. What do you say, baby?"

Eric knew the whole "resistance is futile" spiel. At this point, it looked like Aicha would get what she'd been after the hard way, and it seemed she'd been right to feel she could take care of whatever Vanth could deliver. What opposition could he offer that would match power like that? Wordlessly, he rose and walked over to the semi-conscious bird.

"Go on," Aicha urged. "It'll save me a lot of discomfort. Those gloves are fine for most normal metals, but clay from the Abzu is a different matter."

"How will you ever handle them?" he asked.

She laughed. "That'll be up to Iblis. I never planned to do anything beyond securing Vanth's portal and delivering it to him. Your intervention created challenges, but also opportunities. So, here we are. You've done well... basically. Just a bit more to go and both of you will walk free. Come on, Mr. Schneider. I know you can do it."

He bent over Vanth's crushed and beaten body. She wasn't breathing, but then he wasn't certain any of these entities needed to breathe in the first place. There was no blood. Like Charun, Vanth had broken like a hunk of carved marble, little chips and flecks lost where Aicha had pummeled her, leaving a gaping crevice in her demolished wing.

Cautiously, he reached for the key at her waist, where it likely clung magnetically. He remembered the magnetic power Charun had so successfully wielded against the Afrit, but Vanth was in no condition to attempt such a feat. His hand had just touched the artifact when bony fingers grasped his wrist.

'No,' the dazed bird feebly pleaded. 'I should turn my back, but in reality, the Jinn speaks true. I was at fault... we both were, my mate and me. I know not why these items are so feared, and I lament my involvement, but now is not the time to surrender. In a way, it is fitting that the mighty Charun would die here and in this way.'

Aicha condescendingly scoffed. "And why, pray tell, would that be?"

Vanth choked out her meek reply. 'Because it gives me one final chance.'

"Chance to what?" the Jinn suspiciously asked.

As if in answer, Vanth's body stiffened with exertion.

Eric looked up and saw shadows in the sky, little clouds that dappled the sun as it set in spectacular brilliance behind Aicha's—or Olive's—naked form. Above the Jinn's head, small black clusters had formed. They grew quickly larger as the small shards and stones that had floated loosely in the air began to coalesce.

Looking down at Vanth as she did, Aicha couldn't see them. Instead of dematerializing, she lifted her foot to once again, and likely with finality, smash the great bird's skull.

A terrible mistake.

Both Eric and the unsuspecting Jinn screamed as thousands of little glass-like shards tore into Aicha's naked flesh. Her body was encased in a mist of blood as they whipped her from all directions. Crimson tears streamed from eyes, pierced and pulped by the whirlwind of razor-sharp fragments. The overwhelmed Jinn convulsed in unimaginable agony, and collapsed with torturous spasms, shaking uncontrollably, as she had when Eric had stabbed her.

For him, it was just as horrible, realizing he watched his friend's body being flayed. "Stop!" he cried, beating Vanth's chest to get her attention. "Make it stop! You've done it, she can't move! There's no need to kill her, and if you do, my friend dies too! Please, we'll do anything! We'll make sure you get home. Just don't kill her."

He felt the scrutiny of those orange-yellow eyes as Vanth pondered his words. He noticed Lotte dart to where Aicha had collapsed. She madly assessed the damage to Olive's body and cried with dismay at what she saw. To their relief, however, the storm of rock fragments ceased, and only Lotte's heaving sobs were audible on the little ridge that had witnessed such great woe.

As if in a trance, he crawled to Lotte's side. The flurry of Aicha's movements had stilled somewhat. She appeared frozen, paralyzed by the magnetic particles that had penetrated virtually every inch of Olive's skin. The wounds were neither deep nor large, but the concentration of material had clearly been enough to immobilize the Jinn and wreak catastrophic damage to Olive's soft tissues.

"We have to get her to a hospital," he whispered. "She's gonna bleed to death."

"No," Lotte replied, fighting back her near hysterical distress. "Look at her eyes, Eric. She'll be blind, and horribly scarred for life. No hospital can help her. There's only one possibility."

"Enki. That was the original plan anyway, assuming we got the key and the scroll from Vanth, which isn't looking all that promising right now. Maybe we should just take Olive and get out of here. What about Aicha, though?"

Lotte turned to face the great bird, who still lay on her back staring into the sky, broken wing jutting awkwardly outward. "Great one, can you hear me? Are you still with us?"

'I hear,' Vanth croaked. 'What reserves I once had have been depleted. I must return to my realm, or I will soon perish. I'm not certain I have the strength for the journey.'

"There is energy in this body," Lotte said, gesturing at Aicha who still occasionally flinched and jerked. "The Jinn is trapped here by the magnetism of the stone shards imbedded in her body. We've seen Charun extract the life essence of a person. Is it possible for you to take Aicha's invasive energy and leave Olive's body and her consciousness intact? They're two separate entities. Can you distinguish between them?"

'I know not. Never have I done so. I could try, but I cannot guarantee success. There is a problem, however.'

"What?"

'My torch. I need it to call forth the power of another creature, and in my state, it is beyond reach.'

"I can find it," Eric offered. "Aicha didn't kick it that hard. It's probably just at the bottom of the hill. But Lotte, are you sure this is such a good idea? What if she can't separate the two beings? That means certain death for Olive. Don't you think taking her to Enki is a better bet?"

Lotte looked him in the eye. "I think we have to take the risk. Healing Olive will require removing the magnetic shards. That will free Aicha and she could more than likely dematerialize and slip away again. Enki is powerful, but he's not a creature of earth. I'm not sure he has any innate powers that could do what Vanth has accomplished. We've got Aicha exactly where we want her right now. We simply can't take chances."

"But... but what about Olive?"

"Oh, Eric. You know I don't want anything to happen to her, but this is done. We have to think of the bigger picture. There's no going back on what happened."

Well, actually, there is. It just comes with its own set of problems. The bigger picture didn't include you getting killed two years ago, either. I saw to that personally.

Distasteful as it was, however, he realized Olive and Siddique's fortunes were as provisional as his and Lotte's. Death could strike at any moment for any of them, and in some sense, it wasn't even a question comparing Olive's life against the possibility of Aicha again escaping.

"All right," he reluctantly agreed. "What you say is probably true. It just sucks. Sometimes, all this just really sucks."

"I know it does. I'm sorry. I truly am. I just don't see any other way right now. We can only hope for the best."

He easily retrieved the triangular portal piece, which he found lying in the clear area between the base of the cliff and the thicker brush and trees. The only hinderance was his now weakened and aching hip from Aicha's unanticipated strike. It resonated painfully amongst the chorus of his other injuries as he labored back up the grassy slope. This was the spot where Charun and the Afrit had once battled, though all evidence of that titanic struggle had long since vanished.

When he returned, Vanth was slumped feebly over Aicha's body, which she, or perhaps more likely Lotte, had dragged near the center of the magnetic area.

"Here," he said as he handed the piece to Lotte.

She took it and then went to fit the displaced rectangular portal segment back into its makeshift flowerpot stand.

"What are you doing?"

"I'm turning the portal back on. Vanth shut it off because the power of its magnetic field overrode her ability to call up the shards of the destroyed gateway... but remember what we learned with Charun. Like the Afrit with the flames, these beings use magnetism to extract their victim's energy. That's exactly what Vanth is about to do, and the portal has the strongest magnetism of anything, as long as she's in the field. She clearly needs all the help she can get. So, as I say, I'm turning it back on."

With that, she swiveled the curved rectangle to face the doorway. The magnetic arc again surged to life, and she dropped the white funnel into the bluish-white haze, it floated to the center of the area, where Vanth deftly snatched it from the air. The torch with its purplish flame reemerged in her hand, and the bird creature held it over Aicha's lacerated form.

Unlike Charun's hammer, which he touched to those he consumed, the flame of the torch expanded to encompass Aicha's head and upper body, which once more started to twitch and spasm. The pace of the low hum quickened, and the blue-white aura dimmed slightly, as if Vanth were somehow redirecting its energy.

Eric's heart raced as he took Lotte's hand and watched in helpless apprehension while the great bird fed. Those taken by Charun had been left drained and desiccated, resembling unwrapped mummies, upon whose ossified visages their agonizing final moments were forever preserved. Those bodies had burned like kindling, not even needing the gasoline he had poured on them to start the fires. He imagined doing the same thing now for Olive, and the thought nearly crushed him. All he could do was stand and bear witness. If these were to be his friend's final moments, he would stay beside her. He wouldn't look away.

Through Olive's tortured mouth, Aicha screamed.

She knew what was happening but appeared powerless to resist. Slowly, like a bubble of air rising in water, a transparent orb emerged from Olive's scarred and shuddering chest, parting the purple of the flame as it rose. For a time, this bubble of energy hovered right above the bloody flesh of her breasts, resisting the pull, trying to retreat back into the body where the creature of air found succor.

Vanth also shook with exertion, wobbling unsteadily as she channeled and focused the power around her to overcome her tenacious opponent. Just when it seemed that Aicha would drive back into Olive's abdomen, the violet torchlight withdrew from the body and coalesced around the orb of the Jinn's energy, encasing and separating it from its corporeal shelter.

The bubble darted wildly, as if trying to escape, but rapidly began to shrink in the onslaught of magnetism around it. Simultaneously, Vanth began to strengthen. Her shattered wing rose to join its companion. The mottled splotches on her skin and the scars on her beak and face began to fade, while the colors of her feathers rapidly brightened.

Soon, nothing remained of the clear orb. Aicha was gone, her energy absorbed by the powers of a diametrically opposed realm. The purple flame receded to its position at the top of Vanth's outstretched torch as she rose, victorious and majestic once more, to deliver a deafening screech of triumph.

When they had recovered from this fresh sonic onslaught, Lotte and Eric ran to Olive's tormented and now unmoving body. Her breath was faint, and she didn't respond to any of their desperate entreaties.

"What happened?" Eric apprehensively asked. "Do you think our friend will be OK?"

'I did my best,' the bird creature answered. *'Their energies were separate, but entwined and impossible to fully isolate. Some of the girl's vitality was inevitably lost, and conceivably some of the power which gripped her still remains... that which was invested deeply to seize basic bodily control and would be most difficult to separate without terminating the life of the host. The magnetism of the material in her body keeps this at bay, but were that to be removed, this energy might be able to reassert some level of control. Of this, I am not certain, but I would advise caution.'*

"*Caution*," he muttered under his breath, not wishing to offend the otherworldly being who had clearly done the best she could. "What the hell does *that* mean?"

He stroked the side of Olive's butchered face and gazed into her eyes, only half closed for the bloody viscera which propped them open. If they could keep her alive, Enki could heal the physical wounds, but he worried about the longer-term impact of his friend's unwitting association with Aicha Kandicha.

This is my fault. I called her to be with Siddique, put her on a plane and sent her straight into danger. This is my doing. This is on my *head!*

Nearby, he sensed something moving, but mired in guilty anguish he paid it no heed.

Lotte, however, shot to her feet and addressed the now resurgent bird being. "What are you doing?" she called. "Please, great one, don't leave us like this!" The torch had been returned to the center of the magnetic field and was now gaining momentum as it rotated.

Vanth appraised Lotte with her fearsome gaze. *'I have consumed the energy of this being within the field emitted from The Zone. My form is compromised. I must return and assimilate this energy before I can again venture into your world, though henceforth I see no reason to do so. I risked all to keep the artifacts safe and did my best to save your friend. The threat, it seems, is gone... my work complete. So, to my home I return, by fortune healthier and stronger. Go now and leave me to my eternal peace.'*

"There will be no peace for you. Other Jinn will come for these items. You prevailed this time, but I can't say with certainty you'll ever be safe.

Even if you don't heed the summons, your realm may be vulnerable to the magic and cunning of the creatures of air, just as they have vulnerabilities to the powers of the earth. We can hide this portal in a hundred locations or again risk death destroying it, but that won't necessarily ensure your safety. There may be more of this material out there, or they'll craft another way. The Jinn who hunt these items will never stop. It may be another two-thousand-five-hundred years, but they'll eventually find their way to you, just as they have now. As long as you possess something they want, you'll be in jeopardy forever."

The bird creature inclined her head in thought. *'What alternative would you propose?'*

"Before Aicha, the Jinn you just dispatched, took us hostage, our intent was to come here and retrieve the key and the scroll and deliver them for safe keeping with a powerful being from the Abzu, a place of deep waters. Had that been an option, the man who entrusted the items to you originally would likely have done this instead. If we can get them to him now, the Jinn will lose their interest in you, and the artifacts will probably be safer. Everyone wins."

Vanth laughed bitterly. *'I judge this a rather shabby victory. My realm remains in tatters, and you merely shift the focus of this seemingly endless conflict from one theater to another. Is this the sum of what we have to show for the union of our worlds? If so, all, it appears, are losers... wretchedly grasping for what little can be salvaged in the wake of catastrophe.'*

That pretty much nails it, Eric dismally thought. *It's just like Olive says: the team that loses even when it wins. Looks like we're all under contract.*

'To be free is enticing,' the great bird continued. *'I fear, however, that those who shaped my form and psyche imprinted upon me the imperative to guard these items. It was the unspoken price I paid to access the almost limitless energy of your realm. The power of the rings would ensure their approval of the transfer or would alert them to malfeasance. This is why the ritual remains important. As calamitous as things have become, I still dare not cross them. I need no additional enemies.'*

"There's no one left to be dissatisfied," Lotte asserted. "The Seven Kings who forged the portal are all dead, and we're operating under the instructions of the man who once led them. We risked our lives, small and meaningless as they may seem, to protect our world as best we can, and to try and protect you from the very danger you just experienced. I agree with your assessment that things have gone horribly awry. This may be a small step toward setting things right, but in any case, you *will* be judged. Not by those behind the power of magical rings. The reality of that paradigm is long past. Rather, it will be by the outcomes of your thoughtful action, and by the verdict of those who benefit or suffer from the choice you make... yourself included."

Vanth again regarded her, then looked into the rapidly darkening sky. *'You remind me of someone I once knew. Her name was Rika. She too was dragged unwittingly into affairs beyond her mastery, but she spoke and acted with courage and conviction. She realized the old ways worked no longer. She gave all of herself, and for a time, things were better. In the end, it was for naught, but not all consequences can be foreseen.'*

The resplendent bird from another realm returned her piercing gaze to Lotte. *'I hope you know what you are doing. If not, the fate of this world rests upon your heads, not mine. May you find peace and an end to your conflicts. I have no more help to provide. With this, I too will have given my all.'*

Solemnly, she reached to her waist, removed the key and scroll from where they clung to her now restored flesh, and held them forth.

"We thank you, great one," Lotte said as she reverently took the precious items. "We will try to live up to the confidence with which you've honored us. This won't end the conflict, but it may deescalate the consequences for everyone. I wish we could have met under different circumstances. There's so much we could learn from each other."

'Perhaps someday,' the resplendent entity replied as she turned toward the white-hot light of the open gateway. *'In a universe forged by wiser choices and cooler heads. I sense the wait will be long, indeed.'*

CHAPTER 15

Eric held Olive's limp and bloodied hand. Pasty illumination from fluorescent lamps filtered through the windshield of the van, barely penetrating the hushed darkness where they sat.

She hadn't stirred, even during the excruciating process of transporting her down the hill. Like Lotte, when he had carried her along the same difficult route years before, Olive's head had lolled roughly from side to side as they stumbled clumsily with no light to guide their footfalls. He'd feared injuring her further, but it couldn't be helped.

The contusion on his hip had gotten worse with every step, and this had been his second trip down the hill. The first he used to convey the toolbox and one of the bags containing Vanth's disassembled portal, while Lotte tended to Olive and gathered up the portions of the gateway that remained stuck to the face of the rock. As he had four years ago, he'd driven the van as far as it would go up the trail, to reduce the distance he'd need to carry his helpless friend.

Despite the blanket he brought to cover her mangled body, Olive's blood had seeped onto his shirt and pants. This was the main reason he now sat and waited in the parking lot of yet another Walmart Supercenter, this one just south of Berlin and luckily still open. It was just as well. He could barely walk from the pain and exhaustion that had set in, once he crashed hard from the adrenaline rush of action and exertion.

He needed rest for the drive ahead, but it also gave him time to consider his conversation with Siddique. The minute they'd gotten cell service near Berlin, a slew of texts and voice mails from their worried companion had blazed forth in a frenzied cacophony of beeps, dings, and buzzes on their no longer silent phones.

Lotte was in the back trying to make Olive comfortable, so Eric rang Siddique as he drove.

"Where the hell did you go?" his friend shrieked into the phone. "I was so worried! I almost called the police. Olive texted me and said you were fine, that you'd changed your minds and decided to take her along, but all her things are in my room. That made no sense. It was crazy! I thought you were kidnapped... again!"

Eric bitterly sighed. "We kind of were. It turns out Aicha got inside your body after I thought I'd killed her. Thankfully, she didn't fully take you over, but she kept you out cold and then moved to Olive when she was asleep in your room. We were her prisoners, and she almost got hold of the key and the scroll, but Vanth was able to stop her at the last second. In the process, though... man.... Olive... well, let's just say it's not good. Not good at all."

"Will she be OK?"

"We're taking her to Enki, so he can heal her. We need to give him the artifacts anyway, as soon as possible. I just hope we're in time. I feel so awful about this, and about what happened to you. It's *my* fault. It's unfair that I dragged both of you into situations where you could have been killed, and I'm really not sure where all this ends, or if it ever will... for any of us. I'm sorry. I'm just so sorry."

He feared he'd lost the connection when Siddique was silent for so long, but then the singular lilt of his friend's voice rang loud and clear in his ear. "Man, you're crazy! I thought I was on the team, that we were in this together. You two risk your lives. Why are you sorry for risking mine? I could walk out of this stupid hospital with lousy food, where I can't get any sleep, and get hit by an ambulance. Anybody can die at any minute. This is another one of those things you two don't seem to get. I guess it's just not the world you come from."

"What do you mean?"

"Look, I'm not trying to talk bad about you. You're my friend. I care about you. I mean, hell, I *love* you, but I don't think you really understand how many people in this world live with uncertainty and fear all the time. They work hard, but still don't get ahead. They deal with racism, violence, crime, war. I grew up in the middle of my country's civil war. We had to flee Freetown and go north to stay with relatives. Many people died. Death was everywhere. Okay, that's extreme, but you and Lotte had exactly the opposite—safety, security, all the choices in the world right in the palms of your hands. It makes you think death is far away, but it's not."

"I think we discovered how close death can come, multiple times. We're lucky to even be having this conversation."

"I know, but you *lived,* and it *still* eats at you, just like all this 'accomplish this, accomplish that' eats at your wife. I get it, man, you were born into your lives like I was born into mine, but you *have* to find happiness. Maybe it's easier for me, coming from almost nothing. I get pleasure from all the good things that happen... the little things. I don't worry so much about the stuff that goes wrong because I know how much worse it can be. You both have *big* things... *big* dreams... *big* tasks to finish... *big* universes to save. That's great, but it's like nobody ever taught you about all the sacrifices and compromises it takes to have all that stuff, or all the shit that's still gonna go wrong. You beat yourselves up believing that you're both miserable failures when things don't turn out so picture-perfect, like you grew up believing they would, or that you have this but you don't have that. You gotta let it go, man."

"It's not so easy for me," he whispered into the phone, not really wanting Lotte to hear what he was saying. "It doesn't feel right using you two like pawns in a game, especially one where you're dead if you lose. I'm sorry, it's just not my nature."

"I know. Hard shit is never easy. I get it, but you don't need to apologize to your friends who want to help you. Olive and I knew what we were getting into. Besides, this is where I belong. I mean, hell, it was the stupid shit I did to Lotte that got me here in the first place. You two gave me a second chance. I'm not gonna waste it beating myself up for the rest of my life. I try to move on, do better. This is what you gotta do. You gotta move on, forget about it and just be happy that today wasn't your last day... or mine. Get it?"

The door to the van startled him as Lotte slid it open. "Why are you sitting in the dark? Is Olive okay?"

"I just needed a little quiet," he replied, reorienting himself to the present. "Her breathing seems a bit stronger. I don't think she's getting worse. Did they have bandages? The more of this bleeding we can stop, the better."

"I got a ton of stuff." She tossed a bag on the floor next to him. "Help me unload it so we can get out of here. I have blood on me too. I think the cashier was a little suspicious. I got two gallons of water and a bucket. I'll try to clean your shirt if you like, after I wash out Olive's wounds."

The offer seemed to have been quickly forgotten as she tended to their friend, bandaging her torn and bloody eyes, washing dirt from the wounds on her back, and patching the worst of the lacerations that still oozed blood onto the stolen hospital blankets. She then turned her attention to some other task that he couldn't see as he drove.

"What are you doing?" he called over his shoulder.

"I just had to see," she said with excitement. "I really want to find out what this scroll looks like."

"Not much of a scroll. I don't see how you're gonna unfold it."

"It doesn't unfold, you silly! It's a cylinder scroll. You haven't handled it, so you probably didn't see all the engravings. Items like this date back to Mesopotamian times. It's quite logical Enlil would employ a method of communication like this. I bought some clay in the store. I'm softening it up now. When it's ready, I'll roll the scroll over the clay and it will leave an impression, theoretically with the instructions about how to find the entrance to the Rope of An and Ki."

"Is that such a good idea? Maybe we don't want to know where that is. Not even Utnapishtim looked at it."

"It's in Cuneiform. I can't read it. I just want to give it a look, then I'll squish the clay back together. Hold on... just another second.... Wow!"

"What is it?"

"Well, I'm not certain. There's definitely Cuneiform writing. I could see that before I took the impression, but there's also some sort of squiggly lines and some other markings. I think it's a map. There's a symbol that looks like it might be a city, and another just has three weird little holes in the clay. I'm not certain how to read it. There's no scale, so I'm not sure what the distances might represent. Very interesting. Oh, well, no matter, I just wanted to—"

Olive's scream of pain and terror made them jump with surprise. Eric almost lost control of the van. He pulled to the side of the road and rushed to join Lotte in the back, where she was frantically trying to restrain Olive.

"Don't rip at the bandages! It'll just start bleeding again! Olive, Olive... just stop and try to calm down!"

"Calm down?" she howled "I can't see nothin'! My whole fucking body feels like it's on fire! What the hell happened? Where am I? Oh, God, Lotte, it hurts so bad. Please make it stop. Please, can't you just make it stop?"

"Try to calm her down," Lotte commanded. "I was afraid this could happen. I bought some things that might help."

"Olive," Eric said, taking her hand. "It's me."

"Eric?"

"Yeah. Listen, don't worry about what happened or where you are. We're taking you to Enki. He's gonna fix all this up. You'll be good as new. You just have to hold on. I know it hurts like hell, but this will be over in a few hours. Just try to hold on."

"Here," Lotte said, returning with a cup of water. "Eric will hold your head, and I'm going to put some pills in your mouth. Can you drink them?"

"Hell yes! I'm dying of thirst! Oh, God, I feel dizzy."

"You've lost a lot of blood. The best thing is to take these pills and try to get some rest. I'll stay with you. Eric has to drive. The faster we can get you to Enki, the sooner all this will be over."

It was a drive that, regrettably, Eric would never forget. Olive's miserable sobs brought only searing pain to her mutilated eyes. With patient coaxing, Lotte got her to stop crying, but still she whimpered in anguish, or shrieked in agony when a bump in the road jolted her butchered body. Each outburst pierced him like a dagger in his heart, and it was clear even Lotte's almost inexhaustible resilience was being stoutly tested.

Just past midnight, the sorrowful white van limped into the I-93 tunnel through Boston and exited into Dorchester. By some miracle, Olive had finally quieted, lulled either by the fatigue of suffering, or the over-the-counter sleep aids Lotte had plied her with, along with copious painkillers. Eric steered through quiet streets, eventually bringing their vehicle to rest near the loading dock of the old, converted factory. As quietly as possible, they grabbed the bags with Vanth's portal, along with the section of Enki's gateway that Aicha had forced them to take, exited and locked the van, and dragged off to the loading dock door.

"Where are we taking Enki's portal?" Lotte asked as she fumbled with the keys. "The only pond around here I really know is the one on Holton Hill Road. Good memories there, right? You certainly seemed happy. Maybe it'll be good luck again."

Eric blushed slightly remembering their first sexual encounter. She'd always been more forthright about such things, talking easily about topics that he found uncomfortable or embarrassing. Getting married, he realized with surprise, had made it somewhat easier, almost like being given permission to be franker and more honest. Her casual manner still threw him, however, and it probably always would.

"Umm, I'm not so sure. It'll be awfully dark there, and the trail is too narrow to drive on. I can't carry Olive that far. My leg is killing me, not to mention all the cuts and bruises I got from that damned owl. Plus, that pond is really overgrown with weeds and gunk. I think I have a better idea."

"Do tell," she said, finally pushing the door open.

"You know the cemetery in Southby, not the one by the high school, but the one where my grandparents are buried? There's a reflecting pond there with some benches around it. It's behind some trees, hidden from the road. The grass goes right up to the bank. We can use the van's headlights to see. It'll be after one a.m. when we get there. Nobody should be around. It's the best I can think of."

"It's perfect!" she sang, throwing on the light to their basement space where the Afrit's portal still brooded on the far wall. "It'll take us about an hour to get there, maybe less with the traffic being so light."

They rapidly made the exchange of the bags bearing Vanth's portal for those containing Enki's, reuniting their emergency piece with the rest of the gateway, then quickly locked the door and scurried back to the loading dock. Lotte muttered under her breath as she again fiddled with the wearyingly fussy exterior door. Figuring she had it under control, Eric started toward the van. The door to the vehicle stood open, and he froze in complete shock.

"Lotte? Did you leave the side door to the van open?"

"Of course not!" she derisively shot back as she ran to join him. "We locked it together. It can't possibly be—oh, *Scheiße!* Eric, what in the world is going on? I didn't bring the key or the scroll with me. Did you?"

He shook his head. "We were just gonna be in there for a second, and we needed to take them with us anyway. Why would I?"

"Of course. What about Olive? Is she still even in there?"

"I don't know. Stay here, I'll go take a look."

"Stay here? The hell with that! What happened to sticking together and safety in numbers? Isn't that the one great lesson you took from all those ridiculous horror movies?"

"You have a point. Okay, stay by me and keep a lookout behind us. I'll just poke my head in the van and see if she's there."

Cautiously, the pair descended the short staircase from the loading bay to the ground and crept toward the open side door. No illumination came from the dome light of the van, Lotte having turned it off so as not to disturb Olive. They crouched by the step leading into the vehicle as a train rumbled by on the nearby tracks.

When it had passed, Eric tentatively peered into the darkness. "Olive! Olive, are you there?"

"I'm here," she mumbled weakly. "There weren't nuthin' I could do though. I'm sorry if it messes everything up, but there weren't nuthin' I could do."

"Olive, what happened?" Lotte implored as she hastily hopped into the vehicle and hastened to their friend. "Are you hurt?"

"No more hurt than I was before, I guess. No, he didn't hurt me."

"He *who*, Olive?"

"I don't rightly know. I woke up, and somebody was stroking my hair. I thought it was you, or Eric, but the person didn't... well... *smell* right. He had a kind of... *spicy* scent, like perfume or something."

"How do you know it was a man?"

"Because he talked to me. He had a strange accent. He said he was sorry that he couldn't help me, but that he appreciated what I'd done... what I'd brought to him. It was too weird. I had no idea what he was talkin' about, and I didn't want him touchin' me like that, so I pushed him away. I brushed against his chest. His skin was all rough, like. The guy wasn't wearin' no shirt."

"I rather think he wasn't wearing any clothes at all. He had to dematerialize to get inside the van. Oh, *Scheiße!*" Lotte stood up and clicked on the interior dome light in the cargo space. "They're gone," she said with remarkable calm.

The key and the scroll were not where they'd left them, sitting beside the toolbox behind the driver's seat. Ominously, a bare footprint, slightly disfigured and apparently missing several toes, was impressed in Lotte's clay project, which still sat on the floor nearby. Most of the Cuneiform lettering gleaned from the cylinder scroll had been obliterated.

Hip stiff and painful, Eric gingerly pulled himself through the doorway. "What about the amulet and Charun's rings?"

"They're in my pocket," she flatly replied, "for whatever that's worth now. It's a near miracle we brought the piece of Enki's gateway inside with us. Iblis would probably have loved to get his hands on that."

"How the hell did he find us?"

"So *stupid!* I thought she'd have us take her to the airport. What reason would there be to meet here? Thinking back, though, Aicha clearly said that Iblis would be most interested to see all the *wonders* she'd uncovered. It's my fault. I should have been more careful, more thoughtful, and been able to think it through. Everything's just been so *crazy.*"

"Exactly." He put his arm around her. "When have you had five seconds to think *anything* through? You can't blame yourself for this. Hell, I heard her say that too. I gotta be honest, it went in one ear and out the other. It's all right."

"No, Eric, it's not all right. It's not all right at all. That little mistake just cost us everything we've worked so hard to accomplish. Iblis has the items. It's just a matter of time before he finds the entrance to the Rope of An and Ki and tries to break through the barrier."

"Then we still have time to stop him. Lotte, it's not over."

"I don't even know where to begin."

"I do. We take Olive to Enki and get her fixed up. He'll help us. You're his brazen beauty, remember? He'll listen to you, and you'll convince him to help us. You have all these weird-ass things wrapped around your little finger, right? Plus, it's his stupid family that got us into this mess in the first place. Serves him right."

Despite her distress, she let out a little snort of laughter. "I'm not sure about that last bit, but we'll definitely get him to heal Olive."

"Good plan, y'all. Now can we get movin'? This ain't gettin' no better, and pretty soon, I'm gonna need to pee!"

The cold of the water helped numb the throbbing pain in Eric's hip and soothe the contusions and abrasions from his encounter with the dreadful owl as he and Lotte assembled the portal.

When complete, she used the bucket she'd fortuitously purchased to wash Olive's wounds as a scoop to pour water into the cap at the apex of the arch. The assembled gateway sunk, as anticipated, into the muddy bottom of the pond. Soaking wet, she knelt by the shore, hands in the glowing water, and chanted her appeal for the Lord of the Deep Waters to grace them with his presence. She swiftly received her response.

Eric had prepared himself for the worst, but was flushed with relief when two massive, sweeping, and obviously healthy horns emerged from the still and glowing waters of the Southview Cemetery's repurposed reflecting pond. The last time he'd seen the inscrutable being in this form, one of the great antlers had been savagely ripped from his skull. He had thought the mighty entity dead, but Enki was a trickster, and the agony he endured on Margate Tower's rooftop had certainly fooled their dangerous opponent.

The goat-like head with impenetrable black eyes rose from the waters, and Eric's mind flooded with the power of the great god's projected thoughts.

'*Your pleas have awoken me. Behind your words, I sense tremendous turmoil. You are distressed, and your perturbation is palpable. I know your mind. You would not call me forth for trivialities. Speak, child. Tell me what troubles you, and why you feel such inordinate need for my assistance.*'

As the deity exited the water of the pond and transformed into his human guise, Lotte recounted the events that had led them to this point in gasping breaths full of regret and self-recrimination.

Enki seemed startled when she mentioned Utnapishtim. *'My old advisor still lives? Strange, I cannot sense him.'*

"Well, you did make him immortal," Lotte pointed out. "I hate to say, though, he's in rather awful condition. You can't sense him because he's trapped behind Jinn magic, crafted by the same creature who maimed him, and who, in a sense, is responsible for Olive's terrible injuries."

That ended the tale for the time being, as Enki demanded Olive be brought forth.

Eric barely managed, and collapsed to his knees upon making the transfer of her body into the awaiting god's arms. Lotte crouched by him as they observed the process, watching the waters bubble and splash as the black shards and stones that had caused so much damage disgorged from her body.

"Crap," Eric worried. "With all that magnetic material gone, what are we gonna do about what's left of Aicha's energy still in Olive's body?"

Lotte quickly replied. "I have an idea. I'll take care of it when we get her back to the van. I hope it works. Otherwise, we'll have to take more *drastic* measures."

He had no idea what that meant, but focused his attention on Olive, who clearly seemed to be feeling better.

"Mr. Enki?" she called in a dreamy voice as she floated in his arms.

'What is it, child? The healing is almost complete. Soon you will rest.'

"I know. I'm already gettin' sleepy. I just wondered if you could do one little thing, like you did with Mutig?"

'You wish a different appearance? Greater endowments, perhaps, to better attract a mate, or possibly some of the strength and endurance with which I graced your beloved pet? You are a fighter, like he is. This would be fitting.'

"No, nuthin' like that. It's just... well... I got this stupid tattoo. My dumbass friends talked me into it when I was drunk one time. I don't even date that boy no more. It really does take some explainin' when I'm, well, like you say... trying to attract a mate... if you know what I mean. Can you get rid of it, please?"

The Lord of the Abzu laughed, and Eric began to chuckle as well, until Lotte delivered a rather forceful slap across his arm.

"*Ow*! What are you doing?"

"What are *you* doing?" she shot back. "Why are you just sitting there?"

"I'm watching. What the heck do you want me to do?"

In answer to his question, she gave him the eyeroll to end all eyerolls. "What do you think I want you to do? I want you to get in the water and have Enki heal you. How can you not even for one second think about that? You have injuries from years ago that still bother you, and now who the hell knows what's wrong with your hip. How can it not even cross your mind to ask for one little thing for yourself?"

"I got something for myself. I got... umm...." The words died on his lips. How could he tell her he'd demanded to use the Tablet of Destinies to bring her back from the dead? That would lead to all kinds of questions, which would likely reveal deeper secrets that were best left unspoken.

"What did you get?" she skeptically probed.

"I got.... Well, it's enough for me that Olive's better. That's what I want. I don't feel good about dragging her into this... or Siddique. I'll be fine."

She cuffed his ear.

"*Ow*! Stop hitting me!"

"Get yourself into that water! You're not going to be fine in time to be any good. We need you *now,* Eric! *I* need you! I'll talk to Enki. Just get in the damn water, you foolish, lovable idiot."

Despite his exhaustion, Eric felt better than he had in years.

He sat in the passenger's seat of the van, wrapped in one of the few remaining blankets void of blood, basking in the warmth from the vehicle's heater and the feeling of... *nothing.* The aches, pains, and residual stiffness from years of brutal battering and pushing his body beyond its limits had been wiped away. He felt like a new man, and despite the dire situation, couldn't help the sensation of happiness that was so often elusive in his life.

Siddique would be proud.

In the grand scheme, this was a little thing, but it was *his* little thing, so he heeded his friend's advice and took a moment to enjoy the experience.

Outside the window, a still damp, disheveled, and now barefoot Lotte had recounted the rest of their story to Enki. "So, how do we find him before he gets to the Rope of An and Ki? I assume you can't detect him?"

'Sadly, something in the magic of the Jinn makes them undetectable, even when I have laid eyes upon the human whose body they control. It is at the heart of their power. Jinn work by stealth, surprise and subterfuge their weapons of choice. It is how they have survived here for millennia. Iblis will be difficult to find, and first we would have to know where to look.'

"The only certainty is that he'll be at the location of the entrance indicated on the scroll at some point in the near future. Do you know where that is?"

'The entrance to my brother's realm was never fixed. He moved it as he saw fit, which was wise. However, as Utnapishtim told you, when my brother retreated from this world, he was forced to affix a permanent location. I know not the exact spot he chose. Only this scroll you speak of could tell us that.'

"Wait a minute! I took an impression of the scroll before Iblis got his hands on it. It's gotten a bit squashed, but there might be something left that would give us a clue."

Eric swung around in his seat as she slid open the side door. Olive lay in the back of the van, a peaceful look on her slumbering face despite being wrapped in blankets smeared with her own dried blood. Around her neck, Eric could see the laces from Lotte's discarded shoes, tied tightly together. Under the blanket, they secured the white amulet against Olive's still bare skin in the hope that the magnetism would keep Aicha's dormant energy at bay. So far, it appeared to be working.

"*Verdammt!*" Lotte cursed as they knelt by the flattened clay. "The left half seems to be gone. You can see just a bit of the writing on the top right, and part of what I think is a map at the bottom. There was a little figure, about here. It looked like a ziggurat. I thought maybe that was a city. Then there were more squiggly lines, like these around the three little indentations. Do you know what those represent?"

The Lord of the Abzu pressed close and examined the markings. '*The lines denote where the sea of salt meets the earth. The three holes mark the entrance to a great underground cave, formed in a place where the rushing waters proved more powerful than stone. I know of this place, though I have never been. The Jinn knew of it and used it on occasion as a meeting place far from prying eyes. Ironic it would be if, after all, Enlil had secreted the entrance to the Rope of An and Ki right amongst them.*'

Lotte pulled out her phone and began wildly typing and scrolling. After a moment, she let out a whoop of delight. "Ironic doesn't even begin to cover this! You say the lines represent the coast. Okay, let's assume the ziggurat that got wiped out by Iblis's stupid foot is Nippur, where Enlil's temple was located. There was a coast to the south of that before it came to this one near the three holes. I remember that there was a line that jutted out just above here, but it got squished. That would have been the coast of Dubai, just south of the Persian Gulf, which puts those three little holes in Oman."

"What's so funny about that?" Eric enquired.

"What's so funny is that, if this is right, those three little holes are called the Majlis al Jinn... the bloody *gathering place* of the Jinn!"

"You can't make this stuff up. You have to admit, if we were picking possible places to look from scratch, that would probably have been our absolutely last choice. What does this mean, though, or is that a stupid question?"

"It means that we're going to Oman, and we have to get there as fast as possible. Great one, we need your assistance with this. We don't have nearly enough power to deal with Iblis on our own. How can we get you there?"

'The coast is not far from here. Get me to the waters of the ocean, and I will find my way.'

"We can drive you to the shoreline," Eric suggested, "but Lee Pond is right nearby. That feeds Emerson Brook, which connects with the Blackstone River. That river flows through Providence, then eventually into Narragansett Bay and out to the ocean. Would that work?"

'If the waters can carry me, it will suffice.'

"Umm, all right," Lotte said, a bit hesitantly. "So, that's easy enough, but how will we find you in Oman? I'm looking at the map now. Apparently, there's a town on the shore not too far from the Majlis al Jinn called Tiwi. It has a large beach, just north of a scenic area called Wadi Shab. Could we meet there, on the beach?

'Go to that place, immerse your hands in the waters, and I will locate you. Secure transportation inland. I wish not to walk, and my powers will be terribly limited in this place, as water is sporadic and scarce. You must do one other thing as well.'

"Anything, great one."

'The beast of fire... you must enlist its aid once again. I know not what perils we might face, but Iblis is old, powerful, and devious. He is a survivor, and he will bring all his capabilities to bear in this, his moment of potential triumph. Would that I had the capacity to give the Jinn the release they seek, but I do not, and the prospect of facing my father after all this time terrifies me. So, we also need to avail ourselves of every advantage. I relish not seeing the monstrosity again, yet as unlike as we are, the creature more than proved its worth, and deserved the spoils I granted. Destiny once more calls your Afrit's name, unknown though it may be. It is up to you to convince the creature of this, and your failure may spell our end.'

"I understand, great one. I'll not let you down."

CHAPTER 16

"Okay, so how the hell are we gonna get the Afrit's portal to freakin' Oman?" Eric asked, bewildered.

The Lord of the Abzu had slipped unceremoniously into the waters of Lee Pond, retaking his Capricorn form and vanishing quickly from sight. Now, they drove back toward Southby through quiet streets, Olive in deep slumber after her taxing ordeal and the lengthy healing.

"Where will we set it up?" he went on. "In our hotel room? Are we even getting a hotel room? Will they even let us in the country?"

"That's a good point," Lotte noted from the passenger's seat where she sat cross-legged with eyes closed, the clean blanket around her shoulders. "We probably need a visa. I can't imagine it's hard to get for a short stay. I'll look online in the morning. As far as the other stuff goes, we'll just have to see. Despite what I told Enki, I'm not at all certain I can even get the Afrit to come. We'll know soon enough, after we've talked."

"You sure you have to do that right now? You look utterly exhausted. I am too, even with the way Enki fixed me up."

She deeply sighed. "Yes, it has to be now. First off, we need to know if the Afrit is in or out, and if it's the former, there will be tons of logistical details to resolve. I'll need to get on that first thing tomorrow. Sure, I'm exhausted, but that won't get better any time soon. Serves me right for not properly thinking things through. Seems to be the story of my life, lately. So *stupid!* *Alter!* What a mess I've made of things. Eric, what are you doing? Why are we pulling over?"

"Because I'm *sick* of this!" he shouted, instantly sorry for almost waking Olive, who thankfully didn't stir. They'd come to the center of Southby. The town common, once a cow pasture but now a beautifully manicured park, unfolded to their right. "Get out."

"Here? Eric, why?"

"Because we need to talk, and I don't want to risk waking up Olive."

With that, he shut off the engine, hopped out, and walked angrily to the sidewalk. Nearby, a horseshoe of stonework enclosed a spotlight illuminated statue of Oliver Sturman, patriarch of the family who built the rail cars in Southby's once semi-glorious manufacturing past. The life-size bronze portrayed the man with a large book in one hand, presumably the *Principles of Steam Engineering*, pointing with his free arm toward the horizon, a resolute and all-knowing expression on his monumental visage. He looked like a modern god, promising a brighter tomorrow for all who accepted his gospel of science and industry.

Lotte cautiously joined him at the perimeter of the statue's glow. "Are you all right?"

"I'm fine. I mean, I'm not fine, but that's because it's so painfully obvious to me that something's bothering *you*. I want you tell me what you started telling me in Greece."

"Are you certain you want to have that conversation right now... with everything we have to do?"

"Yes, I'm certain. We need to do it before some other damn creature from the eighteenth freaking dimension swoops in and distracts us again. Now, Lotte... right now. I can't keep listening to you beat yourself up. It's making me crazy. What the hell is the problem?"

"Eric, I don't... I don't know how to say this. I feel so awful. It's all my stupid fault, and I just can't seem to get my head around it. I meant to tell you. I just don't know how."

"Just say it," he pleaded, softening his tone as he saw her look of utter dismay.

"All right. I just... well... it's that... you see... Eric... I'm *pregnant*."

"Is it mine?"

He regretted the words the instant they left his mouth, but there it was — the culmination of weeks of suspicion, anxiety, and self-doubt, all topped off with a healthy dose of jealousy for what he feared might be happening.

Unsurprisingly, Lotte's eyes narrowed, and her lips tightened in a furious scowl. "First off, you little shit, it's not *yours*! It's bloody *ours*! And second, how dare you! Do you really think so little of me? Who the hell do you think the father *would* be?"

Angry as she was, her reaction actually cheered him. Lotte wouldn't lie about something like this, and the degree to which this enraged her made it clear that paternity wasn't really in question.

He backtracked. "I'm sorry, I didn't mean it that way. I just... well... I've been so worried. You've seemed so upset and distracted, and this whole thing with *Sven*... I don't know. I heard he has sort of a reputation for getting involved with his colleagues, especially the young, pretty kind. I should have said something, but I didn't because I couldn't bring myself to believe it could possibly be true. I also didn't want to add to the stress you were obviously already under. I don't know what to say."

Amazingly, his words appeared to calm her somewhat, and her face became pensive. "Where did you hear that, about Sven?"

"Long story. Somebody I met after you gave that talk at the Peabody said something to me, but I can't blame her. It played into certain... well... *fears* that I was having. The truth is, I've always been a little afraid of losing you to someone with more going on than I've got. I don't think little of you, Lotte. You're absolutely amazing! It's me I'm not so sure about."

To his surprise, she took his hand. "Let's sit down."

Together, they sat on the stonework surrounding the statue. It felt to Eric as if Oliver Sturman's outstretched finger followed him, pointing with accusation. He wondered what the charges would be — there were certainly any number of paths the prosecution could pursue — and whether he'd be judged guilty or innocent.

Lotte broke the brief silence. "I have to be honest. Sven did make a pass at me. I wasn't exactly surprised. I sort of got the vibe from him that he might try something like that."

"What did you do?"

"I shoved *this* in has face!" She held out her wedding ring. "I told him this may not mean anything to him, but it means *everything* to me. Utnapishtim is wrong. The rings *do* have power, as long as you believe in them. I believe in mine, Eric, and I made that clear to Sven."

"When was this? Why didn't he send you packing?"

"It happened sometime in July. The truth is, he took it quite well. Sven is opportunistic, and he definitely has a sweet tooth, but he knows when to back off. I actually think he had respect for what I said, and that it helped us forge a more professional relationship. He still took advantage of me, but not in *that* way."

"So, how did this happen? How did you get... like... pregnant?"

"Well, Eric, you know that thing we do from time to time? It can have certain consequences."

"Ha, ha, ha. You know what I mean. I thought we'd agreed, though, that you'd be... well... taking precautions."

"*Alter!* I was! I mean, I am. It was just so utterly *stupid*! You remember in late June I had to go to an interview for the position in Naples? I left my pills behind. If it's any consolation, I left all my toiletries. I didn't even have a toothbrush."

"Yeah, I remember finding that bag in the bathroom. I figured you'd pick up what you needed in Italy."

"Precisely, and for the most part that's what I did. I assumed it would just be a couple of days, but then Werner wanted me to pop up to Berlin, and it turned into almost a week. When I got back, I thought maybe I could squeak by. It's not like I haven't forgotten to take my pill once or twice before, and since we were about to be separated for who knows how long, I didn't want anything to mess up our fun." She flashed him a lusty smile. "Anyway, it was a terrible mistake. Serves me right for saying 'the hell with it' once too often. By August, I knew I was in trouble, so I took a test, and... well... the rest is history."

He sat for a time, stunned. "So, what do you want to do?"

"That's exactly what I've been trying to figure out. It's why I didn't talk to you. I felt like I needed to get my own thoughts in order first, but it's been absolutely impossible. Sven had me totally overloaded, which was fine because it made me valuable, and I learned so much. It was just a major distraction. It's more than that, though. I'm totally torn. I do want children, but now is such a lousy time for this to happen. It would be disastrous for my career. I just don't know how I'd manage finishing up my program while taking care of a child. I've tried like crazy, and I simply can't make up my mind. What do *you* want to do?"

He completely froze. *What do I want? That's the same stupid question I've been asking myself since I met you, and the only answer I've ever found is...* you! *How am I supposed to know what I want if you don't? How does anybody make decisions about stuff like this, or about anything? It feels like if you're not born with some kind of intrinsic motivation or passion, you just float in and out with the tide. That's me... driftwood. Why the hell are you asking me what —*

A strange sensation stopped the seemingly endless loop in Eric's mind, something... unexpected — a sort of calm, but one in which his heart raced with excitement. In times of stress, he would often think of something relaxing, something that made him happy in the most rudimentary and primal way, something that brought unconditional joy into his sometimes-gloomy existence.

He thought of his turtle.

"Langsam," he whispered.

"What about Langsam? She's with your mother, right? Is everything okay?"

"Oh, yeah, Langsam's fine. You're right, she's with my mother."

"So, what's the point of this?"

"That's exactly the point. She's with my mother. Langsam is with my mother, who had to drive to Boston to pick her up. She doesn't like driving into Boston. Too much traffic. I don't blame her. She's right. But she did it anyway. She did it for me."

"That was really nice of her."

"Wasn't it? That's the way she is. She's a nice person. She does things for other people. In fact, I can't think of the last thing she did for herself. I guess this substitute teaching she's started sort of qualifies, but even that's focused on helping people get better. She does it for others. I do that too. Being involved with Schneider, and I guess being a guy, I've always identified more with my dad... but he's ambitious. Not in a bad way, but he's driven, like you are. I'm just realizing, though, maybe I'm more like my mom. The things that make me happiest are the things I do for other people. I wouldn't even be working at Schneider now, certainly not full-time, if it hadn't been for Margot. I didn't want her and Keisha, and maybe others, to lose their jobs. When I thought about what I wanted to do in Germany, I thought of teaching. Helping people. Maybe that's who I am."

"I think that's *exactly* who you are. That's why I love you so. I call you my heart, and that's not a lie. I have to constantly remind myself there are actually other people in the room. You always put others before what you want, especially me. So, what are you trying to say?"

"I'm not sure. In a sense, I'm not trying to say anything. I just have this... *feeling*. The only thing I can compare it to is you. I want you so much. I don't give a crap about the consequences. We face almost certain death, but I might as well be dead if I couldn't be with you. I made that decision a long time ago, and it's just as valid now. So, there's not really all that much I want, but... I think I want this, Lotte. No, I *do* want this. It just *feels* right. This is what I'm built for. I don't know why — genetics, upbringing, warping my brain with too many horror films and video games as a kid, whatever — but I want this, and I'm willing to carry the load so you can have what you want too. I don't want you to sacrifice your career either. It won't be as easy, but people far less capable than us figure shit like this out. You asked me what I want to do, there it is."

She seemed astonished. "Are you certain?"

"I'm Pergamon Museum certain." The bronze statue gazing sternly down at him seemed to waver slightly, as if overridden by the invocation of a more august and supreme monument. "I've never wanted anything more in my life... except you."

"So, you're saying you want to have my baby?"

"Hey, I thought it was *our* baby!"

"I'm just joking, my love. It *is* our baby, or it will be. It will be our gorgeous baby. I just never imagined you'd react this way. You can't believe how this makes me feel. What a relief it is. I feared I'd destroyed everything by being so careless. It was ripping me apart. I felt like such an *idiot*! This is like a weight being lifted." She smiled slyly. "I knew I kept you around for some reason."

He just smiled back and took her into his arms. He too felt glad she kept him around, and that this time, the reason brought a sense of purpose to his life he'd never imagined possible.

Eric watched with fascination as the surreal vision of the Afrit's portal blazed to life once more.

He'd been exhausted, and assumed he could nap in the van with Olive while Lotte spoke with the creature through the gateway, something hitherto impossible until the ashen being had devoured Ninurta. He was surprised, however, when she told him she intended to summon the beast, and not just the little impish thing that had been taking periodic joyrides in their world. She wanted the entire monster in front of her, feeling that was the best way to plead her case, and she wanted him by her side.

Well, I'm awake now.

The tendrils of ash had just begun to emerge from the cloudy face of the ancient glass, when he noticed something amiss.

Lotte saw it too. She pointed at fiery orange streaks that wove and danced in the billowing cloud. "What is that? It looks like fire!"

As if in response to her words, sparks shot out with a fizzy pop from the undulating mass, and both of them jumped backward. This happened several more times, seemingly discharges of excess energy like lightning, before the tentacle of ash reached the large central bowl and the familiar swirling action commenced.

As the massive head and shoulders of the mysterious beast began to assemble, she exhibited even greater worry. Blazing streaks shone like molten lava through the thin, black veneer of the creature's skin, as if bulging veins and arteries made of fire coursed through its body.

"Maybe this wasn't such a good idea after all," Lotte said, "but it's too late to turn back now. Extinguishing the flames at this stage will trap a substantial portion of the Afrit in our world, and that would surely enrage the damned thing."

Eric steadied himself for whatever might come next.

In one sense, it was incredible. The monster, once fully formed, now stood more than eight feet tall. Its entire body rippled with the blazing energy of the Eternal Flame. Eyes once black as night now shone like tiny suns from under horns that pulsed from blue, to orange, to a hot yellow. A spiderweb of incandescent veins lit the creature's wings, and crackling discharges of sparks intermittently flew from its deadly barbed tail.

Eric's awe was tinged, however, by a reawakened fear, one he'd considered conquered though many previous encounters with the otherworldly being. This creature was different—unknown, unpredictable, and by appearance, decidedly more dangerous. He would have stepped in front of Lotte, tried to protect her, but he knew better. With this entity, she was *Sadat Alnaar*, Master of Fire, and his place was to be silent.

'What urgency drives you to call us forth?'

Eric could feel the power in the Afrit's inquiry, stronger than ever before.

'We warn you, that which you see is merely the surface of changes far more... pervasive. Trifle not with us. Our patience with your kind is now as minuscule as the space between our talons and the flesh of your throat.'

To his amazement, Lotte stepped forward. "Great Afrit! Our need is most assuredly dire. You know my mind. I would never summon you were it not of crucial importance. As before, a being from another realm endangers our world. He wishes merely to return to his home, but doing so will unleash the power of a terrible entity, one who is old and angry at having been betrayed. If not stopped, he will surely cause unspeakable damage to our world, and possibly yours. We have enlisted the aid of Enki, who you know. He asked for your assistance and deemed it critical to our success. As always, it will be dangerous, but once more, we call upon you to help us."

The towering beast flexed its bat's wings in the cramped space and swayed from side to side. *'Always the bargain, the exchange, the promise of reward that would bring us closer to our goal: to be whole, to be as we were before contact with this pitiable realm was forced upon us. It is no longer so. Behold! We are complete once more. Different, yes – unlike our former state, which we can hardly still conceive – but refashioned and made anew. The energy we now possess sustains us, and when in the presence of the Eternal Flame, we can resist any incursion. Your plight has nothing to do with us. We no longer have need of your paltry world.'*

Lotte stiffened. "With respect, that's not strictly so. You called me and demanded my service to periodically allow you to visit the Earth.

This is obviously important to you, and you risk losing that if you turn your back on us now."

Eric jumped as the terrible creature swiftly brought its face within inches of hers.

'*Do you threaten us,* Sadat Alnaar? *Do you dare withhold your ministrations in the hopes of bending us to your will?*'

She fiercely stood her ground. "No, great one! I merely speak the truth. If Anu, the being we fear so, gets loose, I can't estimate the devastation. It may be total. It's my honor to serve you, and I'll do it to the end of my days, but that end will almost surely come sooner if we're not able to keep him contained."

The monster pulled away and began its familiar swaying once more. When it spoke, Eric could almost sense a sadness in the emanations from its mind.

'*It is the new voice which speaks inside us. It creates an urge to see and do things we once considered irrelevant. Now, we visualize the colors that you once asked us about, hear sounds beyond the beatings of our dying victim's hearts. We yearn to experience more than the existence we know, just a taste, from time to time. That is enough to soothe and mollify, and to calm deeper inclinations which are not nearly as...* benign.'

"Ninurta's energy. It's changed you, as you say, in more ways than one."

'*It is a blessing and a curse. The power is incomparable, but we warned you, our forbearance is reduced, and our restraint limited. Should we lose control, once the killing starts, it is no longer clear where it might stop. Tempting as this has been to us at times, a bloodbath is not the end we seek, so these compulsions are vexing. Perhaps it is for the best. Never were we truly suited for this world. Now, with little to gain, a total separation may be fitting. Without access to your realm, our impulses would likely drive us mad, but what creature in any world does not possess at least a touch of madness? From what we have witnessed... none. We would exist, and perhaps that is the only thing of importance. So, what offer can you make,* Sadat Alnaar, *that would see us risk our existence once again?*'

She briefly glanced over her shoulder, a bewildered look on her face. "I... I don't know what to say. Your feelings have taken me by surprise. I had no idea. If your power is this great, there is little material worth I have to offer. I can't... I mean, I don't... that is, I just—"

'*It is as we thought,*' the creature said, turning toward the portal. '*You have nothing. We return to our realm. Trouble us no longer with your mortal concerns. We have enough woe of our own to last for eternity.*'

"Wait! There is something! The being who threatens to open the barrier keeping Anu at bay is named Iblis. He's a Jinn, apparently quite old and extremely powerful. We spoke with a man recently who knew of you, and he told us that Iblis is the one responsible for your presence here. He's the one who found you. I don't know all the details, but it seems he mistreated you in some way. The man we met, and his associates who saved you, protected you from Iblis, but they were never able to eliminate him. He's the one we're going after, and we have no intention of letting him survive. If you wish to take vengeance on the one who started all this, now is your opportunity."

The molten glow under the beast's skin pulsed as it stood, immobilized. Slowly, it turned to cast its fiery gaze back toward Lotte, who looked pathetically tiny as she stood in the monster's hulking shadow.

'Iblis. Never did we know his name. Yes, he caused us great suffering. Parts of us languish still in some forgotten place, trapped as we once were, until you had the judgment and courage to free us. We have forgotten neither your clemency nor his cruelty – both have shaped us. Where is he now, this Iblis?'

"In a country far from here. If you choose to join us, it would be difficult, but we can transport your gateway to this place and call you forth."

'That is unnecessary. Long can we now linger in your world. Our energy reserves are vast.'

"So, you'll come?"

'It is ignoble, but to see Iblis pay for his misdeeds entices us. That we might save this world in which we have, to our endless wonder, found some minimal qualities of redemption, is perhaps of peripheral benefit. Let us fly free. Go to this faraway land, and we will follow. The death of Iblis, and if possible, our consumption of his energy, will be our bargain. Let the rings bind –

"No!" Lotte shouted. "No rings!"

"What are you doing?" Eric asked, shocked. "No rings, no bargain. That's the way Chuckles has operated for centuries. Why interfere with that now?"

"Because it's a lie, and it's time to end it. If we're going to establish true trust with such an alien mind, it has to be built on a foundation of honesty." She turned her attention to the seemingly bemused Afrit. "Great one, the power behind these rings is long gone. Those who you once called 'judges' exist no longer. They died by Iblis's hand. It would be wrong to let you think they still protect you, or that they will sit in judgment if we somehow fail each other. It simply isn't true. We're on our own. I'm bound to this agreement by my word, and I'll do everything in my limited power to see Iblis dead. If you ever feel I've done otherwise, I put myself at your mercy. I just want you to trust me, like I trust you, and trust isn't built on a falsehood. You're free to choose, always a difficult thing, but your choice shouldn't be colored by inaccurate information."

'You wear a ring... two, in fact, both intertwined. One looks like the doorway through which we traverse realms. Its colors we have never noticed until now. They are vibrant, unlike other things in the nature of this world. Does your ring have power?'

Lotte gave a soft laugh. "It does, but the power isn't magical. It's symbolic. It's a representation of Eric's and my love for one another. Our rings have meaning to us, and they do bind us, but the strength behind them is in our minds. They're physical manifestations of our beliefs, our convictions, and our trust in one another."

'Then let our rings so bind us. You have proven your word in the past and done things no other we have witnessed would have attempted. Let us now seek Iblis together. The taste of his blood is already sweet in our mouth.'

CHAPTER 17

Eric navigated the surprisingly sturdy Pajero 4x4 up the dirt track that passed for a road in this remote area. The darkness of night enveloped them, hindering their progress, but fortunately, they didn't have far to go.

The Majlis al Jinn was only about an hour inland from the Tiwi beach, where they had recently rendezvoused with Enki. The great god had located them easily when they waded into the surf and reached out to him. Now, he sat in the back seat, adorned in a white *dishdasha* and a red-checked *keffiyeh*, which obscured his somewhat unusual appearance in case they were stopped for some reason.

Once out of the range of the small settlement of Fins, they stopped the car so Lotte could light a lantern, the signal for the ashen creature to come forth. It was hardly necessary. The beast had been tracking her for days as they laboriously trekked halfway across the globe. It already waited nearby. All trace of the flame in the Afrit's body had disappeared, likely suppressed intentionally so it could meld with the darkness of the night sky.

Enki expressed pleasure. *'We meet once more, creature of fire. Odd that beings whose realms are in opposition would forge and maintain an alliance. It gratifies me.'*

'You honor your word,' the Afrit dourly replied, *'and again, we seek the same outcomes, though each for reasons of our own. May we once again enjoy the fortune to meet with a similar result... for the most part.'*

The monster glared at Lotte.

"What the hell is *that* all about?" she asked, confused.

"Who cares," Eric replied, knowing full well the Afrit spoke of his hope to avoid a repeat of her death, as it had occurred two years ago, and which Eric still hadn't told her about. "Let's just get going. We may be too late already."

It had taken them two days to work out all the arrangements for this trip. The visas couldn't be finalized until Monday, which meant flights couldn't be booked until then. They'd finally gotten out on Tuesday night, and after losing Wednesday to the flight and the eight-hour time difference, they spent most of Thursday resting and securing their SUV before driving from Muscat to Tiwi. They couldn't assemble with their supernatural associates until after dark. So much valuable time had been consumed.

The travel logistics hadn't been the only obstacle. In addition to having endured the inevitable "told you so" from Margot, who dutifully cancelled Eric's appointments for the next two weeks, Siddique, who had finally been released from the hospital on Sunday, had desperately wanted to come along, and had hounded Eric when he met up with him at the hospital.

"You're gonna need me, man. Even if it's just to drive, or whatever. Something will come up. I'm fine, really."

"You're not fine," Eric protested. "You still have a bandage around your head and the doctors told you to take it easy. You got hit with a block of concrete. You're lucky to be alive. Now's not the time to be fighting interdimensional monsters. Anyway, it's the same as before. If we fail, and something happens to us, someone is gonna have to go to the authorities."

"And tell them what? An ancient sky god is coming, and he's pissed off, so they better get out the nukes? They'd think I'm crazy and lock me up. What good would I do from the loony bin?"

"They'll believe you when the shit starts hitting the fan. You have details that might be important. Plus, we need you to do something else. I hate to ask you this, but we just couldn't see any way around it, and you need to know what's going on."

It crushed Eric's soul to tell Siddique that he wasn't certain Olive could be trusted. The misery felt almost as bad as it had been to listen to her howls of agony in that van ride back from New Hampshire. They had no idea if Lotte's idea with the amulet would work, but if enough of Aicha still remained inside Olive and got control, it could spell disaster for their plans to stop Iblis. She needed to be monitored, subtly, but almost completely, and there was nobody else to do it. He and Lotte would have their hands full and couldn't watch her all the time.

After the explanation, Siddique shook his head and said, "Shit man, poor Olive. Where will she stay?"

"Your place. It's small, so you can keep an eye on her more easily. When she wakes up, we'll tell her our landlord is coming home and would be confused by people staying in our apartment, which is at least sort of true. Make like you need help for a few days, but if she goes out, you'll have to go with her."

"What about the bathroom? I can't go in there with her."

"Yeah, I know. Watch to see if she takes her phone in with her. If she does... I don't know. You'll just have to play it by ear. Do whatever you think is best. Believe me, this is the last thing I want to be asking you, but for now, this is our only hope."

Olive had been equally resistant when she awoke from her magically induced slumber on Monday, and had pestered Eric in the car all the way to Siddique's apartment that afternoon.

"This sucks! Pardon my French, but I don't think talkin' to stupid authorities makes the best use of my God-given talents... especially with an AR-15. I want revenge on these damn things for what they did to me! It don't hurt no more, I swear. Enki fixed me right up, although I do still remember all that pain in my head. That part's still kinda awful. Then Lotte said I should never take this dang necklace off... ever again! Do you know what that's gonna be like? Just when I get rid of that rotten ol' tattoo, now I get this boat anchor to wear. Won't that be enticing? Not!"

Eric chuckled. "We might be able to figure out something else. There's just not time right now. I know it stinks, but this really is for the best. Remember, Siddique is there for you as much as you're there for him. If you feel funny in any way, let him know."

"Funny, huh? Yeah, I'll be a real comedian, locked up in that little place with him... sleeping on his dang couch while you two are out saving the universe. I don't like you no more, Eric Schneider. I don't like you one bit."

Eric snorted a little laugh at the memory of his friend's words as the Pajero cleared a steep incline. He knew she wasn't serious about not liking him. She was just venting. As with Siddique, she wanted in on the action. He wondered if they truly understood the consequences, but that could be said of Lotte as well. There had been a moment in the airport when he'd stopped her, held her from stepping forward as they'd slogged through the interminable boarding line.

"Are you sure this is such a good idea in your... condition? Maybe you should just stay home."

"The Afrit will be looking for me," she coolly explained. "I can't back out. Plus, you know full well this is what I live for. This is why the decision was so incredibly hard. I want a child, but I'm not willing to give up my life, and this is a part of my life — a really big part. I wouldn't miss seeing this for the world, and if we're needed, then it's both of our duties to be there. That's my bargain with the Afrit, and I intend to honor it. I'll be careful. I promise."

Like you were on that beach in South Carolina? It doesn't work that way, sweetheart. I wish it did, but things happen that we can't anticipate, can't control — even you.

Unfortunately, the matter was settled. She wasn't going to change her mind, ever. This was her life, and by extension, his. His only solace came in knowing that within this odd and dangerous rubric, he now had a role to play, which brought him a sense of genuine happiness. He hoped they'd both live to enjoy their distinct, yet intertwined, desires.

The 4x4 rocked slightly as the Afrit landed on the roof with remarkable delicacy given its hulking appearance. It had chosen to fly ahead while those in the SUV crawled toward their destination. The creature's head appeared in the open passenger's window as it conversed with Lotte.

"It wants us to stop," she announced. "It says there's a turnoff just ahead that leads to a small settlement, but the road there is guarded. They also appear to have rounded up all the villagers. Two, or perhaps more, are holding them in a walled area behind a house. This isn't good."

"I thought Aicha said Iblis liked to work alone," Eric bleakly observed as he pulled the Pajero to the side of the road and shut off the lights. "I guess you make exceptions when the stakes are high enough. What does Chuckles want us to do?"

The Afrit answered, apparently ignoring Eric's quip. *'To the other side of the buildings, illumination comes forth from the ground. This is where we must go, but should you travel farther, you will surely be seen.'*

"Can you... well... how do I put this... *incapacitate* the people watching the road?" Lotte asked.

'They are in a vehicle similar to yours. We can eliminate the hazard they pose, but there will be noise, and there are more of them than we can eliminate in a single strike. They will likely retaliate with their weapons.'

"That definitely won't work. If you make as much noise as you did when you rammed into Blake Harris's SUV, they'll hear you all the way in bloody Muscat."

'That is a great distance. We are unlikely to create such a disturbance.'

She did a facepalm. "I was being facetious... never mind. The problem is, if these people sense trouble, they might start threatening to harm the villagers. We may have to deal with that first, but we obviously can't just drive up there. We need to get closer, try to get a better sense of what's going on."

'There is a building outside the village. It is dark and appears empty. From there, you can observe more. It is not far. You can walk, or we can transport you by air.'

'There may be Jinn amongst them or flying above,' Enki interjected from the back seat. *'They cannot see you for your stealth and camouflage, but encumbered with one of us you may be detected. You claim it is not far. We will walk from here.'*

"All right," Eric said. "Hold on a minute, though." He carefully drove the SUV farther off the road, where it was less likely to be seen, then went to the back of the vehicle, opened the hatchback, and retrieved the tire iron from under the floor of the cargo space.

This may not do jack shit, but it makes me feel better having it.

The three cautiously navigated the road in the darkness of the desert night. Eric found the canopy of stars in this isolated and desolate area even more impressive than it had been in the mountains of New Hampshire.

The Afrit guided them, swooping down periodically and kissing their minds with the barest whisper, *'This way.'* Before they reached the turnoff to the village, the ashen creature stopped them. *'Depart the road here and cut across this open terrain. It will be rough, but we will direct you, and you will not be seen by human eyes. We will stay alert for Jinn. They may be impossible to detect until it is too late, but we see no other way.'*

Enki managed the topography without difficulty, even wearing only the light slippers they had purchased in Muscat, but Lotte and Eric stumbled in the dry, rocky dirt. Eric worried about snakes and scorpions, Jinn or not. They were a long way from a hospital, and with so little water around, the Lord of the Abzu's powers would be severely limited—healing completely out of the question.

The Afrit guided them into higher terrain, well to the north of the road, where they would avoid being seen or heard. Upon cresting a rise, the light the Afrit had mentioned came into view. A mysterious blue-green glow radiated from three fissures in the earth. The nearest loomed near the small settlement that had grown up next to the great cave. Electric lights and parked vehicles indicated some sort of encampment had been established around this cleft in the earth.

The Majlis al Jinn, one of the largest underground caves on Earth, measured over 1,000 feet by nearly 750 feet, with a domed ceiling rising almost 600 feet at its highest point. There were only three entrances, great gouges in the surface formed by water seeping through the limestone below. Eric recalled the map he'd looked at, and figured the camp was set up around "First Drop," the shortest descent at just a bit less than 400 feet, and the one closest to the road and the village.

As they walked down the slope, dim illumination backlit the structures of the tiny settlement to their right, which appeared to be merely a cluster of six or eight houses and sheds. He didn't even see the building they were headed toward until it was upon them, a mere hundred yards or so from both the village and the encampment around First Drop. The Afrit took a position on the roof while Eric and the others cautiously observed from around a corner.

About a half-dozen men milled about, a few near the road, two spread out at points near the ledge of the opening, and two or three more near the back of a large truck with a canvas-covered cargo bed. A thick metal cable extended from the back of the vehicle, held taught as it descended from the tailgate to the ground, and then into the maw of the glowing hole. The sputtering coughs of a generator came from behind the truck, and electric lamps on poles were interspersed throughout the area. A Jeep, two black SUVs, and a ubiquitous white van were also parked nearby.

"Well, we're not getting in that way," Lotte observed. "We'd have to neutralize all those guards, and I can't imagine that happening without making noise."

"So, what do we do? Should we just have the Afrit fly us down one of the other openings?"

'There may be more men below,' Enki cautioned. *'If they see us and raise the alarm, the ones above will hear, as well as those in the village watching the prisoners. We must investigate.'*

The great god mentally whispered for the Afrit, and soon, the ashen creature landed softly behind them.

Enki said, *'Where the light emits from the larger fissure just over there, away from the encampment, can you fly inside without risking detection and report back to us with what you see?'*

Without answering, the beast took silently to the air.

'While it is gone, I will determine the situation in the village. Stay here and make no noise. Both the Afrit and I shall return shortly.'

Enki shed the garments he wore, down to a pair of sleek briefs Lotte had the foresight, and the modesty, to purchase in Muscat. He scampered from behind the house and into the darkness.

They waited wordlessly, the distant thrumming of the generator the only sound. Without warning, the Afrit landed gracefully nearby and furled its bat-like wings.

'There is much illumination in the cave. Its source is deeper within. We could not fly past where the opening gives way to the curvature of the roof lest we risk being seen, so we could take in only that which was directly below. There are three men, perhaps more beyond our view, all armed. There is too much light and too great a distance to travel for us to take them by surprise. They will fire their weapons and the result will be as the Goat-Man stated. Those on the surface will hear.'

Enki returned shortly thereafter, and they related what the Afrit had told them.

He nodded. *'It is as I feared. Those below will need to be neutralized, and that shall not be easy, nor silent. If you value the lives of the innocents who are held hostage, they must first be freed.'*

"What did you see?" Lotte asked.

'They are detained in a walled enclosure behind a house, perhaps twenty in all, including women and children. There are two guards that I could see, though another may be inside. While I watched from over the wall, one of them brought a prisoner inside, then brought them out again.'

"They seem to be letting them use the bathroom. That might be an opportunity. If you snuck inside the house, do you think you could surprise one guard? If we take him prisoner, maybe the other will surrender as well."

The Afrit gruffly interrupted. *'Why do we not simply terminate these petty inconveniences? With the aid of the Goat-Man, it would be a simple matter to accomplish. None of those whose lives you value would be lost.'*

"That's a very kind offer, great one," Lotte said with the utmost decorum. "That would definitely solve our most immediate problem, but it would create quite a stir among those we're trying to rescue and generate a lot of questions I'd really like to avoid, if possible. Let's keep that as a Plan B, shall we?"

'*As you wish,* Sadat Alnaar.'

'*In answer to your query,*' Enki continued, '*I could unquestionably isolate and subdue one guard with ease when they go inside. I will, however, need someone with me to keep the prisoner from panicking and raising alarm.*'

Eric realized all eyes were suddenly on him. "Umm... that would be me, wouldn't it? Yeah, okay, I can do that. What could possibly go wrong? I mean, a god is on my side, right?"

Despite the minor encumbrance, Lotte convinced Enki to put his clothes back on as this would hide his unusual, scaled skin. When the great god had dressed, Eric gave Lotte a quick kiss and turned to leave, but then stopped.

"We have so many moments like this, times I'm not sure we'll ever see each other again, or at least where we're aware of that possibility. I mean, I know in reality I could be walking down the street and get hit by an ambulance at any moment."

"An ambulance? I thought it was hit by a *bus*?"

"Yeah, it is normally. I've gotten to sort of like *ambulance* better. Anyway, you know what I'm talking about. Anything can happen at any time, but it's probably *way* more likely to happen now than on a typical day that I go to work, and you go to school. We go through this so often, though, that it starts to seem, I don't know... *normal*, I guess. Despite the casual kiss, I just want you to know how much I love you and how happy I am, even with all the craziness in our lives."

Her face dissolved into a pensive smile. "I know. Believe me, I know that very well. In situations like these, there's never time to express everything, but trust me, I feel exactly the same. Now give me another casual kiss and go save the world."

"With pleasure."

He felt better for having given voice, however briefly, to the growing realization that he accepted, and was satisfied with, their unusual existence together. He'd said it as much for his own benefit as hers, an acknowledgement that henceforth he would at least try to find happiness within the seemingly endless maelstrom of turmoil. Smiling, he joined Enki and they slipped into the darkness.

The wait seemed interminable. Though cool outside, the cramped little house felt stifling, windows still shuttered and holding in the heat of the day. It was well past midnight now. Eric guessed they'd been hiding behind some furniture in the darkened living room for close to an hour after slipping through the unlocked, and unmonitored, front door.

At least they're not expecting company.

A window in the kitchen at the rear of the house looked out on the enclosed area where the villagers had been herded. They sat forlornly near the stonework wall probably eight feet high, too tall for them to climb, in an area lit by a spotlight from the porch. Two men wearing black fatigues and armed with Uzi submachine guns and other weapons monitored the prisoners.

A hallway led off to the right of the living room, illuminated by a light that had presumably been left on in the bathroom. There didn't appear to be anyone in the house. That was the good news. The bad news was, nobody had been taken inside to pee, and it wasn't clear if, or when, that might occur.

If this goes on much longer, I'll need to pee.

As if summoning the God of Urination by speaking its name, the door to the kitchen swung open and two people entered—a woman followed by one of the guards. He shut the door, then motioned with his gun for her to move toward the lighted hallway. She deferentially hurried inside and disappeared down the corridor.

The guard followed but seemed to stop in the hall. His shadow silhouetted the wall and floor of the living room. He called out something in Arabic, but his prisoner didn't respond.

With catlike stealth, Enki crept toward the hallway, put his back to the wall near the corridor's entrance, and peered around the corner. In the blink of an eye, the Lord of the Abzu vanished. For a brief instant, shadows flickered with movement. Then, all was still. Finally, the guard emerged, held immobile by the great god, one lanky but superhumanly powerful arm securing his torso, and a scaled hand across his mouth.

'*Come!*' he hissed. '*Quickly disarm this one, then take position in the passageway for when the woman emerges.*'

Eric did as instructed, leaving his tire iron behind the old sofa where they'd been hiding, for fear it might unnecessarily frighten the prisoner. After relieving the immobilized guard of his Uzi and pistol, he moved softly down the hall toward the open door of the bathroom. He heard running water, then the sound of footsteps.

The woman emerged, and he grabbed her firmly but not aggressively by the upper arm, then brought his other hand to his lips, motioning for silence.

The woman gasped with surprise and started to pull away, but he loosened his grip, forced his face close, and whispered, "*Shhhhhh....*" He tried to be as reassuring as possible.

She looked past him and seemed to register that the guard was no longer in the corridor. This calmed her, and she ceased her struggle.

"Can you understand me?" he asked.

"Little English," she answered, her accent thick. "You help me?"

Remembering his own pathetically limited ability in conversational German, he tried to keep things simple. "Yes... help you. We capture guard... you safe. I go to my friend. You come, but very quiet... *shhhhhh.*"

She nodded in understanding.

He guided her back to the living room where Enki had dragged the guard near the front door, well away from the kitchen and the back of the house.

'*You did well,*' he said as they approached. The god had pulled his *keffiyeh* across his chin, hiding from the unwitting guard that his lips didn't move when he spoke. '*I have impressed upon our captive that his life is in my hands. Like the other watching the villagers, he is a local mercenary, hired by a man he knows only as* The Turk *— not Iblis, but one of his chief minions who arrived with other foreigners under his command. These men likely serve the Jinn with greater avidity. It is unlikely they will be as tractable, but our prisoner says he has no wish to die. He will try to convince his comrade to drop his weapons and let the hostages go.*

"Okay, what's the plan?"

'*Stay behind with the woman, out of sight. I will take this one outside to negotiate. If this fails, you will need to watch him while I dispatch the other. I hope it does not come to this, as we will lose our element of surprise and there may be risk to the prisoners, but we shall portage that vessel should necessity dictate. Make ready.*'

Eric returned the woman to the hallway and instructed her to stay low in case the bullets started to fly. He then took a position behind a counter that faced the kitchen, where he could see and hear what happened through the door and window.

The great god directed the captive guard to open the door, and both walked out onto the porch. At first, the other guard didn't appear to notice, but then the man Enki restrained called out.

A highly agitated conversation ensued. The other man stood in the middle of the enclosed space between the porch and the clustered prisoners near the wall. He hefted his weapon, shouting in Arabic, though he quickly softened his tone when it became obvious his companion's life was in jeopardy.

Back and forth the discussion ping-ponged, frustratingly all in a tongue Eric couldn't understand, so he had no idea what they said.

At one point, however, Enki spoke, and his words coalesced in Eric's mind. *'You fear I will kill you if you drop your weapons. You know it not, but you are already dead. If the man who pays you is successful in his endeavors, all here will perish. He has no incentive to keep these villagers alive, save as bait to entice a power you cannot begin to fathom to come forth and feed. Those who serve him may successfully flee, but I venture that you and others hired as mercenaries will share these people's fates. I offer you the only chance you possess. Feel the sincerity of my words and choose wisely.'*

The man hesitated briefly, then dropped his submachine gun, reached for his holster, and tossed his pistol aside.

'Excellent. I will take charge of you while my servant directs the villagers to safety.'

Hey! Eric thought, slightly stung. *Servant? And to think, when I spoke to that woman, I called you my* friend.

Eric strode through the kitchen and opened the back door to join Enki on the porch, but the second he did, a man rapidly emerged from the cluster of prisoners, grabbed the pistol from the ground, and started firing. It happened so quickly, Eric could barely process what he saw, and Enki was unable to react in time. At near point-blank range, even a rank amateur couldn't miss, and this captive seemed to have some experience with guns. The hapless guard clutched at his chest and neck from two bullets, then his head exploded in a haze of gore from one final shot.

Without hesitating, the man turned toward Enki and the other guard and raised the pistol. Most of the other prisoners began to wail in distress. They cowered into the corners of their makeshift prison, but a lone woman ran out from amongst them. She wrapped her arms around the man's waist and fell to her knees, crying hysterically.

Eric hit the deck. *Well, so much for surprise! What the hell is going on?*

It appeared Enki had the same question.

'You fool! Why have you done this? You put your life and those of your settlement in tremendous peril. Drop your weapon immediately!'

The man shot back an angry response in Arabic.

"What did he say?" Eric desperately asked.

'He says he will take revenge on all those who... who killed his baby.'

"What?"

"That is right!" the man screamed, this time in English. "I'll have all their heads for what they did! Why? How could someone do such a horrible thing? A woman, no less! She smiled as my precious son died in her arms. Allah forgive me for what I have done, and what I must do, but these monsters must die!"

Eric didn't disagree with this poor man's assessment, but he definitely took issue with the thoughtless method of extracting justice that put everyone else in great danger. They were in the soup now, though, so they had to act fast. Throwing caution to the wind, he joined Enki where he stood, interposed between the man with the gun and the remaining guard.

'This guard says he has no knowledge of what occurred,' Enki explained. *'He says that it happened before he was tasked with watching the villagers. He has seen a woman. She rides with a man he describes as* The Scarred One. *Surely, this would be Iblis.'*

"Do you know who the woman is?"

'I may, but there is no time to explain. The other warriors are surely on their way. Hold our captive. I will subdue the man with the gun.'

Another shot rang out and Enki staggered backward, clutching at his shoulder. The guard he held slipped free and bolted back inside but stopped short when the woman he'd left inside the house emerged, holding the surrendered pistol that had been left in the living room.

Nicely done!

Eric gave a quick glance at the injured god, who seemed more surprised than seriously injured, then he turned his attention to the man in the courtyard with the gun.

"Stop! If you want revenge on these people, we'll help you, but we've got like thirty seconds before all those guards at the cave entrance are here. They're the ones you want, not this guy, and certainly not the person you just shot! We could have taken them by surprise, but now they know something's up. All these people have to get out of here, right now. Otherwise, it's gonna be a massacre. Believe me... I'm a father too, or I will be, soon. I understand how you feel, but you've put everyone's life at risk. Let's focus on getting them to safety first, then we'll get your revenge. Trust me."

He'd walked toward the man, then stopped just a few feet away, staring into his anguished eyes. The woman at his feet, his wife presumably, had stopped crying. Only the repeated squelch of the dead guard's walkie-talkie, followed by some frantic words in Arabic on the device's speaker, broke the silence.

"I trust you," the man finally said, lowering his gaze. "I have behaved shamefully, put others at risk. My grief and anger have consumed me. If what you say is true, I am unfit to carry on. Do what Allah brought you here to do, and may he have mercy on my soul."

He pointed the pistol at his chin.

Enki's fist appeared like a bolt of lightning. It came from seemingly nowhere and struck with a loud snap. The gun flew from the man's hand, and he collapsed to the ground, wincing in agony and clutching his likely broken wrist.

'*Be gone!*' Enki commanded. '*All of you, while there is still time!*' He turned his attention to the man's wife as she frantically attended to her husband. '*He is fortunate I did not kill him for his imprudence. Assist him and flee this place. Perhaps the pain will clear his mind and when this is over, you can begin your lives anew. Hard as that may be, it is the way of things. The prospect of such an outcome is the sole gift I have to offer.*'

She didn't need to be told twice. With the aid of another woman, they helped the injured and distraught man to his feet, then joined the others who streamed out of a side gate in the wall.

"Thanks for the rescue," Eric said. "I didn't anticipate that what I said to him would have that effect."

'*You spoke from your heart, as one who understands what a loss of that nature truly entails. I did not know you expected a child. My heart floods with joy. Now, however, we must hasten.*'

Truer words were never spoken, as just at that moment, a Jeep sped by the open gate, headlights illuminating the area to the north where the villagers fled.

Enki turned toward the porch where the guard still stood, immobilized by the woman with the pistol. '*You must choose! Join with us or run out of this gate and take your chances with those you serve... those who may be angered that you failed in your assignment. Betray me, however, and your death is assured.*'

To Eric's surprise, the guard didn't hesitate. He spoke some brief words in Arabic, and the woman next to him lowered her pistol.

Enki nodded. '*Excellent. Take the woman and run to the front of the house. Your other weapon is there. Let no one enter.*' He turned to Eric, pointing to the submachine gun that lay on the ground near them. '*Take that weapon and watch the gate. Hold out here while I dispatch those pursuing the villagers. I shall return as quickly as possible.*'

The great god vaulted with superhuman power over the wall in pursuit of the vehicle. Eric grabbed the dangerous-looking little Uzi, which he had no idea how to operate, and ran toward the gate. Suddenly, a scream and the crackle of machine gun fire rose from inside the house.

Shit!

Unsure what to do, he scurried back to the porch and peered inside. He heard a noise and saw shadows from down the corridor toward the bathroom. Then, another shot rang out, this time a pistol. In response, another short burst rattled from a machine gun, and he heard the sound of falling plaster and splintered wood, followed by a man angrily shouting in Arabic. He appeared to be in the hallway.

Eric crawled into the kitchen and stole a quick glance past the counter and down the corridor. The first thing he saw was the original guard, the man who had just agreed to help them, lying on his back in pool of blood. Beyond him, a new man, also wearing black fatigues and similarly armed, stood by an open doorway into a darkened room at the end of the hall past the bathroom. Eric was just bringing his gun into position for a shot when the woman appeared, hands above her head.

Shit! Now What?

He couldn't risk shooting for fear of hitting the recaptured prisoner. *Wait a minute....*

He put down the gun, scampered into the living room, and quickly dove behind the couch, hoping the man was too busy securing his captive to notice. The tire iron rested where he'd left it, so he grabbed it and moved silently and swiftly to the entrance of the corridor where Enki had stood earlier. The guard's dead body lay at his feet, riddled with bullet wounds. His empty eyes stared at the ceiling while blood oozed from the side of his mouth.

The woman emerged first, pushed roughly forward by the soldier who kept a firm grip on her *hijab*.

Eric wasn't sure what propelled him—anger, fear, desperation? Perhaps all of those. It didn't register consciously, but the threat of the man's weapons must have helped to guide Eric's strike. Somewhere in his mind he knew a blow to the arm or shoulder would hurt but wouldn't ensure incapacitation. For that, he had to aim for the head, and he had to put some force into it, which he did.

The sound sickened him, a dull *whump* as the heavy iron drove into the man's black-checked *keffiyeh*.

He crumpled without a sound, dropping his weapon and releasing the startled woman.

Together, she and Eric stared down as blood began to stain the headdress and dripped down the man's cheek to the floor.

"You kill him," she whispered.

He nodded. *I kill him. That's what I did. With my own hands, I kill him. What have I done? I wonder if he had a wife and children.*

He had no further time to mourn, as fresh bursts of machine gun fire split the silence of the desert night. They came from north and south but didn't seem to be near the house where he and the woman, whose name he didn't even know, now shared space with two dead bodies, with another in the courtyard.

Fearing to return to his position near the back wall, he stationed the woman by the counter to monitor kitchen entrance with her commandeered pistol, while he kept an eye on out the open front door. For a time, the fighting sounded distinctly fierce, full of guns firing, shouting, and at one point even an explosion. The noises coming from the north ceased first, then slowly those in the direction Eric monitored became fewer, until finally all grew still.

Into the dim light, a figure rounded the corner of the large building that abutted the house to the south. The person appeared unarmed and walked unhurriedly toward the front door.

Eric readied his weapon, but put it away when he realized Enki stood before him on the threshold. He'd lost his slippers and *keffiyeh*, and his beautiful white *dishdasha* was tattered from the impact of multiple bullets and drenched with blood. A mortal would not have survived such wounds, and even the Lord of the Abzu seemed drained of energy after the engagement.

Still, he smiled and extended his hand. *'Come. Together, the creature of fire and I have dealt with the menace of Iblis's minions. It is now time to complete the task that called us here, should it still be within our capacity to do so.'*

CHAPTER 18

"*Malaikah,*" the woman whispered as Enki walked away.

Damn, Eric cursed. *Didn't mean for her to see that. Oh well, too late now.* "Sorry, I don't understand that word."

"*Malaikah...* angel. Very bad wounds, but he lives. Is he... angel? Or is he God?"

He laughed. "Not your god. He's kind of... well... *retired.* He's just here to help clean up a big mess."

"I... I not understand."

"Neither do I, really. I can't explain—too complicated, too hard. Go. Join your people and hide. Still danger here. Forget what you saw. Forget him. Forget... *me.*"

Understanding slowly came to her. She brushed his cheek with her hand. "You save us... I think. I go. I say nothing... but I *not* forget. Never forget." She turned and exited through the kitchen and out the rear gate, not looking back.

He spied the tire iron where it lay beside the dead soldier's body, and reluctantly went to retrieve it. The object hung heavy in his hand. He felt stupid for not really thinking through the ramifications of bringing it along, that it would in all likelihood become the agent of dealing death, which it had with alarming efficiency. He realized that the consequences of this action would ripple on, like a haunting, but still he swung the strap of the Uzi he wielded over his shoulder.

I don't really know how to use the damn thing, but if we get into another fight this is probably more effective than a tire iron.

Now that he was in, it felt difficult to step back out, perhaps impossible.

He jogged to catch up with Enki, who had disappeared past the large building. As he rounded the corner, the remnants of the battle came into sight. Dead bodies lay in the street. The overturned husk of a vehicle smoldered near the roadside. He saw the great god silhouetted in the light from the encampment near First Drop. Beyond, the Afrit and Lotte conversed near the large canvas-covered truck. He rushed to join them, but his heart sank as he approached.

The Afrit's wings were in tatters, one almost completely severed. A large gouge had also been ripped from the beast's abdomen and upper leg. The creature wobbled as it fought to stand erect.

Lotte cried out when she saw him. "Eric, there you are! Help me build a fire. The Afrit's badly injured."

The ashen creature glowered at Eric as he ran to her side. "What happened?"

"It was awful. You wouldn't have believed it. After we heard the shots, the whole camp started going crazy. A couple of men jumped in a Jeep and sped off in your direction, but then a bunch more followed on foot. We had to make a call. I told the Afrit that you and Enki could probably handle those first two and to go after the others. He took a couple of them by surprise, but some of these men were trained mercenaries, well-armed and wearing night vision goggles. They took defensive positions and started firing. Their bullets shredded the Afrit's wings so that it could barely fly."

"What about that big hole in its side?"

"It just got worse from there. The men in the SUV, who were watching the road, showed up. They started shooting as well, so the Afrit was caught in a crossfire. It decided to dive down and take out the vehicle. It smashed through the back window and was fighting with the men inside, when one of them got out and tossed a bloody hand grenade under the car! The explosion virtually blew off one wing and a chunk of the Afrit's body. Then even more men arrived from the camp. I think some of them had been in the cave below and had come up on some kind of elevator. They just started blasting the SUV to pieces, and the Afrit couldn't fly away."

"Jeez, what happened?"

'The Goat-Man interceded,' the Afrit testily replied. *'He is swift, and they did not expect the threat he posed. With their attention turned to him, we were able to slip away. Soon, our adversaries were trapped between us, and we defeated them, though as you can see it cost us both. Far easier it would have been to do as we had originally suggested. Is our visage so horrifying, and knowledge of our existence so blasphemous, that those you deem* innocents *should never gaze upon us, even if we bring them salvation?'*

Lotte went to the creature and put her hands on its chest. "Great one, this is my doing. I know the consequences for you were grave, but the ignorance and prejudice of humankind knows no bounds. Twenty credible people witnessing you in action would raise questions that would be extremely difficult to answer, and threaten the secrecy that protects us all. In the end, widespread knowledge of your existence could be more devastating to you than bullets or exploding grenades. I judged it safer to take this course. If you wish to blame someone, blame me."

The pathetic remains of the monster's wings twitched as it swayed ever so slightly, though whether from consideration, or the result of its weakened structure, Eric couldn't determine.

Finally, it turned and stumbled away. *'All will be moot should we fail to stop Iblis. Let us put this aside and focus on what must be done. Produce flame so we can heal to the best of our ability.'*

Enki came to stand by Lotte and Eric. *'Its consciousness is troubled. Ninurta's energy burns brightly within. The creature is no longer at home by its Eternal Flame, nor can it find solace here. It is trapped between two realms, and I know not how it will resolve this conflict. As with so many things, the consequences of feeding my ungovernable nephew to the creature could not be foreseen. Build the fire as it wishes, but do so quickly. Time grows ever shorter.'*

In the white van, they found three large wooden crates, two long and thin, another squat and squarish, which had been emptied of their contents. The boards and straw packing material served well to create a fire quickly, which the Afrit used to dematerialize into glittering ash, then to reform and repair parts of its broken body. It still couldn't fly, but it stabilized the gouge in its abdomen, and appeared ready to continue, expressing hope that Iblis's energy would restore its wings.

While the creature completed its repairs, and Enki meditated, Lotte and Eric gaped over the ledge of the drop into the cave.

The thick metal wire that trailed from the back of the covered truck connected to a coupler from which four sturdy cables extended. Not unlike the basket in Metéora, each of these attached to one corner of a roughly five-foot-long, rectangular, treaded aluminum platform with a chain-linked railing. The apparatus hung just a short drop from the ledge.

"*Scheiße!*" Lotte moaned. "This looks familiar. There's probably a winch in the truck to raise and lower the lift. They must have pulled up the platform when the fighting started. We'll have to use this to get to the bottom, since the Afrit can't fly, but there may still be soldiers down there."

"Great! Can't wait to get more blood on my hands."

"What are you talking about? Did something happen? Did you have to kill one of those men who drove toward you and Enki?"

He nodded, hefting the tire iron for emphasis.

"That must be awful. I mean... we've been party to deaths before, responsible for them, really, but it's different when it's by your own hand, isn't it?"

Again, he nodded, holding back tears. "Yeah, this feels different. Even with Aicha... I didn't mean to kill her. I just wanted to get her off me so I could get away. She didn't even turn out to be human, though, so it didn't seem the same to me. This time, I knew what I was doing. I knew I had to take somebody's life."

"I understand. I'm so sorry. There probably wasn't any alternative, just like now. Whether or not soldiers are down there, what choice do we really have but to carry on?"

'None,' Enki said, surprising them. *'Enough time has been wasted. If there are more warriors to deal with, we shall do so. Can you operate this mechanism?'*

Encouraged by a supportive hug, Eric pulled himself together as best he could. The three of them went under the large truck's canvas covering and examined the winch. It sat securely bolted to the bed, mechanically powered, and clearly fed by the generator that still hummed at the side of the vehicle. The controls looked simple enough.

"The problem is," he puzzled, "if we all go down on the platform, how do we stop it when we reach the bottom? This, of course, assumes we actually reach the bottom. This thing looks old. It probably doesn't have any kind of auto-stop. If it just keeps going, it might start winding back up again. It'll end up getting tangled or jammed and then the motor will break, or the wire will snap. We'd be stuck down there."

'Lower the apparatus,' Enki calmly stated. *'The creature of fire and I can climb down, each with one of you on our backs. I will scout ahead to see if we face opposition.'*

Jeez, and I thought Metéora was bad. This time we won't even have a basket.

Eric nervously engaged the lever. The metal wire scraped against the rocky ledge but seemed constructed to withstand such abuse. They waited as the platform descended, which took time. The winch moved slowly, and the distance was great. At long last, the cable started to slacken, and he stopped the motor.

They returned to the ledge, where the Afrit squatted like a gargoyle, brooding. To Eric's surprise, Enki hopped casually over the side, but a tug on the cable told him the lithe and powerful god had secured himself. After a few moments, he returned, pulling himself up the rope as if on a Sunday stroll.

'I see no one in the cave. Either they all came up when the fighting started, or those remaining retreated into the doorway.'

"Is it down there?" Lotte asked with wonder. "Is the entrance to the Rope of An and Ki actually right beneath us?"

'It is the source of the light you see, portions of the Abzu and the An themselves, intertwined and manifest in your world. It is glorious. You will be dazzled, but remain focused or all will be for naught. You!'

"Me?" Eric squeaked.

'Yes. Put your arms around my neck and cling tightly to my back. Raven-haired one, do the same with your Afrit. In this way, we will descend.'

"Are you gonna do that little trick where you jump in again? That looks kind of, well, let's just say... *risky.*"

'I disapprove of your lack of faith, but as it clearly terrifies you, I will proceed more gently.'

Slightly chastened, Eric discarded his tire iron with little regret, locked his arms around Enki's neck, and held on for dear life. The great god grasped the cable and walked backward into the gigantic hole. Once past the ledge, he used only his arms to lower them both with great ease.

Now this is how you climb a rope. I guess I just need more upper body strength. Yeah, never gonna happen.

Secure as he felt, he kept his eyes shut until he heard Enki's light footfalls. He then turned and took in the majesty of the enormous cave. They stood on a huge pile of rocks and debris, likely the remains of the roof that had collapsed when the cave entrance was formed, along with additional effluvium that had flowed in over the centuries. He had never been in a space like this, as close to an alien landscape as he could possibly envision, both unimaginably beautiful and inconceivably terrifying.

The *object*, however, if that's what one could really call it, completely overshadowed the cave's effect. An impossible and stunningly beautiful funnel of incandescent blue-green light unfolded before them, dominating the center of the cavernous space. Gigantic near the domed ceiling from which it appeared to emanate—though Eric knew that wasn't truly its source—it narrowed as it neared the ground, along which it briefly trailed before ending in a huge arched entryway, fifteen feet or more in height. The great funnel danced and swirled like a tornado of rippling water, its glow illuminating the entirety of the vast cave large enough to accommodate twelve jumbo jets side by side.

"It's absolutely incredible," Lotte whispered as she dismounted the Afrit's back. "If somebody told me they'd seen this, I'd laugh in their face. It's impossible, but maybe the impossible is possible after all. I told you I wouldn't miss this for the world."

Cognizant of the imminent danger, Eric wasn't so certain, though he found the vortex equally mesmerizing. Together, the pair clambered down the mountain of debris in the footsteps of their nimbler companions. Their feet sank with each footfall on the sodden floor of the cave. Water collected here, forming an intermittent lake during torrential rains, before evaporating or slowly infiltrating the fine-grained, mud-cracked sediment.

'*Stay close behind us,*' Enki commanded as they approached the gigantic doorway. A mist shrouded the opening, so the interior, as well as the presence of any challengers to their entry, remained unseen.

Eric tightly held Lotte's arm as they walked into the fog. He expected some sort of *tingle*, or perhaps a slight breeze, or a difference in temperature, but experienced no perceptible change at all, save visibility being reduced to the point where he couldn't see the beings that walked before them, or even Lotte's face beside him. They took just a few steps before the bluish-green glow began to restore shape and form to the world, but he knew they'd traversed a far greater distance, and that he no longer walked in the realm of his birth.

Almost imperceptibly, the ground had changed. Carved stonework interlaced with decorative and brightly colored marble now met their footfalls. A long, thin chamber emerged from the gloom, and two immense creatures took shape at the far end. To Eric's relief, these turned out to be statues.

Two great winged bulls, carved in exquisite detail from polished marble, flanked an archway through which a corridor sloped upward and then curled away. Each bore the heads of men wearing thick, rectangular beards. Their eyes sparkled like diamonds and seemed to monitor the party with their empty and ominous gaze.

Magnificent as these sights were, his and Lotte's gazes were drawn to the ceiling. Rising in an arch above the stone walls, water bubbled and rippled, casting its otherworldly glow into the cathedral-like room and the corridor beyond. What held it suspended above them was unknown, some field of energy that defied all expectation and explanation, the majestic power of the Abzu on exhibition for two exceptionally privileged mortals.

"Where is the door?" Lotte asked, eyes blazing and face aglow. "There was a key, but I see no door here in the entryway, no lock to put it into."

'*The mist through which we walked is what remains of the door itself,*' Enki explained. '*To make it substantial once again, the key must be borne out of this place. It cannot be closed from the inside, except by Enlil himself.*'

"Where is Enlil? Do you think he might have stopped Iblis?"

The great god walked cautiously toward the statues and stared into their faces. *'They are... inactive. Something has happened, something terrible, and I fear I know what it is. When someone enters, the eyes of these monoliths should send a signal to the guardian of the Rope of An and Ki, but there is no life in them. I fear that Enlil still slumbers, and it may be beyond our capacity to contact him. Come, there is but one way to go. We must proceed, and all will soon be revealed.'*

Enki and the Afrit strode forward between the glaring but inert Lamassu and into the corridor beyond. Here, the stonework of the walls possessed a bluish hue upon which great golden lions and griffins danced, claws extended and fanged jaws wide with menace. Lotte and Eric followed, less boldly and far more cautious and, at least in her case, curious about their surroundings.

"Who constructed all this, and why?" she whispered as they ascended the curving ramp of the corridor. "It looks like an ancient Mesopotamian temple, but who other than Enlil would ever see it?"

'This was the seat of Enlil's earthly power,' Enki replied. *'His priests would visit here when he caused the entrance to manifest itself in the Ekur temple in Nippur, as would those traversing between your realm and the An... until the gateway was sealed. It is not* constructed, *as you put it. Enlil and my father imprinted familiar forms into the energy of this transitional area, floors and walls that would help orient his mortal servants while simultaneously inspiring reverent awe. Ever the showman, my brother. It is the model and influence for many structures in your world.'*

It reminded Eric of the Ishtar Gate and the Processional Way he'd seen in the Pergamon Museum many years before, though those attractions seemed crude copies compared to the lifelike and detailed representations now before him.

They scare the hell out of me, so I can only imagine how someone who'd never seen something like this, or a zillion horror films, might have felt.

"You say your brother and father made this place," Lotte probed. "Were you not involved?"

'All our power was needed to sequester the plane of air. There, my interests ceased. I left it to my father to conquer and harvest the energy of his adopted realm, and my brother to rule as a living god in your world. I remained Lord of the Abzu, and offered my gifts to humanity not to govern, but to foster the ability to independently answer the questions that plagued your kind. As you know, a failed endeavor, but so too my brother and father in the end failed to —'

The shot resounded like the burst of a cannon and echoed in the tall, stone corridor. Blood spattered Eric's face as the great god before him stumbled backward, the top of his head ripped open by the passing bullet. Had Eric been a bit taller, it would likely have caught him as well, and there would have been no chance of survival. Knowing Enki's superhuman capacities, he grabbed the injured deity and pulled him to the wall.

The Afrit already stood there, shielding Lotte behind the bulk of its body.

"What the hell was that?" she cried. "Great one, are you all right?"

The injured god sat, back to the wall, blood streaming down his face. *'I live, if that is your question. It will take more than these wounds to vanquish me, but my reserves are rapidly depleting.'*

"Can you heal yourself? There's water all around us!"

'Yes, and mighty waters, indeed. Much of the force of the Abzu is diverted to the Rope of An and Ki. This is why the rest of my realm regenerates so slowly. Sadly, its potential remains beyond my reach, trapped behind the barrier Enlil and my father created from the power of the An. I cannot penetrate it without access to far more energy. We must find Enlil's gateway. Like the Afrit and I, he too has a portal where he enters this place from the portion of the Abzu which surrounds us. There, these waters must be able to flow, though I suspect we will discover obstacles to this as well.'

Another shot rang out. A bullet ricocheted off the curvature in the wall near the Afrit, and then struck the stonework on the opposite side of the corridor. Curiously, it left no mark, attesting to the supernatural make-up of the architecture.

'We cannot dally here,' the Afrit grumbled. *'We shall be picked to pieces. What course do we take, Goat-Man? Storm forward... or withdraw?'*

'Neither,' Enki said, shaking his bloodied head. *'Direct assault will cost us much, as we learned from the battle we fought on the surface. We parley. It is no Jinn we face. Perhaps this one is convincible.'*

The great god got shakily to his feet and called out. *'Stop! Cease your firing and hear my words. The one you serve has tricked you. He promises riches, eternal life, or great power, but he will bring you none of those things. Only death awaits you, and quite possibly us, from behind the blocked gateway. Once it is opened, the truth will be as clear to you as rainwater in a shallow pool. By then, however, it will be too late. All our fates will be sealed. Throw down your weapons and let us pass. I reveal myself to you so we can converse, face-to-face and eye-to-eye. You will see that I do not lie. Come forth and let us speak.'*

Enki boldly stepped out into the corridor. To Eric's amazement, he saw a man slowly emerge from behind a curve in the hallway ahead, dressed as usual in black fatigues and wielding a large, semiautomatic rifle.

Olive would be jealous, he mused.

For a brief instant, he considered employing the Uzi that dangled at his side, but then thought better of it. He'd be as likely to hit Enki as their enemy, having never fired a gun like this.

Hmmmm... maybe we should have brought Olive, after all.

The man spoke curt and threatening words in a language Eric couldn't understand.

'*He wants us all to show ourselves,*' Enki translated. '*To establish trust.*'

"He's lying," Lotte retorted. "He'll shoot us for sure, and we can't withstand the kind of punishment you've endured."

'*Stand behind your fiery companion along with your consort. We need what energy we have left to deal with Iblis. The warrior has made himself vulnerable and appears willing to listen. This presents our most promising course of action.*'

The Afrit wavered briefly, but then stepped out to stand next to Enki. Lotte and Eric were just beginning to file out behind when the man began shouting and pointing.

"*Seytan!*" he screamed. "*O Seytan!*"

Well, no mistaking what that *means. I guess he didn't get a good look at the Afrit before.*

Enki tried to calm the shaken soldier, and for a moment, it seemed to work. He dropped to his knees and placed his rifle on the ground, praying fervently as he frantically pawed at his chest. Sadly, this was no gesture of supplication. Without warning, he had something in his hand, something as black as the uniform which had hitherto concealed the item. He jerked at it with his free hand, and then lofted the object directly toward them.

"Grenade!" Eric cried, thrusting Lotte back to the wall and then forcing her to the floor where he desperately smothered her. He turned his head when he heard the dense metal contact the beautiful but illusory stonework of the floor.

One bounce, then two, then....

The bomb exploded at the feet of the Afrit. The flash caused Eric's eyes to reflexively close as he braced for the impact that would likely kill him. He felt Lotte beneath him, her body almost as familiar to him now as his own. He buried his cheek in her black hair, no longer uber-straight and cut to draw, or perhaps more likely repel, attention with its jagged and threatening angles. It was softer now, like Lotte herself. Lotte, who carried their child, and who he hoped would tell that child about him, and how he'd given his life to save them both in this oddly familiar place so unfathomably far from home.

He'd seen the flash, he heard the sound, but as Marvin the Martian asked with his singular catchphrase, he found himself wondering, "Where's the kaboom? There was supposed to be an Earth-shattering kaboom!" Warily, he opened his eyes.

The Afrit stood before him, head tilted backward on an arched spine, arms spread wide, cloven hooves braced, one slightly forward, one slightly back for stability. The metal casing of the grenade lay scattered in shards on the ground in front of the ashen creature, but there was no smoke, no fire, no indication of concussive impact. Enki stood wide-eyed at the beast's side, unharmed.

Almost as if throwing a great, unseen ball, the Afrit thrust its head and shoulders forward. A jet of flame streamed from its body. The man shrieked in terror as the fire engulfed him, searing away the exposed flesh of his face and hands. It only took an instant, not even long enough to ignite his black uniform. Nonetheless, the charred remains of the hapless mercenary's head slumped to the ground, and he collapsed forward, dead, as if bowing on his knees in eternal prayer.

"Eric... *ouch.* Can you please get off of me?"

He realized he still had Lotte pinned hard to the stone floor. "Sorry, sorry. I just... I thought it would blow up and kill you. I didn't know what else to do."

"*Dummkopf!*" she snapped as she laboriously sat up.

'*In fairness, my raven-haired lovely,*' Enki intervened, '*he was attempting to save your life, in all probability at the expense of his own.*'

"I know," she replied, throwing her arms around Eric's neck. "He's a *Dummkopf* because he doesn't realize this is why I love him so, and why for me, no one could ever measure up to him." She put her lips to his ear and whispered. "*Do you hear? Do you understand?*"

He held her tight. He heard. He understood. In that moment, he knew with absolute clarity what an utter fool he'd been to have ever doubted her, and to a large extent, to have questioned his ability to measure up in her eyes.

The Afrit's words intruded on Eric's moment of bliss. '*Great power in such a small device. It would have been problematic had it caught us unaware, as did the previous blast. Instead, it gave us valuable energy – a fitting end for the duplicitous mortal.*'

Enki smiled and put his hand on the beast's shoulder. '*He was merely scared, creature of fire – afraid of what he could not comprehend, or that which his superstitions led him to fear. So it is with many humans, and why it is so hard for them to progress beyond their petty squabbles and primitive ways in order to embrace the true gifts of the* Me. *I fight for these querulous beings because the interventions of my kind have unwittingly put them in peril, but in the end, they must decide who and what they want to be, or whether they continue to exist on this tiny rock in space at all. You fight for them too, for reasons of your own.'*

The Afrit scowled down the corridor. *'Unless there are more like this one, nothing now stands between us and Iblis. Let us continue and complete the task for which we journeyed to this place.'*

"All right," Lotte agreed, "but if there are more soldiers, we need to be better prepared." She turned to Eric and tapped the Uzi at his side. "Gimme."

"You want this? Do you think you can handle it? Are you sure you want to?"

"It's smaller than that man's rifle. You take that. I know what you're saying. I'm not excited about the prospect of taking someone's life, but if they stop us, the whole world will be in danger. I promised the Afrit I'd do everything I could. We have to put our feelings about this aside and just do what needs to be done, no matter the cost."

She extended her hands, and he passed her the weapon, which she briefly examined before draping the strap across her shoulder. "Wow, I look like Patty Hearst in that famous photo of her. All I need is a beret."

Who the hell is Patty Hearst? Didn't matter; he smiled anyway. "I'll buy you one when we get out of this, assuming we do."

She gave a brief laugh, then motioned for the group to proceed down the hall.

When they reached the gruesome corpse, Eric bent down and picked up the dead man's rifle. "It doesn't look like it's been damaged. I think we're good to go."

She put a hand on his shoulder as he began to rise. "One more thing. The grenade gave the Afrit power when it was able to channel that energy. See if there are any more on his body."

"You want me to turn him over?"

"I know, it's gross and kind of ghoulish, but they might be really helpful. If I'd known they'd have this effect, we'd have brought some from the surface. I think it's too late, and too much trouble, to go back now, so this is our best chance. Can you do it?"

It wasn't totally unlike retrieving the pistol from the body of the man whose head had been pulped by Charun in the New Hampshire gravel quarry. Back then, he'd done it to seem brave in front of Mason, and, of course, to impress Lotte. He hadn't felt any great need for the weapon itself, though it had come in handy later, buying a bit of time that ultimately saved his life. Lotte was probably right, a grenade or two might seriously come in handy, and his desire to look good in her eyes hadn't diminished a bit.

He took a deep breath. "All right, here goes."

He tried not to look as he guided the corpse's shoulders to the side and then turned the dead man on his back, but it was impossible. The empty glare of skeletal sockets stripped bare of flesh, as well as the eyes through which this man had seen the world, inexorably drew his attention. It was like an accident on the roadside that grabbed the grim curiosity of all passersby. Charred teeth, void of lips, gums, and most of the cheeks, made the final grimace on the man's face even more harrowing. The image burned into Eric's brain, like the sight of blood quietly soaking the fabric of the *keffiyeh* of the man whose life he'd taken.

Lotte's gentle touch brought him back to the present. The man wore a black harness on which three grenades remained hooked. Having no way to transport the dangerous items, he unfastened the clasp and slipped the thick strap from under the lifeless body. The soldier's seared head flopped to the side at the motion, and his bony jaw swung wide as if crying out in violation.

The ghastly task completed, the party ventured forward, though with far greater caution. If ever-curious Lotte had questions, she kept them to herself. Despite trying to put what had just happened out of his mind, Eric couldn't take his eyes from the gaping wound on Enki's head. Miraculously, it had stopped bleeding. It was the second such injury he'd seen the great god suffer. Scars in the scaly skin on the right side of his face still attested to Ninurta's ferocious assault.

Eventually, the corridor widened, and over the rise above them Eric could see they were approaching a huge chamber. The party stopped short of the great space, crouched down, and surveyed the breathtakingly incredible interior.

To the left, they saw an immense, semicircular recession that contained a tremendous but empty pool. The depression spanned the roughly hundred-yard distance to the far wall. At the center of the basin loomed a familiar archway, almost identical to that of Enki's gateway in construction and material, but vastly larger, and clearly not intended to be portable.

A mighty stone throne majestically surveyed the impressive space from a dais behind the pool, accessed by great ramps that ran along the wall. Its design echoed the archway of the portal below, representing the flowing waters of the Tigris and Euphrates rivers, so central to life in the ancient Fertile Crescent. Directly beneath the great throne sat an enormous pedestal, decorated by the faces of two lions with huge, spicket-like oval mouths. These seemed to be conduits for water, but the openings were sealed with the same golden stone, or the illusion of stone, from which the carvings were constructed.

On top of the pedestal rested the gigantic body of another marble Lamassu. The statue reared up on its hind legs. Its great cloven hooves extended intimidatingly forward, but there appeared to be a problem.

"What happened to its head?" Lotte whispered. "It looks like it's been knocked off into the pool."

'Indeed,' Enki answered with regret. 'It was as I feared. This is the work of Sharur. Look there.' He pointed to the right, where a stone structure, or one crafted to appear as stone, stood in ruins in a small, curved alcove. 'The repository for the Tablet of Destinies, created after it was retrieved by Ninurta from the Anzu. Now, it lies decimated by the power of Sharur's mace. First, however, he had to dispatch the guardian.'

"Why didn't it come to life? You said the statues in the entryway below would send a signal if anyone was detected."

'Sharur had no need of the doorway. He likely materialized in this very room, as he had done countless times in the past. The statues in the entry did not detect him, and as a creation of Enlil, he was never feared, and never suspected of the treachery his master, the son of Enlil himself, would demand. Similar to Sharur, the great Lamassu exists as a stone statue, but can animate when necessary. Sharur struck before it could do so, and his power in mace form was perhaps the only thing that could shatter the rock and break the enchantment. Now the Lamassu is dead, and it was by its command that water would flow from the mouths of the lions into the pool to open Enlil's portal. We are, as I suspected, on our own.'

'Fire,' the Afrit said, pointing toward the far end of the room. 'Iblis must be there.'

On the wall directly across from their position stood another opening, completely occluded by a great barricade of ice. A cloud of steam-like smoke streamed from the barrier, partially obscuring the surrounding area, but the orange glow of flame clearly shone from within the mist. Occasionally, streaks of fire erupted near the wall and soared upward.

From the shadows of this mist, a figure wearing a hooded cloak emerged. Slowly and gracefully, the person walked toward them. Somewhat past the middle of the great room, the mysterious being stopped, bowed deeply, and threw back their hood.

Eric beheld the visage of a woman with long, black hair, a hawk-like nose, and skin the color of bronze. She spoke, and to his surprise he could understand her words clearly, delivered in a perfect English-from-England accent. The buoyant lilt of her voice, however, failed to mask the palpably underlying menace of her tone.

"Welcome, Brother, or perhaps I should say, Half-Brother. You were not expected. My heart fills with joy at your presence after such an unspeakably long time... though I imagine you are as displeased to see me as Iblis is to see you. No matter. It shall be nice to converse one last time before you are either brought to heel or die alongside these wretched beings who inexplicably stole your heart so long ago."

CHAPTER 19

Enki shuddered. *'Dimme.'*

"Who is that, great one?" Lotte enquired. "Her name isn't familiar to me."

'She is as she says, a child of my father's, but her mother was a mortal from your world who had been possessed by a Jinn. The union was, shall we say, not entirely successful, her powers distressingly less than the sum of her potent parentage. Stunted and sterile, Dimme acted with a malevolence that appalled even the most detached and uncaring of the gods. For reasons of his own, it was Pazuzu, cheerful bringer of disease and famine when not properly honored, who uncharacteristically took it upon himself to keep her in check. This she detested, but it was the only answer short of terminating her existence – not the easiest task, even when dealing with the weakest of Anu's offspring, capable of vanishing like a Jinn.'

"What on Earth is she doing here helping Iblis?"

'Woefully, that is what I must now determine. You have to stay here, child. You are in greater danger than you could possibly imagine. Dimme desires to speak with me, and I will honor her wish.'

The great god rose and, with a look of grim determination, strode into the enormous room. *'Dimme! Of what crime have I been deemed guilty that the punishment is having to now speak with you? Higher probability you would be found lurking in some forsaken swamp, hiding from Pazuzu and licking blood from the bones of a baby crocodile, than standing before me now. Yet here you are. Speak, wayward and woebegone daughter of my father, and explain your presence in this place.'*

The woman laughed heartily as she stood her ground. "Oh, Enki, you use a name I have not heard for millennia! Lamashtu, and in some cases, Lilith, are the monikers they used for me after you took to your slumber, which apparently wasn't as eternal as you promised. No matter. I remain pleased to see you. I assume you're here to stop Iblis from opening the passage to the An? Truly, you'll receive no resistance from me. I have as little interest in seeing our father again as you."

This seemed to take Enki aback. He stopped to within about ten feet of her and paused before speaking. *'Then why are you here? For what purpose would Iblis bring you if not to help open the gateway?'*

"A fair question. In short, I had little choice."

Dimme threw open the upper part of her cloak, revealing a dark collar made of heavy iron that ringed her neck. The top and bottom of the ungainly contraption were rimmed in gold, and connected to lines of gold that ran vertically at periodic increments to seal the various curved iron plates together. Short, spike-like nails jutted outward all around the metal band, like some Punk Rock nightmare, and Eric saw the stains of blood on her low-cut shirt.

"You see?" she said, gesturing to the macabre apparatus. "I am but a helpless prisoner. This is meteoric iron, highly magnetic and capable of stifling my Jinn-like ability to vanish into thin air. Should I disobey my captor's commands, the results are even more distasteful. Just a little push of air and these nasty little iron spikes easily find my neck. Obviously, from the condition of my shirt, I remain a bit headstrong and don't like being ordered about. I go through a lot of shirts."

'It surprises me you would let Iblis close enough to trap you in such a way.'

"Close enough," she scoffed. "What would you know of it? No closeness for the girl who was exiled and ostracized, reviled for taking what few pleasures were left to one deemed unworthy of her divine title. No pity or kindness ever shown to me. I was hunted!"

'You feasted on the blood of mortal babies, some not yet even born! Had there existed a purpose, it might have been comprehensible — punishment for a lesson that needed learning, or transgressions of the laws that kept the peace. These actions, however, have always been of your own accord, and you reveled in the devastating sorrow left in your wake!'

"I did no such thing! I gave as little thought to the emotions of these beings as the great gods gave to mine. Little wonder I was tempted by one who offered some measure of sympathy and aid, who didn't recoil from the very sight of me. I know now that it was a clever ruse designed to lower my guard, but for that brief time, I felt the love and acceptance ever withheld from me by the brood of entities that constitute our incomparably maladjusted family. Be that as it may, Brother, I see things differently from you. Mortal beings are food for the likes of us, plain and simple, and the tastiest morsels are those whose energy is not corrupted by the tortured and conflicted thoughts and emotions that later plague their souls. Many Jinn have long seen this, and perhaps it is my Jinn ancestry that renders me immune to the fantasy that has ever held you in thrall. These are not your children, great Lord of the Abzu, they are your *lunch!*"

'*You disgust me! I believe you lie and that your predilections result from jealousy over your infertility and paltry capabilities. Our conversation is through. Bring forth Iblis and we shall settle this matter without your interference!*'

"Brother, I'm trying to help you. Put aside your prejudices and listen. We came here fully prepared to battle the Lamassu, guardians of Enlil's domain, but it appears someone has already taken care of that for us. Looks like they stole the Tablet of Destinies as well. *Bummer*, as the kids today like to say, but that's not really my concern. What I'm trying to tell you is that Iblis wields great power, much of which he draws from me. I'm like his little battery, or to put it in terms you'd understand, a reservoir of energy he can use and has been using for centuries."

Lotte whispered in Eric's ear. "*This* is the exceptional power that Utnapishtim told us about, the one that allowed Iblis to hunt down and kill the Seven Kings. No one could ever figure out its source. He literally had access to the energy of a god!"

The normally affable Lord of the Abzu forebodingly scrutinized his imperious half-sister. '*Perhaps, then, it is you to whom I should turn my attention?*'

"Ha! Good luck with that. I assure you, the second you threaten me, you'll feel the potency of Iblis's capabilities. You are not a warrior, and I know your abilities here are limited, being so far from water — well, water that you can access, anyway. You cannot stop Iblis. He's opened a gateway to a realm of fire. As we speak, it burns through the frozen barrier that separates us from the An. It won't be long now. I give you this chance to flee, the opportunity to encounter your father later, after he's eaten and perhaps gotten over having been imprisoned. Okay, that's probably unlikely, but if you want to be the first thing he sees after thousands of years of being locked away at your behest, I suggest you give your fishy tail a big kiss goodbye now, before it's too late."

'*I did not come alone, Dimme. I bring one who is most powerful indeed, and who bears a grudge against your captor.*' The great god turned and faced the doorway where Lotte, Eric, and the Afrit still crouched.

She squealed with delight. "Ah, the legendary Afrit! I've heard so much about this creature. Iblis thought it dead, or lost forever, imprisoned by Aicha Kandicha's sorcery. Bid it come forth so I can see the beast with my own eyes. Have your other little friends come out as well. I presume one is the clever girl with the impressive portal collection who somehow dispatched Aicha?"

What am I, chopped liver? Eric wondered with annoyance. *Whatever.*

Reluctantly, Enki made a motion.

The Afrit began to rise, but Lotte grabbed its arm. "This is a trap! Don't go. Force Iblis to show himself. We'll be exposed out in that room. There's no telling where he could attack us from, and we're not as capable of resisting as you and Enki."

The tiny suns of the Afrit's eyes met the bright black holes of Lotte's gaze. The beast almost imperceptibly tilted its horned head, as if curious at what it beheld.

*'Have no fear, **Sadat Alnaar**. Iblis knows not what we have become. Nor, perhaps, do we, but never will we possess the opportunity to ponder such things if we cannot stop what is about to happen. If they want you, they can take you at any time. You are safest by our side. The first strike may well be his, but the last will be ours. May it come swiftly. The words of this woman irritate us.'*

The Afrit gently removed Lotte's hand and walked purposefully into the great chamber, cloven hooves landing silently on the mirage of the marble floor.

With resignation, Eric filed in behind Lotte, who strode close behind the hulking monster, Uzi at the ready.

"Incredible!" Dimme gushed. "So much bigger than Iblis had described. The idiot mortals depict me with wings, the claws of a bird, and the head of a lion. Were it only so. You, however, are quite a wonder."

The trio stood next to Enki, who turned back to the demi-goddess. *'As you can see, this being is formidable. The presence of fire in this room from the creature's own realm makes it only more so. If you are quite satisfied, can you please summon Iblis, and then stand aside as you indicated you would?'*

She shook her head. "Well, it can't be said I didn't try. Very well, creature of fire, why don't we go have a look at the 'flames of your realm.' Let us see if you can summon their power and make the one you seek pay for his ancient injustices. It will be most interesting, indeed. Come. We'll all go." She turned to Lotte. "Especially you, my darling. Don't you just smell absolutely delicious."

'Touch her,' the Afrit snarled, *'and we promise it will be the final act of your wretched existence.'*

"So adorable," she chortled. "Iblis told me you always had a thing for your keepers—conniving little wenches, the lot of them. Don't worry, I'll be good. The prospect of my father returning to this realm revolts me, and despite my unusual heritage, I don't have the capacity to dwell elsewhere. I'll probably get a little stick for this, but I'm telling you the truth that I'd like you to stop him. *Ugh –* "

The spikes on Dimme's collar vanished as they drove through the metal band and into her throat. She spasmed briefly before the nails abruptly returned to place, dripping with blood.

"You see?" she sputtered. "Don't be an idiot, Iblis! They'll soon see the hopelessness of their cause. Bastard. Now... shall we?"

Dimme led the way as the group warily trekked toward the cloud of mist at the far side of the huge chamber. "What Iblis and I would really like to know is how in blazes did you find us? He said himself, this was absolutely the last place on Earth he would go looking for the entry to the Rope of An and Ki—quite an inspired choice by my other half-brother. How did you locate it so quickly?"

"I took an impression of the cylinder scroll before Iblis stole it," Lotte explained, voice defiant despite the charged situation. "I wanted to see it before we gave it to Enki for protection. Iblis stepped on the bloody thing, but Enki could still interpret the map."

"Bravo! I applaud you, but in the end, this may turn out to be a case of curiosity killing the cat. How about the missing Tablet of Destinies and the rather shattered Lamassu? Do you have any light you'd care to shed on that, darling?"

"Not that I'd especially care to share, no... but thanks for the offer."

Dimme shot a furious glance over her shoulder, but the Afrit interposed itself, so she angrily turned and resumed walking.

About thirty feet from the wall, the great hissing cloud of steam billowed upward before them, originating at the doorway frozen over by Enlil's power. The intense heat of the Eternal Flame bored into the ice, which violently and noisily evaporated amidst periodic eruptions of fire.

Eric absorbed various details in snatches through the swirling mist. Two great pillars towered in front of the doorway, ringed with snaking channels from which a lava-like liquid glowed and bubbled. They were exactly like those he remembered from the Reynolds Treasures room of the MFA, though seemingly made of some modern synthetic material rather than stone. They loomed to either side of a cauldron, filled with more of a similarly glowing liquid.

These must have been the items that were in those boxes in the van. This is why they needed that lift, and all those men to move this stuff here.

Above the cauldron, and between the pillars, shimmered a tiny, undulating sun, barely bigger than a golf ball. It shone almost white-hot through the mist. Had most of the energy from this puncture into the realm of fire not been directed toward the doorway, it would have been impossible to view directly.

Barely visible amidst the vaporous veil, a man sat between the radiant point of light and the wall, cloaked and hooded as Dimme had been. Across his lap lay a staff forged of gold. Attached to the top of this item, encased in a decorative golden spiderweb, rested a globe of dark metal which echoed the spiked collar around the daughter of Anu's neck.

"Iblis," Lotte intoned.

"The one and only," Dimme cheekily replied.

"He doesn't look especially concerned that we're here," Eric gloomily observed.

"As I said, his power is great. You'll see. Right now, he maintains most of his focus on the portal."

"How can he tap the power of the Eternal Flame in this place?" Lotte queried.

"As long as the entryway to the Rope of An and Ki is open to your world, the realm of fire is accessible to him. When the frozen doorway is finally seared open, his task is complete. It's a matter of wearing down the ice before it has a chance to regenerate. At any moment, a small crack might give way... and that will be that."

'More reason to dispense with words and act,' the Afrit groused.

The beast raised its arms upward in the motion that had become familiar to Eric when it summoned energy from a fire. Strangely, nothing happened. The orb of intense light continued its assault against the frozen doorway. Neither the periodic streaks of flame nor the gurgling liquid exhibited any discernable change.

Seemingly unconcerned, the Afrit strode brazenly forward, directly toward where Iblis indifferently sat. Just shy of the misty perimeter, the creature slowed, and then came to a stop.

'There is... a wind. It makes progress difficult. Help us, Goat-Man.'

Enki ushered Lotte and Eric away from his dangerous half-sister and joined the Afrit at the edge of the cloud of steam.

'You are strong,' the ashen creature said. *'Push us forward. Perhaps together we can penetrate this barrier.'*

Enki gave a slight bow and pressed his back against the Afrit's mangled wings. The two powerful beings shoved into the invisible wall of wind, straining mightily to gain headway against the unseen but potent force. Working in tandem, they propelled the Afrit a step or two farther than it had achieved on its own, but there, progress halted. The exhausted entities recoiled with frustration.

"See?" Dimme smugly interjected. "I tried to warn you, but do you listen to me? Of course not. No one ever does."

The Afrit cut her off. *'Silence, shrew! Perhaps this barrier has a top and the way is over, not through.'*

"That ceiling is high," Lotte said, looking upward, "and there's no telling how far up the wall of wind goes. You'd almost surely need your wings."

The Afrit swayed briefly, seeming to ponder her words. *'You may be correct, but even if not, it would suit us to be whole. Prepare one of the energy stones.'*

"Huh?" Eric asked, confused.

"It means a grenade," Lotte clarified.

"Umm, okay. What do you want me to do with it?"

'Throw it at us as did the warrior we recently dispatched, so it releases its power at our feet.'

"Right, of course. Throw a grenade at the Afrit. Makes perfect sense. Why didn't I think of that before?" In truth, Eric realized, it did make some sense given the creature's ability to channel the energy of the little bomb. "Hey, whatever you want. We're just gonna stand over here, if that's okay."

Everyone moved back a bit.

Enki sternly accompanied Dimme in the opposite direction of Lotte and Eric.

Eric then removed a grenade from the harness, pulled the pin, and gently lobbed it toward the impatiently awaiting brute.

He covered his ears and squinted his eyes, but neither were necessary. A dull thump sounded as the explosive shattered, and broken shards of metal fell to the ground. The Afrit, however, vigorously sucked the force of the blast into its body, which pulsated with an intense orange glow before the beast violently fragmented into a blazing cloud of swirling ash. Like a firestorm, the glistening particles that constituted the creature's makeup chaotically raged. Gradually, its hulking form began to take shape once more.

Incredibly, when the fire and ash had settled, the ashen monster unfurled its bat-like wings and gave a mighty howl. It stood perhaps just a bit smaller than before, some of its mass given to repair what had been lost. Now, however, it could fly, and the reinvigorated Afrit vaulted into the air without hesitation.

It danced along the edge of the misty cloud, probing for a spot lacking resistance. When it reached the transparent ceiling of the chamber, the creature darted from left to right, an ocean of water hovering mere inches above its head. The perimeter of Iblis's barrier of air arced around where he sat with his staff near the pillars, and the simmering cauldron of liquid.

The Afrit's motions became ever more frantic. There appeared to be no top or opening in the wall that separated them from their nemesis. Eventually, the creature landed among them with its usual grace, but noticeably perturbed.

'The wall is strong, but it is only energy. We feel it flex and give. Through this barrier we cannot summon the power of the Eternal Flame, with which we could easily break through, but we will not be denied. Prepare another energy stone.

Eric turned to Lotte, who simply shrugged. Cautiously, he removed another grenade from the harness, pulled the pin, and again tossed it toward the Afrit. This time, he didn't close his eyes, choosing to take in the wonder of the ashen creature's ability to instantly dominate and manipulate the force of the blast. A halo of fiery energy quickly encircled the beast, pulsing with explosive power.

Twice, the Afrit batted its wings, then rocketed headlong into the invisible wall of wind. Fire and air clashed as the luminance of the monster's burning cocoon rammed a visible depression into the barrier. The wall stretched like rubber, straining at the might of the onslaught. For a moment, it seemed the obstacle would crumble and the Afrit would slash its way through, but remarkably and distressingly, it refused to give way. The monster clawed and thrashed its powerful wings, pushing ever deeper, but appeared unable to penetrate Iblis's unseen shield.

"So near, and yet so far," Dimme casually observed as she stepped forward. "Brother, I know you detest me, but our fates are intertwined, and I fear neither of our futures will look especially cheery if Iblis succeeds. Seems a shame for you to have come all this way for nothing, but it was certainly nice seeing you once more. Perhaps our paths will cross again."

Dimme winked, then closed her eyes, lowered her head, and tensed all the muscles in her body. Almost instantly, the horrible spikes in her collar again drove into her neck. Blood cascaded down her chest. She began to spasm and then collapsed in a shaking heap to the floor.

Iblis's sinister restraint, however, had come just a nanosecond too late. The perimeter of the deep bulge in the barrier where wind met fire suddenly gave way, having been oh-so-briefly deprived of the energy that sustained its might.

The Afrit blasted through, tumbled to the ground, then slammed hard into the far wall, the fiery aura around its body extinguished.

Iblis, once sedate and peaceful as a meditating monk, now surged into action. He shot to his feet, brought his golden staff to bear, and pointed the metallic tip at the intruding Afrit. A colossal gust of wind pinned the creature to the wall and threatened to thrust it back outside the boundary of the protective barrier of air.

Somehow, the beast withstood the assault, and with one three-clawed hand, it grasped toward the orb of light emanating from the portal.

The small globe pulsed like a strobe, and a white-hot jet of flame soon burst forth. With superhuman speed, Iblis redirected his staff toward the oncoming blast. The plume of fire engulfed his body, pushing him backward and throwing off the hood of his cloak. The flames, however, washed harmlessly around him, redirected by a barrier of wind from his staff. At the same time, the glow from the orb dimmed, and the hissing steam and streaks of fire from the doorway behind him abruptly ceased.

Iblis was a stocky man, bald, with one thick black eyebrow over his right eye. The left side of his face appeared misshapen and disfigured, as if horribly burned. His left hand bore similar scars and lacked two fingers, but he tightly clutched his golden staff with the bony remains of his other digits.

He turned to the Afrit and laughed with obvious glee. "My creation! I am overjoyed to see you once again. I thought you dead and buried. Well, you *were* buried — still are, really — somewhere out there in Syrian desert. This part of you, however, now stands before me, and what a sight you've become! All the things I made you, and so much more. Well do I understand. The power of your realm has flowed in the blood of this scarred body for centuries. I am loath to abandon it, because herein lies much of my power. Like you, I am a creature of fire."

'You are not like us,' the Afrit disapprovingly retorted, *'and we refuse to be as you, selfish and power-mad. You threaten an entire world, and possibly others, with your actions. This we would never do.'*

"Really? You mean to say that the assassin for hire that slayed hundreds, if not thousands, over eleven centuries, would simply shrug its shoulders and walk away from its home forever, should returning there cause a slight inconvenience for a few bags of meat and water? Well, a few billion bags of meat and water, but you get the idea. You think I am power-mad, and yet I have never used my abilities to dominate humans. True, I have allied with those whose aims intersect with mine, helped those who in turn could help me, but never have I ruled as did Anu and Enlil, arbitrary and self-proclaimed god-kings, or your unlikely ally from the Abzu who you've brought along. I wish only, as you surely did during your various imprisonments, to return to my own realm. As you once were, I am trapped here against my will. I grow weary of this place and the boisterous and ignorant beings that dwell here. Look deep, Afrit of the Jinn, and you will see we are much alike."

The Afrit bellowed in anger, then launched itself at Iblis, who swiftly raised his staff. For a brief moment, the two were suspended a mere foot apart. They glared menacingly at one another as they strained against forces unseen. Finally, Iblis stepped aside and withdrew his barrier of resistance. The Afrit stumbled clumsily forward, and his opponent delivered a powerful shove from his staff to the creature's back. It sent the monster careening to the far side of the space. Another blast of wind drove the beast against the wall, mashing its body against the beautiful illusory stonework.

Eric watched as Enki hurled himself into the invisible wall of air, trying with all his might to penetrate in order to help his ally. Despite his efforts, the shield held firm, and the great god reluctantly ceased his apparently useless expenditure of energy.

Iblis jubilantly shouted. "You think you are a match for me? I have had centuries to prepare for this moment, millennia to plan how I could dispatch the Lamassu and stop the waters from opening Enlil's gateway, should the key and the scroll come into my possession. In the end, someone did the job for me, likely Sharur, who made such a spectacular exit from the Louvre two years ago. Why he, and most probably his master, Ninurta, did such a thing is as unknown to me as why they suddenly fell silent, but it leaves me with power to *burn*. She may not be able to use it properly, but poor little Lamashtu is certainly endowed with the capacities of a god. Bad news for you, my old friend, because it will now spell your death!"

The crush of force from the staff appeared to double, and the Afrit's torso began to ripple and fray, strands of ash whipped away in the violent vortex of energy.

Eric ran to Enki's side and looked desperately into the wounded and impotent god's face. "Isn't there anything you can do? He's gonna tear the Afrit to pieces!"

The Lord of the Abzu sadly shook his head. *'Without access to the waters all around us, I am powerless. Dimme was right, Iblis is incredibly – '*

The burst of a machine gun interrupted Enki's words. They both turned and saw Lotte firing the Uzi she carried into Dimme's supine and still twitching form. The bullets tore into her chest, adding to the gory mess from the collar that shackled her.

'Stop, child!' Enki cried out. *'What are you doing?'*

She shot him a desperate look. "You heard Iblis! It's *her* energy he's using to power all this. We have to kill her. It's the only way to save the – Ugh!"

Lotte hurtled backward as if swatted by a giant, unseen hand. She fell hard, and her head gave a resounding crack as it bounced on the stonework of the floor. Eric turned and saw Iblis with his staff pointed in her direction. Incredibly, it appeared Lotte's action had distracted him, perhaps by interrupting the flow of energy from Dimme's body. Now, however, the Jinn had trained his full attention on her.

"That was unwise," Iblis declared, "but perhaps you've given me the answer to our little standoff. The *Sadat Alnaar* clearly adores her Afrit. Let's find out if the feeling is truly mutual." With a wave of his hand, the shining orb between the great pillars brightened and began to throb.

'Quickly!' Enki cried. *'We must flee!'*

Eric didn't need to be told twice. He joined step with his supernatural companion as they ran toward Lotte, who lay unmoving on the ground. A glance over his shoulder verified that something rapidly approached them: something big and extremely dangerous. He and Lotte would be incinerated if struck by even a small amount of fire from that portal. The far door stood a long way away, and he had no aspirations of outrunning the blast. He trusted that Enki had a plan, but it looked pretty hopeless from where he stood.

There was no sound, but the orange-white glow told him the flames were rising behind them. They had only just reached Lotte. Enki gently but hurriedly lifted her into his arms, but Eric knew they were too late. He turned to meet his fate.

Even had he wanted to witness the end, the light was too bright to view directly. Eyes shut, he felt the warmth of the approaching flames while he struggled to stand fast against the incendiary wind that blew death at both him and the woman for whom he'd sacrificed everything.

At least we die together.

Lotte's face was all he saw in his mind, strangely still adorned with the squiggly eyebrows she hadn't sported in nearly a decade.

Something caught him from the side and knocked him painfully to the ground. Sparing a glance, he opened his eyes and saw a bleeding gash in his left bicep. Ignoring the excruciating sting, he looked up. The Afrit loomed above him, dark, cloven hooves anchored to the floor, wings beating furiously to steady the bulk of its body.

Eric assumed he'd been struck by one of these appendages, hopefully unintentionally, but he wasn't about to complain. The creature had interposed itself between the projectile of fire and its three companions. Now, it battled to control and contain the surge of force that would surely have killed Lotte and himself, and possibly the injured and diminished Enki.

'Run!' the Afrit commanded. 'We cannot assimilate this flame that Iblis conjures. It is under his control. Another blast is sure to follow. If it is stronger than this, we will struggle to contain it.'

Eric ran.

Enki had already scooped up Lotte and now moved with great speed, not toward the far door, but toward the alcove in the wall containing the shattered remnants of the structure that once housed the Tablet of Destinies. He rounded the corner and disappeared.

Eric still had about fifteen yards to cover before he reached safety, when the wall and floor again shone with a threatening orange glow. He couldn't run any faster. He could only hope that the Afrit could absorb this strike as effectively as the last.

He tried to slow himself in order to make the sharp turn, but the illusion of polished marble on the floor proved to be as slick as its material world counterpart. He started to slide past the gap between the wall of the alcove and the shambolic structure it housed. Again, he felt the heat from the oncoming blast.

At seemingly the last second, strong hands grabbed the front of his shirt and pulled him in. A streak of flame engulfed the air behind him, singing his back and igniting his hair and clothes. Enki quickly smothered him while he batted madly at his head to extinguish the flames. The pungent stench of burnt hair permeated the air around them.

"Damn. Thanks. How is Lotte?"

'She was unconscious, but now recovers. Go to her. I will signal to the Afrit that we are safe, or as safe as we can be.'

Eric navigated the narrow alleyway that curved between the outer wall of the chamber and that of the structure nestled in the alcove. Sharur had broken in at the top near the front, so the back and side wall of the repository remained sound. When he reached her, she sat propped against the azure blue tiles of the wall, still decidedly groggy.

"What... happened?" she slurred. "All I remember... well... I was shooting that gun. Now, everything's just spinning around."

"Try to sit still. You hit your head pretty bad on the ground. You probably have another concussion, really not a good thing for that oversize brain of yours."

She didn't laugh. "The Afrit... what happened?"

"It's fine, or at least it was the last time I saw it. Shooting at Dimme like you did probably saved its ass, and it returned the favor when Iblis went after us. That was a brave thing you did... and smart... and dangerous, too, I guess."

"It was... it was the only way. That woman is the key. Iblis... *milks* her. Stop her... and you stop Iblis."

'*She is right,*' Enki said as he rounded the corner, the rather beleaguered looking Afrit in tow behind him. '*Iblis spoke true... he came prepared. Now he has retrieved the body of my incapacitated half-sister behind his protective shield. We no longer have her assistance in lowering the barrier, and he again focuses the energy of his gateway on the ice blocking the doorway.*'

"What if we get more grenades," Eric ventured, "try to break through again? Can't you control the fire of the portal against Iblis?"

'*The energy of the fire stones will not be enough,*' the Afrit sourly replied. '*Iblis's power over the force from the Eternal Flame is insidious. He merges the realms of flame and wind in a way that is unfamiliar to us. In this case, fire cannot not fight fire. Even should we again penetrate the barrier, his might here is too great.*'

Enki cut in. '*Only because we cannot break through to the waters of the Abzu all around us. Again, Iblis spoke true. He knew he had to both eliminate the Lamassu, as well as prevent the flow of water that would release Enlil. Failure to do either would not permit him to focus on the doorway. With the Lamassu gone, there is no one who can open the tributaries and let the water flow. If there were, I could penetrate the barrier and stop him. Fire may not be able to fight fire, but water can, especially the waters of my Abzu, in the service of their master.*'

The Afrit turned and placed its clawed hands on the chamber's outer wall. Its talons ran gently across the surface, and the creature's wings flexed with small spasms in the cramped space.

Finally, the beast spoke. '*Where water might flow from the felines' mouths at the base of the pedestal in the great pool, the energy would be no stronger than here?*'

'*No stronger, perchance weaker,*' Enki suspiciously replied. '*That is the barrier of energy that the Lamassu would release when necessary to activate Enlil's gateway. What do you have in mind?*'

The Afrit didn't respond. Instead, it sidled past Enki and Eric to where Lotte sat, eyes closed and still largely despondent. The hulking creature bent and touched her cheek with its terrible claws, then brought its massive, fanged mouth to her ear. It appeared to whisper something—something guarded, quiet, and unintelligible. She shivered and began to aimlessly wave her arms as if grasping for some unseen object just out of reach.

Eric bent down to try and calm her, but the Afrit grabbed his arm. *'Come... now. We have need of you. Goat-Man, be ready. Your window will be brief and surprise your ally. In this, you cannot fail.'*

Enki nodded, a somber look on his face.

The Afrit guided Eric down the alley toward the entrance near the door where they had entered the chamber. Enki slipped off in the other direction.

"We're going out there again?" Eric nervously asked. "Aren't you afraid of more firebombs from your old buddy?"

'Iblis's focus is elsewhere. He believes we now pose no threat, so he has returned to his melting of the ice.'

"So, what are we gonna do?"

'Your task is simple. On our command, you will throw the last of the fire stones.'

"Gotta admit, that's pretty simple. I'll do my best."

The Afrit brought its unfathomable gaze to bear on him. *'Please do, as always you have.'*

After one cautious glance around the corner, the creature strode into the chamber and bid Eric follow. They skulked across the room in the direction of the massive pool in which Enlil's gigantic arched gateway lurked. The dais and throne, and the great lion-headed pillar that supported the now headless Lamassu statue, rose majestically behind.

The pool formed a depression in the illusory stonework, with no ledge or wall to contain it. The shining marble of the rest of the floor simply gave way to an imaginary mosaic of tiles, which sloped gently downward toward the circular basin at the center. Here, when the water covered this lowest area, the gateway would open, and one could converse with Enlil as they once had with Enki. When it crested the arch above, the god so holy that supposedly even other gods could not look upon him would be able to come forth.

Eric spared a glance back in the direction of Iblis and the frozen doorway, again engulfed in steam and fire. Enki stood midway between, his sober and determined gaze focused upon them, hands clasped in front of his chest as if in prayer. Eric flashed a slight smile and waved, but the great god made no rejoinder.

'Focus,' the Afrit grumbled. 'How close do you need to be for the stone to strike the pillar when thrown... without being too close by?'

"Umm, I guess I'd need to be about even with the basin to be certain of hitting it. I'll need to circle a little wide. It gets steep the closer to the middle you get. I don't want to fall in. Like, right about there.... Will that work?"

'Perhaps, perhaps not. Be certain of hitting the pillar. The rest... we shall see.'

That appeared to be all the answer he was going to get, so they carefully maneuvered to the spot Eric had picked.

'On our command.... Are you ready?'

He nodded, and the beast took to the air. Eric readied the grenade and locked his finger in the pin. Thrice, the creature circled the great pool, approaching the faces of the lions on the pillar, then turning away for another pass. On the fourth circuit, the monster called down to him.

'Now!'

Eric pulled the pin and threw the heavy little pineapple-shaped bomb. He'd never had the best arm in Little League, nor the best swing or fielding abilities, for that matter, but this pillar was gigantic. At this distance, he really couldn't miss. Anticipating that the Afrit would absorb and shape the energy of the explosion, he completed the arc of his throw, crouched on the sloping floor, and watched. His aim wasn't perfect, but it seemed good enough. He hit the stone of the pillar a few feet below the gaping maws of the lions from where water might flow when the energy barrier was removed.

The Afrit timed its strike in perfect concert with the blast. Again, the dull thud of the grenade sounded in the cathedral-like chamber, and the metal casing fell to the ground and skittered into the basin of the pool. The ashen monster channeled the force of the blast inward and the lattice of glowing veins in its body surged with a molten radiance. Almost instantly, the creature became a flaming missile of fiery energy, and it slammed with incalculable force directly into the mouth of the rightmost lion.

This time, there was a kaboom. A big kaboom.

I guess I should have run, Eric idly thought as his body lifted skyward. Deep inside, he understood that he'd never have gotten far enough away to avoid an explosion of this magnitude, but the idea of getting away had always appealed to his sensibilities.

A cacophonous sound accompanied the impact that sent him flying. He landed on his back with a bone-rattling jolt, then slid agonizingly across the mosaic floor of the pool. It took him a moment to regain his senses. When he did, he saw the air above him engulfed in flame. With excruciating effort, he rolled onto his stomach to protect his face from the heat. Ears ringing, back screaming, and bicep bleeding, he fought to retain consciousness. Lacking other options, he closed his eyes, covered his head, and waited for the worst to pass.

There was no telling how much time had gone by: a minute, an hour? Perhaps a lifetime.

Sound slowly returned to Eric's world: a strange noise, somewhere between the crackling of a fire and the rustling of dry leaves in the wind.

Water. Flowing water.

He tested his back and shoulders, probing for dislocations or broken bones, but found nothing save the deep bruises and abrasions he'd fully come to expect with excursions such as this. He lay near the edge of the pool, just beneath the border where imaginary tile met the mirage of stone. Carefully, he lifted himself up on his elbows and looked behind him. For all the turmoil of the mighty blast, the pillar seemed largely unscathed. Only the mouth of the rightmost lion bore a crack, and a softball-size hole from which water gushed. The basin of the pool had already filled, and the familiar glow of the open portal cast its illumination upward.

What the hell? How long have I been lying here?

Ignoring the protests of his battered body, he shakily stood and peered over the edge of the pool.

Enki stood near the frozen doorway, but nothing looked as it had before. The steam and fire had vanished, as had the glowing light from Iblis's portal to the Eternal Flame. The wall and doorway were now largely visible, obscured only by a giant block of ice that creaked and cracked in response to Enki's wild gesticulations.

Eric dragged himself out of the pool and stumbled toward the great god. As he got closer, he realized the body of Iblis was trapped and unable to move in the great mass of ice.

The Jinn stared outward, the look on his face a mixture of incredulousness and an almost happy resignation at his failure and fate. His hooded robe lay in a heap at his feet. Clearly, the Jinn had tried to flee in his immaterial form, as Aicha had, but Enki's magic had rendered this impossible. His nude form displayed the ravages of the fire that had immolated his hapless and unknowing host thousands of years before. With each thunderous crack, the ice compacted, growing smaller and denser around the once mighty Jinn.

'You live,' Enki said, obviously distracted by the task which engaged him. *'I feared the implosion would end your life along with that of the creature of fire.'*

"What? What are you saying? Are you telling me the Afrit is dead?"

'Naturally. What did you think it planned to do to penetrate the wall of force that separates this place from the Abzu beyond? Unlike Iblis's barrier, this energy is unable to shift and redistribute itself at its master's command. Additionally, the source of its power is ultimately water, diametrically opposed to the potency of flame. It is exactly this prescript I use now to contain and destroy Iblis. The Afrit knew this, but also knew that it would take every grain of energy that it possessed to break through. Just one moment....'

Eric attempted to process what Enki had just told him while the Lord of the Abzu clasped his hands together and tensed his body. He then threw his arms wide and thrust forward. The block of ice cracked and compacted once again, and Iblis's body shattered under the pressure. The inside of the shining boulder became a sickening scene of crushed flesh, bone, and innards.

"Wow. I guess that's it for Iblis now, too."

'Indeed. Once I had the power of the Abzu at my disposal, breaking through Iblis's barrier was simple. As your mistress deduced, Dimme was the key to his power. Without my half-sister's resources, he could not prevail.'

"Umm, speaking of Dimme, where is she?"

'I have her likewise trapped in the ice, right over there.'

Eric looked to where Enki distractedly pointed and saw the woman's cloaked form encased in a somewhat opaque mound of frozen slush. It looked almost as if the great god had used the steam from the doorway to form the prison that now entrapped her.

'Sequestering her was my first priority. The power of the frozen waters of the Abzu diminished Iblis's ability to draw on her energy. Once she was largely out of the way, I turned my full attention to him. He fought me with the powers of flame from his portal, as well as wind from his staff, but without Dimme's energy, he was no match for me. The fire I countered with a barrier of ice as stout as that guarding the doorway to the An, and a blast of water washed the staff from his hands and shattered the delicate latticework that held the magnetic stone in place, depriving the item of its magical properties.'

Eric looked at the wall near the ice-filled doorway and saw the twisted and broken staff. The ball of meteoric iron rested some fifteen feet away.

Hmmm. Solid gold staff. That's probably worth something. Sure would be nice to offset some of the cost of those ridiculously expensive plane tickets to Oman. Eh, forget it. I don't think Enki will take very kindly if I walk out of here with that under my arm. Too bad.

Enki interrupted Eric's idle musings. *'Iblis knew he was defeated and tried to flee. I froze the air around him to prevent his escape in immaterial form. Now, the job is nearly finished. When I am certain Iblis is no more, I will turn my attention to Dimme, or will perhaps leave her fate to Enlil, who will soon emerge from his slumber when the waters crest the arch of his gateway.'*

Eric walked over to examine the frozen body of Enki's disquieting half-sister. His Nike sneaker made a sloshing sound. He stopped dead still. A stream of blood, likely from the sharp, thick spikes that had pierced the fearsome woman's neck, or else Lotte's machine gun bullets, oozed from the mound of frozen slush that encased her unmoving form and expanded into a rose-tinged puddle.

Why is this ice melting?

He clearly registered the damp chill of Enki's magic all around him. He leaned over Dimme's figure to try and locate the source of the water. A narrow tunnel seemed to snake through the frozen mist, and he tracked it from the near the floor toward her body. In a panic, he threw his hands on the top of the mound and frantically wiped at the snowy slush so he could see.

The emptiness of the hood of Dimme's cloak felt to Eric like a confrontation with the abyss. Iron sections of the spiked collar lay in disarray where her neck had once been, the gold seals having seemingly melted away. He recoiled in horror and tried to scream, but breath had abandoned his body. A wave of nauseating dizziness dropped him to his knees.

'What is it?' Enki demanded. *'Are you injured?'*

"She's... she's... gone."

'Gone?' The great god turned his attention from the pulped ruin of Iblis and ran to where Eric knelt in the bloody puddle. *'Oh, child of Anu, how I underestimated your prowess. The shattering of the staff undid the magic from the collar that held her captive. She was able to melt the gold seals, and slipped away while I battled Iblis.'*

"Lotte," Eric whispered, barely able to speak. "Her baby... our baby... Dimme! She can't get to Lotte! She'll kill our child!"

'I will run to her. Follow as you can.'

Enki moved with such great speed that he virtually vanished before Eric's eyes. It wasn't long before he emerged from the alcove behind the ruined receptacle building, Lotte draped lifelessly in his arms. The Lord of the Abzu moved quickly but carefully across the room and descended out of sight into the great pool that the stream of water from the mouth of the lion still gradually filled with water.

Eric crawled out of the puddle and hauled himself to his feet. His injuries, as well as his state of shock, prevented him from moving quickly, but he forced himself forward, dreading what he might find. He crossed the border of stone and tile, and carefully navigated the downward incline.

In the basin of the pool, Enki had lowered Lotte into the water. *'Your fears were warranted. Dimme has gotten to her. Your love lives, but she bleeds. Inside. Here in the waters, I can heal her. She will survive, but your child....'*

Blood blossomed from between the thighs of Lotte's black cargo pants. Eric watched in mute dismay as it flowed away from her in delicate, inky coils, tinting crimson the clear and glowing waters of the Abzu. He watched until he could watch no more, until his eyes closed of their own accord, and all for him faded into a haze of overwhelming bleakness.

CHAPTER 20

Tears of exhaustion and frustration streamed down Lotte's face. Her head lolled to the side as sleep tried to assert itself, but then she jerked to attention and continued her marathon of torturous concentration.

"Maybe you should take a break," Eric offered. "You've been at this for hours."

She wiped her nose and eyes with her hand and looked forlornly up at him. She sat cross-legged at the apex of the black marble board, the great gleaming frame of the Afrit's portal above her against the brickwork wall of Siddique's apartment. The curtains were drawn to the gorgeous late-October day outside, the candles gleaming in their bowls providing the only illumination.

With their secret location in Boston likely compromised, they'd stashed the portals at Siddique's place until a new storage facility could be secured. Their friend hadn't exactly been thrilled with the disruption, especially on the heels of hosting Olive, who fortunately had displayed no suspicious symptoms of Aicha's presence in her body, and who, with Lotte's approval, had flown back to Georgia.

Now, the cases and bags of the various portals dominated Siddique's tiny living room and minimal closet space. He'd been equally unenthusiastic to see them at his door at 6:00 this morning, but Lotte had been insistent, so he'd grudgingly let them in before he wearily left for work, calling them both "crazy," as usual.

"I... I can't," she snuffled. "I know it's in there. I felt it. It called to me... I'm certain. I have to reach it. It seemed... lost. I have to stay here until it can find me."

Eric rose from the couch, where he'd retreated when the floor had become unbearable, and sat once again beside her. "I know, but this is killing you. You're literally falling asleep, and you must be starving. I know I am. It's three in the afternoon and we haven't eaten anything since that crummy little breakfast bar in the car at five a.m. on the way over here. Plus... I mean... maybe... well, never mind. Forget it. Can't I just make you something to eat?"

"Plus what? What were you going to say? Tell me."

He sighed deeply. "All right, but don't take this the wrong way. I'm just wondering if maybe... I mean, it might be possible that... well, like, what if this is kind of... sort of —"

"Eric, just say it already."

"Okay, sorry. I'm just worried that this may be... well... in your head... kind of wishful thinking, or even displaced emotions. I mean, the Afrit is dead, right? How could it really be calling to you now?"

She sat motionless, and he felt the icy glare of her black-hole-sun eyes bearing down upon him.

"The return of *Doktor Freud*, I see," she finally scoffed. "Actually, much as I hate to admit it, that isn't fair. I'm a scientist, and empirically, I know my personal experience isn't worth a damn. I had a dream, an especially vivid one. It felt a lot like the dreams I had back in high school, and maybe a bit like the one the Afrit sent me after he'd absorbed Ninurta. This was different, though. As I say, the creature seemed lost, like it was searching for something — possibly me — but it didn't know quite where or how to look. That's all I really know. I thought by opening the portal and reaching out, it could find me."

"Or you could find it."

"Meaning what?"

"Meaning that you could find... well... what was lost. Maybe this is your way of coping, of dealing with what happened — having a dream where you're reunited with... well... you get the idea. I don't know. It just seems like you've taken things pretty much in stride. You haven't really talked about it since it happened, and you started right back with school. Yeah, you're working from home a lot more now, but it seems like you've sort of... moved on, I guess. I just wonder what might be going on with you, like... inside."

Only once had he gotten any inclination that something for her might still be percolating since their experience in Oman. He'd come home early from work one day, a fairly regular occurrence in the month or so since they had semi-victoriously limped home, and had found her in the living room. She stared at the far wall while she silently danced, listening to one of her old vinyl albums through headphones, wearing nothing but her underwear and a faded black t-shirt. He couldn't determine which band. The logo was on the front. Not wishing to disturb her, he'd slipped quietly back out through the kitchen.

That had been the only instance where he'd sensed anything might be out of sorts, except for that horrible morning, after the battle with Iblis, and after Dimme had broken free. The despair of that ordeal would forever dwell in his mind. Unbidden, emotions now rose from the depths of his soul, where he'd valiantly but futilely tried to entomb their miserable memory.

Eric was shaken from his stupor by Enki, who vigorously tugged at his shirt while projecting stern but measured words.

'Do you hear me? Do you understand?'

The great god had said a number of things, but to be honest, little had registered with Eric. He'd complied when Enki had pushed him forward, and he carried some vague recollection of walking back the way they'd come through the curving azure corridor, but he couldn't attest to anything beyond that.

"I'm... I'm sorry. Can you repeat what you told me?"

The Lord of the Abzu flashed a sympathetic look, and patience came to his tone. *'I instructed you to stay here and to watch over your mistress.'*

Unsure where "here" was, he glanced around. They stood in the entryway to the Rope of An and Ki. The colossal diamond-eyed Lamassu statues towered above them. Lotte lay at the base of the leftmost pedestal, where Enki had placed her, clothes still damp from her immersion in the waters of the great basin. He realized his clothes were also wet, and a hazy memory came to him of suspending her as she floated unconscious in the glowing pool.

'She sleeps, and will do so for some time while recovering. I must speak with my brother, who will need to hear of what happened and address the damage Iblis has wrought. I dispatched what remained of the nefarious Jinn while you bathed your mate in the healing waters of the Abzu. I retrieved the key and the scroll from his cloak. Enlil and I will decide the fate of those items. It is best if you stay well away. My brother has a temper, and it would not be surprising if in some way he attempted to force you into his service. I shall return, and we will leave this place together.'

It was all the same to Eric. He sat quietly by Lotte, hand on her shoulder, unconcerned by whatever destiny might await him.

He had no idea how much time had passed when Enki came back. The Lord of the Abzu offered nothing about his conversation, and Eric didn't ask—he didn't really even care.

He simply followed as Enki carried Lotte out through the mist of the doorway, back into the echoing silence of the Majlis al Jinn. Together they ascended the rocks of the breakdown to where the aluminum platform still dutifully sat vigil. He clung to Enki's neck as he effortlessly climbed the cable, reluctantly leaving Lotte below, but that would be brief as Enki would quickly return to fetch her.

Once at the top, Eric morosely activated the winch, and waited despondently as his companions rose to the surface.

Dawn promised itself in the sky to the east. The sun rose as Eric drove the SUV down the mountainside and away from the great cave, and the small village, and the events that unfolded in these no longer faraway places that he would never forget.

"Why?" he asked as he navigated the Pajero down the rough trail. He wasn't actually aware he'd spoken out loud until Enki responded from the back seat, where he cradled Lotte's still unconscious body.

'Why what, young prince?'

"I just don't get it. The Afrit could have taken Lotte and flown away, forced her to return it to the Eternal Flame, or just found somebody else to do it. It doesn't make any sense, especially if what you said is true... that it actually knew it was gonna die. Why... why would the Afrit do what it did?"

The great god replied after a pause. *'I have no firm answer. The Afrit was a creature of its word, but all beings have their limits when it comes to their own continued existence, even me. I sense that more must be at play. Perhaps, in the end, the creature of fire judged your kind worthy of continued existence, though I imagine this was predicated upon the behavior and actions of a precious few. Doubtless, the beast has seen the very worst of human behavior in its time here. Against all odds, it chose a different course, surely guided by the hand of those who looked past their own predispositions of fear, or want of material power, and were able, in their own ways, to show the creature compassion, integrity, and perhaps in some cases... love.'*

They reached the beach and disembarked from the rented SUV. The vehicle had survived the ordeal remarkably unscathed, losing only its tire-iron, which Eric had forgotten to retrieve.

Oh, well.

Enki carried Lotte to where the waters danced against the night-cooled sands.

Eric followed, though he knew not why.

The great god placed her down and faced him. *'I take my leave. I have business for a time in your world, as does Enlil. We have both been... selfish, shortsighted. The changes we sought to contain, or control, have only accelerated during our slumber, but change defines your kind, as does your capacity to learn.*

This was perhaps our greatest mistake. I, too, have learned, and there is more knowledge to be gained. We cannot go back. Even the Tablet of Destinies cannot rectify all past misdeeds. We can, however, go forward, if we so choose. I know there will be pain in your hearts, but as your sun rises above us, a new day brings the possibility of future joys. I will not experience them in eternal sleep, nor you and your love in eternal misery. Mourn, but come back to us. We have need of you... both of you. You remain the guardians of my portal, as well as others, and though it has cost you, may the day soon come that you will rejoice at what you have accomplished, and have yet to achieve together. You will see me again, when the time is right.'

The Lord of the Abzu shed what remained of his shredded and bloody dishdasha, bowed deeply, and then turned to face the ocean. He walked serenely forth until the waves washed over his head. Eric barely caught a glimpse of the sweeping horns of an ibex, propelled forth by the serpentine tail of an enormous fish that slashed through the sparkling water, before they disappeared into the depths.

The sun had risen high in the sky when Lotte finally woke. Eric agonizingly told her what had happened. This time he couldn't spare her the disturbing details or protect her from the harshest of realities.

She sobbed when he told her about the Afrit, pounding her fist repeatedly on the sand in doleful anger, but that soon ceased.

The other news brought a cold calm to her face. She silently rose to her feet and followed Enki's footsteps into the tide. There, the roar of the surf drowned out her racking and violent howls of anguish, and carried her bottomless sorrow out with it into the vastness of the ocean.

Lotte hiccupped a little laugh. "Really? This is what you think my dream is all about... that wanting to find the Afrit is just a disguised surrogate feeling for wanting to have our child back?"

"I don't *think* it. I just... wonder."

"Well, I suppose it's a fair enough hypothesis with the current lack of any corroborating evidence on my end. It's just that... well... it happens to fit in with something I thought I heard... though maybe I didn't really. I don't know. It's all so odd."

"What do you think you heard?"

"It'll sound strange."

"Stranger than waking up at four in the morning screaming about the Afrit looking for you?"

She rolled her eyes. "Quite possibly. Let me ask you: did the Afrit say anything to me? I was in and out of consciousness after Iblis's strike when I hit my head. I remember talking to you in that alley, but then I sort of lost it. Do you remember anything?"

"Now that you mention it, yeah, I do. It was right after Chuckles made the decision to turn itself into a guided missile and blow through that lion spout, though I didn't know that was what it planned to do at the time. It bent down and whispered something in your ear. I couldn't hear what it said. Are you saying you remember it speaking to you?"

"I recall something, whether it's real or not. I keep thinking it said, *'Remember us, in your dreams.'* Those words are just so clear in my mind, like they've been burned there—no pun intended."

"Well, like I said, I didn't hear anything, but that's awfully coincidental, don't you think? Are you sure you didn't dream that, too?"

"No. As I said, I'm not sure of anything. It *feels* real to me, but you could well be right. All this could simply be a dream, and maybe it *is* related to my feelings. I don't really know what's happening. There, are you happy? I've admitted that possibility. But let me ask *you* a question. Where were you last night, and who were you with?"

"Are you kidding me? You know where I was. I went to the Pats game. I asked you if you wanted to go. I'd have gotten you a ticket, but you said you were too busy. You also reminded me how you think American Football is so 'bloody boring.' Remember?"

"Oh, I remember. I'm not accusing you of anything. I just want you to think for a moment. Who did you go to the game with?"

"Nobody. You know that. I went by myself."

"Why? Why didn't you ask Siddique to go, or somebody else from work? They'd have loved to have gone. You've gone to baseball games with them, and we've all gone to see the Bruins and Harvard play hockey together. It seems unusual that you'd go solo, don't you think?"

"I... I don't know. I didn't really think that much about it. I just wanted to go."

"Like you want to come home early from work every day, or go in late... or both? Like you want to lie on the couch in the living room every night and all weekend? Have you thought at all about any of those things?"

"I'm... I'm just tired. I haven't felt like reading at night. I just want to watch TV. I don't want to bother you."

"Well, that's very considerate, but this isn't exactly like you, is it?"

"Okay, now it's my turn. What are you trying to say?"

"Eric, I'm not angry. Quite the opposite, really. You wonder if my dream is a way of dealing with feelings I haven't confronted. You may be right. I'm wondering if your behavior is the same. Maybe this your way of *not* dealing with it. Look, I get it. It's only been a month. I'm not rushing you. I'm not saying you're doing anything wrong. I just hope that you're paying as much attention to *your* inner feelings as you are to what you think *mine* are. I also know we suffer from the same debilitating affliction."

"And that would be?"

She laughed. "Only-child syndrome! Neither of us are particularly good at communicating. We just tend to go our own way and keep our own company, especially when things get difficult. It's exactly what I did in high school, but do you know what? That was stupid. You can't do it all yourself. You need someone to talk with, someone to bounce ideas off of, someone to trust, who trusts you back. That's what you gave me, and without that I'm not certain I'd be here today. Guess what? We still have that, and it's not a one-way street. Why do you think I'm working from home so much?"

"I don't know. I don't understand all the ins and outs of what you do. I figured it just worked better for you to do things at home."

"Well, it does, at least for now. I have a ton of stuff to catch up on, including the work for Dr. Henriksson I didn't finish when I had to leave for Greece, but it's more than that. You seem really down. I wanted to be here if you needed me, if you wanted to talk. I wanted to keep my eye on you, make sure you were okay."

He felt exposed. She was right, of course. His behavior was strange, even for him, and that was saying something. He'd attributed it to jet lag, then to his various injuries, though in truth, the waters of the Abzu under the arch of Enlil's semi-open gateway had inadvertently cured most of his ailments while he'd tended to her. Really, though, there hadn't been any rationale behind it. He just couldn't concentrate on anything. Everything just seemed so incredibly difficult and... so utterly pointless. Seeing her return to normal so quickly had also made him feel alienated and somewhat incompetent.

"Aren't you down too?" he asked. "Why is it so easy for you to just... move on?"

She closed her eyes. "Oh, Eric, there's nothing easy about this at all. I am down—*incredibly* down. What happened is awful, but think about it: we might have saved the entire planet. You know what that means? It means we get to try again, this time more thoughtfully, when we're *really* ready. That's why I want to work so hard, so I can be done with this bloody program and get on with our lives, live the way we've always dreamed. Despite how things turned out, we learned something that we might never have known otherwise—we both want children... a lot! How about that? Now I want them even more than ever, because I know you're in for what that really means to us. I'm working to get to a place where it's truly possible."

He was stunned. "When the hell did you become so well-adjusted?"

She beamed. "It was after I met you, that's for sure, and believe me, I'm still a work in progress." She hugged him, and then quickly stretched out and put her head in his lap. "You never told me who won the game. Did you have fun?"

"You were sound asleep when I got in. Those eight-thirty starts are brutal, and I took the train home from the stadium after. Then you woke up screaming that we had to drive to Worcester like two hours later. Pats won 23-7. You'll be sorry to hear they beat the Falcons. I know how you love your black birds."

She giggled slightly.

"Did I have fun?" *Jeez,* did *I have fun?* For a time, he replayed the game in his mind, though really nothing that happened on the field came to him.

"I guess I did. It was good to go, good to be there, be one among many. I felt invisible. I suppose that's probably what I was after. I wanted to be in a crowd, but if I couldn't be with you, I wanted to be alone."

A spike of sorrow pierced his heart.

That's a lie!

Tears filled his eyes.

"No, I didn't. I didn't want to be alone, and I wasn't. She was there with me... or *he* was, but I usually picture her as a little girl. She has black hair and black eyes, like yours, and she's curious about everything—not like you, though. She doesn't *devour* knowledge. She just wants her question answered, as if it's a game, as if knowing is both the means and the end. Then it's time to get ice cream. Yeah, she likes ice cream too, just like you. I told her what was happening on the field, every play—told her she was watching Tom Brady and Bill Belichick, two of the greatest ever. I remember my dad doing that. I remember, and somehow, I sensed she'd remember too—not the details, but just being together, lost in this sea of cheering people... all the lights, the noise, the smell of the concession stands, the feel of her father wiping ice cream off her chin with a paper napkin. That's what dads do, right? She'd remember. She'd remember all that, wouldn't she?"

Lotte didn't answer. He bent over and saw her eyes were shut tight. She was fast asleep.

Seriously?

It didn't matter. He felt better. He didn't need to confess to her. He needed to be honest with himself, admit that his heart had been ripped out in that giant underwater chamber, and that the sense of purpose he'd felt so strongly had left a gaping hole in the tattered fabric of his life when it had been torn away.

It definitely helped to know how she felt about it. He could see a path forward, as Enki had said, a "tomorrow," which held the promise of being better than today. He was starting to realize, though, that this would take some work. It was work that he'd been avoiding, because it was just too painful to confront. For all the dire and life-threatening situations he'd been in, he figured he'd be better at confronting things than he was, but as Bill Belichick liked to say, "It is what it is."

Lotte twitched. She was dreaming.

He resigned himself to sitting in this position until he lost circulation in his legs. There was nothing to look at save the candles flickering in their bowls. He let them lull him into a welcome calm as he softly stroked her arm. He wasn't okay, not yet, but for the first time in a month, he sensed "okay" might actually be in his future.

A movement caught his eye. At first, he thought it was something on the brick wall behind the thick, ancient glass in the resplendent frame. Then he realized it was coming from the glass itself.

Lotte's movements intensified. Her entire body became a cacophony of small spasms.

He reached for her shoulder, intending to wake her, but stopped short.

Remember us, in your dreams. The words froze him. *Could she be right? Could it be possible? Only one way to find out.*

He sat without moving a muscle, taking shallow breaths as he focused on the glass of the un-mirrored mirror — a slight wisp here, a puff of what appeared to be smoke or ash there. They were sporadic and chaotic, totally unlike the purposeful and organized coalescing of particles he'd witnessed in wonder so many times before. It's basic appearance, however, seemed identical, and after what appeared to be a series of aborted trial runs, a glittering mass of black ash took form in the center of the rectangle of glass.

It took its time, but soon a small tendril extended tentatively forth, probing the air like the flittering tongue of a snake. Seemingly satisfied, it quested outward, and reached with hunger toward the light of the candles in the large bowl at the center of the arced black marble board.

Lotte began to softly moan as the fragile coil of ash drifted upward, carried by the amplified heat of the flames. Slowly, it began to rotate.

Sluggishly, the visage of the beast attempted to form. Particles fused then broke apart, spilling clouds of mist into the air, which the spinning, ashen column gruelingly reabsorbed. Finally, something appeared to gel, and a ghost of the creature's horned head materialized. From there, the rest of the beast's body and wings incrementally unfolded, while its cloven hooves pawed at the fabric of Siddique's faux Turkish rug.

The monster was miniscule in comparison with what Eric had most recently seen, more like the tiny imp that Lotte had gathered into her rucksack and let fly free in Boston's night sky, or the one he'd battled in the kitchen of 246 Holton Hill Road twelve years before. Mingled in the darkness of the ash, however, he still perceived streaks of molten magma, and its horns still pulsed from blue to orange to a hot yellow. The beast might be slight in stature, but nevertheless burned with the intense energy of a demi-god. Its lava-like eyes darted furtively around the darkened room, as if it were seeing a realm other than the Eternal Flame for the first time.

Now that the creature had fully materialized, Eric figured it was probably time to awaken Lotte, who still trembled in his lap. He grabbed her shoulder and shook her gently.

"Stop," she sleepily groaned. "You wanted me to sleep, and now you wake me up."

"Umm, I think there's something here you might want to see."

She opened her eyes. *"Scheiße!"*

She slowly lifted herself up, stared for a moment, and crawled hesitantly forward.

The tiny beast spied her. It unfurled its wings, which twitched as it began to smoothly sway from side to side.

Eric filled her in. "It came after you fell asleep, after you'd started dreaming. Do you remember anything?"

"It's kind of a jumble. I felt the same sense of searching. It was just as intense, but somehow not so disturbing. It felt like the first time I summoned the Afrit, when I had that overwhelming sensation that I was doing exactly what I was supposed to have been doing all along, but it was all mixed up with something else."

"What do you mean?"

"Well, I'm not sure. I felt like I was in this crowded place, people everywhere yelling and screaming. For some reason, I was eating ice cream. I got some on my chin, and a nice man wiped it away with a paper napkin. It made me feel... I don't know... *safe*, somehow. What do you think *that's* all about?"

He didn't answer. She had crawled within two feet of the miniature simulacrum of the once mighty and terrible Afrit. He knew how much this meant to her. Her sorrow at losing her connection to the beast had been almost as terrible as losing their child to Dimme. He also had to admit, he actually missed the curmudgeonly thing as well, and he wondered how much of the Afrit they'd known carried on in this small sliver, which the monster had apparently left behind.

She reached out her hand, and the impish beast's wings fluttered. It flinched and cowered slightly, but then haltingly stretched forward, extended its taloned hand, and gently brushed the fire opal on her golden wedding band. She started to simultaneously laugh and cry, and Eric crawled toward the woman he so loved to lend his support.

The little monster suddenly screeched and hissed as it recoiled, raking at him with its tiny claws and raising its barbed tail above its horned head.

Eric laughed.

Some things, it seemed, were simply never meant to be.

THE END

(**...although Eric's and Lotte's adventures will continue. To help ensure that happens, please consider leaving a review on whichever site you typically purchase books online. Your support is critical to the success of independent publishers like Evolved Publishing, and independent authors like William E. Noland. Reviews send a strong signal to potential readers and encourage online booksellers to promote the titles. If you'd like to see more books like this one, leaving an honest, heartfelt review is one of the best, and most sincerely appreciated, forms of support that any loyal reader can offer. Thank you so much.**)

ACKNOWLEDGEMENTS

As always, my great thanks to the team at Evolved Publishing, especially my editor, Dave Lane (AKA Lane Diamond), and cover artist Kris Norris.

My sincere appreciation goes to all my friends and family who have read earlier versions of this book, and the other books in the series, and to all my readers, whose support is indispensable.

And as ever, thank you to my wife, Madeleine, whose energy and spirit buoys me through the challenges of the creative process. All my love to you.

ABOUT THE AUTHOR

William Noland combines a lifelong love of speculative fiction with a passion for history, sociology, and psychology. Engaging and entertaining, Noland's stories carry his hallmark of strong character development that weaves through every book in this page-turner series. In addition to writing, William plays in multiple rock bands and loves international travel and reading. He lives in Massachusetts with his wife and two cats.

For more, please visit William E. Noland online at:
Website: www.WENoland.com
Goodreads: William E. Noland
Facebook: @WENoland.Author
LinkedIn: www.linkedin.com/in/william-noland-103804140/

WHAT'S NEXT?

William and his team at Evolved Publishing are fast at work on Books 5-6 of the "Uncommon Bonds" series. Stay tuned to the web page referenced below to keep up to date.

www.EvolvedPub.com/UB

MORE FROM WILLIAM E. NOLAND

PLAYING WITH FIRE
Uncommon Bonds - 1

An ancient entity, trapped and suffering; a girl who inexplicably hears cries of anguish in her dreams.... What's their connection?

HAMMER TO FALL
Uncommon Bonds - 2

A grainy photograph and a cry for help begin a new descent into terror for long-separated friends Lotte Schwarz and Eric Schneider.

FROM THE BEGINNING
Uncommon Bonds - 3

A devastating flood and a chance encounter trigger a rapid-fire series of events that again pit Lotte Schwarz and Eric Schneider against challenges both mortal and supernatural.

MORE FROM EVOLVED PUBLISHING

We offer great books across multiple genres, featuring high-quality editing (which we believe is second-to-none) and fantastic covers.

As a hybrid small press, your support as loyal readers is so important to us, and we have strived, with tireless dedication and sheer determination, to deliver on the promise of our motto:
QUALITY IS PRIORITY #1!

Please check out all of our great books,
which you can find at this link:
www.EvolvedPub.com/Catalog/

Thank you!

www.ingramcontent.com/pod-product-compliance
Lightning Source LLC
Chambersburg PA
CBHW020548020726
47494CB00006B/1965